Lorelei Mathias grew up in 'Metroland' before studying English & Philosophy at Birmingham University. Since then she has worked in Publishing and Advertising, and has written articles for various magazines. She lives in East London.

Her first novel *Step on it, Cupid*, was published when she was 25, followed by *Lost for Words*. *Break-Up Club* explores the importance of friendship, and was inspired by her experiences in an accidental break-up club of her own. One day she'd like to set up an official refuge for the broken-hearted, so that no one should ever have to go through a break-up alone.

In her spare time she enjoys making films, running a fictional bakery called Niche Quiche, and asking people where the nearest lido is. She's also named after a mythical German mermaid, which might explain the obsession with outdoor swimming.

Follow Lorelei and her blogs at:

Loreleimathias.com
facebook.com/Lorelei.mathias.author
@loreleimathias
breakupclub.co.uk

LORELEI MATHIAS

Break-Up Club

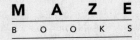

A division of HarperCollins*Publishers*
www.harpercollins.co.uk

MAZE

A division of HarperCollins*Publishers*
1 London Bridge Street
London
SE1 9GF

www.harpercollins.co.uk

First published in Great Britain by HarperCollins *Publishers* 2016 as *Reader, I
Dumped Him . . .*

This edition published by HarperCollins *Publishers* 2016

A catalogue record for this book is
available from the British Library

ISBN-13: 9780008197957

Set in Minion by Palimpsest Book Production Ltd, Falkirk, Stirlingshire

Printed and bound in Great Britain

MIX
Paper from
responsible sources
FSC® C007454

FSC™ is a non-profit international organisation established to promote
the responsible management of the world's forests. Products carrying the
FSC label are independently certified to assure consumers that they come
from forests that are managed to meet the social, economic and
ecological needs of present and future generations,
and other controlled sources.

Find out more about HarperCollins and the environment at
www.harpercollins.co.uk/green

This book is dedicated to:

Katie and Mark

The memory of my Dad and Evie

And anyone, anywhere, who has ever had a break up.

PROLOGUE

'What does not kill me makes me stronger'

(Nietzsche)*

* just how many break ups did you have, Freddy?

The Rules of Break-up Club – *'To our members, we're the first emergency service'.*

#1 – The first rule of Break-up Club is, you do not talk about Break-up Club.

#2 – The second rule of Break-up Club is, you do not talk about Break-up Club with your ex.

#3 – If this is your first night at Break-up Club, you will be expected to cry.
Uncontrollably.

#4 – Meetings take place once a week, every Sunday.

#5 – Each member must be prepared to perform Initiation (otherwise known as Brunch Duty). You shall deliver croissants and a smile to the residence of a new recruit on their First Weekend As A Singleton.

#6 – No Face-Stalking. Exes should be de-friended no later than 48 hours after a break-up. Phone numbers should be deleted or re-saved under the name 'Don't Answer'.

#7 – Members must be prepared to drop everything in the event of a Crisis Meeting. Common triggers range from a member relapsing with an ex, to an outbreak of F.I.H. (Facebook-Induced Hysteria).

#8 – Members must be willing to accept phone calls from co-members at any time of day or night, and talk them down from the bridge.

#9 – Hook-ups between co-members are strictly prohibited.

#10 – For their own protection, members must respect the N.G.Z. (No-Go Zones) imposed by a break-up. N.G.Z.s fall into three categories – Locational, Musical and Gifting. However, your ex does not have long-term sole custody of Bob Dylan or Streatham Hill, and a time will come when you'll be able to assert the first major bastion of Break-up Club (BUC) law: The Reclaim.

#11 – Understand the two absolutes of break-ups:

i) Eventually, you will be OK. You will recover.

ii) You absolutely cannot imagine ever feeling OK again. Ever.

Signed: Bella, Olivia, Harry
249A Fortess Road, Tufnell Park, London.

*

'Go on then,' Bella said, holding an old-fashioned fountain pen up to Holly's face.

Holly stared at the pen, watching it go in and out of focus, her eyes thick with tears. Everyone was staring. It was not unlike being back on the school playground. She was half expecting a football to come and thwack her round the head. She looked down at the epic list of rules and wondered how it had all come to this. What was next? Laminated membership cards? A ten per cent loyalty discount at Thornton's?

'Yeah, Folly, sign,' Olivia said. 'What are you waiting for?'

'Please don't call me Folly. Lawrence calls me that.'

'*Called* you that,' Olivia corrected.

'C'mon Holly. Let's face it now, the only way is up!' Bella sang while doing a move that wouldn't have been out of place on *Top of the Pops* circa 1990.

Maybe they had a point. Holly wiped her green eyes for the tenth time that day and reviewed the evidence. She had only slept three nights out of the last twelve. Currently, her top three activities were: binge-drinking, insomnia and unabashed howling on public transport. And, these days, the face that stared back at her in the mirror was none other than the bastard sister of Freddy Kruger.

Olivia held out a plate of baklava. Holly recoiled, feeling a bunch of moths practising the high jump in her belly.

'Christ no. Nothing against Harringay's finest delicacy, I'm just not really doing food at the moment.'

No one commented, but it was obvious what they were all thinking. Things must be bad if Braithwaite was off her food.

Oh no you don't, she thought as her eyes welled up again – the tear jar is full today.

Bella put her arm around her. 'Let it out, Hol. That's what we're here for.'

'But that's all I've done today. Cry. Blow my nose. Watch American teen dramas. And repeat on a loop. I have no brain cells left, and the most overworked tear ducts in all of North London.'

'Sweetie, you're supposed to indulge it at first,' Bella said.

'Yeah. That's the point,' Olivia said, holding out the tray of baklava. 'Here, get your strength up.'

Holly tried a tiny morsel.

'It's really just a formality at this stage,' Olivia said, sounding a little too much like she did in her day job. 'In the eyes of BUC law, you and Harry are already members. You both joined by default when you did a Synchronized Dump.'

Holly winced at the ridiculous slogan and scanned the room for any trace of irony. She looked across at her best friend from childhood, Harry, who had signed only moments before. The wry

5

smile on his freckly face said that yes, he appreciated how ludi-crous this all was, but the alternative was too bleak to comprehend. Going it alone. Venturing into the Valley of Unrelenting Doom in a seat for one. No, that was too horrendous a thing to imagine. Much better to travel on a bicycle built for two; or in this case, four.

Holly wiped her nose and took a deep breath. 'All right. Gimme.' Bella did a small handclap, then passed her the pen.

Even though this was all madness, there was still a part of her that felt like she was betraying Lawrence. Somehow signing on a dotted line made it all seem more final. Counting to three in her head, Holly signed her name in funeral black, next to the other squiggles.

'And then there were four,' Bella said.

Everyone cheered and clinked glasses. Holly pretended to look pleased and dedicated to the cause. Pretended she wasn't thinking about Lawrence for the fourteenth time that minute.

She handed the document to Olivia, who returned it to its A4 plastic sleeve, the matter of New Joiners now dealt with. 'We can always add to The Rules, as we see fit,' she said, stretching up to place them high on a shelf as though they were the Dead Sea scrolls. 'I think we're done here, don't you? Unless anyone's got any AOB?'

Bella, Harry, and then Holly shook their heads.

'So then, let's go out and celebrate your inauguration!' Olivia smiled.

As they descended the stairs in the flat, Holly felt her eyes well up again and finally she gave into the tears. She let them fall in time with her walk, leaving little droplets on every second stair. Before long, there were so many lines of black eye make-up down her cheeks that, as she shut the front door behind her and stepped out onto the street, she had the distinct look of a Jackson Pollock No.7.

Of course, none of them had imagined they'd ever need a

thing so absurd as a Break-up Club. None of them had imagined they'd be spending the fag-end of their twenties slumped together in a living room in Harringay, knocking back cheap wine and baklava to a soundtrack of The Cure. Least of all Holly, who had always been such a committed Marxist. Not of the hammer and sickle variety, but the one Groucho

Marx gave to the world when he vowed never to belong to any club that would have him as a member. The kind that has since led to neurotic girls everywhere (Holly among them) running for the hills whenever anyone shows too much interest. Which was why out of all four of them, she was the last to see this coming. But then, there are some things in this world – your first grey hair, an on-time Northern line train, a pig flu epidemic – that you just never see coming.

PART ONE

(Two months earlier)

'Your heart is a weapon the size of your fist.
Keep fighting. Keep loving.'
('Pure Evil' Street Art, East London)

1. *Tunnel Vision*

I love him; I love him not.

I love him… Holly decided, tearing off the virtual petals and staring across at the handsome man with the brown curls and big blue eyes… the one who'd first rocked her tiny world five years ago.

Yes, I one hundred per cent definitely love you, Lawrence Hill. Holly put the imaginary pile of 'love him not' petals to one side and stared at his silly face with fondness.

'Stand clear of the doors. Mind the gap,' came a brusque female voice, puncturing the moment.

'Wow. She's in a grump today.'

Lawrence smiled from across the carriage. 'You realise it's just a recording? She's not real?'

'She probably was, once…' Holly mused, a scene unfurling in her mind of a glamorous actress in a Soho sound booth, trying out different tones – from jovial to breezy, to downright matronly.

'Fair,' Lawrence said, staring at the Tube map like it was some kind of exciting code to be cracked. 'But in other news, we need to get off in a minute.' He grabbed his denim jacket off the floor.

Holly pressed pause on the sound session and looked up at the map. 'No we don't.'

'Yes. Ours is the next stop,' he said with the over-focused determination of Rain Man.

'But we're nowhere near Tufnell Park.' She gave Lawrence a knowing smile, her left dimple popping out as she did. 'Ah, but my dear Folly, that is a simplistic way of looking at things.'

'Why's that then?' She moved into the proverbial brace position.

Adopting an old-fashioned BBC accent, Lawrence went on, 'We should alight at Stockwell and change to the Victoria line.'

Holly's brow furrowed. 'Or, surely we just get the Northern line all the way to Tufnell Park?'

Lawrence smiled knowingly and shook his head. He began picking at the dilapidated shell-top of his left trainer. He pulled at the rubber flaps until they were dislodged, at which point he looked up.

'Of course,' his eyes widening with his trademark blend of smugness and childish excitement, 'that is what London Transport's Flawed Journey Planner would have you believe. However, I might remind you that there are a limited number of secret shortcuts and portals on the underground network, which only the truly seasoned Londoner is privy to.'

'Wow. You have literally never been sexier.'

He grinned with pride. Lawrence, for all his charms, suffered from a rare yet socially debilitating condition known as Tube Tourette's. Having grown up in the Midlands, Holly was distinctly less interested in Tube trivia than Lawrence. His fascination for it was so all-consuming, she firmly believed that under his skin were not veins or arteries, but a full replica of the London Underground map (first designed by underground electrical draughtsman Harry Beck in 1933, he'd hurry to tell you, too).

'The Northern line boasts two such changes,' he went on. 'One at Stockwell, and another at Euston. While they might appear pointless at first, these two changes will actually shave off a substantial section of your journey time. Not to mention the fact that the Northern line is heinously unreliable, frequently beset by the twin evils of signal failure and engineering works.' Holly let out a small sigh. Being an avid book-reader (a fact she loved about Lawrence), he had a habit of talking as if he was choking on a thesaurus (a fact she loved less so). There was a time when this had charmed her. Now it just niggled at her sanity.

'Lawrence you douche, just give it to me in English.'

'We'll cut out loads of time if we change lines here. FACT.'

'I have seventeen bags with me after staying at yours. I don't fancy changing trains and schlepping all this about.'

There comes a moment in most long-term relationships when you realise your identity has irreversibly eroded. You might have been a relatively normal individual once, breezing in and out of buildings, nothing but a shoulder bag about your person. But five years into a relationship in a big city, and you're The Bag Lady of the Northern Line – lugging around so much in the way of work clothes, unwashed gym wear and toiletries that you practically need your own carriage. Holly had recently begun duplicating all her worldly goods for North and South London. She'd had to call time on the doppelganger cosmetics project shortly after shelling out for the second set of GHD hair straighteners. Still, anything to avoid actually moving in with Lawrence.

As the train drew nearer to Stockwell and the first of Lawrence's shortcuts, he shifted about in his seat.

'OK, if you're so bothered, why don't you go?' Holly said sarcastically. 'I'll meet you there.'

Lawrence's big blue eyes widened. He stood up. 'OK, here's the plan. No really, this'll be fun. You take the Northern line all the way. I'll change to the Victoria line and back again. Then finally we'll know the DEFINITIVE answer of which is quicker! This age-old debate will have been answered, once and for all!'

'Oh, Lawrence... I was kidding. Please sit down,' she scolded before noticing that they now had an audience the size of a small fringe venue. All they needed now was a man in a tux selling programmes and overpriced ice creams.

'Aren't you just a bit curious to know who's right?' Lawrence said. As he dispatched one of his daintier breeds of kisses onto her forehead (the ones he liked to call 'fairy kisses' when no one else was listening), she couldn't stop the smile from creeping across her face.

Lawrence shot up from his seat, his eyes pogoing with excitement. The doors were opening. The old lady across the carriage seemed, from her enormous grin, to be egging them on.

'You're a freak,' Holly replied by way of acquiescence. Then, reluctantly: 'But listen, this has to be a fair test. We walk at a normal pace. No running up the escalators!'

Lawrence nodded. 'I love you,' he whispered, the doors beeping.

'Love you too. Twat,' she said as he bounced off the train and the doors began to close.

Flushed with a mixture of anxiety and humiliation, Holly Braithwaite watched as Lawrence stepped onto the platform and grinned back at her. Then she pulled into a tunnel deep beneath the River Thames, sank into the tired upholstery and leaned against the window.

She pictured the scene of her boyfriend sitting on the other train, staring with intent at the stopwatch on his phone. Lawrence's diehard competitiveness was one of the things that most riled her about him. Or was it loved? Who knew, she wondered as she pulled her black beret out of her bag and folded it into a make-shift travel pillow. She wedged it beneath the cushion of her thick brown hair, and rested her head against it. She listened to the voice reading out the names of the stops and closed her eyes. She began replaying the imaginary scene of the actress in the sound booth. She'd had that slightly clipped, RP accent, evocative of another era. Perhaps she'd done the recording many years ago, dressed in forties get-up, her hair in victory rolls? She couldn't help smiling, until a bleak thought occurred. The recording

14

sounded so dated that there was a strong chance the owner of the voice was no longer alive. In which case, these slightly tetchy TFL announcements could be the only echo of her that remained in this world? Her legacy. Holly struggled to think what she'd be remembered for, were she to shuffle off this mortal coil right now. An insalubrious flat-share, a dysfunctional relationship, and an intellectually emaciated TV show about a regional discotheque. Ball bags, Holly thought, looking upwards with pleading eyes and hoping it wasn't too late for her to make a proper contribution to the world.

Half an hour later, the train reached Tufnell Park. Holly rubbed her eyes and breathed a quiet sigh of relief to be north of the river again, and closer to home. Leaving the platform, she found herself jumping the stairs two at a time. She cleared the Oyster machines and ran through the ticket hall, where she could see that – bugger it – Lawrence was standing beside a lamp post on the street. She could tell by the position of his thumbs and the rapid movement of his eyes that he was playing Candy Crush on his phone. As she walked towards her man, she began playing a favourite game of her own, imagining it was the first time she'd ever seen him. She pretended to check him out, to assess if she still wanted to jump the bones of this stranger before her. She surveyed the optimum amount of stubble across his face and the dark brown hair that was perennially in the just-got-out-of-bed style. She studied his tall build – athletic without even trying – and his weathered Che Guevara T-shirt. She smiled. Yep, he definitely still had it. Despite being annoying in a multitude of ways, Lawrence Edward Hill could still turn her stomach to mush.

'See?' Lawrence said without looking up, his voice drunk with 'I told you so'.

'All right, well done.'

He stared at her expectantly.

'Yes, you were right.'

15

He smiled. 'So, since I won, maybe you can get the wine for dinner?'

'You're all charm,' Holly said, poking him in the ribs, then beginning to walk up the road.

'But not just yet...' he said, tugging at her arm. He bent down to kiss her and they smooched under a street lamp like teenagers.

'Hey,' Holly said, breaking away. 'Don't laugh, but, if for instance I should, you know, die in some sort of freak accident tomorrow – what would you remember most about me? My eyes? My voice?'

Lawrence's thick brown eyebrows crinkled towards each other. 'Well, since you ask, your laugh. I think it's the most beautiful sound ever. But what is this? Have you gone wonky with motion-sickness again?'

'I just got a bit hypnotized by that Tube announcer's voice, hearing it over and over. I didn't have a book to read, so for some reason I went off on one, and started overthinking things.'

'That doesn't sound like you,' he said, before smiling, 'although, you did have a much longer journey than me.'

'Ha ha, very funny,' Holly said, as they walked hand in hand towards Boozenest – the 24-hour convenience store she lived above with her two flatmates.

'But just imagine, what if you actually knew her? What if you were her boyfriend and she'd up and left you one day? Would it be really painful hearing her voice every time you travelled? Or – what if she did these recordings years ago, and now she's six feet under?'

Holly crouched on the pavement and began opening bags at random. Lawrence bent down to assist her in The Great Key Hunt. 'Well, if that were true, it'd be a bit like she's been acci-dentally immortalised by Transport for London.'

'Exactly! I mean, imagine if she'd left behind a widower. Do you think the poor guy would ride the Northern line, just to hear her voice again, as a way of being with her again in some way?

Or maybe he'd always avoid it, as it would be too painful?'

'The Northern line is always painful,' Lawrence said as his fingers pulled out something sharp and metal. 'Et voilà!'

Holly smiled, took the keys from him and began unlocking the door, just as her phoned beeped with a message.

'Shut the front door!' she said, stopping on the stairs to re-read the text.

'I just did,' Lawrence replied, shooting her a puzzled look before noticing her mouth drop open. 'Oh. What's up?'

'It's Olivia. No wonder she wanted to come over for dinner all of a sudden. She's just broken up with her boyfriend. I can't believe it. She and Ross were an institution at university.'

'How awful. Who's Olivia?'

'You know Olivia. From Uni. Wow, I really thought they were in it for the long haul,' she mused as they stood up and began to hike up the stairs.

'Hello?!' Holly shouted over a booming Ella Fitzgerald song as they reached the internal front door and she pushed it open. They headed up more stairs, past a tapestry of Blu-Tacked posters of film and music icons. On first moving in to 249a Fortess Road, Holly's long-term flatmate Bella, had been outvoted on the motion to only display pictures in frames from now on 'We're not students anymore', Holly and her other flatmate Daniel had pointed out. But slowly, as if by osmosis, new Blu-Tacked posters had begun appearing every few months.

Holly wandered into the lounge and through the kitchen, looking towards the small roof-terrace where Bella was smoking. Seeing her flatmate, she thought again how fine the line was between fancy dress and Bella's style preferences. A slave to vintage, Bella was dressed head to toe in fifties housewife chic, from the red and white polka-dot apron pinching in at her waist, to the Routemaster-red lips and heels.

'We have wine!' declared a triumphant Holly, opening the bottle and popping it onto the kitchen table to let it breathe.

Then she bent down to the speakers, turned down the insanely loud Ella, and headed outside, kissing Bella on the cheek. She stood on the terrace and took in the staggering view of North London trees and rooftops, remembering again why they'd chosen to live at the top of so many flights of stairs.

'Sorry, it took forever to get here from zone twenty. We've left you to do all the dinner. Can we help now?'

'Oh, crap!' Bella stubbed out her cigarette and headed back into the kitchen where some pots were just starting to bubble over. Next to the hob there was a cavalcade of crumbs, empty tofu packaging, stray lentils and shards of purple sprouting broccoli. Bella began stirring the lentils with one hand while applying mascara with the other, using the kitchen window as a mirror.

'No, it's all under control. Just open some wine. Who's this friend of yours that's coming over again?'

'Olivia. We were in halls together at university. She's down in London this weekend,' Holly said, attempting to fold napkins in a way that didn't look entirely eighties. 'She stayed up in Manchester after graduation, which is why we don't see that much of each other. That, and she's been mummified in a relationship for the last seven years. But apparently they've just broken up, so…' Holly looked at Bella to make sure she was paying attention, '…so she's probably going to be a little fragile right now,' she warned just as the doorbell rang.

'Liv!' she squealed into the intercom. 'Hey love. Come on up.'

Some moments later, Olivia Mahoney appeared under the curved archway next to the kitchen. Unlike Holly and Lawrence, who had both emerged from the stairs looking like they'd just been traversing the Pennines, Olivia was barely out of breath.

'Hello!' she sang, with a smile that made everyone stop what they were doing. Olivia had always been disarmingly stylish, but today she appeared to have actually been curated by Dolce & Gabbana themselves – if her freshly straightened mahogany hair and immaculate shift dress that perfectly highlighted her curves

18

– were anything to go by. In short, this was not the look of a recent refugee from Dumped Ville, Tennessee.

'Holly! It's been so long! Oh my days, you look so healthy!' she said, going in for a hug.

'Thanks,' Holly smiled, wondering mid-hug whether to take this as a compliment, or some sort of backhanded suggestion of weight gain.

'I'm so sorry to hear about you and Ross,' Holly lamented as she squeezed her tight, 'how are you coping?'

'Oh! I'm fine, really,' Olivia said, disentangling herself, 'actually, I'm sort of loving all this free time I've got now. And it's given me a great excuse to move back to London. Didsbury is lovely and all, but it can be a bit provincial.'

'Liv,' Holly said, 'this is the lovely Bella, one of my flatmates. We met when we temped together at a bleak call-centre after uni.'

Bella took Liv's hand and shuddered. 'Oh God, don't remind me! "Good afternoon, may I speak with the named home-owner?"' she said in her best admin nasal. '"Are you entirely happy with your current broadband provider?" Aaaahh! Kill me now!' she yelled, curtailing her skit at the sight of Olivia's muddled expression.

Meanwhile Lawrence had wandered in. Apparently in some kind of hunger trance, he walked towards the fridge, opened it and leaned in to study the contents.

'And this is Lawrence,' Holly said, sounding apologetic. 'We'll be eating soon, Lawrence.'

'Nice to meet you,' Lawrence said, shutting the fridge and turning to face Olivia. 'Sorry to hear about your break-up and all.'

'Oh, thanks, but as I was just saying to Hol, I'm fine about it, really. We'd definitely reached the end of the line,' she said, blinking while running through a word-perfect speech about all the benefits of being single – and how her newfound free time meant she could now take up all the things she'd secretly been craving. Just as she was immersed in the virtues of learning your way round the stock market, Bella inserted a glass of wine into her hands a little too forcefully.

'So Liv, tell me to shut up if you'd rather not go there, but what happened?' Holly said. 'Last I remember, you and Ross were really happy?'

Olivia inspected her nails. Sensing a girl chat brewing, Lawrence grabbed his bag of tobacco and retreated to the terrace.

Olivia sighed. 'All right. I'll talk about it – for five minutes, max – then we'll move on to something more interesting!' She took a large sip of wine. 'So, as you may recall, Ross is something of a computer boffin. Sorry, was,' she added a beat later, remembering with a jolt he belonged to her past tense now.

'Geeks can be hot though,' Bella said, 'what did he do for a living?'

Olivia smirked. 'If you really want to know, he was a "Backend Developer".'

Bella snorted. 'That's never a real job title.'

'I'm afraid it is. I think it means he does coding for websites. But don't quote me.'

A mobile phone on the table began to flash and vibrate, and Olivia's skin tone turned a few pantones lighter.

'Is it he?' Bella asked, leaning forwards. She picked up the mobile and examined the flashing photo. Then she looked at Olivia and grinned. 'Wait, *that's* your Ross?'

Olivia nodded.

'Well, he can backend develop me, anytime…'

'Bella!' screeched Holly, elbowing her in the ribs.

Olivia gave a knowing smile. 'He's all yours,' she said, retrieving the phone and cancelling the call. She put it back into her bag and for a nanosecond looked wistful.

'You're not going to talk to him?' Holly asked.

Olivia shook her head; her eyes belying more grief than she perhaps wanted them to. 'No. When it's over, it's over,' she said as the phone made a loud beep from within her bag. 'Stick a fork in it, I say.'

'You're not even going to see what that is? He's probably left a voicemail?' Holly said.

'Nah.'

No surprises there, Holly reasoned, remembering how at university they'd always joked that Olivia must have been having a cheeky manicure the day God was dishing out the batches of needy female hormones. Which went some way to explaining why the last time Holly had seen her, Olivia had declared herself in the midst of a 'friendship audit'. Although Holly had been spared this time around, Olivia's plan had been to prune away anyone peripheral, Facebook or otherwise, that she hadn't seen in a year. One by one, she had called up each unsuspecting friend for a fond farewell, in the hope that streamlining her social life would have a Zenifying effect. Now that Olivia was newly single, Holly couldn't help wondering whether she might be regretting the mass cull.

'So you were telling us what happened?' Bella said.

Olivia rolled her eyes like a child being told she had to eat her peas before any pudding. 'All right then. Just quickly. So, as you know, he was a bit of a computer nerd – which was sexy in the beginning. You know, he had a proper geek-chic thing going on. But then he went freelance, set up his own company, and it all changed. He started working from home a lot more, sleeping in and working late. Then one day he just stopped getting dressed at all – he'd just sit around festering, in these rancid jogging bottoms. Until eventually, you couldn't tell where the pyjamas ended and the tracksuits began.'

'Wow, that's so strange,' Holly said. 'He was Mr Charisma at uni.'

'I know,' Olivia's eyes moistened as she threw back the rest of her glass of wine. Then like Olivia Twist, she held out the empty receptacle in front of Holly, who immediately filled it up.

21

'I remember,' chimed in Holly, 'he was *that guy* in Fresher's week. The one every girl wanted to… you know, and every guy wanted to be.'

'But it's easy to be nostalgic about Old Ross – before he killed his personality off with a lethal concoction of daytime TV and JavaScript.'

'So what did you do? How did it end?' Bella tipped her head to one side, her empathy palpable.

'Fairly predictable stuff. Me saying I thought he'd let himself go, that I just didn't love him anymore, and we'd grown apart, blah blah… Him saying, "Shit, Olivia, I'm sorry. I wish I could just press Control Z."'

'No way,' Holly said, while Bella's brow furrowed.

'That's Apple Z, for the benefit of Mac Monks. As in, to undo?' she added, and Bella's brow un-furrowed. 'Yes. So then I said, "Ross. I think we both know, it's a case of Control Alt Delete now."'

'Well,' Holly began, 'it sounds like you've done the right thing. It must feel like such a massive shock to your system though, after seven years.'

'It's been brewing for a long time – it's a relief to have finally done it.'

'So where are you going to live now?' Holly asked. 'Do you want to come and stay with us?'

'Oh thanks, but I'm staying with my parents in Hampstead for a bit; just while I get myself sorted with a new job down here. But chances are, I'll only be allowed a week in the show home before I'll have to be out again!' Olivia smiled, then covered her ears as the incredibly loud smoke alarm began to go off.

Bella leapt up. 'That's dinner!' She poked her head in the oven. At the sight of smoke she began turning off all the knobs and dials. Holly began prodding at the smoke alarm with a broom to make it stop. This was all done with complete composure, as though it was an everyday ritual.

'So, everyone, dinner's kind of a buffet type thing. Just pile on,' Bella said, as she handed out partially-chipped plates to everyone.

'Looks amazing, thanks,' Holly said, spooning some of the blackened food onto her plate and assessing it for carcinogens. 'Is Daniel not eating with us?' said Holly.

'No, he's got a night shift at the hospital again, poor bastard,' Bella said.

'Ah, shame,' Holly said, secretly thinking it might have been handy to have a member of the medical profession on standby, but then feeling guilty for being so mean and having done nothing to help prepare dinner. She watched Lawrence digest a whole mouthful before taking one of her own.

Olivia picked up a fork full of food, but then opened her mouth to carry on speaking: 'But anyway, a friend of mine is just about to put his gorgeous flat in Dalston on the market, so if Ross can buy me out of our flat in Didsbury in time, I'll be able to nab that and move straight in!'

Bella's eyes widened. 'Dalston? As in, East London?'

To Bella, East London was a hallowed kind of a place. Legend had it, it was where all the hot men in London were being kept. Bella had stumbled across it one day while navigating a Walk of Shame through an unknown neighbourhood somewhere North of Bethnal Green. Quite by accident, she'd found herself in a quaint little strip called Broadway Market. It was all fancy deli stalls, fit-as-fuck buskers, and dashing men with oversized spectacles on fixed-gear bikes. Ever since then, there was sometimes talk in hushed tones of 'going East', as if it was some kind of promised wonderland. Bella would bring up the notion of warehouse parties in Dalston once in a while, but the thought of venturing somewhere new always lost out to the easy walk home from the local.

'Anyway, Liv,' Holly said, feeling the need to change the subject, 'if I can say so, you seem to be doing very well considering.'

23

'You really are,' Bella said, 'I mean, if it was me, I'd be needing round-the-clock care to help me do basic things like getting dressed and swallowing solids.'

'Yeah well, when you know, you know,' Olivia said.

'Any more, Liv?' Holly said, holding out more food towards her.

'Oh no, I'm stuffed,' Olivia said, slotting her knife next to her fork and laying it to rest. Her plate looked as full now as it had at the start of the meal, only everything on it appeared to be in a slightly different position. 'That was great though, thank you!'

Some hours later, they had retreated to the lounge. Lawrence was snoozing on the faded blue sofa in a post-gluttonous coma. Olivia sat perfectly upright next to him, staring at her phone, and Bella was picking at the yellow strips of foam that were leaking out of the sides of the sofa like oven chips. Over time, the hole had grown so large that these chips were now a regular feature of the lounge décor. Lawrence was forever coming into the kitchen after a big night out, picking them off the floor and going to eat them in his drunken stupor. Then, once Holly reminded him they had slightly less nutritional value than their real-life counterparts, he would drop them back onto the floor. But not before placing one of them on her shoulder and saying, 'Look, you've got a chip on your shoulder.' Every time.

'We really should stitch up that hole. Can anyone sew?' Holly said.

Naturally, Bella did not respond. Her filter for all things domestic was now so advanced, the vibrations of Holly's speech were physically shielded from penetrating her eardrum and making the journey to the middle ear. Instead, she stood up, a puddle of chips at her feet, and began the preparations for a round of Analogue Netflix. This was a game Bella had devised some time ago, borne out of her reluctance to pay for what she called 'special television', and her belief that they should all learn to appreciate the one thousand films they already owned between them. In reality they spent far more time deciding what to watch than they did watching anything, so in many ways it was exactly like the real Netflix.

Bella stretched up towards the Jenga-like tower of DVDs and plucked some out at random, as Holly began laying them out on the coffee table. Bella started calling out titles.

'OK, so what have we here… *The Notebook*.'

'Nope. Boring, saccharine, predictable…'

'It's beautiful!' Bella said, staring daggers at Olivia.

'*Pride and Prejudice*?'

'Too long. And too… period,' Lawrence said, rubbing sleep dust from his eyes.

'How about… *The Curious Case of*—' Olivia began.

'Benjamin Boring? The film that editing forgot?' Holly said.

'*Love Actually*.'

'Um, get a life, actually,' Holly said, and Lawrence nodded in agreement.

'But it's a wonderful film,' Bella insisted. 'So affirmative of the power of love as life's great leveller—'

'If I can just stop you there, Miss Bella. I've nothing against Richard Curtis per se,' Lawrence began to pontificate, 'I mean, let's be honest, *Blackadder* was pure televisual perfection. But the trouble with *Love Actually* – nay, the whole Curtis canon – is that he's clearly being paid by the people at Visit Britain to promote a wildly inaccurate view of London to the rest of the world. Take *Notting Hill*. There is no way the character William Thacker would be able to afford to live in such an attractive period property – with a gargantuan roof terrace – in the real Notting Hill. I mean, let's be real here: HE WORKS IN AN INDEPENDENT BOOKSHOP!'

Lawrence was getting more irate than was probably necessary. Holly felt her stomach constrict, and looked round the room to see if anyone else had noticed him being a little too shouty.

'But maybe house prices shot up after the film? Maybe Notting

Hill used to be like Hackney?' Bella posed, desperately still wanting to believe.

'Hey, you know what would be fun?' Holly began, her eyes on Lawrence. 'We should make a tongue-in-cheek mash-up of all the Curtis films, where the characters live in properties which actually correspond to their income. So, let's see… Will Thacker would live in an ex local authority one-bed in Kensal Rise, with a Juliet balcony at best.'

Lawrence laughed. 'Yes! And we'd replace all the friendly cabbies and romantic Routemasters with those charmless new buses with grumpy drivers that refuse to stop for you.'

'We'll have it raining the whole time! And we'll call it Stamford Hill!'

'Perfect! And *Love Actually* could be – Dumped Actually,' Lawrence said, smirking.

'Or, Shat on from a Great Height, Actually!' Holly added, and they both fell about laughing.

'Yeah, yeah. Whatevs,' Bella said. 'So. Anyone for *Four Weddings*? Oldie but a goodie?'

Holly began to realise she and Lawrence were outnumbered. An hour and twenty minutes later, she was feeling her usual bout of nausea at the scene where Hugh Grant and Andie MacDowell kiss in the rain, when she noticed Lawrence's eyelids closing out of the corner of her eye, his wine glass hanging off his fingers at a precarious angle. In slow motion, she saw his fingers relax and the glass slip, sending Shiraz cascading to the floor. As everyone leapt up to try and stem the tide with a whole roll of extra-quilted kitchen roll, Holly reached a conclusion. It was time to take Lawrence to a place where other people were not.

Twenty minutes later, she emerged from the bathroom and smiled. Once again Lawrence lay on top of her bed, eyes closed, with all his clothes on. His muddy Adidas trainers hung off the edge of the bed. A trickle of drool was slowly wandering from his lips and onto her freshly laundered pillowcase.

'Lawry…' she said, peeling off her clothes and hopping into bed beside him. She kissed him on the back of his neck, noticing that, as ever, he smelled very strongly of unwashed hair. She told herself this was sexy and manly, and not that Lawrence was a disciple of the 'your hair starts to clean itself after a while' gospel of hair care.

She began unlacing his shoes, rolling down his jeans and unbuttoning his shirt.

'Hey, I'm fine,' he said, as though bidding his manservant off duty.

'Oi,' she said, resorting to prodding.

After a few more inaudible grunts that sounded like 'No… sleeping…', he turned his back to face the wall and resumed snoring. Following a couple more failed attempts at erotic coercion via the means of spooning and shiatsu, Holly gave up and turned around so they could do that less talked about but equally popular sexual position – the back-to-back 'we're in a strop' position, where they remained for some time. Occasionally, their bare bottoms made contact, but they quickly moved apart on impact as though electrically repelled.

An hour later, she felt someone kissing the back of her neck.

'Hey. I miss you.'

'I'm right next to you,' she said, but she knew what he meant.

She felt his arms tighten around her. She turned to face him and they shared a slow, sleepy kiss.

'Meet me somewhere?' he said when they stopped. 'Old Havana?' His eyes closed again, his last words dispatched.

Holding his head to her chest, she closed her eyes and thought of vintage motor cars, cigars and salsa dancers and everything else they knew about the city they planned to visit together. She attempted to teleport herself there, to join him in his sleep-world. This wasn't a low-budget version of *Inception*; it was a game they'd invented when they first got together. It had been one of those nights where they'd laid together talking and cuddling all night, amazed at having found each other and wondering how other couples ever got any sleep. This had been their way to make parting for sleep just that bit easier: to pretend they would meet in their dreams.

Sometimes it didn't work so well. Tonight in particular, there was heavy congestion on the teleporting highway. Five hours later, Holly was staring vacantly at the ceiling, listening to the busy traffic noises of Holloway, not Havana. She closed her eyes as she heard the recycling van belting out its one-hit wonder, 'Stand Clear. Vehicle reversing'. Sometimes the traffic was so unfeasibly loud that she had to check her mattress wasn't actually in the middle of the road.

After a while, she became aware of how spectacularly un-tired she was, and lay watching Lawrence snoring blissfully away. Attempting to locate some inner yogic calm, she tuned in to the rise and fall of her boyfriend's snores. Loud to soft. Heavy breathing to quiet breathing, then back to blissful silence. Another chorus of heavy breathing, a guttural snort, then back to more quiet breathing. Holly listened to this on a loop for hours, wondering when she'd first become an insomniac. Gradually, the room stopped being so dark, and Lawrence's snoring solo found some backing singers in the baby blackbirds outside her window.

Two hours later, she switched off her alarm and wanted to weep at the time. She stared down at Lawrence sleeping and whispered, 'Lawry, I've got to go. See you later.'

A freckly and toned forearm emerged from under the covers, attempting to pull her back into the warm, feathery world under the duvet. Half asleep, he planted kisses on her cheeks, moving down to her neck.

'Hey, I've got to go to work,' she said as he drew her further inside and pulled the duvet high above their heads. He tucked it round them, so they were hidden from the world, in their own dimly lit universe. And then she remembered. When things were good with Lawrence, there was nowhere she'd rather be than under the duvet with him. Hiding from responsibility, from pretending to be a grown-up.

'Stay.'

'I can't. It's only my second week!' she said as he planted kisses on her stomach. She pulled in her non-existent abdominal muscles. 'I've got to try and be in early as I don't think my new boss is terribly impressed with me. My first episode ended up over length, when I forgot to allow for the extra ad-breaks they have on Sky!'

Lawrence looked at Holly, his eyes hazy with sleep. 'But you can't go – I'll miss you too much.'

'But I need to try and make a better impression.' Mustering all her willpower, she lifted the lid on their private universe, letting the cold air to their faces. It was a wrench, but slowly she untangled herself from the covers and peeled herself out of bed. She kissed him goodbye, feeling a tinge of pain.

'I love you,' mumbled Lawrence through slumber, his eyes closed.

'Love you too.'

'Love you three,' he said as he sank into sleep.

Holly smiled and tucked in the covers around him so he was all sealed up and no cold air could sneak in. She stood watching him sleep; his brown curls splayed out over the pillow, his long eyelashes twitching as he dreamed. She thought how adorable he looked, all wrapped up like a lanky, stubbly bundle of cute. He was exasperating at times, yes, but Lawrence-on-form was so full of life that she struggled to imagine a world without him.

In a way, knowing it was hard to leave him gave her a kind of comfort. Maybe Shakespeare was onto something with that whole 'parting is such sweet sorrow' thing. Sweet because somehow it made it OK that they were still together – that even five years in, it still hurt a little bit to say goodbye. Yeah, we're all right, Holly told herself as she tiptoed out the room and down the hallway. Then quietly, she snuck through the front door and went to work.

2. Airbrushing

'OK, that's it, a bit closer, Chardonnay, we can't quite see your pores,' Holly said in her broom cupboard of an office. 'There we go.'

Holly picked up the clip of Chardonnay and dragged her into the timeline of her Final Cut editing programme. Then she began to mix, chop and change the scene around, in the hope of making something good out of the weekend's footage.

It was hard not to talk to yourself in the broom cupboard. Having no one to share her new 'office' with, Holly's self-discipline had to work extra hard just to stop herself from taking naps or ringing her friends. Still, she was only two weeks into the job – she'd get used to not being open plan anymore. It was all part of being a more responsible adult, this promotion to actual Editor. Even if her old job assisting the Drama Editor at a small, artistic production company now seemed infinitely more creative. Mark, her lovely old boss, had always referred to the edit suite as the 'shit to ice-cream department'. But as Holly played with the colour levels, adjusting Chardonnay's tangerine skin tone to something more natural, she wondered whether she would ever manage to submit an episode of *Prowl* that had anything like the appeal of ice cream.

The latest in a craze of brain-dead reality TV shows, *Prowl* was a docu-soap set in a suburban nightclub which screened on Sky's Channel 653 (she couldn't say for sure, never having watched it). Much of the content came from the 'fly on the bog wall' footage from within the ladies' lav. Not actually inside the cubicles (they weren't *that* desperate for content… yet), but in the communal wash-basin area, where the perfumes, lollipops and Brandii, the guilt-mongering towel lady, were gathered. The 'unsung hero of the UK club scene' (so sang the press release), Brandii was effectively the eyes and ears of 'Prowl' in East Sheen. So, quite literally, the show Holly edited was unadulterated crap.

No, she decided, cutting this negative thought and pasting it at the back of her mind. Taking this job in Daytime TV had been a triumphant career move of epic proportions! It paid twice as much as her last job. Not only that, she was going to use her evenings and weekends to pursue Proactive Creative Projects. Like making short films. Yes, with Lawrence's help she would edit a fabulous film to enter into festivals. Together they would use their spare time to win industry awards, like the creative powerhouse dream-team they were truly meant to be. Hurrah, she thought, stemming the tide of career anxiety and picturing her lovely, talented boyfriend back home, tucked under her covers – his long-toed man-feet poking out of the bed.

If Holly had mastered one skill so far in her small time on Earth, she reckoned it was the ability to cut and paste the things of life into little compartments in her brain. She was as good an editor of her thoughts as she was of daytime television. As she returned to editing the scene in front of her, a new face filled the monitor; that of Luke Langdon, the show's main male 'character', Phil the Barman.

Luke was a trained actor, reduced to the status of a barman on a reality TV show. But because the premise of the show was that everything must appear real, to all Luke's luvvie peers, it looked as though he was actually a barman. As he bent over to lift the beer barrel in the fictional-but-real-world bar that he ran, Holly couldn't help staring at the muscles on his upper arms as they flexed in and out. Playing around with the slow motion effect (in a purely artistic way, of course), she realised the job had some perks. Although, it was unlikely to propel her to Baftaville any time soon. Nor was it getting her any closer to her dream job of editing a feature. But she might as well enjoy the scenery along the way, she mused as she heard a beep from her emails.

Jeremy.Philpott@TotesamazeProductions.com to
Holly.Braithwaite@TotesamazeProductions.com

Morning Holly,
Could you bring me a coffee when you have a minute? Just my usual! Also, just a heads-up that we had to do some major re-cutting on some of the scenes at the end of the second episode. Bit woolly in places. Too many indulgent shots over the graffiti on the toilet walls, for one. The ending has much more punch now we've taken those bits out. Less is more.

Also, small point: What was with the Wagner soundtrack??! Maybe artistic if this was a film festival, but let's try and remember that this is DAYTIME TV. Your audience are ASDA MUMS with 2 GCSEs or less, who eat KFC for breakfast and smoke while breastfeeding. They don't need to see pretentious shots set to opera. The only music they know comes out of the X Factor.

Did you get a chance to type up those minutes? Would like to get them circulated before lunch.

Many thankings,

Jezza.

P.S. Oh – almost forgot! A little niggle's come up regarding your contract. I'll tell you when you come in.

Getting to the coffee machine involved traversing a mixed terrain of sets, wardrobes and dubious props. Being a very small production company, TotesAmaze often had to shoot some of their scenes in-house when they couldn't get into the actual locations. So there were a number of makeshift replica locations to wander through – down the pretend hallway, past the pretend cloakroom, and through the pretend chill-out room. As Holly arrived, she found herself staring at the same muscular arms she'd been admiring from before, only this time less pixelated. TV's 'Phil the Barman' was fixing a drink in the real world. He was resting one arm on the coffee machine, staring vacantly into his plastic cup as it filled up with tan coloured foam. Holly couldn't help wondering whether he had one too many buttons of his checked shirt undone than was really comfortable for a work environment. She wondered if the open-chested look was a decision from the Wardrobe department, or if it was Luke's own style. But after a few moments of staring at the chest hairs that were peeping out, she decided it definitely wasn't a problem.

'Hi. Sorry. All yours in a minute,' he said, and she stopped gawking and looked up at his face.

'Oh, don't hurry. I'm in no rush to get back to the broom cupboard.'

'The what?'

'My windowless edit suite.'

A penny dropped behind Luke's retina. 'Oh, I thought you were a runner, I don't know why. Sorry, I don't think we've met.'

'That's OK. Flattered you think I look young enough to be a runner! The anti-wrinkle cream must be working!' she said, wishing she could cut that last sentence as soon as she'd delivered it.

'Oh, definitely,' Luke said, his smile that bit more genuine in the flesh.

'And you are?' she said, immediately wishing this shabby attempt at humour could also be relegated to the cutting-room floor.

'I'm Luke. I'm – "the star of the show"', he said with a reasonable dose of irony.

'I know. I was joking. Sorry. My bad joke filter isn't working today.'

'And you call yourself an editor,' he said, and Holly smiled nervously.

'Is this fake?' Luke said, staring at her.

Holly was flummoxed. Was her conversation that dull?

He took his coffee out of the machine. 'You know, the coffee? Is it pretend, seeing as it's all smoke and mirrors round here?'

'Oh!' Holly said, relieved. 'Like it's actually just boiling water with food colouring in it? No, I'm pretty sure it's real. It's got a fraction more flavour.'

He smiled and took a sip. 'I wouldn't be so sure.'

Holly pressed the cappuccino button.

'So, you're the person who dishes out the close-ups?' Luke delivered another of his really quite smouldering leading-man grins.

'Well, in between being an accidental PA to the Head of Programming, yes, deciding between shots is one aspect of being editor.'

'So I should keep you sweet, shouldn't I?'

Holly took the plastic cup from the machine and grappled with not swearing about how hot it was. She didn't want to shatter the illusion she wasn't totally potty-mouthed. Yet.

'So there's no non-cheesy way to say this – but how about I take you for a real coffee some time?'

Holly hoped her smile covered the fact that inside, her heart was having minor palpitations. 'I wouldn't have said cheesy. Transparent, maybe…'

Her phone began to ring in her pocket. She looked down to

see a flashing thumbnail of a girl with jet black hair and red lips holding a microphone.

'Oh sorry. This is my flatmate, I'd better…'

'Sure. Let me know about that coffee another time.' Luke smiled as she turned to walk away.

Those teeth have almost certainly been bleached in a Hollywood salon, Holly decided before answering the call.

'Hey hon, you OK?'

'Holly! Oh my giddy fuck! The world has just ended.'

Holly sighed. The world was always ending in Bella's world.

'What's wrong? Have you and Daniel had another flatmates squabble? Have you thrown the laundry rack at him again?'

'It's so much worse than that,' she said, breaking into sobs.

Putting her hand over the receiver to drown out Bella's crying, Holly headed down the corridor. She rounded the corner to her office and closed the door behind her. 'OK. Sshhhhh. Deep breaths. What's happened?'

But all Holly could hear now was broken speech, not unlike a child's hyperventilating playground tears.

'My beautiful Sammy! He's shitting well dumped me!'

Through the phone, Bella began to rant, oscillating from desolate to indignant with every breath. One moment it was all 'How-dare-HE-dump-ME!', the next it was 'He's the love of my life, my soulmate!'

'Oh, hon,' Holly said, 'I'm so sorry. Where are you?'

'Guildhell.'

Ever since her first term at The Guildhall – a prestigious Drama School that worked its students very hard – Bella and her coursemates had referred to it as The Guildhell School of Music and Trauma.

'Do you want me to come and meet you after work?'

'Can't-You-Meet-Me-NOW?' she wailed. 'Yes. Sorry, can I just have a chai latte extra hot please, takeaway. Thanks. Can I pay by card? Oh sorry, where's the nearest…? OK never mind. Sorry…

sorry… Hol, I'm back. Oh no, hold on, Daniel's ringing. Sorry Hol, wait one second.'

Holly cleared her throat. Before long. Bella returned to the phone line with renewed focus. 'Sorry Hol. That was just Daniel wanting me to buy loo roll again. The man's obsessed! I mean – can you honestly believe he thinks he's exempt from buying bog roll just because he poos at work?! I mean, who thinks like that?!' Bella giggled despite her trauma.

'He's probably expecting one of his lady callers.'

'Yes, that figures. But anyway! Can we do a movie and Prosecco tonight please?'

'I really should be working late on fixing this new episode. I'm still two minutes and twenty-three seconds over length.' She looked at Chardonnay's tangerine face, frozen mid-pout, and thought for a moment. 'But of course, B. I'll pick up some pizzas on the way home.'

'Christ, no. Shan't be no solids passing my lips for at least a month now.'

'Oh, right. More for me then.'

'Actually, maybe pick up some chocolate brownie Ben & Jerry's? I can probably digest that. At a push.'

'Done. See you later for some *Sex and the City* therapy. Love you.' Holly had an unrivalled talent for prescribing the exact most fitting episode for when her friends were going through a personal crisis of any sort. Despite being almost a decade old, many of the show's scenarios were still so on the nail that viewings became like a workshop session.

What would it be this week? Definitely not the 'he broke up with me on a Post-it' one, she decided as she hung up the phone.

She grabbed the cup of black coffee that was now only partially warm, and headed down the hall towards the gargantuan corner office. She knocked on the door.

'Enter.'

Once Holly had recovered from being momentarily blinded by the light from Jeremy's floor-to-ceiling windows, she handed him his coffee. He took the cup without looking up from his screen, which was quite clearly displaying an inter-marital dating site. A dialogue box was open, in which Jeremy was filling out his physical characteristics with a generous dollop of artistic license. Holly stared at the back of his head, where a bald spot was forming like a threadbare patch on an old rug. She waited for him to stop typing, minimise his screen and turn to face her. When that didn't happen, she began to talk in that garbled way she did around people she thought didn't like her.

'So um, thanks for your comments on the edit, I'll remember that when I'm cutting this week's show. Note to self, Toto, we're not in Drama anymore!' she attempted humour, but Jeremy was too busy writing about what a good sense of humour he had to hear her.

She tried again. 'So, what was the "little niggle" you had to tell me about?'

'Oh, yes. Well, the headline is that it looks like *Prowl*'s going to be axed after this series. I know you were signed up for two series but, should it be axed, I simply can't justify keeping two full-time editors on.'

Holly's mouth fell open. 'Oh. If only I'd known that when I left my old job.'

'This is telly, Holly. It's about as secure as a two-man tent from Lidl in a torrential hurricane.'

'Quite. Is there anything I can do to help my chances?'

'Well, I'm not sure when, but at some point I'm going to have to make a call between you and Pascal…'

Holly's heart sank. Pascal, the gay (strictly in the modern sense of the word) editor from Romford who cycled in every day at the crack of dawn, was as much a part of the furniture as the Coke-stained sofa in the green room. Incidentally, that sofa had shown Holly a much warmer welcome than Pascal ever had – she could count the number of times he had acknowledged her existence on one finger.

'...So I'm going to need to see you both really adding value. Whether that's getting a first pass done sooner, or coming to me with proposals for the channel that can replace the *Prowl* slot. Or just bringing me more coffee. Ultimately, though, it will mean you putting in a lot more of your evenings, and some weekends.'

'I'm guessing you won't be paying us any extra for all the overtime?'

'I know it's unusual, but we're a small outfit and we have to do what we can. Of course, if you don't like it...'

'No! I can definitely try and help come up with some new show ideas.'

'Great! Just email them through, any time of day, it doesn't matter.'

'Actually, there is this one thing I thought of yesterday, that I guess could be a documentary. I was on the Tube, listening to the old-fashioned voice that calls out all the stops, and I got to thinking how she must have been a real person once... and how there are probably a few disembodied voices like hers who may have since passed away, and how strange it must be for their loved ones to hear their voices when they've gone? Maybe they take the trains and buses more than normal – more than they need to – as a way of seeking comfort in the vocal leftovers of their lost loves? Maybe we could find if there are any real-life examples... perhaps interview them?'

'What are you calling it, *Britain's TFL Widows*?'

'Mmm, I was thinking *Mind the Gap*.'

Jeremy spat out his coffee. 'Sorry, did my email say Frappuccino?'

'No?'

'Thought not. And yet strangely this cappu is ice cold,' he said, pushing the cup back into her hand, managing to spill just enough on her to demonstrate he was being hyperbolic at her expense.

'Sorry. I'll get you another one,' she said, as he turned back to complete his profile. 'So what do you think about the voices thing? Could it be a goer?'

'I think it's somewhere between utterly far-fetched and BBC2.'

'That's a no then?'

*

Arriving home after a Boozenest stop-off for emergency ice cream, Holly could hear The Cure blasting from upstairs at full volume. She walked into the lounge just in time for 'Pictures of You' to finish and start up again.

'Nothing in the world, I have ever wanted more, than to feel you deep in my heart!' Bella screamed out at the room.

The lighting was scant. Creeping into the lounge, Holly could just make out Bella sat in the far corner, in her favourite little alcove. She was cross-legged on the floor, surrounded by cushions. In front of her lay newspapers and an array of broken objects.

'If only I'd thought of the right words, then I wouldn't be breaking my heart!... over...' She broke into tears, mid-wail.

'Um... how are you doing, Bella my dear?' Holly began, thinking again what an exquisite singing voice her flatmate had.

Bella looked up. Her face was streaked with thick black lines, indicating hours of heavy-duty sobbing.

'Yeah. Good thanks,' she said, the smile on her face a touch maniacal. Holly sat down and took Bella's palm in hers. It promptly became stuck. Holly slowly unpeeled Bella's hand to discover it was covered in a filmy substance and that Bella was now picking at the layers of skin. After a brief jolt of panic, Holly realised it was just congealed glue, as Bella exploded with tears. She sobbed in Holly's arms for a full minute, and then broke away, not before leaving a pearlescent trail of snot on Holly's shoulder.

'Poor B. I'm so sorry. Want to talk about what happened?'

'Not so much.'

'OK. Shall we talk about all this then?' Holly asked, looking down at the *Blue Peter* project that was unfolding at their feet. Was it toxic, this stuff? she wondered. Should she be calling the FRANK helpline for advice on solvent abuse?

'I'm just trying to fix stuff. I tried to make a cup of tea earlier and I accidentally smashed this mug Sam gave me. It was so upsetting, seeing it all in sad little bits; I just had to try and mend it. See – it's much better now.'

Holly nodded. There was a huge crack down the middle, and solidified lumps of gloop lined the area where she'd wedged the handle back on. 'Best girlfriend in the world' now read 'best end in the wor'.

'Good as new.'

'Shall I make you a cup of tea now?' Holly asked, reaching into one of the cupboards and taking out the only non-chipped mug. She switched the kettle on.

'Please,' Bella said, allowing a smile to sneak out through her tears.

As was often the way, Holly looked into the mug and saw that, like most of its peers back in the cupboard, its rim had a beard of dried-on dust, giving a whole new meaning to the old adage 'drinking from the furry cup'. She ran it under the tap as she waited for the kettle to boil, trying to suppress two thoughts, which were: 1) why am I the only one here who notices dirt, and 2) surely I am too old to live like this?

'Anyway,' Bella went on, 'I realised how strangely therapeutic it felt to mend stuff, so since then I've been looking for other things to fix. This Superglue, it's fucking miraculous! You must need something mending?' she asked, her eyes brimming with possibility. She jumped up and ran towards the cupboards, coveting like a kid in a sweet shop. 'Let me at your broken stuff!' she said while scanning the rows of crockery.

'Right… clearly tea is a waste of time,' Holly said. 'I think another trip to Boozenest…' She grabbed her wallet from her bag and then selected *Sex and the City*, series five. She'd thought hard about which episode to prescribe and had settled upon 'Plus one is the loneliest number', which although it sounded maudlin was actually rather uplifting at the end. She looked at Bella who was puffy-eyed and catatonic. Holly opened the ice cream and stabbed at it with a big serving spoon.

'Here, take this and apply liberally. And, when the DVD menu page loads, just click on episode two; I won't be long. I'll get us a bottle of Prosecco. Don't go sniffing too much glue.'

Bella's eyes lit up as though this had given her an idea.

'And when I'm back if you're ready to talk about what happened, just say and we can pause the DVD, OK?'

Bella nodded, staring at the ice cream as though she didn't quite understand it.

'Better make it a box of wine,' Holly muttered as she headed out.

Arriving home armed with supplies, Holly made a pit stop in her bedroom, to hunt down her pink duvet slippers for Bella. Hands down, they were the best thing to put on your feet in a crisis. As she got back to the lounge she could hear the *Sex and the City* theme music playing, but it was just the same tiny segment of it, on a loop.

Bella was staring blankly at the television.

'B, hon! You could have pressed play! You must be so sick of that same ten seconds of music?'

Bella moved her head slowly to look at Holly. Her eyes were red. 'Hmm? I hadn't noticed. Now you mention it, yes, it is kind of annoying. Can you booze me up please?' she said, her eyes desperate. 'I don't think I should be sober in my condition.'

'What am I thinking? Here…' Holly pierced open the box of wine and filled a large glass, before pressing play on the remote. 'Get this down you,' she said as the title credits dissolved to a shot of Carrie standing in a beautiful high-ceilinged bar in Manhattan.

Bella glugged the whole glass in one go before topping herself up again. Holly curled up on the sofa, pulled a blanket over them, and prepared to let the world drift away for a wonderful twenty-three minutes.

Or as it happened in this case, three.

'You know,' Bella spoke up mid-scene. 'There were times when I thought I could've married that fucker! I thought he was… don't hit me for saying this but – The One!'

Holly turned to face Bella and tried to decipher whether this had been a one-off comment, or a prelude to a whole conversation. She grabbed the remote and pressed pause, just in case.

'Oh love, I know. I'm so, so sorry.'

'But, now he's gone and fucked that one up hasn't he? Or, maybe I fucked it up,' she said, randomly picking up foam oven chips from the floor and stuffing them back into the hole in the sofa.

Holly put her arm around Bella, who began squirting glue into the gap in the sofa.

'Belle, you can leave the sofa broken for now. You know, it's OK if some things go unfixed.'

'All I know is, my life's no longer the life it was. This whole pathway I had mapped out in my head has just dismantled itself.' she said, sobbing again. She downed another glass of red wine like it was water. You know?

'I know. But you'll be OK. You just need to do some recalculating of which path to take – you know, like the SatNav says?'

Holly grabbed her pink sleeping-bag slippers and slid them onto Bella's feet. 'There. These should help in the meantime.'

Bella was quiet for a moment. 'Oh, my, god. What are they? They're incredible! They're SO comfortable! They're like magical duvet cherubs!' Bella laughed, her eyes lighting up for the first time that night. 'My feet have literally never been happier!'

'I know, right!' Holly said, relieved something was helping at last. 'They're the equivalent of having a gigantic mug of tea at the same time as a massive hug from your mum!'

Bella's eyes glazed over as Holly remembered that Bella hadn't seen her mum in about a decade, on account of the fact that their parents had left some years ago to go and live in a transcendental meditation retreat in New Zealand.

'Sorry. SHIT choice of words,' Holly said, quickly giving Bella a hug.

'That's OK,' Bella said with forced stoicism. 'I'll try to remember what a hug from my mum would feel like. Seriously though, you're never getting these babies back.'

'OK. Word of advice though – DO NOT try to walk in them. No good can come from walking in them.'

Bella looked completely unfazed by this; clearly it had not been her intention to move from the sofa ever again. She glugged more wine.

'So, do you want to tell me what happened?

Bella took a deep breath. 'I'm so humiliated.' Her eyes welled up. 'I've started having flashbacks of the lowest low point.'

'What was the lowest low point?' Holly asked.

'Well, the trouble was, the location of our break-up really wasn't ideal. Although we'd started "the break-up chat" at his house, we both had this hideous Guildhell event in town that we had to get to. Which meant that we had to sort of, carry it on, en route? You know, while commuting together into town, on a cramped Tube carriage like normal, except that I'm bursting into tears every other second, wanting to kiss him one minute, and punch his lights out the next!'

'No…' Holly gasped.

'Yes! And then to make it worse, there was one of those nice homeless guys on our carriage, giving it the whole "let me tell you a joke or sing you a song, in exchange for money or a cup of tea", and I was like, jeez, now really isn't the time! But then, once we'd made it to Covent Garden, I reached whole new levels of humiliation. I…' Bella broke off, her eyes filling with tears.

'What?' Holly asked.

'I begged him,' she grunted inaudibly. Clearly the shame was such that Bella couldn't bring herself to fully formulate the words.

'What?'

Bella sighed. 'I BEGGED him, Holly! In the STREET. I clung to him. With my ACTUAL arms. There I was, grasping his legs like a slobbering bloodhound.' Her eyes clouded over at the memory. 'I'm just always going to have this godforsaken image of me ON ALL FOURS. I can never go back there! The whole of Covent Garden is now a walk of pain to me!' she sobbed 'But then, soon it was clear he'd already started floating away from me, like a helium balloon drifting upwards and I was this devastated child grasping at the string. Yeah, I've lost him all right.'

'God, that's so sad,' Holly said, pouring her another glass of wine. 'But I don't understand, where did this all come from? Did he give a reason?'

'He said, "I think I need to be by myself at the moment. My course is just getting so demanding that I don't think I can manage both my career and you,"' she said, as though the words were still rotating round her brain on a loop. 'Then he started banging on about "needing his focus" and how he "has to put his passion first" – and I was like, but I thought I was your passion and he said that yes I am but he loves me too much to be fully committed to his "ART"??'

'What a cock.'

'I know. Like my own course isn't demanding?!' she cried, then burst into tears some more. Holly folded her up in her arms and stroked her hair as she sobbed.

'Arsehole,' Bella sobbed.

'Yes,' Holly agreed. 'Although, maybe this is just something he needs to do? Something he needs to get out of his system? Chances are, he'll want you back, as soon as he realises he can't function without you, and you're his muse after all.'

'That's what I keep hoping. It's like that saying, "if you love something, set it free"', Bella said, as a tear slid down her face and splashed into her wine. She picked up the glass and downed it regardless.

'"And if it comes back, it's yours forever!"' Holly finished.

'Although helium balloons don't come back, do they?' Bella said, her shoulders slumping.

Holly thought for a minute, then shook her head. She topped up Bella's drink. 'So, if it's not too soon to say this, I'd like to impose a rule?'

'A rule? Really? OK, hit me with it.'

Holly grinned. 'No more self-involved actors for Bella! Seriously, your last three boyfriends have been thesps, and they have all caused you untold pain. I think you need to find someone a little more reliable, with a sturdy job.'

'That's a good rule. From now on, I'm going to activate my actor-radar, so I can always see them coming!'

'Wait. You mean your RADAr...?' Holly said, pronouncing it Raardar, and Bella snorted.

'Yes! My RADAr!!!!'

After giggling raucously for a good minute, Holly took a tissue and began to mop up Bella's face, feeling a bit like a grandma with a slobbery handkerchief.

Bella craned her neck to the mirror on the wall. 'Oh god, look at the state of me! Ugh. Never mind the mascara streaks, why am I still getting so many bloody spots? I am twenty-seven. Give me wrinkles, not pimples, surely!?'

'You're gorgeous, don't be silly,' Holly said.

'I'm serious though. I mean, look at this one, it's like one of those conjoined twins. There's another one brewing right next to it! Maybe I shouldn't be doing this Vegan Pledge – maybe it's a sign I'm suffering with malnutrition...'

'But you've only been doing it for five days? Your skin is fine,' Holly said, hoping she sounded convincing.

45

'I think I'll start painting eyeliner on top of them. I had a friend who did that once, to make them look like beauty spots.'

'That's always an option,' Holly offered.

'What am I saying? I'm never going out again anyway... it's fine!' Bella said, remembering her life was over, her eyes welling up.

'Shall we watch the rest?' Holly said.

They turned their attention back to the TV screen, where Samantha was frozen, in the middle of complaining about a chemical peel that had gone awry.

'All right then. I do love this episode. There is still SO much wisdom in this show!'

'I'll just grab us another blanket. It's feckin' freezing in here.'

Holly pressed play on the DVD.

But now Bella was curled up in a ball on the sofa, fast asleep. She'd obviously worn herself out from crying, like children did when they were overtired. Holly grabbed a pint glass, filled it with tap water and put it beside Bella on the floor. She draped the extra blanket over her, planted a kiss on her cheek, and left her to sleep. Then she headed to her own room and drifted into a perfect, snore-free sleep filled with surreal dreams about an imaginary celestial lost-property bureau.

Waking at dawn to the sound of the reversing vehicle, she picked up the notepad on her bedside table. In her muddied state of consciousness she wrote down 'The Helium Depot'. She had no idea why, but she rather liked the sound of it as she rolled over and went back to sleep.

3. *Holloway*

A week later, Lawrence stood at Holly's door, an olive green beanie grappling with his unruly curls. Holly leaned forward to kiss him on the lips.

He broke off halfway. 'Look, I bought Georgia!' he said as he unhooked himself from the enormous, unwieldy guitar case that was strapped to his back.

'Who?' Holly asked, looking around her.

'My new acoustic! Isn't she the sexiest thing you've ever seen?'

Holly nodded as Lawrence clambered through the door, bashing Georgia on the already scratched walls of the entrance hall.

'What's not to love?' Holly said as they headed into her bedroom and he started bashing out a tune.

In truth, Lawrence plus guitar equalled total subservience on Holly's part. She could be furious with him about something, and all he'd have to do was strum three notes, and the drawbridge to her lady-garden would drop there and then. Right now, he was playing 'You've Got To Hide Your Love Away' – but singing the chorus over and over because it was the only bit he knew all the chords to.

Lawrence perched on the edge of the bed, his muscular frame

stooped over his guitar, his brown curls falling into his eyes like a slightly crustier Jim Morrison. He was playing a new chord sequence now, which Holly couldn't place in his usual repertoire. After a few more beats she recognised it as 'My Boy Lollipop'. Only, when he sang the chorus he changed the lyric to 'Hollypop, Hollypop' for attempted comedic gain.

'Oh, that's cute, Lawry! Although, am I a boy?'

Lawrence grinned. 'Yes. For the purposes of this song you are. Anyway, it's not quite ready yet.'

'It's lovely. Thanks, baby.'

She sat on the bed and watched him slowly pick out the chords. Lawrence had never got round to learning how to read music. But what he lacked in patience he made up for with a most amazing ear. He could usually pick out most requests just by listening for the notes that sounded right. As a result, having Lawrence and a guitar around was sometimes like having a slightly hyperactive human jukebox at your disposal.

'Play it again, Lawry,' she said, brushing some sleep out of his eye.

'No. I'm bored of that one now,' he said, pulling her towards him for a kiss.

'Hey,' Holly said, breaking away after a minute, 'do you remember the other day, when I got a bit fixated on the woman's voice on the Tube?'

Lawrence squinted, trying to recall a memory lost in a distant fog.

'Well, I've been thinking about it some more, about whether it could make an interesting story – all about the comfort people might take in the voices of their loved ones after they've gone? I wondered if there are any real-life TFL widows out there that we could make a documentary out of?'

'Bit morbid, but there could be something in it.'

'That's what I thought, but Jez blew it out. But then I got to wondering; could it be the kernel for a short film instead? A heart-wrenching little film, about someone's journey through grief, guided by voices…' she looked at him, her eyes dancing with possibility, 'but you know more about shorts than me.'

Lawrence had been tinkering with a chord sequence all this time. He stopped for a moment and looked into her eyes. 'It's definitely interesting, Fol. I mean, I like the irony that to most passengers the voices are just these robotic murmurs; a necessary and repetitive part of getting from A to B. Yet, to a few people they are these ghost-like traces of someone they used to know. Someone they used to share their world with.'

Holly's eyes widened. 'Exactly! I just have this feeling it could be really poignant. What do you think about us developing this into a film together? It'd be lovely to spend our time doing something creative, as opposed to box-set bingeing.'

'But we love box-set bingeing!'

'We could actually make it though – you direct, I'll edit! It would be great for both our reels! Put it into festivals. Stop our careers from flatlining?'

'Sounds like a plan,' said Lawry while picking out the opening bars to 'I Wanna Hold Your Hand'.

'You're better at writing than me though,' she said, taking one of his curls and twirling it around her finger. 'Will you help me script it sometime?' But her voice was drowned out by a strange robotic tone coming from the bed, which sounded not unlike 'Live'.

'What the bejeezus?' Lawrence said. But then it happened again. 'Where is that robot voice coming from, and why is it telling us to live? Is it a new Existentialist phone line?'

'It's my new upgrade,' Holly said, retrieving her phone from the top of her bed. 'It's the world's most complicated mobile. It insists on telling me who's calling, in a Stephen-Hawking-on-weed voice.'

'Why don't you read the manual?' Lawrence said, infuriatingly.

'Oh, you ARE my father!'

Everyone in the world – except from Lawrence and her father – knew that life was too short for reading the manual.

'Live,' bleated Stephen Hawking.

'Can you make it stop?'

'Oh, hang on!' Holly said once she'd found her phone, 'He's saying Liv! As in, Olivia! She tapped the answer button. Hey Liv, how you doing?'

'Bored,' came Olivia's voice. 'Can we go to the pub?'

'Well, it would be good to walk Bella again. She's been surgically attached to the sofa for two days and is starting to grow mould. I'll go and prod her.'

Holly hung up the phone and turned to face Lawrence, who was picking out another new song on Georgia.

'Lawry… Do you mind if we go and meet her?'

He looked up. 'Actually, I'm really close to mastering a new song. I might stay here and finish it if that's OK?'

'OK. And maybe when I'm back we can have a go at writing the script. I've even thought of a name for it! Mind the Gap. What do you think?! It works on two levels…'

Lawrence looked up from his guitar and into her eyes. 'Yeah, I get it! But if I'm honest, Folly, I'm not totally convinced it's film fodder. It seems a tiny bit far-fetched to me.'

Holly's heart sank a little. 'The name, or the idea?'

'That's a point though, it's that short film festival in Paris in March. We best get tickets soon. Remember, you said you'd come?'

'I did?' she said, wishing he could stay on topic for more than five seconds, just once.

'Yes! It's the European Independent Film Festival? It's like, the undisputed Mecca of Indie Films? I have to go and do the whole networking thing, but it'd be so much more fun if you came with me.'

'Are we not doing Cuba this year? Surely we should be saving all our pennies for that?'

'Yeah, we definitely will. We can totally do both.'

'With what, exactly? When did you start sweating tenners?'

'I'll sort it out, I promise… chill, Winston! How about, I start having a look at flights and stuff, while you're in the pub?'

'OK. Deal. Thanks.'

In the lounge, Bella was now mummified in duvets. There were flecks of crisps in her hair, and her laptop lay ajar on her knees. Her face was dotted with white blobs of toothpaste in a bid to dry out her spots – a technique she'd long referred to as the 'poor woman's facemask'. As she stared, transfixed at the laptop screen, the pantone of her cheeks began to change from peach to pillar box red.

'What. A. Cock,' Bella shouted at the screen.

'What's happened?'

Bella turned to face Holly. 'Here I am, screaming my guts out, mourning the death of my relationship, not knowing if I'll live to see another day, and Sam Cocknamara is joining groups like "Bring Back Superted!"' Bella lifted up her laptop as if to throw it across the room, then seemed to change her mind and rested it back on her knees. 'Oh and get this – Sam's status update, 48 hours after breaking up with his girlfriend of just over two years…'

Holly walked towards the iconic pale blue and white webpage. 'Sam Macnamara…' she read aloud, '"can't decide which is better – crunchy peanut butter or smooth?" Mmmm. That is a bit of a kick in the teeth.'

'Especially when, as any douche knows, it's crunchy,' Bella said, scowling.

'Although maybe it's some really clever metaphor, for life?'

'Nice try. But no, I don't think he's that clever. The last time I tried to discuss metaphor with Sam he thought I was talking about bull-fighting. He really is that thick.'

Holly shook her head, her eyes landing on the empty vodka bottle and half-eaten bag of jelly babies at Bella's feet. 'Right well, I'm not sure you'll be up to it, or that you need to add to the alcohol that's already colonising your veins, but some of us are

51

going to the pub. I'd like to recommend you take this opportunity to try and do outdoors – take a short intermission from moping?'

Bella shook her head. The prospect of having to act happy again so soon did not appeal. After crying for so long, she felt snug as a bug nestling at sorrow's bosom. 'No, no. Not out there, not yet.'

Holly walked over to the window and peered through the gap in the dark blue blinds. There was still some daylight left; the sun wasn't quite setting. She grabbed the string and pulled.

'Hey!!! What are you doing?' screamed Bella, clamping her hands over her eyes.

'You have a date in the bathroom. There's someone in there I'd like you to meet. He's called Mr Shower Head. Now. Come on!'

Reluctantly, Bella relented. But instead of hoisting herself up on the sofa in order to stand up, she went for the roll and land technique. Still swaddled in blankets, she slowly rolled onto the floor in the manner of a depressed pancake. Then Holly began to peel off the blankets, Bella whimpering as the cold air hit her pyjamas. She stood up, shook her hair free of some of the crisp crumbs, then hobbled towards the door in the pink duvet slippers.

'YAY. Well done you. Listen, you get in the shower, I'll make you a cup of sugary tea and put it in your room for afters, OK?'

'Thanks,' mumbled Bella, stepping out into the hallway and walking like something from *Dawn of the Dead*. Holly went to put the kettle on. Moments later, there was an almighty shriek, followed by what sounded like a herd of elephants jumping on top of each other.

Holly ran to the landing. She looked down to see Bella in a crumpled heap at the bottom of the stairs.

'FUUUuuuuuuCK! I've broken my arse!'

Holly ran down the stairs. 'I did try and warn you! No walking in the slippers! They are strictly for loafing!'

'I forgot I had them on!'

'Sorry!' Holly said, folding Bella into her arms.

'Hey, at least I can't get any lower now, can I?' Bella said, shrieking with laughter, tears streaming down her face.

Forty minutes and thirty millilitres of soothing Aloe Vera gel later, they set off. After wandering down the long and winding Tufnell Park Road, Bella and Holly arrived at Holloway Road. Aesthetically, the contrast never failed to bring a shock to Holly's system. The way the charming Victorian conversions morphed into grey concrete 1960s blocks and stalls flogging mobile phones. Slowly they strolled down the rows of off-licenses and discount clothing shops, with dated shopfronts.

Just as they turned right onto the road, Holly felt the wind tugging at her hair, forcing her to wrap her charcoal-grey duffel coat tighter around her. Holloway Road appeared to have its own microclimate – it was always cold and windy, no matter what the weather was doing anywhere else. As if on cue, it then began to rain. Holly pulled her coat above her head to protect her curls from going fuzzy.

'Ah, home sweet booze,' Bella said, as they walked through the doors to the Big Blue and she leaped towards a cluster of free sofas, draping her long red coat over the biggest armchair.

'I'll have a Vodka and Red Bull if you're going up to the bar,' Bella said, slumping into a chair and resuming the affectation of a broken-hearted creature.

'Of course. Although, I can't believe you still drink that university shite. You'll be after a Snakebite and black soon!' Holly said, looking at the door and seeing Olivia walk in.

'Hi, Liv,' Holly said, moving in for a hug.

'Oh my days, Holly, what's happening to your eye? It keeps jittering! Are you developing a nervous tic?'

'Oh, my eyelid? It's been doing that for days now. I didn't realise anyone else could see it twitching. Do I look like a circus freak?'

'No more than usual,' Bella said.

'That's stress, that is,' Olivia said, 'when your eyelid gets a trapped nerve. It's stress, or lack of sleep.'

'Oh well, I'm sure it will go away. What's everyone drinking? I'm getting this round.'

'Hendricks and slim-line, please,' Olivia said. 'Remind me again why you guys drink here?' she added as she sat down on the only non-saggy bit of sofa, surveying the scattering of Arsenal-shirted, skin-headed punters. As her eyes took in the peeling upholstery and the lighting that hid a multitude of nicotine stains on the walls, her expression read, 'Take me back to West Didsbury!'

'Because it's cheap, and we can always get a seat,' Bella began, 'and because when you're here, you can't sink any lower. Lower your expectations, and you lower your propensity towards disappointment.' It wasn't entirely clear whether she was talking about their surroundings or something more. Either way, as was sometimes the case with Bella, there was a kernel of wisdom buried deep.

'So how's the exciting new job?' Olivia said. 'Is it getting any better?'

'Nope. Starting to really wish I'd stayed where I was. Far better to be a junior editor in a company I liked, than a senior one in a clusterfuck of an omnishambles! Not only is it such a small outfit there that I'm doubling as general office gofer, and doing all my own grading as well as the editing, but Jeremy's also got me and the other editor there competing to pitch him ideas for new shows in our spare time!'

'Bet you'd be good at that though, wouldn't you?' Bella said.

'Not the sort of rubbish he likes. From what I've seen so far, he's got the creative judgment of a discombobulated goldfish. But I'm going to give it my best shot.' Holly's voice slowed as she noticed a Vesuvius of tears erupting all over Bella's face.

'What happened?' she said, stroking Bella's hair.

'Dylan,' Bella said, as if this explained everything.

Holly's eyes narrowed in confusion.

'It's bloody, bastarding Bob, on the cocking jukebox. I was doing fine until this!'

'What's wrong with Bob Dylan?' Holly asked, regretting it as soon as she had.

'Bob Dylan is Sam's favourite singer. It's like they know!' Bella said, scowling across at a cluster of innocent bystanders at the jukebox. Then she looked hopelessly from Holly to Olivia, her eyes bloodshot.

'Oh, dear,' Olivia said, leaning forward to give Bella a hug.

Holly rubbed Bella's shoulders. 'Poor B. It is awful now, I know, but it will get better. I think. It has to, doesn't it?' Holly looked for direction from Olivia, who smiled and nodded unconvincingly. 'Um, will it help if I say something about focusing on the good times? Like, you know, it's better to have loved and lost than never to have—'

'Oh don't you dare start with that BOLLOCKS!' Bella cut in. 'Nothing but propaganda, perpetrated only by the likes of Moon Pig, to sell pointless cards! I can honestly say that I feel so much worse for having been shat on by Sam than I would do if I hadn't ever met him!' She was now swaying, having dispensed with any attempts to conceal her level of inebriation.

'Are you calling Alfred Lord Tennyson a liar?' Holly asked.

'Well surprise me, it was a bloke that said it!' Bella yelled, ever more irate. 'And since when is Lord a middle name?'

'OK,' Holly said, stroking Bella's hair again. 'Let's take some deep breaths now.'

'I'll bet Alfred didn't have any useful advice on what to do with the stupid little leftovers you have after a break-up, did he?' Bella said in between deep breaths. 'For instance, I have this weird little pack of break-up detritus that I've been carrying around all day. It's basically the contents of my "drawer" at his house. You know, the shit I'd leave at his for when I stayed over.' She paused for a breath, mid-rant. 'When I left, I just shoved the lot into my

55

rucksack, and now I don't know what to do with it all. Do I unpack each and every sad bit of toiletry and make sure I use them one by one? That might make for really sad showers?'

'Can you even say the word toiletries in singular form?' interjected Olivia, prompting a scowl-ette from Bella.

'Or, do I pack it away and save it until we ever get back together, or until I meet someone else who is ready to give me a drawer again? Is that sick though?'

'Little bit,' Olivia said.

'Haha,' snorted Holly, realising something. 'You've got a BOYFRIEND PACK! You beautiful nut-nut!'

'Just throw it all away, surely?' Olivia said. 'Buy new stuff. I don't know why you didn't just leave it all there!'

'Where is it all? Let me at it!' Holly said.

Reluctantly, Bella produced the Boyfriend Pack from within her rucksack. She opened the bag and upturned it so that the contents splayed out all over the floor. Shampoo miniatures, a small travel hairdryer, hairbrush, manicure set and suchlike.

Holly dived in to claim some of the miniatures. 'These will come in handy for the gym!'

'When have you ever been to a gym?' Olivia said, who had started going to Gym Box every morning at 6 a.m. without fail since moving down to London.

'I'm going to start. This will make me start!'

'I guess I could use that hairdryer if you're not going to use it,' Olivia said, grabbing it with both hands.

Before long, the bag was empty, save some weathered nail-files, and the problem was solved.

Fuuuuuuuuck, was all Holly could think as she stared at the empty bag. What if she ever broke up with Lawrence? After nearly five years, it would be her life in duplicate. Her Boyfriend Pack would be more than some tiny Dick Whittington pouch; it would probably stretch to three suitcases' worth.

'So,' Bella said, turning to Olivia in a bid to deflect the embarrassment away from herself if only momentarily. 'How are you, Liv? How have you been coping?'

'Yeah, fine. Ross has been in touch a few times over the house stuff. He's finished buying me out, so it feels good not to be tied together by bricks and mortar anymore! I had to see him the other day, just to give him back a few of his things and sign all the papers. I'd thought it would be good to clear the air a little. But it turned out to be like a kind of exit interview, you know, like when you leave a job? He kept telling me all the things I could have done better!'

'I hope you made sure you gave him ample "360 degree feed-back" in return,' Holly said.

'Oh I did! I can't help still missing him a bit though. You know, there are just so many reminders of him everywhere I go. Ridiculous things! Like, a pop-up online advert turned up in my face the other day, for this anti-virus software he used to go on about. It reminded me of how I used to find it so chivalrous, the way he'd spend hours installing updates on my laptop, and programming my phone for me. Now I've got no one to do all those things. So I couldn't help missing the little dweeb when I saw that – just a bit. And oh! Then the other day this big lorry drove by and stopped by me at a traffic light. As I walked past, the driver started singing the first song we ever kissed to!'

'Weird. What was it?' Holly asked.

'Oh God. This really old track from the eighties, by Simple Minds, called "Don't you forget about me".'

'Oh I love that track!' Bella said, bursting into song, prompting stares from people nearby.

'But it's such an old track! That's why it weirded me out so much that some random lorry driver was singing it, at that exact moment.'

'Do you think it's a sign' Bella said, 'that you shouldn't forget him just yet?'

'Is it fuck,' Olivia said, taking a sip of her drink.

Bella laughed. 'I so know what you mean with the reminders though, Liv. Every other day, there's something else to remind me of an in-joke with Sam.'

'But you know, it's easy to go too far with that stuff. You know, drag it out beyond the point of silly,' Holly said. 'For instance, do you remember Lucy, our flatmate from uni, when she broke up with Rob?' she broke off as Olivia nodded in recognition. 'He dumped her on graduation day, the poor lamb. While the rest of us posed for photos in our gowns, Lucy was hiding in a ditch behind the university library, weeping into her mortar board, slowly dismantling the visions in her head that she'd had of them going travelling, of moving to London, living out their careers together. From her ditch, she had sat and watched as her dreams scattered into the air with all the mortar-boards. Well, that's how she put it to us after three gins later that day, anyway.'

Bella's eyes began to well with empathy for this poor girl she'd never met. 'Wow that's a ceremonious stinker of a dumping!'

'Exactly,' Olivia said, 'see, at least Sam didn't do that to you!'

Holly nodded. 'But yeah – my point is, it was so terrible a dumping that even for weeks after it happened, we'd be like, "Do you want a cup of tea Lucy?" and she'd be all, "Oh, Rob used to make me cups of tea…" and start bawling again.'

They all laughed.

'Poor Lucy, she really did milk it, no pun intended.'

'So yeah, to some extent you have to be a bit disciplined about this stuff,' Olivia said. 'You almost need a rule. Something like a "no mentioning their name more than five times a day… or, "no listening to songs that remind you of your ex" rule. Just til a certain time has passed.'

'Sounds a bit regimented, surely?' Bella said.

'Ha! Liv invented regimented. She's the most disciplined person I know!' Holly chuckled.

Olivia grinned with pride. 'Everything in life is easier to deal with if it's compartmentalised and under control!'

'But – but – we can't be that hard on ourselves straight away,' Bella said. 'Surely we're allowed some wallowing time? For instance, I know I'll probably fall apart when I see the first dandelion clock of the season.'

'Why?' Holly said.

'Oh, there's just this funny thing Sam used to do with them.' Her eyes began to water.

'What, tell the time?' Holly said.

'Well. Yes.'

'Everyone does that, B. That's not so special,' Olivia said.

Bella looked as though Olivia had just trampled all over her palatial sandcastle. 'No they don't. Not the way he did it. He used to pretend to be the speaking clock voice, and do the whole "time sponsored by Accurist" bit, like it used to say in the nineties. You had to be there.'

'Evidently,' Olivia said.

'OK, Bella darling,' Holly began. 'I know you don't want to hear this, but I'm going to say it in case it will help. Your Sam was a complete ARSE! I mean, he used to call you MISS PIGGY behind your back.'

Bella snorted.

'He didn't!' Olivia said. 'So that's where your Miss Piggy Complex comes from?'

Holly stared at Bella and thought that, in spite of her dark brown hair, her round, symmetrical face bore an ever-so-small resemblance to Jim Henson's most famous creation. And yet still there were some things you must absolutely never say to a person, and 'you look a little bit like a brunette Miss Piggy' was chief among them.

'You absolute Muppet!' Olivia punned, unwittingly. 'Why would you put up with that?'

'Blimey,' Bella said. 'Listen to us, whining on about our break-ups like a couple of miserable reprobates. We're like some lonely hearts club, only without the band.'

'Sad Bastards Anonymous, more like,' Olivia suggested, smoothing out her hair, which had become crumpled from all the recent hugging. She began foraging for her handbag under the coat pile.

'No...' Holly said, 'you guys are like some kind of bizarre break-up cult!'

Bella's eyes dilated with excitement. 'Break-up Club, surely? That's got a better ring to it? Yes! That's what we are!' Bella lurched forward, while Holly and Olivia exchanged looks of concern. 'HAHAHAHaaaa!' She clamped a hand over her mouth. 'Um, has anyone got a tissue? I think I've just been a bit sick in my mouth,' she mumbled through her fingers.

'No,' Olivia said, clearly disgusted, while Holly dug around in her bag for a tissue and handed it to Bella.

'Ha! And that can be our strapline!' Bella said through giggles, having wiped her mouth of anything offensive. She pulled out a moleskin notebook and began to jot things down in it. 'The Break-up club..'

'You cannot be serious,' Holly said.

'LOL. LOL,' Olivia said.

Everyone slowly turned to face her.

'Liv. Did you just say "laugh out loud" – like, as an acronym?' Holly asked,

Olivia nodded. 'I'm afraid the answer is yes. Yes I did.'

Bella groaned. 'Liv, you div. You can just laugh, you know. You don't need to, like, declare the laugh.'

'I'm sorry. I can't help it. It's Ross. He barely said whole words in all the time we were together. He spent so much time in those chat rooms! You'll need to bear with me while his geek vernacular wears off.'

'Anyway, we can always think up another strapline for the club,' Bella said, deadpan.

'You nut-nut; there isn't really a club. We were just twatting about,' Olivia said, looking at Holly. 'Seriously, we're not that unhinged.'

'Yes, seriously, hon, we'll be fine,' Bella said, her eyes bloodshot, mascara all over her face, and snot congregating around her nostrils.

'I don't think you should be so quick to knock it, actually,' Holly said.

Bella squinted at her in confusion.

'Yes. In fact, I was just thinking how it's kind of serendipitous that you guys have coincided. It's nice that you're there for each other, to help each other through this difficult time.'

'Next you'll be saying you're jealous,' Olivia said.

'Ha! No, you're all right,' Holly said, taking a large sip of her drink and accidentally finishing it.

4. *Habana*

'Ride horseback through the world heritage site of the Vinales Valley. Salsa through the streets of Trinidad, Cuba's museum city....'

Holly looked up from the 'Havanatur' leaflet and watched the travel agent, Cheryl, tapping away at her screen. Holly read on, beginning to swoon at the very idea of getting away. 'Lose yourself in frenetic La Habana Vieja. Enjoy home-cooked cuisine in a cosy "Casa Particulare". There's more to Cuba than Communism and Cohibas...'

'OK,' interrupted Cheryl. 'The cheapest thing I've got for you guys is with Iberia, change Madrid, for seven nine six including taxes and fuel surcharges. How about it?'

Holly gulped. 'Wow. It's four months from now, and it's that much already?'

'Or can do you a nice package deal to Varadero, if you like, for let's see – eight nine?'

Holly turned to Lawrence. They both had the same policy on package holidays: a resounding 'Hell, no.' Holiday Reps were 'for wimps from Wilmslow' was Lawrence's saying and he was sticking to it.

'No, that's OK, we'll take the flight and play it by ear when we get there.' Holly smiled at Lawrence, a scene playing in her mind of the two of them on a motorcycle, cruising up a highway lined with palm trees, whizzing past wild horses and tobacco plantations, her hair blowing in the wind, her arms clasped around him as he rounded corners at break-neck speed. Obviously, for the purposes of this daydream, Lawrence looked a lot more like Gael García Bernal than he did in reality.

'OK, if you're sure,' said Cheryl. 'Actually, you get in quite late from this flight, would you like me to book your first night's accommodation?'

'Makes sense – thanks,' Holly said, looking at Lawrence, who was nodding.

'Well, here's one hotel we recommend. The Saratoga. A lot of our customers have loved it there.'

Cheryl rotated her monitor to show a maroon webpage displaying a dreamlike wonderland straight out of a catalogue for Paradise. It was all gilded interiors, high ceilings and colonial architecture. There was even a lavish rooftop pool overlooking the whole of Havana. Basically, gulp.

'Wow,' Holly said, 'that's Havana heaven.'

Lawrence squeezed her hand. 'Imagine getting into that pool after a nine and a half hour flight. That's not Havana, that's Navana.'

'Ick, Lawrence!' shouted Holly. 'Did you just pun?'

'Yes. You're right I did. I'm sorry, it was a proper stinker too; I just couldn't hold it in.'

Lawrence pretended to 'fan' the air around him, as if to rid the air of the stench, while Cheryl looked on, bemused.

'Sorry. How much is it per night?' Holly asked.

'200 convertible pesos. I'm not sure what that is in sterling at the moment.'

'Let's take it!' Lawrence said. 'It's a poor country, isn't it? Pesos probably aren't worth much, are they?'

Holly knew how ridiculous Lawrence sounded, but she just

couldn't take her eyes off the rooftop pool. 'If you say so… It's only one night anyway; we can rough it the rest of the time to make up for it.'

'Smashing. So with the hotel included, the grand total comes to one seven nine fifty. Now, I will be needing the whole amount now on either a credit or debit card,' she said, looking to Lawrence.

'Wow. Flights to Paris for only £59.99!' he said, staring at a poster on the wall. 'That's so much cheaper than Eurostar!'

Holly shifted about in her seat. 'One thing at a time, dear,' she said in that way they sometimes did when they pretended they were an old married couple. Tentatively, she reached for her purse and dug out her credit card. 'Anyway, I'm sure it'll be more than that – see how it says "FROM" £59.99… that's the trap to lure you in. Chances are, it'll actually cost more like £159.99.'

'Actually, the price is what it says it is,' Cheryl added helpfully. 'Sorry. I'll just go and get the card machine.' She smiled and then headed out into the back room.

'So,' Lawrence went on, 'I'm just thinking, it might be good to book our tickets to Paris while we're here. And maybe they can do us a special deal, since we're spending so much already?'

Holly felt a tiny knot form in her stomach.

'Um, Lawrence, I already said, I'm not sure I want to go to the film festival. I thought you understood. Also, have you SEEN how much we're about to spend? Sorry – *I'm* about to spend, since you can't pay me back til next month? When for all I know I'll be out of a job by the time we go?'

'I know, Folly. And don't think I'm not hugely, massively grateful, 'cause I really SO am! Don't worry about the job stuff – I'll help you come up with some ideas for shows. But I also just think it's really important to spend money on something that might potentially help both our careers?'

'I'm sorry, I just don't think it will. Surely we've both got more chance of improving our careers if we actually use the time to make a film, rather than schmoozing about drinking champagne and watching other people's work?' The knot was growing in size. Now she was wondering if this whole thing wasn't a huge mistake.

Lawrence opened his mouth to protest, but Cheryl came back to the counter. She tapped some buttons and stared at the screen. 'Oh. Computer's frozen. I was just about to confirm your seats. Hang on, let me just reboot.'

Holly could feel the Gobi desert relocating to her throat. Was it unfeasibly hot in here suddenly? Was this I.T. fail some kind of sign not to book the tickets? No... signs were nonsense. They'd been dreaming about this holiday since forever! Well, since their first date at a bar in Waterloo called Cubana, where they had danced salsa and smoked cigars until 3 a.m. As first dates went, it was up there with the best of them. It had started out with them watching a play at the Old Vic. Afterwards, they'd strolled along the Thames looking for somewhere to drink, completed the obligatory circuit as every bar was closing up, before heading back to the Cubana Bar with its reassuringly late license. They'd been the last to leave, but not before promising the Cuban musicians they'd all go and stay with their relatives in Havana one day. Which is how they came to be sat here now, in Tooting Bec Discount Travel Centre.

'Holly,' Lawrence interrupted her reverie.

'Yes?'

'Did you hear any of what I just said?'

'What? Yes. Sure.'

'So you don't mind lending me the money? Oh, you're the best girlfriend ever!'

'For the Cuba flights, sure. I already said I'd put that on my credit card. So long as you'll pay me back when you can...'

Lawrence looked down at his dilapidated trainers. 'No, I was just saying that if I don't get the flights to Paris now, they'll be astronomical next month. So, if you lend me the money for that now, I'll then have more money to pay you back for the Cuba money next month when I've been paid for that corporate filming job I did? Basically, it just makes good financial sense to get them now before they double in price?'

The knot in her belly, previously conker-sized, was now more iceberg in scale.

'Holly?' Lawrence took her hand. 'You'd just be helping me out so much. Remember last year, when that rep from Red Green films was so positive about my work? I think if I can just get talking to them again this year then I might honestly have a shot at being taken on.' He stared at Holly with his 'look, I'm a reasonable man' face on. 'Folly, it's only £50. If I had it and you needed it I wouldn't think twice! You know, when I've made it, you won't know what's hit you, you'll be sooooo spoiled!'

How did he do that? Not only manipulate her into lending him money, but also insult her by simultaneously insinuating that she was mean with her money? There was no winning.

'Besides, you can just use Lawrence Logic and pretend the Cuba flights were £25 extra each. I know, I've got it! You're always saying you'd go to the cinema more if only you had the time, aren't you?'

'Yes.'

'Well… our plane will have in-flight entertainment on it, won't it, Cheryl?'

Cheryl nodded. 'Yes, it should have a full programme of the latest movies.' She turned to stare at Lawrence, as though intrigued as to where he was going with this.

'Well, an eight-hour flight is like going to the movies at least three or four times. So, at standard central London prices, you're looking at £10 times four, plus if you indulge in popcorn once or twice, well, you're already way over the £50 mark already!'

Cheryl looked impressed at Lawrence Vorderman. 'That's a funny way of looking at things. I might start doing that…'

Holly nodded weakly. 'Yes it is. He's a bit special, this one.' She turned to Lawrence. 'Have you checked there'll be popcorn on the plane then?'

'Ha-ha. You get the point, don't you?'

Cheryl was smiling at them, clearly having fallen for Lawrence's Odd-box charms.

Lawrence looked at Holly, hope flashing in his blinking, puppy-dog eyes.

'Please, Fol? You know I'll pay you back.'

Holly sighed.

'OK. Sorry, Cheryl, can we just get another flight on there too? One return to Paris?'

'Just the one?' said Cheryl, looking to Holly in surprise.

'Yes. I'm not going, I can't afford it.'

As Lawrence went through the finer details, Holly picked up her other credit card and handed it to Cheryl. 'Whack the whole sorry lot on there please.'

Lawrence grinned his schoolboy smile as Cheryl totted up the bill. Holly was practically shaking as she typed in her PIN and the receipt whirred and printed the four-figure amount that was pushing one month's salary. It's just pretend money, she told herself. And it'll be a great chance for us to put the spark back. And he'll definitely pay me back before my contract finishes, so it's basically all good. Plus one day, Lawrence actually will be a red carpet sensation able to treat us and I'll feel much less like a gargantuan mug, so thinking about it, we're totally fine and dandy here aren't we, she decided, just as Lawrence leaned over and kissed her on the cheek.

'Thank you so, so much. Right, I'm taking you home for a mojito to say thank you!'

'Oh, thanks.'

'And Hol?'

'What?'

'You're sure you won't come with me to Paris?'

'ARRRRGH. NO!' she squawked. 'My love,' she added, seeing the hurt in his eyes.

As they walked up the road towards Lawrence's flat, Holly's

phone beeped with a text message: 'You are cordially invited to an "Eff-Off Valentine's Day party". Next Saturday at Flat A, 249 Fortess Road, Tufnell. Bring booze, snacks and your sexy (ideally single) selves, 7 p.m. onwards. Love B xx.'

'Oh right? I think I've just been invited to a party at my own house. How very Bella!' Holly said as they walked through Lawrence's cluttered but high-ceilinged hallway. Once again, as she walked into the tiny bedroom she'd dubbed The Lawrence Pit, she had to restrain herself from calling 999 to inform the police of a burglary. It looked like someone had taken a machine gun, pointed it at the room and splattered it with jumble-sale bullets. In the far corner of The Lawrence Pit was a not-quite-double bed. Next to that, a desk bowed inwards with the weight of the enormous monitor, currently doubling as TV and computer. Next to that stood the leaning tower of Ikea – a cream canvas wardrobe that was perpetually lopsided: having begun life as a temporary storage solution, it had become permanent as time went on. It was empty bar a few discarded items; among them a suit jacket that hadn't seen daylight since 1997. The rest of his clothes were hung neatly… on the floor. Holly tried not to let any of this bother her as they kissed, fell into bed in a mojito-fuelled slumber.

The next morning, Holly was playing one of her favourite weekend games: setting her alarm at least an hour before she needed to get up, then pressing snooze every nine minutes and drifting back into legalised, blissful oblivion. On this particular Saturday, things were getting a little out of hand. She'd been snoozing for almost 90 minutes when Lawrence interrupted her by planting a kiss on her nose.

She opened her eyes one at a time. Lawrence was dressed in his Che Guevara T-shirt again, some rogue chest hairs poking out of the top.

'Folly, sorry to wake you. I have to go now. Is it OK to borrow some cashish?'

'Mmm? Sure. There's a load of change in my purse. Help yourself,' she said through slumber, before rolling back under the covers, wishing that his broken blinds would magically fix themselves in order to cover the gap where the sun was streaming through.

'Oh,' he said, surveying the coins. 'I need a bit more than that. I've got to pay for my website hosting tomorrow or else it will all come crashing down.'

'Is anything actually on your site yet?'

'Well, no, but I have to pay rent on it still, otherwise I'll lose the domain name, or something. Sorry. My Solo card is up to its limit, and mum said she can't give me any more money this month. Can you lend me, like, fifty, that should cover it? Sorry, I hate to ask…'

As if on cue, the opening beats to *The Littlest Hobo* bleated out like a cacophony into her left ear. And the snooze fest was over with a thud. Holly punched the 'stop' button on her phone, and resolved to change the once-nostalgic-now-infuriating alarm tone at the next available opportunity. She sat upright, shook her hair, and rubbed the sleep dust from her eyes. Keep calm, she told herself. Yes, he's the only person she knew that still took money from his parents. Yes, it was the third time she'd lent him money in as many weeks. But these were all things she should think and not say, in order to prevent an outbreak of world war three.

'Um, how to put this without sounding like a naggy old hag. Did you not hear me the other day when I said my job is currently hanging in the balance? This is radical but – have you ever thought about getting a part-time job, or something? Just for a bit, so you can catch up on your finances a little?'

'Oh here we go. By the way Holly, it's really NOT sexy how much you sound like my dad sometimes. "I don't know why you don't go in for bar work, or take a Saturday job as a labourer,"' he said, mocking his dad's West Country accent. Holly couldn't help giggling at his performance, even if it was designed to wind her up. Bollocks, why did he have to be funny, even when he was being a knob?

'Folly,' he said, back to his normal accent, 'we've been through this before. I need all the time in the day to work on my films. On my reel. On keeping in shape. So I don't have time – that's reason number one. Reason number two: If I have a part-time job – for example – an usher at a crap musical, I'll just feel shit about myself, and I'll be too tired and deflated to work on my directing stuff. Then before I know it, I'll actually BECOME an usher. That will be my life. People will look at me while I shine a light to their seats at We Will Rock You and they'll say, "Oh there goes that nice usher man again. I wonder how many years of training he took to get there."'

Holly rolled her eyes and tried to call to mind all the reasons she was with him. Funny. Intelligent. Caring (sometimes). Gorgeous. She checked them all off, and then began to dig around in her hard drive of happy memories. The day he'd taken her to the seaside as a surprise, and they'd ended up sleeping on the beach under the stars. The time she'd been to stay with his family in Cornwall and they'd all played guitar karaoke together out in their garden. And... and... But the images were beginning to fade; the more Lawrence wittered on, the more pixelated the halcyon days became...

'Don't you see, Holly? The money saved will be nullified by the psychological damage incurred – which will slowly become my undoing.'

...until they were gone entirely, and all she could see standing in front of her was an absolute tool.

'Surely you can understand that, Hol?' the tool was saying.

She sat up in bed and stared at him.

'Lawrence. Just for a second, pretend that your parents aren't around to help you out, and to pay your bills. You wouldn't just give up on being a director, would you? You'd find a way?'

Lawrence appeared to have stopped listening. He was shoving clothes into a bag, no discernible logic to his approach. He calmly upturned the entire contents of his underwear drawer. In amongst the pants and old coins, there fell a bottle of lighter fluid, some cigarette filter tips and an old Pringles tube. He pocketed the change, and left the drawer and its offspring all over the floor.

Whenever Holly watched him packing for anything, or getting ready to go out, it was like watching small hand grenades being detonated one after the other. And yet none of this bothered Lawrence, who remained calm throughout as he moved on to dragging a massive holdall down from the top of the wardrobe. As he did, a thousand more things came cascading down all around, knocking other things flying.

'You know, Lawry, maybe you'd even feel proud of yourself, for getting there on your own? Besides – when did you last actually do a proactive film anyway? I'd really love for us to work on Mind the Gap. If you could only help me write it. I know you had some doubts about it, but I can really imagine it having a powerful twist at the end!'

'All right, maybe.'

Holly felt the good kind of butterflies kick off in her belly. 'Yay! How about we try and make it in time to enter into the next Future Shorts?'

'Okay. Sure. Just as soon as I've finished wading through corporate sludge for Barclays. And once I've built my website.'

'You've been saying that for years.'

'Have you ever tried to understand HTML? It's, like, harder than Mandarin! Anyway, we both know this isn't really about coding, is it? This is about that giant chip you've got on your shoulder, isn't it? That, just because my parents have been supportive, it's somehow my fault that yours aren't?'

'All I'm saying is, I've always had to do part-time jobs to get by, and it's not done me any harm.'

'But I don't have time! No offence Folly, but editing's nowhere near as competitive or hard to get into as directing, is it?'

'I'm sorry? What did you just say?'

Lawrence inched away, a look of fear on his face.

'Do you think I just filled out an application form? Did my job just fall into my lap from the sky? No – I did twelve months of unpaid internships while also working in an effing call centre!'

Holly climbed out of bed and began throwing things into a bag. She cast a look at herself in a nearby mirror. Catastrophic bags under the eyes, and a spot the size of Copenhagen brewing... but she could probably just manage the journey home looking like this. Provided she held her head down and avoided all eye contact. Anything but stay here a minute longer. She had just hit her Lawrence Limit. And in her experience, it was always better to walk away when this happened. She pulled on her jeans, and shoved her red hoody on over her head. 'I'll do a transfer when I get home,' she said, her voice measured.

Lawrence looked humbled for a moment. 'Thanks baby. Look I'm sorry; I didn't mean it to sound like that. I'll walk with you to the bus if you wait five minutes. Don't you want a shower or something?'

'No, I'll have a bath when I get home.'

'Holly,' he said, taking her by the shoulders and looking her in the eye.

'Womble.'

Holly broke away and picked up her bag.

He grabbed Georgia and started to pick out a familiar tune. 'Feels like nothing matters... in our private universe...' he sang.

Arses, thought Holly, trying to keep her armour in place. It was, to use so saccharine a phrase, 'their song'. It was also so ludicrously moving that it could engender a tear in the most stony-hearted of folk. But not today. Right now, the dulcet early-nineties tones of Crowded House just weren't up to the job.

'Goodbye, Lawrence.'

'You know, Holly, it's actually not my fault that I have supportive parents,' he began.

Oh, here it comes, she thought. Any moment now he'll step on the hidden tripwire and blow her resolve into smithereens.

'Just because they help me out, doesn't mean I don't work hard myself. But it's like, for some reason, nothing I do will ever be enough for you. You know, they'll never say about me that, "Oh, that Lawrence Hill, he had it so tough, he grew up on a council estate and triumphed against all adversity,"' he said, as though he was quoting from an imaginary *Sunday Times* Culture section. '"He got himself through university before he became a Bafta-winning success." No, Holly, I'll never be able to say that, because yes – I had help – I had a privileged upbringing – I went to a fee-paying school! I'm sorry! But for the love of shit, it's not my fault!'

Oh. She'd never actually thought about it like that before.

'Lawrence, are you honestly expecting me to sympathise with you that you've not had it tough?'

'In a way. I think a lot of people trade off their poverty, and make themselves sound all holier-than-thou that they lived in a council estate, had to do ten jobs at once just to live, and wore nothing but ill-fitting hand-me-downs. It's annoying.'

'Jesus, who are you? I wore nothing but ill-fitting hand-me-downs! I don't understand why we are together!'

'Shit, sorry Holly. That came out all wrong. I love you baby. Please don't shout.'

She stared at him as her arms folded themselves.

'I'm sorry. Listen, I'm so proud of you, you know I am. You're an amazing editor, and you've done so well to get where you are…'

'Yeah. Because *Prowl* is really about reaching the absolute zenith of my creativity, isn't it!' Holly said, gathering her bags and stomping out of the room, stubbing her toe on one of the distended cupboard drawers. 'AAARRRRGH!' she exclaimed; the

73

final chip in her resolve against hissy fits. She walked down the hallway and slammed the door behind her for maximum impact, before feeling her eyes fill up with warm saltwater.

As she stepped out into sunny Streatham, thought number one was, bollocks, why had she inherited her dad's temper? Thought number two, holy crap, she was about to lend Lawrence even more money! And thought number three, how many rows had they had this year? Which was closely connected to thought four: when was their sell-by date?

*

Holly.Braithwaite@TotesamazeProductions.com to
Jeremy.Philpott@TotesamazeProductions.com
Subject: Possible series idea

Hey Jeremy
Sorry to email on the weekend but I just had an idea for a series that I wanted to run past you: THE HELIUM DEPOT.

This is a story about a celestial lost property bureau. A control centre where all the helium balloons that children have ever lost go to. See, when you're a kid, losing a helium balloon is one of the saddest things that can ever happen to you. Wouldn't it be great if they all ended up somewhere safe though?

In this story, they go to a great big balloon depot in the sky – think TFL's lost property bureau, only more magical. Maybe at the centre of it all is this one character, Engelbert, who's been running it for years. He's got big red cheeks from re-inflating all the balloons and then gradually returning them to their original owners, who are all grown up now as it takes him so long to find them. After a while, he gets a little bit disillusioned, because,

74

while some of the kids are delighted and moved to tears, others are strangely aloof as they're so disconnected from their childhood self.

That's as far as I've got with it, Jez – possibly a bit bonkers but I wanted to run it past you. Look forward to hearing what you think either way,

Holly.

Jeremy.Philpott@TotesamazeProductions.com to
Holly.Braithwaite@TotesamazeProductions.com
Subject: Re: Possible series idea

Braithwaite,
Were you on helium when you wrote this?

I've got two words for you... ASDA MUMS.

Our current audience have a simple goal in life – either to be famous, or to be able to afford a timeshare apartment in Benidorm.

In other words, you're aiming too high with this. Go LOWBROW. Think of the lowest common denominator you can, then go EVEN LOWER. What was it that Oscar Wilde said? Shoot for the gutter, and you might just end up in the drain.

Also – and this is fairly key – try and move away from fiction and into factual.

Better still, Reality.

Hope that helps.

Keep 'em comin. I'm having a meeting with the channel next week, so I need you and Pascal firing on all cylinders and all hands on deck!

Jx

P.S. I've mentioned this already but just a small reminder for your next episode of Prowl: there are a few more ad breaks to take into account than in terrestrial. (Yesterday's ep. was exported over length AGAIN.) Let's get this confusion ironed out for next time? Happiness?

P.P.S. NEVER apologise for emailing over the weekend.

Holly.Braithwaite@TotesamazeProductions.com to
Mark@RedGreenFilms.com
Subject: Apple Z! APPLE Z!

Dear Mark,

Sorry, what I'm about to say is probably professional suicide. But… please can I have my old job back? I've made a gargantuan error and things are really not working out.

Love and big slices of humble pie,
Holly x

5. *Unexpected Item in the Bagging Area*

'Hol, have you got the glass-effect champagne flutes?'

Holly was staring down at her mobile phone while leaning against an overflowing trolley. They were in their local supermarket, doing a last minute dash for party supplies.

'Sweetie, the flutes.'

Holly, as Head of Disposable Catering Equipment, nodded. 'Yep. I'm on it.'

Bella looked Holly in the eye. 'What's wrong?'

'I've just had an email from my old boss. It seems any chance I had of escaping my job at TotesAwful has now gone.'

'Oh no! What did he say?'

'I'm actually quite hurt! All he said was, "Sorry, the position's been filled. I'm sure you'll work it out one way or another. Good luck, M x".'

'That's a bit cryptic! Oh well. Looks like you'll have to style it out with weird old Jez. Poor Hollychops!'

'Thanks hon,' Holly said as she clocked a flash of Bella's stomach, which was now looking considerably concave. 'But never mind me, how are you feeling?'

'Mmm, I think today is a good day. I managed to eat a whole apple.'

'Good!'

As they pushed their trolley past a window, Bella caught sight of her face in the reflection. 'Christ, look at this new one coming through. Are you sure I won't scare away all the guests? People will think it's a Halloween party! More to the point though, WHY AM I STILL GETTING SPOTS? I am three years shy of 30!' she sighed and looked skywards to the God Of Acne Redemption.

Holly stifled a laugh and pretended to scan Bella's face. 'Where? I can't see it! You look fine.'

'Two words you must never say to women! Fine or Nice! You know that!'

'Sorry. OK, well, it's not as bad as you think.'

'I thought you couldn't see it. It's a proper big momma. And I can already feel it's got a little baby one coming through just next to it.'

'You mean it's "with child"?'

'Yes!' Bella said, laughing. 'But aside from the horror that is my face, I'm really looking forward to getting to work on The List.'

'List?'

'Everyone has a list.'

'The only list I have is a to-do list. It begins with "back up my photos", and ends in "clean out the cupboard under the stairs".'

'No, not that kind of a to-do list. No, THE LIST is the secret wish list you have in your head, of guys you'd sleep with if you were single.'

'Not me. I've never had one of those,' Holly said, but at the exact moment Leading-Man Luke's face popped into her head.

'So yeah. Bollocks to Sam – I'm just dead excited to be single again! I'm like, let's get out there and shop for sweets! Yeah, instead of thinking, "bollocks, I've just lost the person I wanted to spend the rest of my life with," I've decided to flip this fucker around!' Bella stood in the centre of the frozen foods aisle and looked up towards the overhead lighting, her eyes dancing with anticipation for what the future might bring. 'I'm free! I can dance on my own like nobody's watching me! At any given moment, wherever I go, whatever I do, I could meet my next love interest! It's just totally invigorating to know I've not yet had my last first kiss!'

'Well that sounds utterly rubbish,' Holly said, trying not to be swept away by how entirely exciting singleton-dom sounded, suppressing the tiny voice inside of her that was whispering, 'I want some of that! Take me with you!'

'Have you heard from Lawrence?' Bella added, jolting Holly out of her reverie.

'No. It's been a week since we rowed! I think maybe I was too harsh on him. I don't even know if he's coming to the party. Should I break the silence?'

'No, darling. I expect he's gone into his cave, which means he'll probably not reply and you'll feel like shit. No, let's get the rest of this shopping done so we can get home and crack open the rosé. Everything will seem brighter then.'

Half an hour later, Holly, Bella and their flatmate Daniel were hauling shopping bags up the stairs. Daniel attempted to open the internal front door, but it appeared to be blocked by an incoming tide of coats.

'OK. Bella that's it. This is officially no longer a functioning thoroughfare. No one can feasibly need this many coats,' he said, gesturing to the suspended jumble sale and the full-to-bursting Morrisons plastic bag that hung by a plastic thread on top of them.

Bella looked up and blinked innocently.

'He does have a point, B. And this Morrison's bag really has to go. WHAT IS IT?'

Bella frowned. 'Don't be mean. It's the break-up bag. It's all of Sammy's shit. I can't bear to have it in my room, but I also can't bear to throw it away. So it's in no man's land until I can work it out.'

'Well it's blocking entry to the flat, so you'll have to find another place for it,' Daniel said. 'It's practically a Health and Safety violation. Just think if there was a fire…'

Bella, who had already made a start on the rosé on the way home, began to laugh. 'Hey, it's the Break-up Bag! From the Break-up Superstore!' She took the bag off the hook and began sifting through Sam-remnants. Her face became overcast.

'What's in it anyway?' Holly peered into the bag. One pair of trainers, beyond toxic. Two packs of cigarettes, one half empty. Some boxer shorts. A curling toothbrush. A Lynx deodorant. And lastly, a framed piece of paper bearing what could only be described as an actor's manifesto.

'What is this…?' Holly said, reading the manifesto. '"The Theatre speaks to the Actor…"' she began, clearing her throat, '"I will give you hunger and pain and sleepless nights… Beauty and glimpses of… Heavenly light, all these I will give to you."'

'Give me that!' Bella wrestled the frame from Holly's hand. Then she read aloud with pretend-gravitas, '"None of these things you will have constantly… All these things will be momentary: Adventure, and be bold!"'

Holly doubled over on the floor laughing. Bella slumped down next to her.

'Well, that confirms it then,' Holly said.

'What?'

'More reasons to break up with Sammy…' sang Holly, aping the old 'More reasons to shop at Morrisons' jingle.

Bella had tears down her face, but was unable to resist joining in with the singing. As they sang in loud, unabashed hollers, their arms doing improvised actions, three coats came cascading to the floor, proving that perhaps the Break-up Bag had been serving a more practical gravity-defying purpose than they'd realised.

Daniel re-emerged from his bedroom and cleared his throat. 'Right, well, I'm going to start setting up the party. You're welcome to give me a hand when you've finished your pantomime.' He squeezed past, knocking even more hats and scarves flying. Holly and Bella looked at each other and giggled.

'In all seriousness though, when will you actually do the break-up exchange? It's surely not good feng shui to have all these memories around, cluttering the hallway like this?'

Bella laughed, taking another swig of rosé before heave-hoing some of the coats into the hall cupboard. Then she slammed the door after them, oblivious to the stray mitten-on-a-string that kept getting caught in the door frame. 'Oh why won't it shut? Why? Why!'

Holly looked up to see that Bella's face was beginning to crumple – a sign she was on the threshold of hysteria. Uh-oh, not a crying fit, please. That could set them back hours in terms of party preparation time. Holly leaned forward, grabbed the stray mitten and tucked it inside the cupboard. 'There,' she said, kissing Bella on the forehead.

'Thank you,' Bella replied, slamming the cupboard shut. 'Why aren't there people around to help with this stuff, to make life easier? Why aren't there professionals you can employ to mediate between you and your bastard ex?'

'You make a good point. Yes, they could be like Break-up Bailiffs! You hire them for a nominal fee, and they do the awkward exchange of stuff, so you don't have to!'

'Yes! Hell, they could bring me my sleeping bag that I left at his! And my purple tights! And my...' Bella trailed off, her face flushed. 'Oh my giddy Christ. I've left my COCKING rabbit at his. Is there anything in this world more ridiculous?'

The image of Sam cleaning out his drawers and discovering one of Bella's many battery-operated devices was too much to prevent them from collapsing into giggles again.

'Or, here's a thought,' Bella said when they regained composure, 'instead of Break-up Bailiffs, maybe there should be some kind of art exhibition, like a kind of heartache amnesty? It'd be like TFL's lost and found, only much, much sadder!'

'Oh yes! And we could call it "Loved and Lost", like from that Tennyson poem you hate!'

'And people could auction off some of the stuff! Like, it's too sad for me to wear those red LK Bennett shoes that Sam bought me, but someone else might just get loads of use out of them and maybe the money could go to a charity like Relate, the marriage guidance people! And hey, we could source all the artefacts through Facebook! And we could do a spin-off TV show that you could pitch to TotesAwful and buy yourself another six months work with! And, and…!' Bella stopped; her eyes popping with excitement. At this point, Holly knew from experience there was every chance Bella would go into hyper-drive, get locked on and not let up until they'd quit their jobs and held the auction right then and there.

'Yes. It's an awesome idea and WE WILL DO IT, but for now, we have a party to set up, capiche?'

Bella nodded, busy scribbling in her pink notebook.

'Look, I'll take custody of the bag for now. Just try not to think about it, or Sam, OK?'

'Thanks Hol, you're a legend,' she said, hugging Holly.

Holly took the 'Break-up Bag' and tied the ends together tightly, as though this would lock in all the memories and keep them away. Holding it at arm's length, she carried it to the cupboard and shoved it in, right to the back. Then she headed to her room and began to think about what dress she could wear that wouldn't require a bringing forward of the annual event that was ironing. She opened her wardrobe.

After a few minutes of sifting, the doorbell rang.

'Fuck sticks,' Holly said as she tripped over the half-detonated shopping bags on the way to the door.

'Oh no! Who's here already?!' Bella said, emerging from her room with a homemade egg and oatmeal face mask on. 'Why would people be early for things? It's the height of rudeness!' as she spoke, a large dollop of oatmeal-yolk fell off her cheek and landed splat on the floor.

'And I'm sure they'd be charmed to hear you say so, lovely. Anyway, calm yourself! It'll just be Liv; I asked her to be an early person.' Holly stepped over the yolk and opened the door.

Olivia strolled in, carrying a holdall filled with food in tins and plastic containers. 'Here you go ladies, I had a bit of a bake-off with myself and got a little carried away,' Olivia said. 'There's some cupcakes, flapjacks, some pies and things.'

'Wow, amazing, thank you Liv!'

'This is so generous of you!' Bella said, opening up the boxes and peering in.

'It's amazing there's any left though, I kept on sampling the goods as I made them. I must've eaten my own body weight in butter! Definitely need to go to the gym tomorrow! Anyway, who's coming tonight?' Olivia asked with a definite subtext of 'will there be any Olivia-types?'

'I'm not sure to be honest,' Holly said. 'It was all so last minute; whoever shows up will be a bonus.'

'Harry's coming though isn't he?' Bella said.

'Oh yes, I can't wait to see him!'

'Who's Harry?' Olivia asked.

'My oldest best friend from school. You won't fancy him Liv, before you even go there. Plus he's practically married and is rarely allowed out – we lost him down a domestic abyss in Suburbiton some years ago. Which is why it's so blooming exciting he's even coming!'

There was a knock on the internal front door. Holly opened it to reveal a smiling man with a navy trilby hat perched on a bed of ginger hair.

'The man himself!' she threw her arms around Harry, knocking his hat flying. He was always wearing hats of some sort. Possibly to divert attention from his slightly receding hairline, or possibly to give himself a sneaky bit of extra height.

'Come in, come in,' Holly said, gesturing to the cramped hallway while stripping Harry of his duffel coat. He wandered further into the hall and was quickly swallowed up in hugs and how-are-yous from Bella and then Olivia.

'Liv, this is The Great Harry. Me and him go way back to primary school, but I hardly ever see him anymore, now he's gone south of the river!'

'I have an Oyster, I will travel, you know! And you're always welcome in Surbiton,' he said.

Then he looked Bella – in her face mask and dressed in her only size six dress – up and down. 'Christ, Belle, have you lost weight?' he said while hugging her. 'There's nothing of you!'

Holly stared at Harry, remembering why people often mistook him for being gay.

'What?' he said, reading her expression. 'I'm a sensitive guy! I notice these things!'

'It's true, your face is gaunt,' Olivia said in admiration, 'it's all fallen off you!'

'Well, since you mention it, this is my skinny dress. I've not worn it since I was a teenager!'

Olivia's eyes scrunched together, as though her brain was trying to process the idea of anyone still possessing clothing they'd bought in the nineties.

'So what's your secret?' Harry asked in his best mock-Gok.

Bella smiled. 'I'm calling it the Break-up Diet. All the slebs are doing it. Last month was the Five-Two diet – this month it's the Misery Plan.'

Harry and Holly laughed, and then slowed to a stop, realising this was possibly inappropriate.

'The ideas is, you eat nothing for two weeks, then in a rare moment of gluttony, you load up on carbs. And it doesn't even show!'

'Well, melancholy looks good on you,' Olivia said, in the same tone as if she was admiring a new pair of Louboutins.

'No it's awful really. I miss food; it's one of my biggest pleas-ures. But nothing looks in any way edible when you've got a heart as wretched as mine,' she said, drawing out each word and looking skyward as though she was giving a soliloquy at The Globe.

Harry put his arm around her. 'Ah, poor Bellarama.'

'I'm serious. No food has passed my lips in days. Unless you count my own mucus, from crying so much.'

Holly looked at the vintage Coca-Cola clock on the wall. 'Um, guys. Not to sound insensitive, but now really isn't the time for one of your impromptu Break-up Club meetings. We still have a party to set up?'

Olivia's eyes darted to the ceiling. 'Don't be ridiculous. There's no such thing as Break-up Club. It was just a wind-up.'

Behind Olivia's back, Bella was nodding and mouthing the words, 'Yes there is.'

Despite herself, Holly couldn't help feeling a tiny bit left out.

'Anyway, Harry, how about you come and chat to me while I get ready? Tell me how've you been?' she said, heading to her bedroom.

'Aye, no' bad,' went his warm Edinburgh accent as he followed Holly and dumped his Howies bag onto her bedroom floor.

'Aw, your lovely accent is back – have you been back home again?'

'Yup. A week with the McGregor clan is all it takes to eradicate my silly Southern accent. Speaking of silly, how are things with you and Lawrence?'

'Yeah, fine. Apart from all the rows.'

She pulled off her top and realised she was now only in her bra and jeans. She didn't bother to try and cover up though; Harry was like a brother to her. They'd seen each other half naked so many times before that it didn't bother either of them. Or, as Harry liked to put it, she was safely inside 'the circle of sexual disgust'.

'But hey, everyone rows at least three times a week, don't they?'

'Um, no Holly. Three times a week is sex. Arguing is less, ideally.'

'Bollards. We're shagging less than average too then!'

Holly attempted to pull on her dress, quickly finding herself all tangled up, before remembering that you needed a PhD in contortionism to put on most All Saints dresses. 'Um, can you give me a hand?'

'Here you go, doofus.' Harry began grappling with the many complicated layers. Then he deftly realigned it, somehow managing to reposition the intricate flaps and hangy-downy bits in such a way that Holly could now manage actual breathing.

'There. Bootiful,' Harry said.

'Thanks,' she said, assessing her reflection in the mirror and giving him a quick kiss on the forehead. 'Brilliant. Shall we go upstairs?' she said, shoving on some lip gloss. 'Hope you're hungry. There's shitloads of food.'

Three hours later, 249a was at capacity. People were lining the stairs from the hallway to the kitchen, to the extent where it almost looked as though their kitchen had a one-in-one-out policy. Most of the faces she knew, but some were Daniel's work colleagues, who were mostly the wrong side of dorky. Dressed in shirts and smart shoes, they were downing vodka like they'd never been hung-over before. Holly headed to the kitchen and spotted Daniel, his head in the freezer, wading through bags of frozen peas and fish fingers.

'Have you seen the ice?' he asked. 'It can't have all gone?'

'No, sorry,' Holly said. 'Do you ever wonder whether we're too old to have parties like this now?'

Daniel nodded. 'Every minute,' he said as they watched someone run and be sick into a bin.

'Have you seen Bella?' Holly asked and Daniel shook his head.

Moments later, Holly was pushing her way through the randoms in the hallway. She peeled two drunk girls off Bella's bedroom door, then hammered on it.

'I'm not here.'

'Bella? Are you OK? Everyone's been asking where you are. It's me, Holly.'

'Oh, OK. Come in. But don't bring anyone else.'

Holly walked into the room and was affronted by a crockery-based Armageddon. Dirty plates, half-empty mugs of furry tea, and pizza boxes lined the floor, along with piles of dirty washing. At the centre of it all was Bella, lying across her bed, staring at her laptop.

'Oi! You're not stalking him again?'

'I'm not, really, I promise!!!'

Bella's fingers leapt to the screen, and minimised the tab she had open. Holly snatched the laptop off her and opened up the History column in the toolbar, which yielded about a hundred search results for 'Sam Macnamara', and some pages of IMDb. Holly cleared her throat. 'Yes you are. You're on the International Movie Database.'

'But he's just been released from Guildhall and I need to check up on him! See what girls he's working with and how pretty they are!'

'Step away from the Macbook, Isabella Allen.'

'In a minute! Just as soon as I've finished looking at his new Spotlight photos; he's had a load more done, and he looks so hot in them! In black and white, too. LOOK AT THEM,' she said, scrolling through the pictures. 'I can't bear it. I can't bear to think that that used to be mine!'

'He looks gay in them to me.'

'Really?' Bella's cheeks brightened. 'Not edgy, hunky, manly?'

'Gay as a Tahitian pineapple.'

Bella's eyes lit up like a Catherine wheel. Then she stared at Holly as if to say, 'Please sir, can I have some more.'

'And old. Just look at those new wrinkles round his eyes. All that chain-smoking is bound to add years to his playing age.'

'Oh, you're a good friend,' Bella said, smiling.

'Seriously, friend, this isn't good. Is your RADAR not switched on?'

'I know. I'm a certified nut-nut. But you'd think with all the modern-day inventions, someone would invent an app to stop you Googling or Face-stalking people?' she looked at Holly, her eyes desperate.

'They have, you numpty,' Holly said. 'It's called the application of willpower.'

'Oh very funny. But…' she trailed off, realising something. 'Aha! You can't stop me watching his reel though, can you! HAHA! I've got that on an actual "duvuda"! Bet you don't know where that is, do you?'

'No, I don't. But, honey, you MUST stop monitoring his progress. It's a little bit bunny-boiling, and it isn't going to help you get over him.'

'Get over him? Why should I want to do that?'

Holly sighed. There was a knock at the door.

'Girls?' came the concerned voice of their flatmate.

'Come in. I could do with some back-up in here.'

Daniel strode in just as Bella began pressing the refresh key over and over again, her eyes widening.

'OH flipping lord, NO. Holly, your dongle has gone flaccid! The Internet has shut me out! I was just about to see who was playing the leading lady in his new play! Daniel, please can I borrow your wireless code thing? I promise not to use it for porn.'

Daniel shook his head adamantly. 'It's a no from me, Bella.'

'Please??!'

'No way. You went over my download limit last time.'

'Please??!'

Daniel was still shaking his head.

'Shit, it's not fair!' Bella said. 'Where is Magic Internet when you need it?'

Bella was referring to the intermittent insecure Wi-Fi they were sometimes able to pick up And because Magic Internet occasionally worked in her bedroom, she had refused to contribute financially towards getting proper broadband installed in the flat.

'Bella, the party is in full swing, why don't you come upstairs and actually socialize? It's eleven thirty!' Holly said, looking at Bella's clock on the wall.

'Oh that one's really fast. It's not as late as that.'

'Well what time is it?' Daniel asked, his patience waning.

Bella pointed to the alarm clock on her bedside table. 'Let's see, that one's only seven minutes fast, I think. So if that one says it's twenty past, then it must be just coming up to eleven fifteen.'

'Bella you lunatic, why are none of your clocks set at the right time?!'

'I've told you before; it's to stop me being late!'

'But if you never know which one is which, how does that even work?!'

But Bella was still absorbed with tapping away at her screen, pressing refresh and trying to make the Internet come to life. She sighed.

Daniel was now fractionally red in the face. 'Seriously, Belle, what are you DOING? There's a party going on upstairs. A party YOU insisted on having. Our house is getting crapped on from a great height. The least you could do is get up there and ENJOY IT.'

Bella's face began creasing. Gradually, something similar to the Iguazu Falls came gushing out of her eyes, down her face and onto the bed, leaving watery deposits of mascara all over her pink duvet. And so began a tantrum-ette. To the uninitiated, a tantrum-ette wasn't quite a full-blown hysteria fit with fist-on-floor thumping action, but it was tiptoeing over the edge of what constituted 'normal' adult behaviour. Amusing to watch though it was, it didn't last long, and Bella would be back to her charming self within minutes.

Holly put her arm around her. 'Come on, B. It'll be OK. I know it must feel horrendous now, but it will get better.' She watched in silence as her hand rose and descended on Bella's back, in time with her sobs.

Daniel dispatched a guilty, 'I think my work here is done,' look at Holly, before retreating upstairs. She started brushing Bella's hair and mopping up her face with tissues.

'Thanks Holly,' Bella said through sobs.

'Hey, anytime,' she said, delivering a big bear hug.

'I'm really sorry for having another outburst. If it's any consolation, I have really been trying to cut down.'

'I know.'

'You're like family to me. You know that, don't you?'

'Aw, thanks Belle,' she said, wondering if Bella wasn't becoming a bit needy lately. 'So, shall we go upstairs? I for one need a drink. Lawrence still hasn't been in touch!'

Bella nodded and brushed herself down. They headed to the kitchen, to join Harry and Olivia, who were with Daniel's friend Jonny – more commonly referred to as Jonny The Archetypal Public School Boy.

'So I had some brilliant news today,' Jonny was saying, placing some cocktail sausages onto his plate. 'I made an offer on a little "pied-à-terre"…' he said, raising his fingers into little animated quotation marks, 'and amazingly it's just been accepted!'

There was a general chorus of 'Wow – that's awesome!' and 'Well done!' and 'Where?'

'Thanks!' he beamed. 'It's in Victoria Park village. It's all exposed brick, high ceilings, and it's got this cool mezzanine level.'

As Jonny began to tell them more about his new flat, Holly felt herself zoning out. She stood up and went to open another wine bottle. Despite her best efforts, buying flats was still something she just couldn't bring herself to feel excited about yet. She returned back to the circle just in time to hear Jonny deliver the sentence all homeowners used to make themselves feel better about stamp duty and a life devoted to choosing bathroom tiles: 'No more throwing rent money down the drain for me now I've managed to buy!' he beamed.

Holly cringed, realising that Jonny – chiselled and charming though he was – was now on the other side of a dotted line. The one separating those who had made it onto that most impossible of rites of passage, the first rung of the property ladder, and those that still hadn't. The ones that were living in sweet denial of pensions, properties and prams... and most of all, the big 'Three Oh' that was hurtling towards them with relentless zeal.

'So...' Holly began, as she poured out more wine, 'does no one else think it's a bit odd... this whole "–uying" thing?'

Everyone looked confused.

'You know. One day in your mid-twenties, out of nowhere, people start talking about "BUYING." But they don't say what. It's like, now it's okay to just say, "We're buying", and expect people to know what you mean. Has no one else noticed that?'

Everyone stared at her with a mixture of raised eyebrows and furrowed foreheads.

'People are just being sensible, that's all,' Olivia said. 'You know, trying to get some security for the future.'

'And then,' Holly went on, 'three years later, the same thing happens. Only it rhymes. You just replace the "B" sound with a "TR" sound. Does no one think this is odd?'

'Oh right, I get you,' Bella said.

'I mean, what's next after that? Lying? Sighing?'

'Crying?' Bella suggested.

'Dying,' put in Harry, emptying the last drops of white wine into his glass, and then opening another bottle entirely on auto-pilot. 'Or, D.I.Y.-ing. Whichever is worse, I guess.'

Olivia placed her empty glass onto the table a fraction too forcefully. 'Well. I'm a long way off ANY of those things. My relationship of seven years has just flatlined, and nearly everything I own is currently residing in a small storage unit in Brent Cross. Mostly I think I'm going to be CRYING.'

As Olivia's face coloured, Holly felt the tact police slam hand-cuffs around her wrists. 'Shit, sorry, Liv. That was insensitive of me, prattling on like that. Sorry. Are you OK?'

Jonny edged closer to Olivia and draped a heavily triathloned forearm around her. Olivia turned to look into his eyes and smiled. 'I'm fine Holly, don't worry,' she said, still looking into Jonny's hazel eyes. 'I was just winding you up.'

'Anyway, I thought you were going to buy your mate's flat, Liv?'

'That's the plan, but it's not gone through yet. The solicitors are dragging their heels. Yawn.'

'Oh dear. But anyway,' Holly went on, 'all I really meant was, we're still young, and there's plenty of time before we have to get all serious, isn't there? It just came out a bit wonky. And if it helps, now that I've made an epic career fail, the only property I'm ever likely to be able to afford as a first-time buyer is a converted Portaloo.'

'Hol, you're all good now, you can leave it there…' Olivia said.

'I'm going to get another drink then. Can I get you one?' Holly said, but Olivia was now engaged in an intense and prolonged session of eye contact with Jonny.

'You OK?' Harry asked, following Holly to the fridge.

She shook her head. 'Not really.'

'Lawrence?'

She paused for a moment. 'How did you guess?' she said, holding out her glass as Harry raided the fridge. 'Booze me up please.'

He smiled and handed her a vodka and tonic.

'Did you know that Bella and Liv have formed something they're calling a "Break-up Club"? Liv keeps saying it's just a joke, but I think it's sort of become real, through necessity. Bella says they meet up, just the two of them, every Sunday night.'

'The most depressing night of the week. Makes sense.'

Harry led them to an empty sofa and sat down at one end. Holly stretched out next to him, laying her head on him. It was one of her favourite places to sit – with her head resting in the nook of his shoulder.

'What you thinking HolFace? You tempted to join the cult?'

'Christ no! Although, if I'm honest, I do sometimes get this teeny-weeny feeling of doubt. But everyone gets that, don't they? Who's ever in a relationship they're totally sure about all the time? I mean, that would be weird, right?'

'I couldn't be surer about Rachel and me.'

Oh yes, Rachel, she remembered, lifting her head off Harry's shoulder. 'Sshhh, show-off,' she said, prodding him in the stomach.

'Ow! Well, to be brutally honest, Hol, it sounds to me like you've heard the bell.'

'The what?'

'The sad bell. Set to go off at the exact moment you first feel those doubts. The second something in you knows maybe it's not right. And the thing is, once you've heard it, there's no way back. It's time for the bin. Anything beyond that point is classified as denial. Or, pressing snooze.'

Shit. She did so love to snooze.

'No, no, no. I'm just drunk. It's fine, really,' she said. 'I love that man to pieces. We've got far too much history for me to just run at the first hurdle. And he's so good at helping me in my career, too. Plus we've got Cuba coming up!'

Harry nodded. 'Of course.'

'Gawd, I've got these horrible nerves in my stomach now. They feel like butterflies, but more uncomfortable. Like an invasion of nasty ones that have gone to the dark side!'

'So, moths, then?'

Holly laughed. 'Yeah! Moths is right! Anyway, how is it that you know so much about break-ups?'

'Oh, I studied for a PhD in this area… right up until I met The One, in fact.'

Holly felt a pang of envy at how content Harry was in his relationship. And then felt guilty for doing so.

'And how is the lovely Rachel?' she said, hoping it didn't sound too insincere. In truth she'd never really taken to her. She'd always seemed too much of a Grazia-grazing-girlie-girl for her Harry.

Still, there was no denying the fact that he did seem happier than she'd ever known him to be.

'Are we to hear the pitter-patter of tiny sprogs soon?'

'I'm game whenever she is! We've got to get the Big Day sorted out first before all that – Rachel's been so busy we've not had time to go and look at venues yet. It's crazy though; I'm the only one out of all my mates apart from Rick who's not had any bairns yet! Never mind all that though. Holly, I really think that if you're not sure he's "the one"—'

'Oh you're such a girl! I've told you before, and I'll say it again. The idea of THE ONE is – along with friendly bus drivers, men who put the toilet seat down, and the same two socks ever coming back out of the washing machine – complete and utter fiction.'

'I disagree; romantic fatalism has a lot going for it! Look at Rachel and me. She just up and sat next to me on the bus to Oxford one day. Imagine if I'd got a bus fifteen minutes earlier or later? I would never have met my soulmate.'

'Mmm,' she said, feeling oddly moved despite herself. 'Hey, I wonder if there are more stories like yours out there. I wonder how many other people meet the love of their lives in seren-dipitous ways like that?'

'How was it that you first met the love of your life? I don't think I know the story.'

Holly's eyes narrowed in confusion. 'Oh! You mean Lawrence! Well, it's quite a silly one really.'

'Go on.'

'It was a dead man's fart that did it.'

'I'm sorry?'

'I mean, it was less "across a crowded room" and more – across a crowded bowel. We were at this bluesy dive bar in Soho. I was ordering a drink, when I suddenly became aware of this godfor-saken stench. I started to wonder what it was – when everyone began turning to one another. And then people were holding their noses, realising it was a fart. But the nice thing was, there

94

was almost a feeling of camaraderie after a while. You know, the way that normally aloof Brits actually start talking to one another in a crisis. And at that point, I turned to the person next to me to say, 'Hey, it wasn't me!' but as soon as I spoke, I'd locked eyes with this gorgeous man with curly brown hair… And that's when we got into a discussion about how bad the smell was. Lawrence had this theory that this wasn't any old flatulence – it must've been a "dead man's fart", as he called it. Then it was my turn to be served, so I offered to buy him a drink.'

'Wow. And they say romance is dead,' Harry remarked 'That could totally be another one for your collection. Joined together in holy flatulence.'

'Ha! Very funny. Yeah, I guess if I could find a few more true stories then it could be enough to pitch as a show idea to Jeremy? He is after more "Reality" ideas after all.'

'There's definitely something in it. Love can turn up in the most surprising of places. The right person can just suddenly come into your life when you least expect it!'

Holly rolled her eyes, just as the living room door swung open to reveal Lawrence.

'Like I said,' Harry said as Lawrence bounded over to Holly and enveloped her in cuddles.

'You came!' she said, feeling a bit like she'd been caught with her hand in the till.

'Yep! Thought I'd surprise you. Surprise!'

'Hooray!'

'I missed you. Missed my Folly,' he slurred.

'Missed you too.' They kissed again, and the eclipse of moths flew away.

'I'm sorry we fought,' he said, and she was struck again by Lawrence's unique take on the Art of Apology. He would always say something vague like 'sorry we fell out', rather than taking any blame for it. But she pushed this thought aside. It was just so nice to see him. Even if he was hammered.

'Me too. Love you,' she said, kissing him.

Harry stood up to free his seat for Lawrence. 'Well, I'll leave you lovebirds to it,' he said, the irony not wasted on Holly as he snuck away.

∗

Three hours later, the party was winding down. Harry had gone home and all that remained were a few stragglers in the lounge playing SingStar. After watching drunk Bella perform Robyn's 'Dancing on my Own' at the top of her voice, Holly and Lawrence decided to slip away. On the way downstairs, they noticed Olivia and Jonny sneaking out together.

'Oh, really?' she whispered to Lawrence as they went into her room. 'That's an interesting pairing!'

'You're an interesting pairing,' Lawrence slurred as he leaned in to kiss Holly. She couldn't help noticing how much his breath stank of booze. Reasoning that in fairness she probably smelled like an off-licence too by now, she kissed him back. As they kissed some more and he held her in his arms, they could hear Edward Sharpe's 'Home' drifting down through the floorboards. In a burst of spontaneity, Lawrence took Holly's arm and twirled her around. Slowly they danced to the distant music before collapsing onto the bed. She kissed his neck, unbuttoning his shirt while feeling his arms tighten around her back. She worked her hands down towards his trousers and fumbled with his fly. As his jeans came down, revealing the grey boxers – the ones that had more holes in than sense – she felt the hands around her back grow limp. They weren't the only thing, she observed as her hands wandered inside his holey shorts.

She saw that his eyes were closed and sighed. 'Lawry?'

He opened them, one at a time. 'Sorry. I'm just fucked.'

'Or not, as the case may be.'

'I'm sorry Folly, I just can't... Um. I can't... actually... feel anything. Bit too much brandy I'm afraid. Don't hate me. We can still cuddle. I'll make it up to you in the morning when things are back on down there.'

Holly said nothing.

'Love you lots?' he added, because that usually fixed everything.

'Right,' she said, unimpressed. 'Um, is it me, or does this happen a lot these days? If it's not "I'm too drunk", it's "I'm all bloated, I've eaten too much curry".' Holly sighed. 'Whatever it is, Lawry, it's getting old.'

'Baby. That's not nice. It's not my fault I'm tired. I've had a long day. What's the big deal?'

'You know, I wasn't going to mention it, but you smell of tramp. Are you sure you actually didn't just go and sleep on the heath last night and drink whisky 'til dawn? And Lawrence, I hate to break it to you, but your whole hair-washing-itself-after-a-while theory: it's really not watertight!'

'Harsh?!' he exclaimed to an imaginary umpire. 'Holly, could you please, for a second, quit having a go at me? I smell fine. Fucksake.' He rolled his eyes, then took a sly whiff of his armpits just to be sure. His nose twitched in discomfort.

'You're not fine. I'm not fine,' she sat up in bed. 'Baby, let's be honest.... WE are not fine.'

He pulled her back onto the bed and started kissing her. Gently to start, then more energetic. As though he was wrestling with himself to be more awake, he kissed her harder, and started running his hands up and down her dress. As his hands went into her bra, a cacophony of different sentences began to play in her mind, many of them Harry's words from before. It was like she was back in her edit suite, playing different Wav files one after the other... Maybe you've heard the bell and the niggling doubt; is he really the one...? and... and... all the while Lawrence's hands were working their way south. She looked into his eyes and all she could see were blanks; clearly he was sleepwalking his way through all of this.

'Don't, Lawrence,' she said quietly.

'You want me to stop now? For fuck's sake, there's no pleasing you!'

'It's not that. I just think… maybe this isn't working.'

There. She'd said it. Foundations, laid.

'What the fuck?'

'Don't shout – please stop yelling and being over-defensive. You always get like this when you're pissed now.'

'And you're just such a stress-merchant these days. You're nothing like the laid-back, fun-loving girl I met at the Blues bar that night.'

'Oh I'm sorry. What are you going to do? File a complaint with the Advertising Standards Authority?'

'WHAT?'

'Never mind. Maybe you're right. Maybe we just bring out the worst in each other.'

All the while she was becoming increasingly aware of how tight her dress was around the neck and stomach. She tried to remain calm as she wrestled with the complicated All Saints straps and pulley systems. She attempted to pull the layers of dress over her head, but then her arm became trapped. Soon she was entirely entangled, which only added fuel to her fury. She sighed and wondered whether it was the dress that was choking her, or the dysfunctional relationship. She gave it one last go. 'ARRRGH!' she screamed, then gave up.

Lawrence leaned forward and gently pulled the dress over her head. She smiled by way of thanks.

'I am not being over-defensive!'

'You so are!'

'What are you really saying, Folly?'

Holly sat down on the bed in her bra and pants. 'I don't know. I just… Maybe I don't want this anymore.'

Lawrence sat down next to her, beginning to put his arms around her, but, perhaps thinking better of it, he folded them instead. 'I'll tell you what you want. You want Alan.'

'Who the fuck's ALAN?'

'You want Alan Smith. You know, Mr Fucking Straight. Good old Alan Smith the Accountant, who's reliable with money and will make dinner for when you get home from work and treat you to nice fucking holidays and duck-egg bathroom tiles. Well I'll tell you what. I'm not Alan Smith. I'm more interesting than that – I might be a twat about money sometimes, but Alan Smith is boring. I'll tell you this for free, Holly…' he said, his enormous blue eyes staring into hers.

'What?' Holly asked, shaking her head in bemusement.

He sat up straight, put an arm around her, and took a deep breath for extra gravitas. 'You'll never find anyone as fun as me!'

The second the words left his mouth, he was sick all over himself.

Holly said nothing. After a minute, she peeled Lawrence's arm off her, and climbed down from the bed.

'This isn't fun anymore.'

Lawrence was mute. Holly walked out of the room, then came back in with a cloth, which she threw at him just as the chorus of 'Home is wherever I'm with you' drifted down from above.

As Lawrence dabbed at himself with the cloth, she sat on the floor, tears of anger pressing at the edges of her eyes.

'You know what. You're not fun. You're the fucking trailer for fun. Turns out, the main feature is just too much fucking stress. You don't even remember the times when I've had to peel you off the floor and walk you home. The nights that have ended with you passed out under a table, in public! I can't do looking after you anymore.'

Lawrence was shaking his head. He started to cry. 'I'm sorry. I know, I'm a fucktard. I'll sort stuff out. I'm still fun, I'm still your Lawry. I'm sorry about your bed. I'll clean it up. I love you.'

There they were again. She used to think, if we can just snuggle under the three-little-word safety blanket, then everything would be OK... But now she thought about it, she couldn't remember when she'd last said 'I love you' and really meant it.

Lawrence looked up at her, his blue eyes sober now and full of remorse.

'I think maybe we should... have some space for a bit.'

'Space? What is space?'

'Maybe we should have a rest from each other. Just 'til you're back from Paris. Use the time to think about what we both want.'

'I want you. I don't need to think about it.' His eyes fixed on hers lovingly. 'What about Cuba? We're going to have the trip of a lifetime!'

Her heart sank. She'd forgotten about that. 'We still will. Let's just take some time.'

She couldn't look at him. He looked too loveable, even now; despite the fact he smelled of vomit and had little bits of broken Pringles stuck in his stubble. Like a disorientated yo-yo, all she wanted was to take it all back, to press Control, Z.

'But, I love you, you imbecile!' he said through sobs. As he took her hands in his, the front doorbell rang.

'Who the shit can that be?' Holly said.

'Leave it,' he said as it went again.

Now the doorbell was going continuously, as though some one was leaning on the button.

'Why is no one answering it? Christ, it's 6 a.m.,' she said, catching sight of her alarm clock as she climbed off the bed and threw on her oversized Blur T-shirt. 'To be continued...' she said, running out of the room and down the stairs in the dark, bumping into Bella at the front door.

'Oh. You are here,' Holly said. 'Why didn't you tell me you were getting the door? I was kind of in the middle—'

'Hey, what's wrong?' Bella asked, seeing the tears all down Holly's face.

'Nothing,' she said as they both pulled the front door in towards them. Holly wiped the snot from her nose as they peered out into the dimly lit street, looking in either direction. They were just about to close the door again when they caught sight of Harry below them, slumped in the doorway like a vagabond whose world had just ended.

'Finally!' he said, looking up through bloodshot eyes.

'Harry-face, what the hell are you doing here?' Holly yelled, helping him up off the ground.

Harry stood up, and Holly noticed he had been sitting on his big blue Karrimor travelling rucksack. The same blue Karrimor rucksack they'd both bought when they'd gone travelling together after university.

'Are you off somewhere?'

'Long story. Can I come and stay for a while?'

'Of course.'

'What happened?' Bella asked as they cowered in the dark hallway that smelled of rising damp.

'Well, the headline is, I've just walked in on Rachel shagging the arse off of Ryan Gosling's body double.'

'Oh my god,' Holly said. 'Not Rachel? As in "Practically Poppins in every way" Rachel?'

Harry nodded.

Bella was staring at Harry. 'What do you mean, shagging the arse off? Was she wearing a strap-on?'

'Bella! He meant it as an expression! You absolute tool!' Holly said, just as Harry began to hyperventilate and flood with tears. Harry – twenty-seven years of age, her rock since childhood – was doing actual crying. So sobering a sight was it that for a moment she was frozen still, no clue of what to say or how to make it better.

'We were supposed to be getting married next summer!' shouted Harry. 'And making wee bairns together! We had it all planned out.'

'Come here.' Holly folded a dismantled Harry into her arms. 'You poor bastard. I'm so, so sorry.'

'He was seven fucking foot, too. She always said me being short was never a problem!'

'The lying ho,' Bella said, taking position as the second bit of bread in the hug sandwich, inside which Harry was the sagging bit of ham.

'Let's go in,' Holly said eventually, as the last of the sun rose over Fortess Road.

'You're with us now,' Bella added as they headed up the stairs.

6. *Recalculating*

The rules are different on a hangover, Holly consoled herself as she put her hand on her belly and felt her food-baby do a little kick. She had just eaten a whole roast beef with TWO Yorkshire puddings, but was still impossibly ravenous. It was common fare with her hangovers that she would enjoy an unbridled licence to eat all day. As anyone knew, hangover calories carried a value of nil, didn't they? But today she was even eyeing up leftovers on neighbouring tables. Holly tried to distract herself by looking at her phone's idle inbox. Or by seeking solace in the leafy avenues through the windows. She watched a double-decker go past, then turned back to face the table, which was lined with hung-over faces and half-empty plates.

Half-empty plates indeed. How did people do that, she wondered in awe as her eyelid started twitching again. Olivia's caramelised haloumi was staring up at Holly, whispering sweet nothings to her. She felt her hands begin to move independently of her brain.

'Liv, are you not going to eat this?'

Olivia shook her head.

'Mind if I...?' Holly asked, embarrassed, but thinking of the hunger-vortex in her belly. After a quick game of Neuroses Top

Trumps, Hoovering-Up-Leftovers had won out over the shame-faced Ordering-More-Food.

'Of course. I'm not hungry at the moment. This week I have replaced eating with fucking.'

Everyone was startled. From within the soft cocoon of their hangover duvets they weren't prepared for such coarse language.

'What's going on? Who are you knobbing?' Bella said.

'Yes, details please,' Holly said. 'I thought I saw you leaving the party last night with a certain young gentleman?'

Olivia blushed a little. 'Mmmhmm. There may have been some kissing. And I may have gone back for some sexing. And I may have only just left.'

'WHO WAS IT?' Bella demanded.

'Jonny,' Olivia said, taking a sip of her orange juice and lemonade.

'Jonny The Archetypal Public School Boy?' Bella screeched. 'Oooh, nice one, he's hot. He seems a bit into himself, but I wouldn't kick him out of bed. Will you see him again?'

'Yes. But it's no biggie. I'm also seeing this guy Tom from work. Although we're just-good-FBs.'

'Facebook friends?' Holly said.

'No sweetie, she means Fuck Buddies,' Bella said as Holly's mouth dropped open.

'I've got a date with another one on Tuesday. Basically, I'm firing up the hob again.'

'The hob?' Holly said.

'Yup. It's my foolproof dating analogy. You just have to make sure you've always got more than two pans on at one time, and that they're all on alternating levels,' explained Olivia. 'If you only have one pan on high, it's bound to curdle or burn out too soon. You know what they say, you can't date a pressure-cooker...' She trailed off, apparently now less convinced of her theory than when she started out.

Harry's bloodshot eyes narrowed. 'Aren't you basically saying don't put all your eggs in one basket?'

'Eggs? Is there more food coming?' Holly blurted, but nobody seemed to hear.

'No, Harry. It's a bit more complex than that. Sometimes I just think I need a bigger hob.'

'I've always wanted an Aga...' Bella said, a wistful look in her eye signalling that she was no longer with them. Instead she was in a thatched cottage in the Cotswolds, a dog curled at her feet as she stood over the Aga in a plaid Laura Ashley dress, stirring a vat of homemade soup made from leftover chicken giblets.

Meanwhile, Harry took a sip from his craft beer and suppressed a sigh. He scanned the room to check there weren't any men sitting around that he could talk to about laying floorboards, or any vats full of protein shake he could guzzle in a manly way. His eyes landed on a mute television in the corner. He stared at the football match, a last-ditch attempt to preserve any remaining shred of manhood.

Holly saw that he was sinking and put her arm around him. 'You OK?' she whispered.

'No. But I don't want to talk about it either. Thanks, mind.'

He turned back to the mute television, a broken shell of the man he'd been twenty-four hours ago. Holly gave him one last desperate squeeze, before leaving him be.

'So Holly, how are you and Lawrence doing?' Olivia asked, batting the attention back at her like a ping-pong ball.

Holly pulled an expression that could easily have been mistaken for car-sickness.

'Oooh, that good?' Olivia said.

'Put it this way. He passed out last night with puke all over himself.'

'Attractive.'

'And then he left this morning with his tail between his legs.'

'Did you call time on the relationship then? Or at least, ring the bell for last orders?' Bella asked.

Holly put her fork down, took a sip of her drink and slowly shook her head.

'Don't take this the wrong way, Holly, but…' Olivia began.

'Single-handedly the worst way to begin any conversation,' Holly said, drowning another chip in mayonnaise.

'Sometimes I think you're not so much going out with Lawrence as you are childminding him?'

Holly returned the uneaten chip to the plate. 'Sod off. He's not that bad.'

'She's got a point!' Bella chimed, back from the Cotswolds. 'I mean… can you ever imagine having children with him? When he's so much like a child himself?'

Holly bit her tongue, striving to suppress all references to pots and kettles.

Olivia looked alarmed. 'Christ, ick, guys! Not the C word!'

'Yeah, since when are we having children?' Holly said.

'You still want them one day, don't you?' Harry said, turning back from the mute television briefly.

'I don't know – maybe. Anyway… Lawrence makes me laugh. Surely that counts for a lot? And surely I should just be living for now, shouldn't I?' She stared at them with hopeful eyes through the silence. Her eyelid started twitching again.

Everyone was silent, while Holly sat hoping at least one person would defend her boyfriend. That at least one of them would stop the death-knell from sounding. ANYONE???

The silence dragged on.

'So just to clarify. If Lawrence isn't who I want to spend my life with, and isn't who I might imagine having children with if I even want children that is… then that means being with him is a form of time-wasting?'

'There it is!' shouted Harry.

'This conversation is a form of time-wasting,' Olivia said,

drinking the last of her orange juice and lemonade with a discrete slurp. 'I think you need to face it – the end is in the post,' Olivia said. Bella smiled sympathetically. 'But not just yet – maybe it's just second-class rather than first.'

'When did we get to a Royal Mail convention? Give it a rest guys. Just 'cause you're trying to get me to join your stupid club.'

'For the last time, there is no club!'

'Here's a question,' Harry began, 'if you were with Lawrence aged twenty-one, would you still be sticking with him?'

'What do you mean?'

'I think that a big part of why you've stayed with him this long despite his, er, flaws is that you're scared you might not meet anyone else that could be lifer material. And then you'll wish you'd held onto him,' he said, taking out an electric cigarette.

Holly opened her mouth to say, 'Harry, smoking again, really? After three years of being on the wagon?' but she stopped herself, remembering he had a reason.

'I think you've nailed it there, Harry,' Bella began. 'There's such a difference between meeting someone in your early twenties compared with your late twenties. There was no pressure back then! These days, the kinds of thoughts in my head aren't "what shall we go as for fancy dress?", they're "I like the way he just fixed that wonky restaurant table with an old newspaper – he'll be good around the house when it comes to D.I.Y!", or "Oh, he's letting me pay the bill, that means one day I'll have to be the one with the well-paid job and good maternity benefits!"' Bella reached the end of her monologue, now a few shades pinker.

'Of course, you can see that's TOTALLY INSANE, can't you?' Harry said.

'Of course,' Bella lied.

'Listen,' Olivia began, 'I've been working on a theory about all this, after consulting various people, and I think I'm ready to test it on you. It goes like this: all relationships can be classified according to the following "sentences". They're either a three-monther, a six-monther, three years, five years... or...'

'Or what?' Holly asked.

'A life sentence.'

Everyone nodded slowly.

'Wow,' Harry said. 'That's bang on. And there's no irony in the word "sentence" either.'

'I know. So Ross and I, we were just a five year-er, gone long. That's why it needed to end. And by the same token,' Olivia turned to face Holly, 'you and Lawrence, you're a five year-er; you've lived out your sentence. I don't think you have it in you to become lifers.'

Holly gulped, but said nothing. Everyone stared.

Eventually Harry spoke up. 'How did you leave it with Lawrence in the end?'

'Well. We agreed to "take some space" for a few weeks, while he's away at his film festival. That way, we can both give it some proper thought, and make an informed decision.'

'So in other words, you're on a break? I've told you once and I'll tell you again, Holly... breaks are a sham,' Olivia said, her words a small kitchen-knife through Holly's heart.

Bella put an arm around her by way of comfort.

'Cheers, Liv. Did you have a VOICE OF DOOM pill for breakfast? Besides, it's just a mini-break! A semicolon, rather than a full stop?'

'She does have a point, hon,' Bella said, nodding sagely. 'In my experience, breaks are only ever a dress rehearsal for the main performance.'

'But you're all forgetting one thing. Breaking up with someone is TERRIFYING.'

Olivia rolled her eyes. 'I'm not going to sugar-coat it, Braithwaite. You either dump him or stay with him. Break-ups are absolutes. Not hotel buffets where you can put a little bit on your plate to see if you like it first.'

Holly gulped. The last time she'd gone to a hotel buffet, she'd had a self-control malfunction and ended up with three sky-high platefuls, and the waitress had had to move her to a bigger table. She flushed with horror. 'Well, let's just see how this next month goes, shall we…?'

'I mean really. When has a break ever led to happiness? Can anyone show me a happy couple that got through a break, for the better!?'

The question hung in the air like a bad smell that no one knew how to get rid of. Worse than the stench in Holly's room post-chundering.

7. Break-up and Smell the Coffee

He is the one; he's not the one…

A few weeks later, Holly was sat in her windowless office counting virtual daisy petals. After several rounds of this, being no closer to a decision, she tried to get back to cutting down the latest episode.

Today she was doing a marvellous job of being ruthless – Jeremy would be proud! She'd managed to cut a few frames here, another nip and a tuck there – soon she wouldn't be far off the magic forty-three minutes!

But then she got to the next scene and realised it no longer made sense without the bits she'd just cut; now the pay-off had no set-up. She scrolled back and slowly put the frames in again. She looked at the clock, saw that she'd just lost forty minutes to indecision, and sighed.

Choosing between shots was hard enough for Holly at the best of times. But now her relationship was on a life-support-machine, possibly breathing its last – all previous decision-making abilities had been forcibly removed by an impenetrable fog of vagueness, leaving her with all the editorial conviction of a piece of wet lettuce. No, only one thing could help her now. Shopping. Holly leapt up, stuck a note on her door saying 'back soon', and fled up the corridor.

Soon she was face to face with her good friend the stationery cupboard. She looked from side to side. Moments later, she was rifling through supplies. She filled her arms with notebooks, file dividers and shiny new highlighters. She wasn't proud, but this sort of thing gave her unbridled joy. It had all the perks of shopping, only it didn't cost a thing, there were no queues and no charity muggers! But best of all, you had none of the horror of seeing your bubble-wrapped cellulite in the over-lit mirror. Yes. Performing a stationery raid was basically retail therapy, without the heart attack at the end of the month. Westfield, Bluewater, they had nothing on Room G.E.13.

As Holly was midway through foraging for felt-tip pens, she remembered that Lawrence would probably need some more layout pads so he could keep up his storyboarding practice. In her own small way, she liked to help him build up his career by kitting him out with as much free stationery as he needed. Yes. She would give them to him when he was back from Paris. What a good almost-girlfriend I am, she thought, filling her arms with more art and craft paraphernalia than a whole season of *Blue Peter*.

Cradling her bounty, she walked smack bang into her boss Jeremy, who gave her a look that said, Am I not paying you enough?

'Oh... Hi Jeremy. Did you have a chance to read that proposal I left on your desk yet?' she said, hoping to distract him from her lever-arched-kleptomania.

He shot her a look of tepid interest, which she took as her cue to go on.

'No? Well hopefully you'll like this, as it's much more "Reality" based. It's a documentary called "Is This Seat Taken?" We find real-life couples who met in amazingly serendipitous ways, and interview them for a really uplifting film. I did some research on the weekend; turns out there are tons of amazing real-life chance meetings. From a couple who met while staring through an estate agents window, to a couple who married at the age of 22 only to discover they'd been born side by side in the same hospital bed! Isn't that mental! Then there's my boyfriend and I who met because someone next to us did a really smelly—'

'Can I just stop you there, Holly?'

'You hate it.'

'I don't hate it as much, but the tone's still way off. It's far too twee for what we need. Secondly, doesn't the whole world online date these days – why would anyone care about this archaic Brief Encounter crap?'

'Well you say that but, as I put in the proposal… it's precisely because people are changing the way they meet that these stories are so interesting. Surely now is a timely, um, time for all this? Boy meets girl is a story as old as time, but…' Holly stopped, noticing that Jeremy had started to go red in the face, and not from embarrassment.

'Another worry is that it will just depress the fuck out of lonely people. I don't want to be responsible for a rise in suicide rates.'

'No. Absolutely.'

'It's not all bad news though. I've had a good idea in from Pascal, which I think could be a goer. It's not quite there yet but once he's developed it some more, and unless you can think of anything better, we'll be taking that to the channel.'

Holly suppressed a gulp. 'Oh, OK. I'll keep thinking then, and send you something soon.'

Holly walked up the corridor back to her office, thinking, why oh why did I leave my perfect old job, when she noticed a Diesel-clad beanpole leaning by her door in the manner of a catalogue model.

Luke spotted her and smiled.

'Hey. Just finished filming for the day, and thought I'd see how your caffeine levels were doing. If you still fancy going for that coffee?'

Three thoughts were vying for Holly's attention. One, she'd

never actually agreed to have a coffee with him, had she? Two – Luke was looking annoyingly hot. And three – how was she going to explain the fact that she looked like she was driving the getaway car from a Ryman's robbery?

'Umgh,' she said, feeling even more inarticulate than usual. Luke's face puckered with confusion. 'Sorry. That was "yes, great, come in".'

'Been to the sales?' he asked, following her inside.

'Ha ha,' she said, piling up her 'purchases' onto her desk. 'Just needed to stock up on some things.'

'Never had you down as a closet klepto.'

'Ha ha. No, they're for my boyfriend.'

'Oh.'

Luke looked down and began to shift about on his feet.

Ouch. The Drop-In was never a good moment for either party. The awkward moment when you know, and they know, that there's been an unspoken spark between you, and A MOMENT has clearly been had, but one of you has decided to call time and announce that this probably shouldn't go any further.

'Well. My sort-of-boyfriend that is,' she back-pedalled, 'we're in a weird patch at the moment. Anyway. He's a director. He uses them for storyboarding.'

'OH. My. God. You saw this?'

He was staring at Holly's noticeboard, where a flyer from Michel Gondry's short film *The All-Seeing Eye* was pinned up.

'I did! It was incredible. You saw it too?'

'I was on tour with a play, so I couldn't make it unfortunately.'

'It kind of reminded me of those memory games you played when you were younger... you know, "I went to the shop and I bought..." and then you have to try and remember all the items everyone bought.'

'I remember that game! I was shit at it. Probably smoked too much weed as a child.'

'Ha. Well, it was sort of like that, only in reverse. The idea was, you sat in this strange circular room, looking at objects being projected onto the walls around you. Each time the projections went around, the objects in the room disappeared one by one, until there was nothing left.'

'Sounds intriguing.'

Luke picked up some layout pads and moved them aside so he could sit on the desk. Holly's eyes landed on the stuffed toy that was just under her noticeboard. It was a tiny womble holding up a little window frame, which Lawrence had bought her on her second day, when she'd complained about not having a window.

'I'm sure the film must be online somewhere.' Holly jumped onto her computer and began Googling. 'Here… have you tried the mediatheque?

'The what?'

'You don't know the mediatheque?'

He shook his head.

'You commit yourself to celluloid daily and you haven't heard of the mediatheque?'

'No, already!'

'It's only like the best resource in all the land! It's a massive library of films that you can use free, any time!'

'Where?'

'It's in the British Film Institute; you know, on the Southbank?'

'Amazing, maybe you'll take me there sometime.'

'Maybe I will,' she said, avoiding the womble's disapproving gaze.

Luke smiled. Holly looked down at the floor, before daring to sneak another look at him again.

There followed an unfeasibly long silence, where they did nothing but hold each other's gaze while the room became smaller, and the tiny creatures in her belly performed rhythmic gymnastics.

'Unless your sort-of-boyfriend would object?'

Holly looked at the clock on the wall, as though time itself would have the answer. As she opened her mouth to speak, her phone rang and she looked down to see Lawrence's flashing jpeg.

'Oh, sorry, I should just get this quickly.'

Luke nodded and started looking round the room at things.

'Hello?' she said, unable to hide the surprise from her voice. 'Lawry, I thought we were… Can I call you back? I'm just in a meeting…' she said, looking apologetically at Luke.

'Womble,' Lawrence's voice said down the phone. 'Sorry, I know we're not – but I just need help doing this quick email to production company reps, like you suggested. Can you help me write this draft? Listen to this… Dear Monique, I'm writing to you to—'

'But you're great at writing! You don't need my help!' She shook her head to Luke as if to say 'wait, don't go', but he was already halfway out the door, making 'I'll call you' signs with his fingers.

She sighed. 'All right, read the next bit…' and she heard the door close behind her.

*

'How was your day, dear?' a red-eyed Harry slurred later in pseudo-American drawl. He was swinging in a large hammock that was tied precariously to the railings of the roof terrace.

'Marvellous, honey,' she lied as she wandered onto the terrace, 'but where did this come from? It's awesome! We can pretend we're crusty backpackers again!' she said, pushing Harry so that he swung even faster.

'Indeed! I liberated it from my flat just as I was leaving with my rucksack. Rachel and I got it in Thailand. Hope you don't mind it monopolising the balcony.'

'Course not. It makes a welcome addition to the outdoor

furniture collection,' she said, taking a seat on a weather-beaten dining chair. 'Just don't swing too much and go plummeting off the balcony to your death.'

Harry's eyes lit up as though she'd just given him an idea.

'So, I saw Rachel today.'

'Shit, where?'

'She's been begging me to meet up for a drink, so she could explain.'

Holly nodded. 'So how was it?'

'Just awful. It's weird. I always thought I'd be all right about the odd bit of infidelity. I thought that I loved her to pieces and I'd be able to forgive her if she ever did something like that. But it turns out, I'm a right old-fashioned cretin, and she's never going to be the girl I fell in love with!'

'Mmm,' Holly said, no idea what else to say.

'Still, she wants to keep on going, and to try and put it behind us. She invited me back, so I thought I'd try and be the bigger man – give her another chance.'

'In other words, have some nice break-up sex.'

'Right… But when we got back there, I just couldn't stop seeing his face, imagining them at it, replaying it like a bad porn film in my head. I just couldn't get into it. So I ran away like an absolute tit and came to sit in my hammock.'

'Poor Harold,' she said, leaning over the hammock to give him an awkward hug.

'Here. Climb aboard.' Harry shunted along and gestured for her to join him.

'What if it breaks?'

'I'll hold my stomach in so I'm lighter.'

Holly laughed.

'Let it break. It's just a relic of my dead relationship anyway.'

'Oh well, at least Jeremy blew out my documentary idea. At this rate we'd have two less contributors for it!'

'Well, every cloud.'

'Sorry. You're right, I am becoming obsessed. I just so want to beat smug Pascal!'

'I think you're actually quite enjoying all this coming up with ideas malarkey.'

'No, I'm just worried about how I'll pay off my mahoosive credit card bill if my contract doesn't get renewed.'

'Come and join me.'

'Are you sure it's a double?'

Holly slowly lowered herself next to Harry, trying not to panic about falling through the frail netting to the cold stone patio. Harry began stroking her hair, which had the initial effect of feeling lovely, until she realised that it was lovely because it reminded her of being touched. Of having someone. Of having a Lawrence. Her eyes began to well as she thought about ringing him.

'Drink,' Harry ordered, having spotted this. He held the bottle of wine out for her.

'Thanks,' she said through gulps. 'Oh, Harold. This is all too much! I just still can't decide what to do about "The Break". I've even done a bloody pros and cons list!' she said, looking down at her shoes.

'You have not.'

She pulled out a crumpled piece of paper from her jeans pocket. 'The trouble is, it all came out in equilibrium. So what am I meant to do? Roll a dice?'

'What's this point here?' Harry said, pointing to one of the 'Pros'. '"Job under serious threat – L is good with ideas!" Wait, you can't stay with Lawrence because of that – that's just using him! Plus, it's horseshit!'

'But I'm about to be fired, and there are bugger-all jobs out there!'

Harry rolled his eyes. 'Putting the job thing aside, I think if you have to think about something THIS hard, then it can't be right. Can it? Surely if you're already at the pros and cons stage it's as good as over? That must be what your gut's telling you?'

'I wish people would stop saying that! All my gut ever tells me is that I'm hungry.'

'There's Thai leftovers if you want some.'

Holly paused to consider the relative merits of prawn toast and Massaman. But then remembered the more pressing issue at hand.

Harry allowed a smile to seep out while Holly emptied her wine glass. 'You either love him or you don't.'

Holly looked down at her feet and was silent for a long time. 'More wine?' she asked, taking his glass.

'You don't, do you?' Harry said, trying to catch her eye.

'It's good cheap plonk, this,' she said, looking firmly at the wine and topping up his glass. 'You can't beat a BoozeNest special,' she said as they heard the front door slam and footsteps scurry up the stairs.

'You know what I think? We owe it to our future selves to find out if there's someone else out there for us. Someone who can make us happier than we are right now. We owe it to ourselves to take the risk.'

Holly nodded, thinking through his words.

'Hey!' Bella said, running out to join them on the balcony. 'How are my two favourite fuck-ups?'

'Fucked, thanks. Wine?' Holly waved the bottle in Bella's face as she squeezed her bottom next to theirs on the hammock. The tightly wound mesh wobbled under the strain. There began a sound of tearing fabric. Holly jumped up.

'OK, three's a crowd as far as this hammock goes. I'll leave you to it,' she said, deciding this was a perfect excuse to go and investigate the leftover Thai food. Calorie consciousness could wait until this whole relationship business was resolved.

'You know,' Holly said as she came back out and sat on the mildewed dining chair, 'sometimes, when I brush my teeth, I have this old tube of toothpaste that I never know when to give up on, and I'm, like, trying to squeeze the last bit out of it.'

'Where are you going with this?' Bella asked, and Harry 'shushed' her.

'Bear with…' she said, her mouth now full of curry and rice. After a few moments chewing, she went on. 'Sometimes, I look down at the tail end of the tube, and I think, OK, that's it now, after the next time there'll be no more left; nothing to see here. But then… the next day, it's looking up at me going, actually, there's plenty more left if you just fold me down a bit differently, from the bottom; roll me up, give me a good squeeze. So I do, and then loads more paste comes out, just when I'm about to chuck it.'

'Wow. I'm so glad we hang out,' Bella said. 'Dude. Let it go.'

'But don't you see?! It's the perfect metaphor for Lawrence and me. Just when I think it's ready for the bin, Lawrence will pull something cute out of the hat, like make me dinner, or turn up to an event on time, or when my heels were hurting me, he made me some emergency ballet pumps out of pita bread from a nearby kebab van. And then I'll think, shit, there's still a wee bit left in the old tube.'

Harry was shaking his head, while Bella now seemed to understand. 'OK, I see what you mean.'

'You always were a hoarder,' Harry said.

'You know what I think?' Bella said.

'No, but I have a feeling you're going to tell me anyway…'

'I think you should bloody well finish it and stop talking about it, IT'S GETTING OLD! Holly, I love you, but GROW A PAIR!'

Holly began to sob. 'You're compassion personified. Thanks.'

'Just giving you some tough love, my dear. It's all become clear now. Harry's right – you holding on to Lawrence is just another of your failures to declutter. What are you doing being an editor for a living, Hol, when you're clearly so bad at it? For the love of God, your relationship has gone off! SHOW IT THE BIN!'

Holly stared at her in stunned silence. 'I hate you,' she said, downing her wine.

'You know what you guys need?' Bella said, smiling.

'No.'

'A synchronised dump. That'll sort you right out.'

'A what now?' Holly said.

'I'm serious. If you're both going to ditch your carcasses of a relationship, then why not just coincide, do it in sync with another? You know what they say: "a break-up shared is a break-up halved".'

'A synchronised dump,' Holly repeated in wonder.

'Who on God's good earth came up with that?' Harry said.

'Club Secretary. A.K.A. Olivia Mahoney QC. She would never admit it to your face, but she's been getting really into all this club business. She's gone full Nurse Ratched! More importantly though, she's drafting up a written constitution for BUC Law as we speak. I think she can't help it; it's an occupational hazard.'

'Serious? After she was in such denial about it before? Oh well, she always was a control freak at uni,' Holly said.

'Either way, I'll bet she'd love a couple more guinea pigs to test the rules on…'

8. *Don't U... 4Get About Me*

Holly sat in front of her laptop watching the pale blue logo bobbing up and down as it loaded. She attempted to practise the calming Ujjayi breath technique Bella had taught her recently. Breathe in and out slowly, feeling the throat constrict, and make a sound like the lapping waves of the ocean. Or something. She tried it a few times, began to feel light-headed and gave up.

It's OK, she thought. On another side of London, one of your best friends is doing this too. Suffering in sync. A text came through which read 'Good luck. No backing out now. See you on the other side.'

The clock struck twelve. She logged into her account. As the familiar beeps kicked in, she tried to focus on welcoming a large breath into her diaphragm. But her heart was pounding so much, and her eyelid was twitching about like a butterfly on crack, that any further attempts at attaining yogic calm were futile. 'OK, let's do this. Good luck xxxx,' she texted back.

Her heart in her stomach, she watched as LawryHillUK lit up to green. Then she clicked on the telephone icon, and the familiar Skype ringtone started up.

Lawrence's smiley, stubbly face appeared on screen. Right away she could tell that in Lawrence-land, nothing was wrong. This was going to be harder than she'd thought.

'Hi!' she said awkwardly.

But the sound didn't seem to be working. So while she fiddled with her settings, Lawry leaned into the camera and blew tiny kisses to it.

L: Hi womble! he typed in.

H: Think there's a problem at your end. Turn on your microphone? So, how's it going out there? Have you been signed yet?

'Awesome!' he shouted, the sound coming back on. 'Not been signed yet. But I've been to some amazing parties and short films… And I've had an idea for what I want to write my next film about. Oh, and did I tell you I ran into that guy Max that I went to college with? He wants me to direct a film, I think I'll do it even though it's not paid… might be good for my reel… oh you'll never guess what… I met someone called David Bland today. Seriously, that's genuinely his name!! But the funny thing was, he was actually really interesting. I wondered if he has to overcompensate for his name by being extra charismatic?'

Holly nodded and watched his butterfly brain flapping from one thought to the next, closely followed by an image of herself as a gardener hacking through weeds, wanting to hack through the small talk and get to the real stuff.

'You OK?' he asked, his eyes at the bottom left corner of the screen.

'Um, not really.'

'Oh, is work still bad? Has Jez said any more about how long he can keep you on? Has he presented any of your ideas to the channel?

'No. Just Pascal's. But thanks for remembering. But anyway, there's something I think we should talk about,' she said, delivering line one of the script she'd written at last night's emergency Break-up Club. She still couldn't quite believe she was actually

122

taking this thing seriously now, let alone referring to it by its silly
name

But ever since she and Harry were kids, she'd always done
whatever he did, like a sad little lamb following him round the
playground. Today was no different.

As Holly opened her mouth to continue, she stopped, realising
Lawrence wasn't looking at her. He was staring down at the corner
of the screen, adjusting his hair.

'Lawry, are you even listening to me? Can you take your eyes
off your own image please?!'

His eyes shifted to the centre. 'Sorry.'

'Listen. I've got something important to say…' she started, but
there was a break in connectivity.

'Hi, can you hear me?' he said.

'Yes!'

'I've been having a think while I'm out here,' Lawrence said.

'Really?'

'Yep. Been thinking about us.'

'You have?'

So maybe this was going to be a lot easier after all.

'Yeah. I've really missed us. And I think that when I get back,
we should move in together.'

After a few seconds, she switched into typing mode.

H: Sorry baby. I think there was a bit of distortion there. It
sounded like you said 'move in together'?

L: I did say that. I genuinely think it's time. I don't know why
we've been putting it off so long!

Holly's heart did tiny somersaults all the way down to her
appendix.

H: Oh. Really. That wasn't what I was going to say.

L: Holly Braithwaite… I think that… I could really be with
you.

H: Oh, Lawry…

L: We've been together so many years now, and I know we

123

have our issues, but I figure, if it's not going to work then, at least if we try to live together, then we'll know. And we'll know we've given it our best shot then.

There was a really long pause while she took in what he was saying. It should have been so romantic. It should have made her jump for joy. But somehow he'd made it sound more like a laboratory experiment than a grand romantic gesture.

H: Wow, that's really romantic. Ish.

'So what were you going to say to me?' he said, switching back to talking mode.

Holly was silent, frantically thinking... did this change anything? Should she abort her mission now? She turned the page over and scanned through her prompts, feeling like a call-centre worker whose customer had just said something that meant she'd have to veer 'off-script'. She ploughed on, improvising as well as she could.

'I was going to say that... shit... I don't know how to say this now... it's not even in the same postcode as what you were going to say.'

'What is it?' Lawrence asked, his face sinking.

'Well. I think we...' she paused, 'I think that what we have has run its course.'

Lawrence's face stared out at her from the screen, his eyes beginning to water in sync with Holly's. At that exact moment, the kitchen door swung open to reveal Bella, who came marching in, kvetching about her conjoined-twin spots.

'Hey Holly, how was your day? Look at the state of this one!' she said, pointing to her face. 'I'm going to have to have surgery – I need a new face. And I've even got one in my ear? What the feck is wrong with me?' Bella positioned herself next to Holly on the screen. Then she peered into the webcam, apparently using it as a mirror to better illuminate the über-spot. 'I mean, say you're at a party or an audition with a munter like this on your face; do you think it's best to just acknowledge it? Get it out in the open, rather than try and ignore it? What would you do?'

Holly glared at Bella. A beat later Bella noticed Lawrence's deadpan face on the screen, and the tears forming in Holly's eyes; then the penny farthing dropped.

'Oh. Hi Lawrence,' she said, waving at the webcam. 'Shit, sorry. I'll get out of your way. Um, have a fab time in Paris, Lawry. Sorry,' she said, backing away.

Holly turned back to face Lawrence.

'Shit, I'm so sorry about that. You know the only signal I can get in this godforsaken flat is here in the kitchen.'

'What?'

'I said the only signal in the house is in the kitchen.'

'I can't hear you. Hello? Hello?'

'Hi! I can still hear you! Lawry!'

'Hang on. I'm losing you. Hold on. What was that?'

'Let's hang up and try again,' Holly said.

'Oh fuck this. Let's just forget the video and do messaging.'

Disconnected.

Call again?

She called LawryHillUK, her stomach now completely full of moths. Knowing what was coming, there was no backing out now.

H: OK. Let's just do chat now.

L: :(

H: What the fuck? Don't EMOTICON me!

L: Y?

H: Five years of building a meaningful connection with someone, and that's what you're giving me? A SAD FACE?

L: What do you want – a shitting sonnet?

H: Piss off.

'Oh, I just love you,' he said, suddenly reverting to voice call.

'Ah I can't keep up! Pick a mode and stay with it!'

'Sorry. Look Holly, listen. I love you with all my heart. I want to grow old with you. I thought we were going to have kids

125

together, live by the sea, eat fish and chips and push each other round on Zimmer frames…'

Holly was hit by a tidal wave of nausea as she tried to find what to say next.

H: But… you never once said any of that to me?

L: I know, but maybe I didn't want to freak you out by saying it!

H: Oh Lawry, please don't say things like this now; you're breaking my heart!

L: No. You're breaking mine.

Both were silent. The minutes moved past like stoned snails.

'I miss your face,' Lawrence said. 'Your actual face. Not your avatar jpeg thing. Let's try talk—'

The line crackled.

'Lawrence, I can't hear you, you're breaking up…' she said, the irony jabbing her in the stomach.

'I said let's try talking again.'

'Or we could just quit while we're ahead.'

'Fine. I'll call you tomorrow then, same time.'

'No, Lawry. That wasn't what I meant.'

Lawrence looked confused.

'I meant – I don't think it's just Skype – I just don't think it's going to work.'

Lawrence stared out of the screen like a lost child watching his helium balloon float away.

'Lawrence?'

Now his face had frozen in a glazed expression, but it was hard to tell if it was the connection stalling or him. She looked back down at the prompt sheet on the table.

'I'm sorry, Lawrence. But I have been feeling for ages that… that we're not in it for the long-haul.'

Lawrence switched to typing.

L:#DidNotSeeThisComing…

'Lawrence! Can we not do Twitter speak right now?!'

'Sorry, I'm a twat. Carry on.'

'Listen. I love you so, so much. I always will. But, I don't think we're right together. We don't bring out the best in each other; if anything we do the opposite.'

For a full twenty minutes, they both stared at their screens and sobbed like children. They typed more messages to each other, then cried some more. All the while, Holly became aware of people preparing some kind of ritual behind her. Out of the corner of her eye she could just make out Bella, Harry and Olivia, padding about the room like those people dressed in black doing prop changes between theatre scenes.

'Wait, this is too big... are we really doing this?' Lawrence said as the truth slowly sank into his rugged features. 'I feel dizzy. I don't want to do this...'

'But we know we have problems! Our issues aren't going anywhere.'

'We can work through them! Please, let's give it another try.'

'But that would feel like cheating – it'd be dishonest, don't you think?'

'Will we still be friends? Will we still do creative stuff together?'

'Of course! I'd still love for us to make that short.' But deep down she was already wondering when in the world that wouldn't be too painful.

L: When will I see you again? When I get back from Paris?

Holly thought for a moment. She thought about what a mess Bella was after seeing Sam, and how much better Olivia's break-up seemed to have gone in comparison.

H: No. I think it's better if we make a clean break. No contact.

'Shit. You're serious?' he said, switching back to video.

She started crying again, and nodded. 'I'm sorry womble. I just know me, and I know I'm such a wuss that I'll go back on this decision if I see you again. And this sounds like a massive cliché, but it's the hardest decision I've ever made. Even now I want to change my mind.'

'So why don't we?'

'What, change our mind? OK.'

'Well that was the shortest break-up in history.'

L: I love you.

H: Love you too.

Holly rolled her eyes, realising how this was all a bit too much like trying to get out of a warm bath. She knew the water was only getting colder; that they were both too hot and bothered and uncomfortable to really enjoy the bath anymore. But then, it was so cold out there, outside of the bath, with the stone-cold tiles and the crap central heating that didn't work, nothing but a threadbare towel to shiver into. What to do now? Cling to each other for warmth? Or jump out before it got any harder?

H: Wait… Lawrence, this is madness. We've said all these things now, we can't go back, that would be cheating, surely? I don't want to get out of the bathwater, but I know we probably should.

L: What bath???! Oh god, Folly. I hate this. I know I shouldn't beg, but please don't do this. I think you're making a big mistake. You're living up to your nickname.

H: Maybe I am. But I can't go on anymore, living with these doubts. It's not fair to either of us.

L: I can't not have you in my life. No. Just stop it, Hol. STOP BEING SILLY.

H: We'll be in each other's lives again. Just as soon as we've given it long enough to get over 'us'.

L: I can't not know you, Holly. You mean too much to me. You're the love of my life. You always will be. I WILL NEVER GET OVER YOU.

H: I've never loved anyone else either. This is just as hard for me.

L: I hate this. I can't believe I'm not going to wake up with you again in our private universe…

Despite the cheesiness, Holly felt moved to the point of emotional combustion.

H: Goodbye, womble. Don't… forget about me.

The tears were all down her face. She felt sure of only one thing now: there wasn't enough toilet roll in the world to stem the impending tide of snot and tears pressing at the edge of her nose and eyelids.

Hang up?

Her finger hovered over the button. If I can just go first I'll feel stronger, she thought, and pressed it. One click and you're done. And then, silence.

The live transcript from their message chat lay open on her desktop, like a living, breathing object. The words 'I could really be with you' and 'I will never get over you' stood out like Belisha beacons, making her question her decision.

She knew she should go and join the others out on the balcony, awaiting her with medicinal booze, and jeepers… a whole ROW of all her favourite Ben and Jerry's ice cream tubs! But she still wasn't quite able to turn away from the screen. Somehow she didn't want to close down the relationship just yet.

Save as? Holly clicked Yes, and saved her break-up under the default file name, '14th May_Chat_ with_ LawryHillUK?', thinking as she did how morbid this was – like she'd just taken a photo of a beloved dead body for safe-keeping during bereavement.

She lay out on the sofa, the laptop open at her knees. She read and re-read the transcript until the sun had set outside, the memory of his sobbing, pixelated face haunting her while her head began to ache from crying so much. Then, when her eyes had become so foggy she could see no more, she shut the laptop, curled into a foetal ball and closed her eyes. The kitchen door opened and she heard the others come in. And for the first time in weeks, her eyelid stopped jittering.

PART TWO

'There is the old joke made by the Marx who laughed about not deigning to belong to a club that would accept someone like him as a member, a truth as appropriate in love as it is in club membership... how is it possible that I should both wish to join a club, and yet lose that wish as soon as it comes true?'
Alain de Botton, *Essays in Love*

9. *And Then There Were Four*

In the wee hours of a night in early spring, the four musketeers were strolling along Waterloo Bridge, nibbling on street-meat – the deep-fried dirt barely penetrating their taste buds through all the alcohol they had drunk. Holly and Harry having just signed the sacred BUC scrolls that Olivia had stayed up all night making, they had all gone into town to celebrate. They had shimmied along the South Bank, watched skate-boarders, accidentally gate-crashed a Private View at the Hayward Gallery, and cartwheeled along the pop-up beach, before going in search of a night bus home.

'Definitely the Four. Always the Four,' Harry said.

'No way! It never comes!' Bella said. 'It's the Smug Bus! We need the 390 from up the road.'

'If only Lawrence was here, he'd settle this in a second,' lamented Holly. 'He's a pro when it comes to Transport For London.'

'OK, Holly that's TWO,' Olivia said.

'Two what?'

'Two Lawrences.'

'How many am I allowed?'

'Well, because this is your first week in the club, we'll be lenient with you. But you need to be mindful.'

'Christ, sorry,' she said, feeling a little giddy.

'It's for your own good.'

'Right,' Holly said, finishing her hotdog and wishing it was like a bus and there was another one coming right behind it. 'It's true though – he was really good at transport.'

'No – he's like RAIN MAN when it comes to transport – you always complained about that remember?' Harry said. 'You said it was like going out with Journey Planner dot com.'

'Yeah – don't be looking back at him with rosé-tinted glasses now,' Bella said.

'Exactly,' Harry said as he took Holly's arm and started spinning her around to the song of a nearby busker. Together, they twisted and twirled as if they were at a Regency ball as opposed to a litter-lined street in SE1, watched by a gaggle of nocturnal commuters. As she spun around, her hair flying, she caught flashes of the Thames twinkling under the moonlight. As she spun around again she caught the glow of the National Theatre meeting the street lamps, and remembered how much Lawrence had always hated to dance in public – he was always so concerned with looking silly and gangly (which in fairness, he generally did). Hurrah: Lawrence O, BUC 1, she thought joyfully, picturing all the dances and first kisses she had ahead of her now.

Yes! Being single was a good decision indeed, she decided as she spun round some more, until eventually tripping up and collapsing onto Harry. As their bus pulled up, she stood swaying in his arms, concentrating hard on remaining upright while also suppressing a sudden need to vomit.

'So Bella. Did you get that guy's number in the end?' Holly asked as they sat down on the upper deck, claiming front row seats in which to watch London-by-night swing by in its glory.

'The one you were dribbling over all evening?' Bella added.

'He was showing me how to Lindy Hop! And no, of course I didn't get his number.'

'He was gorgeous though,' Bella said, putting her Doc Martened

134

feet up on the windowsill of the bus and staring out. 'Too gorgeous. You know, in my experience, guys like that don't make moves. They're too damn pretty to go after girls. Girls just sort of *happen* to guys like that.'

'I don't know,' Holly began. 'There's a pretty boy actor like that at work, and I think he has asked me out. I think there's a fairly corrosive spark between us. Although as I say, I can't actually decipher these things anymore, it's been so long.'

'Hol, you're not talking about the guy that plays the lead barman?'

Holly's eyes widened. 'Wait – Harry, you don't mean to say you watch my show?'

'I am familiar with your work.'

'OH!' Bella squealed. 'He's *that* guy! Phil the Barman! He looks like a massive douche!'

'He's *acting* the part of a massive douche.'

'Isn't it a reality show? Anyway, I think he's hot!' Bella said. 'As a regular viewer, I'd say he's well worth a punt.'

'No!' Olivia said. 'It's too soon. You need time to get Lawrence out of your system.'

'Jesus – I still can't get over the fact that you guys watch my show!' Holly said, shaking her head in wonder.

'I don't,' Olivia said.

'Anyway, back to me!' Bella said. 'So, there was definitely a happening with me and this guy. We really got on well, I think.'

'So how did you leave it? What did you say to him as you were leaving?' Olivia asked.

'I said, "So I'll see you around." And he said, "Sure. I'll look out for the girl with the red beret." I'm so glad I wore my beret! At least it gave me a defining characteristic. Let's face it, without it he'd have had to say, "I'll look out for the girl who has a face a little too like Miss Piggy."'

'For the last time, you don't look like Miss Piggy!' Holly said.

There was a gap, which ought to have been filled with the others chiming that no, of course she bore no resemblance to Miss Piggy. Instead it was filled with silence and Bella's expectant face.

'Well,' Bella said. 'I'm never taking it off now. Just in case I bump into him again!'

'Watertight,' Harry said.

'Oh yes! What if I don't happen to bump into him again?'

'Did you find out where he works?' Olivia said.

'Ish. I said to him how "the girl in the red beret" sounded like a film title, and then he said that he works in a film shop so he'd try and find out whether it is or not.'

'Which film shop and where?' Harry asked in an 'Mmm, the plot thickens' kind of a way.

'Some kind of arty-farty place in London Fields?'

'Aha!' Olivia yelled. 'That settles it then. Group excursion to my new area, at the earliest opportunity! You can see my new flat too!'

'If only to support the path of true love,' Bella added.

'Oh we're hardly talking love at this stage are we,' Harry said.

'No… I mean, obviously I feel like I'm in love with him right now,' Bella said.

'Because you're a mentalist like that,' Harry said.

'You're right. I mean, I don't even know him from Adam. For all I know his name *is* Adam.'

'You didn't even get his name?' Holly said.

'Um, no. I'M RUBBISH AT MEN, I know! This whole thing is you people's fault anyway! I'll have you know, me and my new hymen were perfectly happy before you made me go out and chat to boys. Now look what you've done – I'm all – frustrated! Besides, he almost certainly has a girlfriend.'

'So what, even if he does, you should still register your interest, so he knows, if he ends up single again,' Olivia said.

'You make it sound like he's an item on Argos that's temporarily out of stock,' Holly said. '"Would you like to be notified when this item becomes available again?"'

'That's what I'm talking about!' Olivia said. 'In a dream world that's how it should work!'

'If only,' Holly said. 'Although, isn't that the point of Facebook?'

'Hang on. Can we just go back a step please?' Harry said some time later, his face riddled with confusion. 'What's all this being "in love" versus "loving someone" gubbins? Surely they're one and the same thing?'

'Um, hello? Of course they're not!' Bella said.

'They're two different things,' Holly said. 'Like, with me and Lawrence, when we first got together I was in love with him… but looking back over the last few years, we were more like best friends. I loved – still love – him as a friend, or a family member… that's why it feels like I've lost a limb right now,' she said, her eyes beginning to water. Maybe it was time for more drunk crying, she wondered, marvelling that she'd gone a whole four hours.

The others exchanged glances.

'Do you want to talk about it?' Bella said.

'It's just so fucking sad. The last memory I have of him is of his sad, blurry face on Skype! We said we wouldn't see each other again – not for a long while.'

'You're so brave,' Bella said.

'No, I'm chicken shit. I just know as soon as I see him again I'll want him back.'

Bella nodded. 'She's right; Sam and I being in contact has been a disaster. But I'm so weak, I can't say no to him!'

'Even when you know you're basically just picking at a scab just as it's healing, only to make it start leaking pus again?'

'Ergh, Harry!' Olivia said, her face creasing in disgust as the bus pulled up outside Tufnell Park Road.

'Oh, this is us!' Bella said, leaping up and hoping that the conversation would also terminate there.

Slowly, they began the wibbly-wobbly dance down to the lower deck. Arriving back at 249a, a unanimous motion was passed that Holly was too fragile to possibly sleep alone. So all four of them piled onto her bed and drank red wine in front of old re-runs of *The Wonder Years*, based upon Harry's conviction that it would be therapeutic to all be reminded of their childhood at a time like this.

By 4 a.m. Olivia declared that she needed her own bed and called a cab, leaving Bella, Harry and Holly to sleep head to foot in one bed. Something which would later lead to the coining of the phrase 'BUC bed' – a contorted yet comforting solution to the onset of break-up-induced loneliness. Despite how cramped it was,

Holly slept more soundly in 'BUC bed' than she ever had with Lawrence. On this particular occasion, she slept right through the traffic noises, not even waking when the 'stand clear, vehicle reversing' melody kicked in. She slept soundly until the following afternoon, when she opened her eyes to see Harry's hairy feet in her face.

'Ugh,' she croaked.

'Och! The brunch fairy hath come!' came Harry's voice from the other end of the bed. Holly peered through Harry's feet to see a fully showered and dressed Bella coming in with the *Observer* and a round of croissants.

'I bring freshly baked joy!' Bella sang.

'Wow. Thanks,' Holly said, rubbing her eyes.

'Climb aboard the good ship BUC!' Harry said, peeling back the duvet by way of invitation. Bella clambered on, causing a tidal wave of snotty tissues to land all over Holly's floor.

'Wow this is amazing!' Harry said, swallowing most of the croissant in about three bites and looking in the bag to see if there was a pain au chocolat for pudding.

'You're welcome. It's your initiation brunch… you know, Rule Number Five,' Bella informed them, deadpan. 'Welcome to BUC!'

'Er, thanks,' Holly said, shooting Harry a look, but then remembering what he'd said to her earlier. 'Yes this is as mad as a bag of snakes, but we've signed up to it so let's just see it through, see where it goes…?'

She forced a smile. 'Cheers guys,' she said, holding up an all-butter croissant and clonking it with Harry's as though they were glasses filled with champagne.

'Shall I make a toast?' Bella said. Holly grappled with every fibre of her being not to make the obvious pun about the fact they were already having croissants.

Harry, sensing this, placed a hand gently over Holly's mouth.

'Fire away,' he said, pulling the duvet up over his ginger-haired chest in readiness to listen.

Bella smiled at the younglings. 'OK then. To all of us – wishing us a swift recovery from our respective break-ups.' Then she swallowed her last bite of croissant. She rubbed her hands together, jumped off the bed like a spaniel, and opened the blinds to reveal the kind of azure, cloudless sky that made you feel guilty for being in bed past two o'clock.

'It's the first proper day of spring out there! We should get out and make the most of what's left of the day. And it's nearly time for our meeting.'

'Meeting? You make it sound like AA!' Holly said, pulling the duvet back over herself.

'Didn't we have a meeting last night?' Harry asked.

'Not really,' Bella said like she was trying to recall Olivia's instructions. 'It's Sunday today. This is when we actually DO meetings.'

'This isn't a meeting now?' Holly asked.

'No, this is our Brunch Duty, to welcome you. Rule Number Five,' Bella said as though they were both a bit slow. 'And last night was your Signing Ceremony. Sorry, Liv's given all of this a lot of thought, and what with her legal training I think she's convinced there's an important logic to it. Anyway, how about we have showers and head to Hampstead Heath? Have a nice picnic in honour of our first proper meeting.'

'Cool. I might just call Big Rick and see if he and Alice want to join us. Not seen them in ages,' Harry said.

'Um, NO? This is BUC? That means, only people suffering a break-up are allowed? You can see Richard and his,' this next word Bella said as though it was the very height of distaste, 'girlfriend any other night of the week.'

Holly put a hand on Harry's shoulder. 'Sorry Harry... Bella doesn't mean to sound like a fascist, but I think she feels it's for the benefit of the group if everyone's in the same boat?'

*

Being the warmest day of the year so far, the Heath had a healthy scattering of girls on picnic rugs in optimistic bikinis, and menfolk with their tops off, tending to disposable barbeques. There were also an unsettling number of couples cuddling in the long grass – a detail the members of the Break-up Club made a conscious effort to avert their eyes from as they headed to the top of the hill, lugging plastic bags that threatened to split at any point. Eventually they settled on the perfect spot in which to lay out their corner-shop picnic.

'Hey!' came Olivia's voice some minutes later. 'There you are,' she said, red-faced. 'Never any cocking phone signal in this place.'

'Where've you been? You look all glowy,' Holly said.

'Yeah Liv,' Bella said. 'Are you really that unfit, or have you been doing business time?'

Olivia nodded. 'I won't lie. You guys are the only reason I got out of bed today.'

'Hold the phones!' Holly said. 'You mean, when you said you were getting a cab so you could get a good night's sleep yesterday, you were actually going off and shagging some guy?'

The BUC eyed their traitorous member with suspicion. 'Just who've you been having sexy-times with, missy?' demanded Bella.

Olivia pretended to study her shellac. 'Don't give me a hard time if I tell you.'

'I think you're the only one of us who's been having a hard time of it,' Bella said, snorting.

Holly smiled. 'I think I know who it is… it's Dan's posh friend Jonny isn't it…'

Olivia nodded. 'Look, I know he's a bit of an arse, but he's just highly skilled at sex. Sorry guys.'

'No need to apologise, darling. Whatever makes you happy,' Bella said.

'But listen! Just to be clear. I'm not leaving the club or anything. There's no feelings involved. We're just good fuck buddies.'

'OH, I MISS SEX!' Bella said, a little too loudly, so that the elderly man walking his dog glared at her, by way of reprimand for spoiling the idyllic park scene.

Olivia delved into her bag and laid out a range of low-calorie snacks from M & S, before sitting down on a sarong next to the others on the grass. Bella began pouring out glasses of Cava.

'So now Liv's here we've got a full contingent. It's time to properly welcome the newbies to Break-up Club!' beamed Bella. 'Here's to Holly and Harry! Welcome to BUC!'

'Cheers,' chimed the others, playing along as they clonked their beakers of Cava together.

'Welcome to the clan,' Olivia said.

'Thanks,' Holly said, lying back on a mattress of thick grass and daisy petals, feeling her hay fever brewing and wondering why she hadn't brought her picnic blanket. But oh, she couldn't have: it was at Lawrence's house and was yet another item lost in the break-up vortex.

'Now, newbies,' Olivia said, catching sight of Holly's eyes welling up. 'If I can just begin by saying one thing: I know the pain you're both going through is much more immediate and raw than the rest of us. And that what's in store the next few weeks is going to be hard; at times even mortifying. But let us all think about BUC Rule Number Eleven: You will be OK, even if you can't possibly imagine so now.'

'Aye, thanks,' Harry said quietly, as Holly nodded.

'Here's a little mantra that sometimes helps me through.' Bella opened up a moleskin notebook and began reading aloud from some jottings. '"Though nothing can bring back the hour…"' Harry's expression turned to alarm. Had he taken a wrong turn and ended up in the AGM of The North London Poetry Society? '"Of splendour in the grass, of glory in the flower; we will grieve not, rather find strength in what remains behind…"'

Despite herself, Holly's eyes began to moisten. 'Who is that? It's stunning.'

'It's Wordsworth. "The Ode: Intimations of Immortality",' Harry said, his English degree coming in handy at last.

'It's really poignant, but surely it's about a death, isn't it?' Olivia said. 'A bit much to apply to a break-up, surely?'

'But a break-up is a kind of death, isn't it?' Harry said, his eyes falling on Holly, her eyes bloodshot, her face becoming gaunt from grief-induced starvation.

'Yes. I suppose it is.'

'In some ways,' Bella said, 'what you're going through is worse than death, because you can't see the person, they're dead to you, and yet they're still alive, going about their life somewhere… you just don't get to see them doing it.'

'No, you're right. In some ways it's even more painful,' Holly said. 'Thanks.'

'And it isn't just the death of love, is it?' Bella said, her eyes welling with empathy. 'It's the death of your future, all the things you'd imagined you might do with that person – marriage, babies, holidays – slowly, you have to grieve all those things, and let them go, one by one.'

While Harry looked like he was about to go and drown himself in the men's bathing pond, Holly felt her teeth clenching and wondered if Bella came with an 'unsubscribe' button.

'Bella, while everything you're saying is great, I think that might be enough sympathy for now,' Olivia said.

'Yes. Actually, I think I've had enough splendour for one day. If no one's got any hay fever remedy on them I'm going to have to head home,' Holly said, standing up and rubbing off tendrils of dry grass.

'Oh no you don't. Here, this is remedy,' Olivia said, thrusting a bottle of vodka in her face. 'You just need to up your dose.'

Reluctantly Holly took the bottle and did as prescribed.

'There, that's better,' Olivia said, but now Bella was in tears. 'What's the matter?'

Bella pointed to a dandelion clock. 'I just noticed it. Another cocking Sam-reminder,' Bella said through sobs.

Harry tore the dandelion clock out of her hands. He blew on it, and then pretended to count how many seeds were left on it. Then, in a perfect rendition of the old-fashioned speaking clock voice he said, 'The time sponsored by Accurist is – time to stop thinking about Sam.'

Bella gave a bittersweet smile.

*

Some hours later, they were surrounded by empty packaging, the disposable barbeque had burned out, and all but one of their bottles was empty. The sun was going down and park rangers were starting to suggest people went on their way now please.

'What do we do now?' Olivia asked.

'What do we do with our lives?' Bella yelled.

'What do any of us do!' Holly said, feeling increasingly hazy from the cocktail of alcohol and hay fever.

'I have a suggestion,' Harry said.

'Does it involve booze? Otherwise I'm afraid I'm just not interested,' Holly said, resting her head in his lap.

'What do you take me for? Of course it does, and I'll thank you not to doubt my alcoholism in future,' he said, depositing

143

little handfuls of dead grass onto her head faster than she could shake them off again.

'My suggestion is this,' Harry began, 'we walk into Camden, then we find a dingy but cheap pub. Sit in it until obliterated. Then we walk the streets carrying bottles of wine, drinking as we go… After which point we go to Proud Galleries or anywhere that will have us by then. Finally, we dance on the tables 'til dawn and come up smiling Monday. Do we all agree?'

'Will there be eating at any point?' Bella asked.

'Eating is cheating,' Holly said.

'Did you really just say that?' Olivia asked. 'You, Head of Gluttony?'

'Oi! Yes I did. I'm not good at ingesting solids lately. Need to be careful. Stomach still in bits.'

'Well, hotdogs will be provided by Camden Council, for those who need to eat,' Harry said.

'Oh good, another meal of street dirt,' Olivia said. 'OK then. Let's go,' she said, dusting off the grass from her black Marc Jacobs shirt-dress.

They strolled back down through the Heath, Holly running on ahead, having suddenly contracted the urge to skip. As they wound their way through the long grass and pathways, they stopped to admire things en route – from the elegant Kenwood House – a fine edifice of Neo-Classical English heritage, to Holly's attempt to climb inside a large oak tree simply because it had an enormous hole down its trunk that seemed to her to be inviting them all in for tea, like something out of Winnie-the-Pooh.

'Haha! Look at me! I'm half woman, half tree!' she said, peering out of the trunk, loving how free she felt now she was single. Getting close to nature again! Yes! Life after Lawrence was fabulous!

The other three stopped and stared in a she's-not-really-with-us kind of a way.

'Take a picture of me!'

144

'We don't have a camera,' Olivia said.

'Use my phone! It's in my bag.'

'HolFace. It looks more like you're shagging the tree, if I'm honest,' Harry said.

'Yes,' Bella said. 'How about you just enjoy the moment while it lasts – maybe we don't need to record it?' Meanwhile a queue of toddlers began forming beside the tree as though it was the latest fairground attraction.

'Hol. Dude. Let's go,' Harry said.

'Oh,' Holly said, beaten. She clambered out of the tree, covered in bark debris, mud and grass, which she began scraping off her jacket and jeans without much success.

'Christ, not sure what that was all about, sorry guys,' she said, falling into step with the others. 'If nothing else, it's sure to have turned my hay fever up a few more notches,' she added, breaking into convulsive sneezes.

Bella, walking a few paces ahead, heard this and held out a vodka bottle.

Suddenly remembering Lawrence and missing him terribly, Holly drank and drank as though her life depended on it. Meanwhile behind her, a girl of about seven with long brown hair climbed into the tree.

*

Hours later, having been declined entry to Proud Galleries or anywhere else on Inverness Street (the doormen had taken one look at Holly's eyes and – despite her protestations that the swelling was allergy, not alcohol-related – sent them packing), they eventually headed to the place where everybody knew their name: The Big Blue. Once installed there for the duration, they commandeered the jukebox and dance floor.

After a full two hours of dancing themselves silly, Holly began to think that maybe, just maybe, this Break-up Club thing was a bloody marvellous idea after all. She felt a speech brewing, and gathered them into a huddle.

'Guys. Can I just say – from the heart of my bottom– THANK YOU,' she hiccupped. 'This has been the most fun time. Looking back, we've kind of had a typical first date weekend, haven't we? We've played on the South Bank…'

'Frolicked along Waterloo Bridge,' Bella added.

'Danced in the street,' Harry offered.

'Learned to do that bouncy thing with your ankles like they do in musicals,' Holly said.

'And got drunk as skunks,' Olivia said.

'It's been emotional,' Harry commented.

'And it's just the beginning. Love you guys,' Bella said, pulling them all into a hug.

'Love you more,' Holly said.

'How much?' Olivia asked.

They all stopped. Holly was being sick on Bella's shoes.

'Oh dear,' she said, wiping her mouth on her sleeve. 'There is no one ranker in this world than me. Sorry Belle. I'll buy you a new pair.'

''S'okay. They're yours.'

'Ah, thanks B! OK. Where to next, boys and girls?'

10. *The Cistern Chapel*

Holly awoke to the sound of loud knocking, followed by a soft banging as the reverberation echoed around her head. Possibly someone had entered the room, but she couldn't see who because her eyes didn't work and nothing computed. She closed them again and realised she had slept in her contact lenses. Her eyes were now drier than a dictionary of ancient Aramaic. She teased the contacts out, apologising profusely to each iris as she did.

'Here. Have some fizzy-make-well,' came a female voice. Holly looked up to see a blurry Bella holding out a cup of lurid liquid, whose orange pantone was off the scale.

'Thank you,' she croaked, taking the cup as Bella inched on to the bed.

'I have bruises in places I've never seen before,' Bella whined.

'What were we doing?' Holly asked, scanning her memory for the last 24 hours and failing to retrieve any footage.

'Mmmm. There was definitely dancing on tables,' Bella said as Harry walked in.

'There may even have been dancing on sofas,' Harry said, joining them on the bed.

'Sofas?'

'Yes. I think we ended up at some all-night jazz bar.'

'Really? I thought we were in Holloway? Last thing I remember—'

'To begin with. But we soon found the Big Blue too small for our purposes. So Olivia paid for us to get a cab into town.'

'Dancing on sofas you say?'

'Specifically, edge-of-sofas. I think that's how you got that momma,' Bella said, pointing to the purple bruise on Holly's thigh.

'Excellent, excellent,' she said, wincing as she pressed down on the purple shiner.

'Here, have some of my arnica,' Bella said, whose handbag was never without a herbal remedy of some sort, or a half-eaten banana.

'Thanks. But hang on – why is your memory so clear?'

'I guess I'm lucky. I don't really get booze-nesia as badly as you.'

Holly tried to swallow a sip of the fizzy-make-well, but there appeared to be a small spiky troll in the way. 'Ugh. I can't feel my throat. Did somebody let me smoke last night? Can anyone tell me how that happened?'

Just then there was a loud vibrating sound, followed by a Stephen Hawkingesque voice. 'Don't answer.'

'What the hell is that?' Bella asked, genuinely concerned.

'Don't answer,' bleated Stephen. Holly climbed out of bed and wiped a trail of drool from her cheek. She pulled her faded Blur T-shirt down over her pants and did a befuddled 360 as she looked around her increasingly untidy bedroom. 'Where's it coming from?'

Bella tried to follow the buzzing sound with her ear. 'Your handbag! It's coming from your handbag!' She handed it to Holly, who tipped it upside down. All manner of Saturday night debris fell onto the floor. Chewing gum, lighter, miscellaneous coins, fags, bits of tissues, receipts.

'OH! It's my phone! It's all coming back to me now. Yes, under

Liv's instruction, I re-saved Lawrence's phone number as 'Don't answer' – to make sure I don't answer his calls. Another BUC rule! And I'd forgotten about the weird man voice that's trapped in my phone. I should get rid of him, I just don't know how the hell to work it.'

'It's still happening!' Harry said as the voice bleated on.

And there, in front of her, was Lawrence with a green face smiling up at her, telling her not to answer.

'But oh no, it's horribly tempting – I SO want to speak to him! Look at his silly, gorgeous green face!'

'No! That's a slippery slope and you know it,' Harry said. 'And why is he green? He looks like a villain from a *Doctor Who* special!'

'It's from when we used to do face masks together.'

'HAH! Told you he was a closet queen,' Harry said.

'You should know.'

The bleating stopped.

'Problem solved,' Bella said.

'Should I call him back?'

'No!'

Holly groaned and stared down at her phone, as though that might make it ring again. If it did, she was definitely going to answer, she decided. She stared at it, willing him to call back.

Wait, what did it say on there? Monday, 9.37 a.m.

'WTF? It's MONDAY?' Holly shrieked. 'Why didn't you tell me?!'

'I don't have an office job, it hadn't occurred to me.'

Holly turned to issue Harry with an accusatory look.

'Don't look at me; I've got a sick day.'

'Well SHIT, if it's Monday, I'm really late!' she said, jumping out of bed. 'Fuck, like I need to give Jez another reason to get rid of me.'

'Soz.'

'Shit fuck bollocks!' she yelled as she limped to the bathroom and turned the shower on to let it heat up.

From then on, everything Holly tried to do – from brushing her teeth to finding a pair of socks to put on – seemed to take seven times as long. Someone, somewhere, had pressed the slow motion button on the world.

Sensing this, Bella brought in a cup of tea. 'Here. Two sugars. Your hangover special!'

'Thank you,' she said as though this was the kindest thing anyone had ever done for her.

Twenty minutes later, she left the flat, feeling proud of herself for this most Herculean of triumphs. And yet, something about Fortess Road seemed further away than usual and harder to compute. Holly shook off this thought as she closed the door behind her and headed up the road towards the Tube. She looked down the road again, reasoning that she was running too late now to enter into a game of spot the difference. But by the time she'd made it past the local dry cleaners she realised what it was: she wasn't just hung-over, she had extreme visual impairment. She had forgotten to put new lenses in.

Holly stood still, leaning against a lamp post and doing deep breaths while she entertained a dilemma: Go back home and be catastrophically late, further enhancing her chances of being fired, or continue her commute and her whole day at work, half-blind? Lateness wrestled with blindness in her head, and won by a slim margin.

Five minutes later she returned to the street, this time with the gift of sight. But after a few more minutes of walking, she discovered, after all, that she was not blind – her eyes were in fact shut. She pressed on a few more paces before realising that until she ate anything, she was actually a walking health and safety violation. She wandered into a corner shop, prising her eyes open with her fingers, and came face to face with a whole row of Mini Cheddars. She stared at the marvels of circular cheesy goodness deciding that they simply must be in her life. She picked up a packet and put them into her bag before realising with horror that she'd just done shoplifting by mistake. She retrieved the packet and scanned the ceiling for a security camera. Phew – nobody saw you do it, she thought, channelling Bart Simpson. Then, she grabbed a disgustingly large bottle of Diet Coke from the fridge and went to the counter.

In slow motion, she headed back out to the street. It was two hours shy of noon, yet she was about to eat crisps and Coke, as though this wasn't revolting and rank behaviour. She kept her head down in case anyone she knew should see her. She gobbled as much of her bounty as she could before entering the Tube. Then, having exited the Tube at Piccadilly Circus with now gargantuan hunger pangs, she resumed the walk to work while stuffing wondrous Mini Cheddars into her mouth. Walking on, now fuelled with caffeine and salt, she felt doubly aware of the outside world, and much more aware of the shop signage than usual. For instance, for the first time ever, she noticed that the grey concrete office block she passed every day was called Rennie House. She'd never spotted this before, but perhaps it was just an unconscious reminder of the increasingly turbulent wind that she was experiencing in her belly on account of the amount of alcohol swishing around it. Next she passed the same florists that she passed every day, and noticed that they had a sale advertising hanging baskets. And yet all she could see was the word 'hanging'. All of this confusion was compounded by the fact that she had absolutely no spatial awareness, and kept veering inexplicably into things and people. The only way to explain the sensation was that her mind thought that she was the size of a Mini, when she was actually quite clearly a Volvo.

Eventually she arrived at work with minor bruising, running down the halls to her office, straight into her boss.

'Jeremy. Sorry.'

'Holly, you're green.'

'I'm also late. I'm sorry... I think I've got that bug that's doing the rounds,' she said. It was a safe bet – there was always something doing the rounds, wasn't there?

'Yes. My wife's been off with that. Dizziness, through-the-night vomiting and a stinking cold to go with it. She's never looked more attractive.'

Holly felt her stomach lurch. 'Yes that's the one.' Then she opened her mouth to ask if he'd had the chance to read her latest idea she'd sent him – this time a light entertainment show called Loved and Lost – but a tidal wave of giddiness prevented any power of speech. Instead she forced a smile and headed to her office.

She closed the door behind her, leaned her head against it and slid to the floor. Then with an almighty push, she forced herself to sit upright at her desk, open up a Final Cut project called 'Prowl13marchDefinitelyFinalVersion4NEW', and start putting the finishing touches to it. Luckily the edit had been locked last week and she just needed to finish colouring it, tweak the sound levels and get it sent off. She was in the middle of doing all of these things at once when, gradually, she felt a small gremlin pushing at the sides of her oesophagus, begging to be released from captivity. She tried to ignore it and carried on working. Tried to start the project rendering so it was ready to export. But the gremlin wasn't having any of it.

Holly did a rough calculation, using the floor plan in her head. At a push, she estimated that she could make it down the corridor to the staff toilet in about twenty seconds – versus the bin in her office, which was only two seconds away. She gave the bin a cursory glance. It was overflowing with tissues, there was no plastic lining and it was made of wicker.

Twenty-three seconds later, she was crouched down in a cubicle, kneeling on the floor, her arms grasping at the toilet sides as she retched with all her might, wondering if that was the last one, or whether there was any more left. Nope, there was more to come, she realised, preparing to heave again. Excellent. That's got to be the last, she prayed, wiping the back of her hand and sighing as a teardrop summoned the energy to slide down the other cheek. Slowly, she folded her arms across the basin and lay her weary head down. She felt her eyelids close, and the lights in the world snap shut along with them. After a moment she realised it wasn't just her eyelids, but the actual lights – shit, she'd been crouched here so long that the security lights had gone out! There were no windows and she now couldn't see a thing. Arses.

Being sick in the dark – was it possible to sink any lower, she wondered, feeling the gremlins starting up again. Her eyelids grew heavy as she hugged the toilet rim, dropped to her knees and worshipped at the cistern chapel. Only one thing could make this worse now – if she were to fall asleep, only to be found hours later by cleaners, in the dead of night. Oh but sleep, she thought, suddenly feeling tired from all the heaving. Mmm, that could work, she mused, as the soporific sloshing of the drains sang her a gentle lullaby.

Low point. Definitely a low point.

*

Waking some time later, she staggered back to the broom cupboard, and laid her head gently to rest on her ergonomic-wrist-support-cushion, which in the circumstances felt exactly like a goose-feathered silk pillow in a penthouse suite at The Ritz. She closed her eyes and was just starting to dream of her duvet and fresh eggy pesto pasta when there was a knock on the door.

It was Luke, looking inconveniently attractive.

'Hullurgh,' she said as she stood in front of him. She only dared open her lips a fraction, lest he should pick up on any unfortunate mouth-fumes.

'Hey! Sorry to just drop in, but the Director mentioned the film rushes from the weekend have been uploaded already?'

'They have indeed.'

'Well, I just wanted to check on the scene where I'm training the new girl. They're talking about having to re-shoot some of

153

the lines, so I thought it'd be good to see where I'm going wrong with it.'

'Oh right. So much for reality TV!' she said, her hand hovering near her mouth by way of a force-field against any bad breath leakages. 'I've just locked last Saturday's episode, but let me dig the new ones out. Oh, arses it's crashed again. Have a seat,' she said, pulling a spare chair out from under the desk, and pushing it towards Luke. Once Final Cut had come back to life, Holly opened up the project named 'Prowl13marchFinalVersionNEW'. She set it to begin exporting in the background, while starting to open up the weekend's raw files for Luke to look at.

'Phew. There we go, they're just loading up now.'

'I mean, it's farcical really. The producers never leave enough time in the shooting schedule. And then they complain when we have to do re-shoots!'

Holly nodded, suddenly at the mercy of a thirty-foot wave of nausea. She stood up, holding onto the desk to steady herself. 'I'm just going to get a can of Coke. Want one?'

He nodded.

'Diet Coke or Fat Coke?'

'Diet,' he said, patting an imaginary pot belly.

She pegged it round the corner and ran to the ladies. But by the time she'd got there, the urge to hurl had gone again and she felt fine. Such was the hangover seesaw. She stood panting against the wall, thinking, Lord, take me now. Her first ever chance of a broom cupboard-sexing, blown to smithereens by the Hangover From Hades. She leaned there for a while, holding onto the door handle and taking deep breaths until the room stopped spinning. Then she quickly checked the mirror for any rogue bits of carrot or sweetcorn that might be lurking in her hair.

'Gum?' said Luke, holding out a pack once she was back in the office.

To her mind, this meant one of three things: 1) Luke-with-the-Hollywood-smile had diligent dental hygiene, 2) he could smell her vomit (it was a tiny office, she had been sat here festering for a while now, traces of sick possibly emanating from every pore), 3) he just liked to share.

She decided to graciously accept and hope for the best. 'Thanks. Lovely,' she ventured, taking two pellets and hoping he didn't think her greedy.

She set about finding the relevant shots for him – a task which on any normal day was mundane and achievable in seconds, but today seemed to take approximately four days. Eventually she dimmed the lights, pressed play and sat back down, trying not to notice when his knee brushed close to hers three times.

'OK, I can see what I'm doing wrong there,' he said after watching the playback.

'I thought you got the comic timing just right.'

'Thanks. But I'm concealing Chardonnay as I say it. So I'll need to change position and be the other side of the pump. Bugger. It'll be a re-shoot – Chardonnay's got the number of close-ups drawn into her contract. Ever since she went on *I'm A Celebrity* she's gone full prima donna.'

'Ha! That figures. I didn't know she'd been on that.'

'You don't watch it?'

'Can't stand reality TV.'

'What you doing working on this show then?'

She made a face as if to say, fucked if I know, but instead found herself saying, 'It's not completely without its perks.'

Luke turned to face her, his hand now on her knee. She smiled at him and thought, hold the front page… surely this is contravening the Break-up Club rules somehow? Surely there ought to be a whole clause devoted to the folly of flirting with a gorgeous man, having chundered only hours before?

'Still. I won't be working on it much longer by the sounds of it.'

'Oh?'

'Oh,' Holly said, realising as Luke's smile dissolved that she'd put her foot in the proverbial it.

'What's happened?'

'Arse. I'm so sorry to be the one to tell you. But the show's being discontinued at the end of this series.'

'Wow. My agent hasn't said a word.'

'I'm really sorry.'

'That's OK. It's an absolute shit-show, let's be real here. But are you OK about it?'

'No. Yes. Not really. I'm just a bit all over the place anyway. I finished with my boyfriend on the weekend, and I've been a bit – drained – ever since.' Drained was right. Just don't mention the projectile puke, Braithwaite! You'll be on the fast track to the FriendZone. Luke looked into her eyes and held her gaze.

She put out her hand to hold onto the desk.

'Emotionally drained, I mean,' she added. Then she turned to her computer, checked the export had finished, and began to close down applications. Must wind things up now, she thought. Must get myself to a place where other people are not, and where my only company is darkness and Alka Seltzer. She switched off the computer and slowly stood up.

'Break-ups are the worst.'

Less good, she thought, heading back on the Friendville Flyover.

'How long were you together?' he asked, pushing back his chair and standing up. Luke's eyes met hers.

'Just over five years. We weren't living together or anything, but, I do – or did – really love him,' she said.

'Of course,' he said. And he pinned one arm over her shoulder, so she was tucked in between him and the wall. Just like the 'jock' characters do in those American high-school dramas. 'But hey, when you're feeling better, it'd be nice to get to know you a bit more.'

She felt herself do an inner swoon. Blimey, this one had actual moves. Lawrence had never bothered with moves, he'd just laid back and waited for life to happen to him.

Luke was still leaning in, in that too-close position. Please

156

don't kiss me, she begged in her head. Please don't smell it. Although, please do kiss me, please do come closer, but actually no really, you shouldn't.

After conducting a major war against pheromones, Holly ducked out from under Luke's arm and made some excuse about having to slip away to a doctor's appointment. This was all too soon after Lawry anyway, said her rational self. Also, maybe, just maybe, her hesitancy would be misconstrued as playing hard to get, when really it was just a case of not wanting to thwart her only chance of potential nooky with the sweet smell of bile. Holly smiled, attempting coquettishness as he headed out the office. Luke raised an eyebrow, as if to suggest that maybe he was a man who got spurred on by a bit of chase.

*

Four hours later, as Holly was tucked up in the blissful folds of her duvet, a loud voice boomed out from the floor, chanting 'Jeremy Totes. Jeremy Totes.'

Oh, fuck. Her eyes opened. She scrambled to reach it in time, and cleared her throat.

'Jez! Hi. Sorry – I had to leave a tiny bit early and go to the doctors. Is everything OK?'

'What the shit, Holly? I'm stood here looking at an exported episode, with an ungraded picture. Is there anything you want to tell me?'

Holly sat up in bed and rubbed her eyes. 'Um. I don't know why. I definitely, definitely did the colour on it, right when I did the sound levels, earlier today. I don't unders— Oh my sh—. Final Cut crashed while I was showing some rushes, and in all the confusion I must have opened up a slightly older version once it restarted! And then that must be the project I exported by mistake.'

'In all the confusion? Have you ever worked in an edit suite before?'

'I'll come back in now and fix it.'

'No, that'll take too long. Just tell me which file name it should be and I'll re-export it. Luckily there're still a few hours left before play-out. If this had made it to air, Holly, we wouldn't be having this conversation at all.'

'I know. I'm so, so, sorry.'

'So, the name?'

Holly's heart rate started to climb. 'So, um. Let's see, it would've had today's date on it. Or actually no, it had Friday's as that's when I started it and I don't think I changed it when I renamed it. So yeah, 13th March, then it'll say "FinalVersion4", I think. Or no, it should say "DefinitelyFinal!" Yes! There were two very similar versions, but the one with something like the words "DefinitelyReallyFinal4" in is the absolute master final one, no question.'

'Really? Do you think perhaps it's time to get a better filing system?'

'Version control is one of my weaknesses, I won't lie. In fact it's something I'm really keen to improve on. Do you think when you have time you could sit me down and explain what your system is and how I can improve? I'd really appreciate that!'

There was a silence, and then a sigh. 'Yes. Of course. Although, I really should give you some kind of verbal warning at this point.'

'I'm really sorry, Jeremy. I wasn't feeling well today, that must be why it happened. I assure you it won't happen again.'

'No. Well, I appreciate you trying to fix it, even from your sickbed,' he said before ringing off.

11. *Love Don't Live Here Anymore*

Holly stared out the train window at the thick grey clouds of Battersea power station as she and Harry rode towards Surbiton. She was listening to the voice calling out the journey stops, and thinking how different she sounded to the one on the Northern line.

'What you thinking?' Harry asked. 'You haven't said much since we left Waterloo.'

'I'm thinking that it's funny; this voice-over is much friendlier-sounding than the Northern line lady – she sounds so harassed and fraught! Do you think the guy in the voice-over booth gave this one direction to sound more laid-back, since these commuter trains are on their way out of the big smoke and approaching the fresh air of the countryside?'

'Do you think you might be overthinking things a little?'

'Me? Overthink?'

Harry took out his smartphone and opened up Google. 'OK. Let's see. Who is the voice of the northern line?... Here we go. One Miss Clara Thomas. There. That's your woman.'

'OK. You stark-raving stalker,' Holly said, while also jotting the name down into her notebook.

'I just think maybe it'll help you write the film if you can imagine your characters as real people first.'

'You might have a point. Thank you. Seriously though, HOW did you do this journey every day? How did you not die of boredom?'

'I don't know. I was always looking forward to what was at the end of it,' he said, his eyes filling with tears.

Holly switched seats so she was next to him, and stroked his hair. 'What, work?' she jibed, in an attempt to lighten the mood, when, in truth, all she wanted to do was sob with him. To lie on the floor and wail to their hearts' content, not a care for the other passengers. But today was about Harry. Today she needed to be the strong one. She kissed him on the cheek. 'Hey. You'll be OK, Harry McGregor. You really will.'

'I don't believe you, but thanks.'

'So how long is she going to be out for? Did she say?'

'Said she'd be back around six. So we should be as quick as we can.'

'No worries. I'm a machine when I get into packing. We'll be done in two hours, tops. The main thing is, just think about what you need for the next few months, and what can go into long-term storage.'

Half an hour later, they arrived at a charming cul-de-sac that was basically the bastard love-child of Wisteria Lane and Ramsay Street. The sun was out, the hydrangeas were starting to bloom and the 'let's not waste the best part of the day' people were out washing their cars already.

'Wow, Harry, I had no idea how old you were.'

'Why do you think I never invited you round for lunch?'

'Because you knew I don't do South?'

'No, because I knew you'd take the piss out of all this…' he said as they wandered into a terraced house that could only be described as a shrine to Emma Bridgewater and Laura Ashley. Holly surveyed the expensive-looking ornaments, from strange poultry-based figurines to miniature tea sets, none of which seemed to tally with Harry's personality.

160

'Harry-Face?!' she began. 'This is all far too middle-aged for my liking.'

'Lady Grey or Ceylon?' Harry asked as he walked under the aspidistra-lined archway into the kitchen. Holly looked around the house, spotting pictures of Harry and Rachel on every shelf. Beautiful photos of them hugging and laughing on happier days. While Harry made the tea, Holly turned all of the pictures face down, so he wouldn't have to see her prim, Doris Day face beaming out at him like nothing was wrong.

'We should crack on,' Harry said, his eyes watering at the sight of what Holly was doing. 'OK. The van's booked for two hours' time. We've got to make the last 27 years of my life look as small as possible, so I can qualify for the cheaper rate at Big Yellow Storage.'

Holly scanned the living room, which was stuffed with books, vinyl and vintage comic books. 'OK then, let's get on with it. I'll be Head of Ruthless. Anything you've not used in the last year goes in this Oxfam sack. Anything recyclable goes in this green bag. Anything you want to keep goes in the cardboard boxes. And it says here on the Big Yellow Storage instructions that you have to itemise everything – which I can do, but it does mean you have to really want each item in your life!' Holly began unwinding a roll of refuse sacks, her eyes brimming with excitement.

'Wow. You should have your own show on Channel 5 or something.'

'Just Channel 5? I'm no good at doing it for myself, but I LOVE dejunking other people's lives. Thanks for the TV idea though – can't hurt to have one more at this stage!' she said, scribbling the words 'Big Yellow Break-Up' onto her hand.

For the next two hours they worked tirelessly, dividing up memories, combing each room in the house, where every nook and cranny was saturated with the bittersweet paraphernalia of Harry and Rachel, the item.

'Whose was this?' Holly asked, holding up a huge rustic bottle of extra virgin olive oil.

'Oh, that stuff was really expensive. We brought it back all the way from the Dordogne. Maybe I'll take it but decant a bit for her into a cup or something?'

'Harry. I think you deserve the oil. I don't think she'll begrudge you that.'

'She did shag another man in our bed. Yeah. You're right. Gimme the goddamn oil.'

Next on the pile were the salt and pepper people. Holly stared at the condiment lovers; one blue, the other purple. Their china arms locked in perpetual embrace, they seemed like the perfect couple. What other couples were there like that? So happy that no one, not even God or Facebook, could tear asunder? The humble knife and fork? The Sun and the Moon?

Holly thought about asking Harry whether they should split them up – perhaps they could take one and leave the other for Rachel? The salt, maybe? Best not to ask him, she decided; if Harry saw the couple now he'd probably just smash their delicate porcelain faces in. So she carefully began to swaddle the salt and pepper people in bubble wrap (arms linked, of course. They would travel together to Brent Cross).

She looked across at her best friend, who was sat on the floor sorting through CDs and old cassette tapes.

Wait, cassettes?!

'Harry. Dude. You know that musical formats have changed about six times since the humble audio cassette? You can probably chuck those away now!'

'But these are all the mix tapes we made for each other when we went travelling!'

'Even more reason!' she held out the bin bag towards him.

'I remember, she wanted to make them all on cassette so it didn't matter if anyone nicked them!'

'That was probably really sensible back then. But you can get them all on Spotify now! Come on, bin!'

'But I still have a perfectly good tape player.' Harry pointed to the dusty red 1980s double-decker ghetto blaster that was somehow playing Radio 6 Music.

'Wow. That's proper retro. It's gone full circle to cool again.'

'No. It's just an example of sturdy electronics – made in a time when things were built to last. Not like Apple things that last a year, tops! Designed obsolescence, indeed!'

Holly smiled. 'He has a point. Keep the Sanyo. And the tapes. They're lovely,' she said, shoving them towards the 'keep' pile. 'Besides, if you ever end up out of work, you can make a mint on *Antiques Roadshow*.'

Which was perhaps a joke too far. Either that or Harry had just had a sudden realisation that things were over. She turned to see him in the centre of the living room, holding up a Smiths LP and sobbing. She sat down next to him, held him tight while he wept. Until eventually he began to complain of a crying headache, like the big old girl that he was.

A while later, a transit van marked 'Rapid Removals' pulled into the drive. With the help of Andy, the Turkish driver (the same one who had recently done Olivia's move, and seemed to be developing a sensitivity for these things), they began to load up Harry's life into the back of the van.

'That's the last one,' Harry said an hour later. He gave the flat one last glance, as though committing every square inch to memory, just as Bob Dylan began to bellow 'It ain't me' on the red ghetto blaster.

'I guess this is it then.' The van beeped. Harry took the final goodbye letter to Rachel that he and Holly had stayed up all night writing together, and deposited it on the mantelpiece, next to the face-down photograph of them on graduation day.

'Wait, the radio!' Holly said. She went to the kitchen and

unplugged Dylan, cutting him off mid-chorus, just after the words 'It ain't me you're looking for.'

She felt torn between two things. On the one hand, selfish relief: at least she wasn't the one having to pack up her life into little boxes, nor dealing with a custody battle over every shared possession. And on the other hand, overwhelming sympathy that one of her best friends was grieving the loss of his future.

Leaving Harry to have one last moment on his own, she cradled the ghetto blaster in her arms and stepped indelicately onto the van. Some time later, Harry climbed aboard, the van door sliding after him with a loud, jolting finality. They set off for Brent Cross, to the Big Yellow Break-Up Storage, where much of Olivia's life was already in boxes.

12. *Status Anxiety*

The next few days, Holly lived a pendulum-like existence, swinging from drunk to hung-over to drunk every few hours while simultaneously lurching between her two jobs of incompetent Editor and unofficial Development Executive. At the end of one very long such day, she was walking through the underground walkway at Tufnell Park station, when she passed a busker playing a trumpet. She did a double take when she saw that this particular trumpet appeared to be made out of a Henry Hoover. Ingeniously, the smiling face and its long, winding cord were emitting a hilarious, happy sound. Her thoughts were, one: am I hallucinating from low blood sugar? And two: awesome, I must ring Lawrence to tell him about this! Followed closely by three: fuck-knuckles, I don't have a Lawrence anymore.

She was halfway to the temple of gloom when her phone beeped with a message. 'Hey, it's D-Day! You bring dinner, I'll bring some vino. Let's get this over with! Harry x'

She bashed out a reply before heading home, a renewed spring in her step: 'Roger that. See you soon x.'

When she got to the flat, Harry was already in his makeshift bedroom (previously known as Holly and Bella's living room). Next to him on the sofa was a rolled-up double duvet and pillow, his pyjamas piled up on it with his towel. Next to that was a black bin liner full of clothes he still hadn't unpacked. Next to that, a pile of library books, one of which Harry had open on his lap as he stared straight ahead at the blank television. As he heard Holly enter, he turned to face her, his eyes grave.

'Tell me, why does this feel so much like a rite of passage?'

'I don't know,' she said, shifting the tower of break-up bedding to the other armchair so she could sit next to Harry on the sofa. 'I feel sick. Do you have the instructions from Bella?'

'Yep,' he said, retrieving a printed email from his bag. 'Here we go then. Rule Number Six. OK now, apparently this is all for our own protection. No Face-stalking. Yadda yadda yadda – be sure to follow the specific instructions below. Now,' he said, looking up at Holly, 'firstly, I need to ask. Are you of sound mind at present?'

'Of course I'm not of sound mind. I just bought two Pot Noodles,' she said, placing two Chicken and Mushroom tubs of dirt onto the table.

'Aye. 'Nuff said,' Harry said, visibly saddened by the sight of their unappealing dinner.

'So, I think you should go first,' Holly said, taking the paper and beginning to read. 'Right. Next, it says that this is your official deletion ceremony and a laptop will be required to make things go a swiftly as possible– none of this squinting at phones and so on. Then, log on to Facebook, open your personal settings. Then, remove the information on personal data from your feed that is viewable to others. Now THIS IS KEY. This is the thing that means that you can change your relationship status without anyone seeing.'

'OK. Done,' he said, clicking a few keys. 'Then what.'

'Then, you have to manually change your status,' Holly said, reading aloud. 'And Bella says not to make the same mistake she did, which was to put in SINGLE. Instead, you want to just put NO STATUS AT ALL. This way, you'll be freed from any dirty-laundry-fuck-ups in the future.'

Harry tapped a few more buttons, then closed his eyes as he pressed the last one. 'OK – DONE!'

Holly kissed him on the cheek. 'Well done. That wasn't so hard was it?'

'And I did it without looking at Rachel's picture. Now it's your turn.'

'OK.' She took a deep breath. 'Let's do this.'

'What's your password?' Harry passed her the laptop.

'Womble123' she said as she typed it in. 'Well, that will have to change! Right, where am I going?' She looked through her homepage for 'settings'.

'Oh. Hang on, Hol. Look.'

Harry was staring at the screen, and Holly followed his gaze. There, at the centre of her newsfeed, was a big neon sign saying NEWSFLASH! Orbiting this sign were some disco lights, a mirrorball and the words 'Lawrence Hill is now listed as single'. Next to it all, a dozen comments from friends, and a glib one from him in return.

'So much for going quietly,' she grumbled. Then, scrolling down her own timeline, she noticed she had a load of new messages from friends – everything from, 'Just seen the news. Soz,' to, 'Give me a call, honey. Hope you're OK'.

'Wow. I wish when I'd joined this stupid thing that I hadn't bothered to say I was in a relationship! This is so weird, it's like breaking up twice!'

'So, are you ready to change your status?'

She nodded and began following the instructions. Moments later, a sentence she never thought she'd see appeared up on her feed. 'Lawrence Hill and Holly Braithwaite are now friends.'

'Are they? Are they fuck?!'

'Maybe you should delete him altogether then, and it won't say that. You said yourself you're not ready to be friends. In fact, I'm going to de-friend Rachel now. And it's going to give me enormous amounts of pleasure!' he said unconvincingly, as he took over the laptop and logged back in.

'Oh.'

'Oh, what? What now?' Holly said.

There, right at the top of Harry's newsfeed was the neon broadcast 'Holly Braithwaite is no longer listed in a relationship' – complete with garish broken heart icon.

Holly groaned. 'Brilliant. Bella's instructions didn't work. It's told every Tom, Dick and Barry that I'm single.' She sighed, while Harry poured her some wine. 'Thanks Haz. Sorry I'm being a grumpy twat. I've just had it with The Facebook.' She took a large swig. 'Actually, give me the laptop again.'

She logged back into her account and went to do a status update. She wrote in the words: 'Holly Braithwaite is now listed as Single. Just in case anyone didn't hear the loudspeaker announcement. Send wine and sympathy to the usual address. Thank you please x x x.'

Next up on the itinerary was full-on deletion. Right, let's do this, she thought, finally hitting the DELETE button. There. She'd done it. Phew. END OF. But oh no. The plaster wasn't quite ripped off yet. Here was another one of those oblong boxes, tempting her to change her mind again. 'Are you sure you want to unfriend this person?'

Yes! I am quite sure thank you, she thought. Although am I ready to sever all contact, even virtual?

'How about we get drunk instead and eat ice cream?!' she said, looking up at Harry in the way a pleading eight-year-old looks up at their dad when they want a bit more pocket money. 'Can't I just have one last supervised stalky stalk?'

Harry nodded reluctantly. 'OK. I'm giving you a 24-hour respite. Only if you promise to do it tomorrow at work.'

'Yes, Harry, I promise.'

'Good. Now, I have a confession to make. I'm guilty of some A-grade cybermentalism.'

'What have you done?'

'Yesterday, I Googled the douchebag she'd been shagging. Chris Haddock is his name – which I managed to deduce from various pictures they were both tagged in.'

'Chris Haddock, you say? I mean, imagine having sex with someone called that?'

'I don't need to imagine it.'

'I suppose it would be like kissing a wet fish?' Holly said slowly.

Harry smiled and gave Holly a high-five.

'But there was fuck-all on him.'

'Well. You know what Olivia says – if someone's not Googleable, they can't be that interesting.'

'Which I always say is such a lovely way of looking at the human race.'

'Well, I'm convinced Lawry's knobbing someone out in Paris. The festival finished days ago, and he's still there! I keep seeing him tagged in pictures with beautiful women with names like Fulvia.'

'You realise he now has every right to knob beautiful women called Fulvia, don't you?' he said, but Holly was back on the computer, typing Lawrence Hill into the blue search bar.

As she waited for Lawrence's profile to load up, she found herself feeling the unique mix of excitement and shame in her stomach that only an impending Face-stalking session could generate.

'Oh, no look at him in this one… and there she is again. I can't look directly at her, she's too stunning,' Holly covered her eyes.

'OK, let's see what else there is – then we're getting out,' Harry said.

Together they scrolled back down Lawrence's timeline, perusing a photo album called 'Gay Pareee'. The same girl was with him in a different picture now, next to a pretty, elfin girl tagged as Anna. They were stood on a red carpet by a sign for the Paris Bibliotheque, glasses of bubbles in their hands.

'As if! Lawrence always said that only posh twats drink champagne! All the romance of being in Paris must be changing him. Look at how gorgeous he looks… and look at all those comments from girls underneath. Gah!'

'You mentalist! YOU ended it with him!' Harry said.

'What have we degenerated into?' Holly asked while shaking.

'I don't know. That Zuckerberg has a lot to answer for.'

Harry shut the laptop and put it onto the floor.

'It's really over, isn't it?' Holly said slowly.

'The writing's on the wall. Or at least, the Timeline. You did the right thing,' he said, huddling up to her as the tears fell in droves.

She nodded.

'I've got an idea,' Harry said. 'Let's take our minds off this by stalking another human being entirely. Let's find out a bit more about this Tube voice-over lady of yours.'

Harry opened up Google. He typed in Clara Thomas, then clicked on the link to an actor's website, where there was a black and white headshot of a woman in her forties with brown hair.

'Wow. She's so pretty! Ha, see! I was right, she does loads of other things besides being the voice of London Underground. Adverts, radio plays, all sorts! Cool!' Holly said, adding the link to her bookmarks before Harry took over the keyboard again.

'But what's this,' he said, opening up another link on the Google results page. 'Bakerloo Bob's forum? Wow, this bloke has catalogued all the different voices, on all the different lines and uploaded all of them as sound files! Some people have too much free time.'

'Wow this is actually really fascinating! A record of all the mechanical voices we hear every day but never think to put a name to, or give any more thought to. Mental.' Holly scrolled down the forum, which was filled with people posting facts about different voices on different train lines. 'This is nerdy as hell, but it's also really useful stimulus for my writing. I'm totally going to use this. Thanks Harry.'

'Why don't you have a stab at writing some of it now, take your mind off things?'

Holly knew he was talking sense. And part of her was feeling excited by the idea that Clara had a real life, and there was more to her than her dulcetly robotic tones. Part of her felt spurred to go and sit in her room and write. But her head felt so heavy, and her facial muscles had started to arrange themselves into the shape of a yawn.

'I'd love to, Harry, but I actually feel a bit run-down, like I might be coming down with something. I'll definitely start on it later. I might just have a nap first.'

'What about dinner?'

She looked at the sad little pots of pretend food on the table, waiting to be activated with hot water, and shook her head.

Harry gave her a cuddle and caught a yawn off her. 'Night then. I might go out for a kebab later. I'll give you a knock in case you fancy one by then.'

'Thanks. And well done on the delete – you're much stronger than I am!'

*

The next day, Holly awoke to a stench worse than death. One by one, she opened her eyes. Lying next to her in the bed was a small brown oblong, wrapped in swaddling clothes of pita bread, two small bites taken out of it. Resisting the gargantuan urge to be sick, she slowly dangled one foot out of the bed and felt for the floor. The foot landed on her laptop, and before she knew it, her whole body weight was now on the screen, causing it to tip up like a see-saw. In a matter of seconds, the laptop buckled and back-flipped into the air, landing with an un-earthly crack.

'ARRRRGGJJJJJHHHHH!' she yelled, not daring to look at the damage. Instead she studied her bedroom, which now looked as though it had been burgled by the same people who regularly did over The Lawrence Pit. She could just make out her bath towel at the other side of the room, engulfed in a tornado of 'going out clothes' that appeared to have swept over what was once her Zen-like bean-bag area. 'Shit,' she said, hobbling over to retrieve the towel, which now had an unsavoury smell of mildew. She pulled off her T-shirt and wrapped the towel around herself before running to the bathroom.

But the door failed to open. Arse. She had missed her slot in the unofficial bathroom rota, which meant that Bella was now full-throttle into her three-hour bathroom beauty regimen.

She pounded her fists on the door. 'Honey! So sorry! I overslept again! Pretty please can I share the bathroom with you?'

The door was unlocked and opened, revealing a face dotted with white blobs. 'Don't scream. It's only toothpaste.'

'Thank you! I'll just run into the shower, and I'll be out of your hair in three squirts.'

'What?'

'It made sense in my head.'

Ten minutes later, she was running out the front door and sprinting to the station. The second she stepped onto the crowded Northern line, she had a sudden visual of the kebab detritus that still lay festering on her pillow.

'Bollocks,' she said into a stranger's armpit.

Once at work, having ingested three plastic cups of espresso, she got straight to business in her office, the stern voice-over in her head informing her that she was a responsible, high-powered grown-up with an important telly job to do, as opposed to the crusty, booze-hound student she'd been impersonating of late. Today, she was going to blow Jeremy's polyester socks off with her editing prowess and complete lack of labelling catastrophes. First things first though, she was under strict instructions from Harry and Bella as to her Facebook protocol: delete the curly-haired-one. Simple, she thought; now she was in Efficient Career Woman Mode, this was going to be a breeze. Just tear off the plaster and BOOM, you'll no longer be tied to Lawrence in a silly, virtual capacity.

She dragged her mouse over to the button, and then hit Delete as her heart relocated to her stomach. One click, and you're done. *Yes, I'm sure.* Five years of singing your heart out to bad eighties ballads on your way home, arm-in-arm at 5 a.m., of dancing on the balcony and spontaneous picnics in the park; of cartwheels on the beach and laughing your head off at in-jokes – five years gone in a nanosecond.

Instead, now what she had to look forward to was a palpable absence. Of not waking up next to his blue eyes, his curly mop, his stubble-face. Of not having someone to make her laugh 'til her sides hurt – of not having someone to save her from episodes of chronic self-indulgence like these.

She stared at his profile picture, the same one he'd had for years. The one where he was stood on the edge of a cliff in St Ives, the sun bouncing off his curls, a sweet half-smile on his lips. It was taken from the side, which, unlike everyone else in the world, was Lawry's best angle. He looked unbearably attractive – a fact she'd also thought at the time as she peered through the viewfinder at him. Leaning on their tandem bike to stop it from falling over, and holding on to his half-eaten pork pie for him, she'd swooned at him through the lens. Back then she'd marvelled at how lucky she was to find him, and wondered – even though it was six months in – whether this was someone she might spend her life with.

She hovered her mouse over the pixelated jpeg and tried to click on it to see more, to make it bigger. But no, she was locked out now. Nothing to see here; move along now chaps. She felt another tear slide down her face and onto her keyboard. Oops. How many more drops before she'd be reprimanded by I.T. for causing 'liquid damage' to company equipment?

Wrenching herself away from the impending gloom cloud, she looked down at the crib sheet. What was next on the list? Ah. Seek out new potential. Bella had advised adding at least three men that she vaguely knew. Just to start the ball rolling. Three men? Holly paused, her mind going blank for a moment, until she remembered.

Seconds later she was rifling through the profile pages of various Luke Langdons. Eventually, she found the most plausible one, based on his Likes. She clicked on him and began reading through his profile. She'd never bothered to fill out all that infor-mation about books and films, but he appeared to have gone to town with it, which she found rather alarming. But still, lots of films to approve of here. *Eternal Sunshine*, tick, *Shawshank Redemption*. Yep. All except one anomaly. *Grease 2*… REALLY?

She looked at the clock and realised she'd given nearly an hour to the Facebook Vortex. OK, time to add him, get the hell out of there, and the hell into Final Cut Pro.

Then she realised: before that, shouldn't she check something?

She clicked on Holly Braithwaite, then looked at her own picture. Was it her best angle? After a while, quite beyond her control, she began reading her own timeline messages, to see what kind of an external impression they might make to others. Essentially, she began stalking herself.

This is ILL. ILL BEHAVIOUR, she realised with a jolt, closing down Facebook with newfound resolve, just as there was a knock on the door. 'Come in,' she said as Jeremy was already halfway across the room. His eyes had bigger bags under them than normal, and she noticed that his usual clean-shave was now a thin layer of stubble.

'Holly. Just doing the rounds – seeing if you'd had any more ideas for the channel? We've got another pitch meeting in a week or so. We're taking Pascal's idea across but it'd be great to have another few in the mix.'

'You didn't like Loved and Lost? Or The Big Yellow Break-Up?'

'I liked the general direction. Could be something in it…' he trailed off, his eyes catching sight of a piece of paper on the wall, and beginning to read.

'Oh!' Holly said, scrambling to take it down. 'Sorry, we're not meant to use Blu-Tack, are we. Don't tell Facilities!' she japed.

Jeremy yanked the page out of her hand and examined it. 'Hold the front page! What is this?'

'Give me that,' she said, but his hand moved away before she could grab it.

'The first rule of Break-Up Club is…' he began, his eyes lighting up.

'It's private, Jez, please give it back.'

'So private it's pinned on your wall?'

'It's to keep me in check... to stop me... oh, God, are we really doing this?'

Jez sat down in her chair, leaned back to read, and put his feet up on her desk. 'Hook-ups between co-members is strictly... who wrote this?'

'My friend Olivia. She's a lawyer. She's a bit um, regimental sometimes.'

'So there's a real Break-up Club?'

Holly shook her head. 'Well... ish. It's just this silly little thing a bunch of us are doing, since we've all ended significant relationships at the same time. It's got a bit out of hand but I'm sure it will all calm down soon enough.'

Jeremy's eyes went from being lit up, to being fully fledged Catherine wheels. 'You realise this would make GOLD reality TV, don't you?'

'It's just a bit of fun, Jez. Please give it back. I promise not to damage company property again,' she said, noticing four little smudges on the wall.

'Can we film one of your meetings? Make a pilot?'

Holly snatched the page back. 'I'm not about to prostitute my friends!' She folded it up and put it in her pocket.

'But don't you see? With the weekly meetings, it's perfectly episodic in nature, and ideal for the format on Channel 653! Actually, if this is replacing *Prowl* then we'd have two slots to fill a week. Could your friends stretch to two meetings a week for me? How about on a Wednesday too? Think of all the viewers you'd help by letting them share in your experiences—'

'Jez, I don't know how many different ways I can say this, but NO! I'll think of another, better idea. Just give me time. Please don't let's resort to this! I'm not that desperate for rent, yet.'

'I am,' he said quietly.

13. *Friday, I'm Not in Love*

'What are you doing home?' Bella asked two days later, her eyes blinking with concern, perhaps both for Holly's welfare and the fact that her flat-to-herself rituals were about to be compromised.

Holly lifted her head up off her mascara-stained pillow. 'Oh, hello. I woke up feeling like death. I've got a temperature, a stinking cold and generalised aching.'

'Oh, I expect you've got a bout of Break-up Flu. It's just your body expelling all the germs, you know, while all your white blood cells are busy fumigating Lawrence. It's totally normal. Get lots of bed rest,' Bella said, pulling back the covers on Holly's bed and shaking off some dried tissue morsels.

'Oh. Good to know what it is at least.'

'Shall I bring you the box set?' Bella asked.

'Please. And a new loo roll.'

Moments later, Bella came back in, holding the *Sex and the City* box set out in front of her as though she was one of the Three Kings bringing a present for the baby in the manger. She placed it on the bedside table next to some Yorkshire Gold, echinacea and vitamin C.

'Oh, B, I just MISS him. He was so lovely to me when I was ill. He'd make me hot lemon and honey and play lullabies to me on the guitar. What am I doing trying to live without him? I'm going to text him,' she said, sitting up in bed.

'Now, Holly,' Bella began, 'this is your weakest time right now. Your immune system is down, so it's doing things to your brain. It's going to make you think that you want him back. You don't. You're just having a low point. Never in our lives do we want to be cuddled by a boyfriend more than when we're ill. So you just need to ride this one out, honey, and remember: the irony is, HE is the reason you're ill. It's your body saying "thank fuck you got rid of that loser, now it's time to clear out all the toxins and make room for NEW BLOOD!" 'K?'

Holly nodded, too weak to respond verbally.

'And if you don't believe me now, let me ask you again if you really want Lawrence back next time you're running around a dance floor having the time of your life, because Lawrence always made you sit in the corner with him. The truth is – we only really miss them when we're down. When you're up, you don't even think about them.'

'Yes, you're probably right,' Holly said, nodding and blowing her nose. 'Thank you, you're amazing. Masses of luck with your singing audition.'

'Ta. The usual rule applies – don't ask how it went. I'll tell you if I get it! Anyway, make sure you get an early night; you need lots of rest. Tomorrow is a big day.'

'Why?'

'You'll see.'

*

Fourteen hours later, Bella was back in Holly's room, fixing a red beret onto her head at a jaunty angle.

'Right, missy moo. It's time.'

Holly travelled further into the duvet. 'Nooo! It's time for sleep! I'm ill, remember?!' she murmured through the togs.

'No you're not. You're coming to East London. We're going to visit Liv in her new hood. And to look for Adam.'

'Who's Adam?'

'My bloke from the other night. Film Shop Fittie. OK, he's not called Adam. But since I don't know him from Adam, now he's sort of become, well, Adam.'

'Woooohoooo,' Harry said sarcastically as he entered the room in jeans that looked skinnier than usual, and began distributing mugs of tea. 'We're going East!'

And then he began to sing the Pet Shop Boys 'Go West', but with an altered lyric, in that way Lawrence used to do, of course. But this was par for the course now. Not a day went by when a song, kebab van or muffled TFL announcement didn't remind Holly of him.

'You don't have to come if you don't want to, Harry. We could make it a girlie expedition if you'd rather catch up with your mates, or stay and make yourself more at home in the lounge...' Bella said.

'And miss the Hackney Hipster brigade? Not in a million! East is beast!'

'Come on Hol, uppy getty,' Bella said. 'If nothing else, it'll be a new cultural experience. You might come away with another gem to pitch to Jeremy – about gentrification among the hipster community, or something.'

'Mmm, maybe. I'll come on one other condition, though,' she added, smiling, 'we can take the Tube some of the way there, so I can listen to the voice-overs?'

'You absolute freakatron,' Bella said.

Holly lifted her head and rubbed the sleep out of her eyes. 'Fair.'

An hour later, the moment had finally come: Holly, Bella and Harry arrived in HipsterVille. They approached from the North side, through a mixture of housing estates and beautiful people, all of whom had one of two props in their hands: a bike with a wicker basket of flowers, or a disposable barbeque.

As they approached a busy park, they passed under a jet-black iron gate and a sign for London Fields, which seemed a grandiose title for what was essentially a small lawn of threadbare grass and mud. It was only midday but already the park was buzzing with drinkers, smokers and sound systems. Here in E8 every day was a festival.

'Wow, we are so not qualified for this,' Harry said, 'we are in no way hip enough.'

Bella frowned.

'OK, except you, Bella.'

'Holy fuck,' Holly said, scanning the park as they wandered through it. 'Is there anyone here who isn't drop-dead stylish? And the men…' she said, eyes almost popping out of her head, 'they're all ludicrously hot. I feel like I'm in some kind of game show! OK, I get it now.'

Bella nodded smugly. 'Thank you.'

Holly stood, gawking at a tall, skinny man who was pulling a bunch of flowers out of his basket and walking into a pub called the Cat and Mutton.

'Don't you just love it here?' Olivia said, appearing from the same pub door and kissing them all hello. 'Granted, everyone is way more friendly up north. But Manc guys, they were all either married with kids, or looked like they played in a Stone Roses tribute band. We have so many more options here.'

The four of them began to wind their way through the smoky throngs and soon found themselves at the edge of a crammed street market.

'Of course, it's much less cool now that everyone's found out about it,' Bella said, adopting the role of tour guide even though she'd only been here a few times herself. 'Now it's getting a bit overrun with yummy mummies, and you can't move for tourists. All the genuine arty types have had to flee to places like Clapton and Homerton. It's like what happened to Shoreditch.' Bella scowled as a double-decker pram laden with squealing toddlers pushed past her, forcing her to jump onto the pavement. 'Used to be cool, now chocka with sprogs and townies.' She said this as though it was a proper human disaster, second only to genocide or Hurricane Sandy.

They began to stroll through the market, past the rows of balsamic vinegar and cheese stalls, pausing to taste samples while pretending to be making purchase decisions.

'I've literally died and gone to heaven,' Holly said. 'FREE SAMPLES OF CHEESE, and more beautiful men than an Abercrombie casting!'

'I know. It's like we're on a film set where, instead of people wearing fat suits, they're wearing fit suits,' Bella said.

'Of course, you can see straight through all this, can't you Hol?' Harry asked, apparently expecting more from his clever best friend.

'What?' Holly said, in a freebie-induced stupor, as she walked along picking at the samples, mesmerised by brownies and baba ganoush.

'Can someone explain the dress code though?' Harry said as he squinted at the people around him. They all seemed to be clad in the same east London uniform – skinny jeans hung low, tight T-shirt, brogues and wacky socks of some ilk, and most importantly, oversized spectacles. In some of the more extreme cases, a thick gold earring could be spotted lurking in the left earlobe.

'They are hipsters, Harry – that's all you need to know,' Bella said, drunk on lust.

Holly made eye contact with one and attempted a smile. The hipster looked away.

'Oh my days! This is Adam's film shop! This is it!' Bella said as they approached what was simply named 'The Film Shop'.

'Go on then!' Olivia said.

'What film shall I ask for?'

'Oh – what about *Before Sunrise*?' Harry said. 'It's romantic, so it might be a tiny clue that you have amorous feelings for him.'

'Yes!' Bella said, practically shaking. 'But wait! We can't all go in. How about, just me and Olivia. C'mon Liv, you're good at this stuff. You can help me.'

'So?' Holly said when they re-emerged five minutes later.

'Hopeless,' Olivia said in the tone of a disappointed parent.

'What?!' Harry said, before sipping on a Vietnamese coffee.

'She didn't have the guts to talk to him. Just ogled him from afar. Then eventually she went up to the counter to ask if they had a DVD, but instead of addressing Adam, she spoke to the middle-aged woman with psoriasis.'

'Epic,' Harry said.

'Hey! Liv was meant to be helping – she was meant to be my social lubricant or whatever! But she did nothing!'

'I did try.'

'Anyway here's your stupid DVD,' Bella said, shoving *Before Sunset* into Holly's hands.

'That's not even the right one,' Harry said. 'You've got the sequel, you absolute numpty. You simply cannot watch this one before you've seen the first one. I forbid you.' Harry gave Bella a look that said 'Tsh, we give you simple instructions…'

'Why am I so hopeless!' Bella's head sank into her hands. 'I used to be GOOD AT MEN. Before that shithead dumped me!'

'I know you did, sweet,' Holly said. 'I remember. You'll get your mojo back, I promise. It's just been a while.'

'She's right,' Olivia added, 'You're not hopeless. But it's very important that you go in there again and ask to switch them. Can you do that for us?' she said, stroking Bella's hair.

'OK.'

'We'll just be here, looking at these floral handbags,' Holly said.

''K. Wish me luck,' she said, adjusting the red beret on her head, and going in alone this time.

'Good luck,' Harry said, his eyes flickering with inspiration. 'Hey, I'm just nipping to that bookshop over there – back in a sec.'

'Sure,' Holly said.

A few minutes later, Bella came out of the film shop.

'Oh, there's a happier-looking lady! How d'you get on?'

'He was serving this time! And he said hi!'

'Good, good. Then what?'

'He recognised me from the other night! So, I asked him about swapping these, and then he said what amazing films they both are, if you're romantically inclined that is. And then he said how there's been a third one, and that they're playing a triple bill of them all at the British Film Institute next Friday!'

'Really? Then what?' Holly said as Harry joined the group with a carrier bag and a big smile on his face.

Bella smiled with pride as she narrated the rest of the happy tale. 'I said that the film wasn't actually for me, but I'd tell my friend about the BFI. And then I thanked him for mentioning it.'

Everyone turned in slow motion to face Bella.

'You said what?' Holly asked.

'What?' Then, a beat later, 'Oh. You don't suppose…'

'Yes. He was asking you out. You absolute TOOL,' Holly said.

'I take it back. You are hopeless,' Olivia said.

'SHIT.' Bella stared hopelessly at the film shop. 'I could go in there again?'

'No you can't. You'll look ridiculous,' Harry said.

Bella sighed. 'Who'd be me? Bollocks to all this! Maybe it's all a sign that I'm not meant to be with anyone else but Sam? Dammit, I just want him back!' She took out her phone and went to dial.

'NO!' they all said in unison, as Harry wrestled the phone out of Bella's hands.

'Come on. Let's just go and get an overpriced cup of coffee and see if we can't explain to you about how to talk to people of the opposite sex,' Olivia said, leading them towards a Bohemian-looking French cafe.

'Shall we sit over here in this little area?' Holly suggested once inside, spotting that rarest of all things: a half-vacant table. They began to close in and loiter next to a group who were starting to gather their belongings. As they did, Holly could sense other people were also closing in around them. Soon a silent, subtle war was raging, but one which Olivia wasn't about to lose. Eventually, the people left and Olivia strode in, splaying her bags and coats all over the seats triumphantly. Soon after, Harry appeared with coffees, as Bella was appropriating a fifth chair to put round the table. They then began the slow process of contorting themselves, their coats and bags into the tight space, in order to sit down without decapitating every other customer.

'What is it about London?' Olivia began. 'A cafe this full in Manchester would be twice the size. I swear they design all the bars and cafes here with impossibly narrow interiors, specifically to make you feel more obese and cumbersome than you actually are.'

'Oh my God this brownie is sensational! Try some!' Bella said with her mouth full. She offered it to Olivia who shook her head and tried to get comfortable in the tiny seat.

'I rather like this place,' Holly said. 'Good music.'

Harry nodded and tapped his foot along to Nina Simone while watching the skinny-jean army queuing for coffee. 'You know, I once heard a story about a girl at a picnic whose skinny jeans were so tight, she actually ripped a tendon in her knee when she tried to get up off the grass.'

Holly laughed. 'Brilliant! Hey, maybe there could be a documentary in this after all?' She grabbed her notebook, which was now almost half full, and wrote down on a fresh page, 'Skinny-Jean Army'. Just then the track changed, and a familiar song started up. 'Oh, for the love of shit. I mean, what are the chances!'

'What is it?' Olivia said.

'I'll handle this,' Bella said, standing up. 'They're playing "Private Universe", a prehistoric song by Crowded House,' she whispered to the others, 'Holly and Lawrence's song.'

Holly nodded, the tears pressing at the edges of her eyes as the 'I will run for shelter' chorus kicked in. Instantly, she was teleported back to Lawrence's old bedroom in St Ives, when he'd first played this to her on the guitar. Just as Holly felt herself sink into another wallowing abyss, the music came to an abrupt stop. She looked up to see Bella talking to one of the waiters.

'Aw. She's a good friend,' Holly said. 'I don't know anyone else who would have the cheek to complain about music, do you?'

Bella returned and Holly gave her a hug.

'You're welcome. Music's unwelcome time-travel sometimes, isn't it?'

Holly nodded and smiled as the track changed to something else.

'You never close your eyes… anymore… when I kiss your lips.'

She looked across the table at the others. 'REALLY? The Righteous Brothers? "You've Lost That Loving Feeling"?'

'Oh well, honey, I tried,' Bella said, erupting into giggles.

'I know you did, and I thank you for it.'

Holly laughed at the ludicrousness of it all and stood up, squeezing her chair back. 'Sorry guys. I'm going to sit this one out. Harry, look after my bag for me?'

'Sure,' he said. Watching her walk away, and checking none of the others were looking, Harry shoved an oblong, wrapped-up parcel deep down into the bottom of the shoulder bag.

Once inside the four small walls of the toilet cubicle, Holly noticed a peculiar transition: from boozy cacophonous cafe buzzing with mates and shiny people, to a solitary, silent, graffiti-lined hole. Suddenly, the aloneness was deafening, as was the reality of a life without Lawrence. Laughter was only metres away but, right now, she was affronted by her own overwhelming solitude. She quickly did what she needed to do, and ran back out to her musketeers.

'OK, guys, just so you know. From now on, I'm incapable of being by myself, even for five minutes.'

'You're not alone, sweetie,' Bella said. 'You've got us!'

'Yeah,' Harry said. 'You can hang around me 24-7 if you like, I really won't mind. Be my lapdog.'

Holly laughed.

'You don't need to be alone again, ever. OK?' Harry said.

'Thank you guys. Sorry I'm such a massive loser. I'll be fine soon.'

'Course you will,' Olivia said.

*

Later that night, Holly was unpacking her bag from the day when she noticed a surprise parcel inside it. Sat with her legs crossed on her bed, she tore open the wrapping paper to reveal the words *Story* by Robert McKee. She smiled as the huge tome of a book fell open onto one of the first few pages, where a message was inscribed in spidery handwriting.

Holface,

Don't worry, I'm not about to write 'follow your dreams' or anything dreadful like that, but this is just something to say thank you so much for your help the other day in the flat. And also that, I know you can't see this right now, but you're going to be fine.

In the meantime, this is something that might help. It's THE book that screenwriters swear by.

Sod all this nonsense about coming up with more shit telly ideas. You're just building yourself another prison for the next six months. Brick by fake-tanned brick! At the risk of going all preachy on you, I think you should set your sights on editing something DECENT.

You've been saying for so long that you'd love to edit a feature or TV drama. So why don't you write your way into one? I know you have it in you. Or at least, start with the short?

*You think you need Lawrence to help write you this script,
but you're wrong.*

*Have a read – it's heavy-going in places but stick with it!
Then, write your way to Hollywood.*

(Actually, make it Pinewood. I'd miss you too much.)

All my love, H x

Holly took out her phone and dialled, even though she knew he
would be out with his mates.

'Harry,' she said to his Voicemail, 'I'm sitting here with tears
all down my face. Thank you. That was so lovely. In fact, it's far
sweeter than any gift Lawrence ever got me. Thank you! I'm
totally going to read it from cover to cover! Love you, bye.'

She put the present on her shelf, on top of a pile of other
dusty books that were waiting to be read, and climbed straight
into bed, passing out as soon as her head hit the pillow, and just
before her phone buzzed with an incoming email.

**Jeremy.Philpott@TotesamazeProductions.com to
Holly.Braithwaite@TotesamazeProductions.com
Subject: Re: Skinny-Jean Army – a Proposal**

Love it.

 As a reality show though, not doc.

 Tendon thing a hoot.

 It's on the list.

 **If I'm honest, I don't love it as much as BUC though,
so that's still there to be beaten. Obv.**

 Happy hunting,

 J.

14. *Bang and the Pain is Gone*

'I'm Barry Scott!' Harry hollered the next morning, pointing a lurid pink spray-bottle at Holly. Then he turned his attention back to the kitchen units, dousing them in more detergent.

'Bang! And the dirt is gone!' she said, spraying another dose of Cillit Bang over the taps in the kitchen, and giving them a good wipe down.

'Correct!' shouted Harry. Being a 'Planner' in an advertising agency, he was so well-versed in advertising slogans that sometimes conversations with him felt like being on a low-budget game-show. Holly surveyed the surfaces in the kitchen, which were now unrecognisable from how they'd looked six hours ago.

'Wow, you've given Mr Muscle a run for his money, never mind Barry Scott.'

'Crikey!' Bella said, walking into the kitchen, looking miserable. 'This place is cleaner than when we first moved in! Harry, you have MORE than earned your sofa-surfing keep now!' She headed into the kitchen to put a sachet of popcorn – the first meal of the day – into the microwave. Then she hobbled over to the sofa, spread herself across it and turned on the *EastEnders* omnibus.

Harry, meanwhile, pulled out a bottle of bleach and held it aloft like it was the answer to all his problems, before taking the lid off it.

'Nice one, Harry. I'd help you out but I've got a steaming hangover; I'd only hold you back.'

Three minutes later, the microwave pinged and Bella cast a whimpering look towards the others. 'Sorry to ask but could one of you please pass me that? I've just got comfy.'

'I thought you'd been banned from that stuff?' Holly said as she handed her the bag.

'She had to actually go to the dentist with an emergency toothache the other day,' Holly explained to Harry. 'It turned out to be a bit of husk wedged between her molars that had started to decompose. How gross is that?'

Bella nodded, her mouth full. 'The dentist couldn't get it out – said it has to come out naturally. I still can't stop eating them though.'

'Even when it's actually affecting your health? Christ, you're like a smoker with a hole in the neck!' Holly said, turning around to look for Harry. She found him on the balcony, holding a bottle of window cleaner and scanning the area around him.

'Wait, you're cleaning the windows now? Seriously, it's time to stop. You've done enough. How about we go for some brunch?' she said, looking at him with concern.

'But I've not finished disinfecting everywhere yet.'

'Seriously, Harry Poppins,' she said, feeling her hunger anger creep in. 'Our house has gone up in value. Step away from the mop bucket.' Then, a beat later she added softly, 'It's not going to bring her back.' Holly placed a hand on Harry's shoulder. 'Come on. The bottle.'

Begrudgingly he handed it to her.

'I just really fucking miss her.'

'I know,' she said as her phone beeped with a message.

'Oh, cool. Liv's at The Breakfast Club and is suggesting starting this week's meeting early.'

'Oh, yum, The Breakfast Club!' Bella said, peeling the blanket off her and getting up off the sofa.

'I thought you'd eaten?'

'There's always room for breakfast dessert.'

'How about it, Harry? A meeting might be the perfect thing for you right now?'

'Listening to three other fuck-ups going on. Mmm, let's see,' he said, scrolling down his contact list in his phone. 'No, that's right, all my other friends are married with kids. OK, you've got me.'

'Admit it, you love it really,' Holly said.

Harry smiled and stared after her as she walked down the stairs. A moment later, he followed them out.

When they arrived, Rick Astley was on the jukebox, while Olivia was nestling in a booth surrounded by eighties nostalgia – from Kylie record sleeves to John Hughes movie posters – and drinking a luminescent smoothie.

'Don't you love this place?' Bella said as they all squeezed into the booth. 'I think we should make it the BUC headquarters. The name's basically the same, and it's just so cheery and nostalgic. It reminds me of being a kid! Of the halcyon days when we could wear Global Hypercolour T-shirts, buy Chewits for ten pence and kiss boys with the carefree zeal of someone who has yet to have their heart ripped out through their arse,' she said, her eyes filling with water as her voice rose in volume.

'OK, what's happened?' Holly said.

Bella wore the sunken face of an addict who had fallen off the wagon. 'I've only gone and done a relapse.'

'A what?'

'I accidentally had break-up sex with Sam last night.'

'And you've only just said something now?'

Bella nodded. 'Why do you think I was compulsive corning again? Look, I know it was wrong, but it was fucking tremendous.' She acquired a dreamy look in her eye. 'LITERALLY, tremendous fucking…'

'Wait. And we let this happen how?' Olivia put to the others, as though they were all to blame for letting slip of Bella's chastity belt.

'Hey, it's no one's fault but mine. I am weak. We were just

meant to hang out at his, watch a movie, but it just didn't really work out that way.'

Holly rolled her eyes. 'Wait, after we left Hackney? You said you were going round to a FRIEND'S house? You sneaky fucker!'

'But we ARE friends. And my self-esteem was subterranean after AdamGate. And break-up sex is HOT. And, and I know he still loves me!'

'He's using you, that's what. He's confused, and he's using you for sex,' Harry said as a chirpy Australian waitress came over to take their order.

'You really need to stop contacting him,' Olivia said moments later. 'It's not fair on you that he keeps ringing. He knows you're weak and that you'll see him. It's contravening about five BUC rules, too. Not least Rule Number Six – full deletion!'

'I know! But when he keeps changing his mind and saying he thinks he made a mistake, what am I meant to do? Where's the rule for that?'

'Next time he gets in touch, just don't engage with it,' Holly said.

'Yes. New Rule. Number 12 – DON'T ENGAGE,' Olivia repeated as though it was now officially added to the Constitution.

'I can't get over him though. He's a hi-vis cyclist! Every time I think I'm starting to forget about him, I see a guy zoom past me in a hi-vis jacket. And every time, I think it's him, and then when he gets that bit closer and it's NOT Sam, a little piece of me dies. Is it too early to start drinking please?'

'It is never too early,' Harry said.

'Then let's upgrade these smoothies. Who's going to join me for a cocktail?' Bella said, looking down the menu.

'Good idea,' Holly said, not sure if it was. 'So anyway, boys and girls, I have something to add to this week's "agenda",' she said, miming speech marks.

'Go on,' Olivia said.

'I have a question about Rule Number Six. So, I'm still friends with a whole bunch of Lawrence's mates. They're all really nice.

I still get their updates on my feed. What's the protocol, am I meant to delete them all too? Should I be deleting all of St Ives?'

'If you want a clean slate,' Harry said.

'Do I need to message them and let them know?"

'NO!' shouted Olivia. 'You mentalist! You just go quietly, like you're slipping away early at a party. Friends of exes are all the part of the baggage we have to shed as we go along. Dating's just like cooking really. Clean as you go.'

Holly gulped.

'So, that's Bella and Holly touched on,' Olivia said, 'how is our very important male member? Are you doing OK?'

Harry took a long slurp on the last of his drink. 'Aye. I'm putting one foot in front of the other. The thing I'm finding really hard? Life's silly moments. Like when I see something a bit bonkers-nuts while I'm out and about – like a girl cycling along while towing a suitcase on wheels – I see that, and I know it would make her laugh. That's when I really wish I could ring her!'

'I'm with Harry,' chimed Holly. 'I miss having someone to share my funnies with.'

'We're those people now,' Bella said. 'And we're the ones you call at the end of the day if you want a good-night chat to replace those hour-long ones you're used to having.'

'Oh God yes. I am really missing the long phone calls,' Holly said.

'But then, isn't it insane how much of your day got used up, just being on the phone to a boyfriend?' Olivia said.

'It's true. Was that really such a good use of time anyway?'

'No. You're right. Break-ups are THE GIFT OF TIME!' Bella said as though it was an epiphany.

'Yes. Let's all start using the time to DO the creative things we always wanted to do! The stuff we never did because our relationships kept getting in the way. Come on then, everyone say one thing now that comes to mind,' Olivia said.

'I want to edit a feature film. Or I'll take a short – that would do…' Holly said, her eyes interlocking with Harry's.

'I want to put out an album,' Bella said. 'An actual one. Not just a page on SoundCloud that four people in Reykjavik listen to.'

'I want to figure out how to get this girl at work to sleep with me.'

'Realistic goals, people,' Olivia said.

'Yeah Harry, creative ways to seduce people doesn't count! You must have a creative thing you want to do?' Bella said.

'Don't know.' Harry looked down at his Converses. 'I guess I've always wanted to write a novel.' Then he shook his head as though it was piffle.

'And I've always wanted to set up a small quiche business.'

Everyone turned to face Olivia.

'Where the jeebus did that come from?' Bella said.

'What? Everyone's got a thing – that's mine! I secretly like to bake quiche. If I wasn't a lawyer, that'd be my alternate career. I find it incredibly therapeutic cooking them for people. I'll prove it by baking you some for the next meeting.'

'You're on,' Holly said.

'OK. Right,' Olivia said, writing down everyone's goals. 'I'm proposing we all devote a few minutes every day to our projects. Structure. That's what we all need.'

'How about every week rather than every day?' bargained Harry. 'I mean, let's be real here – we're all still in mourning at the moment. We need to factor in time for being morose, and getting recklessly drunk,' he said, beginning to sound just that.

'And recklessly hung-over,' Holly added.

'He's right. I mean, I for one need to know that we've got enough scheduled moping hours,' Bella said.

Olivia frowned. 'All right. A few minutes every week then! We set aside thirty – no – sixty minutes a week to DO CREATIVE PROJECTS. That way, all those who complain about their jobs – I'm looking mostly at you, Braithwaite – will have no excuse. Myself included. We shall carve out our own niche in the world, one way or another.'

'Niche quiche!' Bella squealed. 'We'll carve out our own Niche Quiche!'

'HAHA!' Holly said. 'That should be your company name, Liv!'

Olivia's eyes lit up into pound signs.

'Have it. Think of it as my gift to you, and your recovery,' Bella said, affecting the look of a modern-day Mother Teresa.

'I might just check if it's copyrighted already,' she said, getting out her phone.

'Hey, I know!' Bella began. 'Why don't we all go swinging?'

'We're not that middle-aged yet!' Harry said.

'No. Swing dancing. Lindy hop. It's all the rage at the moment. All the cool kids are at it. In fact, there's a class at Dalston Roof Park that my friend told me about. Who's with me?' She looked around hopefully, but everyone else was looking down at their two left feet.

'Holly. I nominate you. I've seen you dance when you're hammered. You've got rhythm! Sort of.'

'I'm entirely mal-coordinated. But all right then.'

'Ace! Actually, thinking about it, she said it was on every Sunday at 8 p.m. So there'll be a class opening in half an hour! We can make it if we jump on a bus now.'

'Oh, I didn't mean go now!'

But Bella was already pinning her hair into a victory roll, and slapping on more rouge. Evidently, swing class was an excuse to look even more fancy dress than normal.

'Really? Oh, what the hell, I'm drunk enough now. Let's give it a go,' Holly said, faffing with her bags and following Bella out the door. 'Only you'll have to shout me the money.'

'Sure,' Bella said, rooting around in the bottom of her handbag.

'Thanks. I'm just not really managing at the moment.'

'I can see that, darling. You're wearing a scarf and it was the hottest day of the year today!' Bella said as they headed out onto a busy main road.

'I meant financially, but thanks...' Holly looked down at the stripy Doctor Who-style scarf, which her mother had made her. Her mum and stepdad had a bit too much free time now they were retired, so they were often sending her strange yet exciting packages. This month's handcrafted horror went down to her feet and was made of wool, even though it was spring.

She removed the scarf and stuffed it into her shoulder bag.

'There. I've put the stupid thing away now. OK?'

As Bella nodded, they heard the screeching of car horns, then the sounds of a huge double-decker bus grinding to a halt.

'What was that?' Holly said, her eyes scanning the Islington traffic for a clue.

'Look!' Bella pointed to the other side of the street where a red bus was parked halfway into the road, its hazard lights flashing. The bus was being emptied of its passengers, and people were crowding round.

'Someone's been hit,' Holly said, racing across the road. Bella hobbled behind in her enormous heels.

Her first thought when they got to the other side of the bus was, fuck-sticks, why hadn't she paid attention when they'd done first aid in school? Then she might've been more prepared for the fact that there, in the triangle of road between pavement and bus, a man was lying on the ground, contorted under a mangled bicycle. His bruised arms were tangled up in a bike chain the colour of Sunny Delight, and his body was beginning to erupt into small quakes.

'Shit, we should do something!' She looked around, noticing a whole audience of people staring and gawping, none of them actually helping.

'We're trollied, Holly. We'll only make things worse.'

'But no one else is doing anything! OK how about you ring for an ambulance, and I'll try to make contact.' Tentatively, she stepped forward and crouched down. 'Hello. Are you OK?'

As she got closer, she could see that the young man's leg was bleeding and a small paddling pool of blood was appearing next to it.

'Sorry. Stupid question.'

He nodded and gave a half-smile. Then he winced, and a tear slid down his cheek. 'How bad is it? I can't feel my leg.'

'It's OK. You're OK,' she lied, blindingly conscious of her own ineptitude. 'We're getting you some help. Try not to worry,' she said, taking hold of his hand and squeezing it.

'An ambulance is on its way,' Bella announced, crouching down next to them, 'so try not to worry.'

As the two friends exchanged concerned glances, a rotund woman emerged through the crowd of gawkers. Luckily, she looked the spit of Matron from the old *Carry On* films. Holly hoped with all her might that she could act the part of Matron as well as look it.

'Has anyone got anything we can wrap around his leg?' Matron said, crouching down to join them.

'How about this?' Holly grabbed the stripy woollen scarf from her bag. 'If you don't think the bits of fluff will cause damage or anything.'

'I think there's more risk of fashion damage with that than anything else,' Matron said.

The man managed a small smile as they wound it around his leg like a tourniquet.

'Should we try and put him into the recovery position or something?' Holly asked, feeling her brain kick in a little more as she gradually sobered up.

'No, it's best not to move him just in case,' Matron said.

Halle-fucking-lujah. At last, someone who wasn't a total numpty when it came to life-saving. Holly vowed to take up first aid the second she got home.

She squeezed the man's hand again and took a proper look at him for the first time. His hair was splayed out in matted tendrils over the tarmac. In normal circumstances, were his cheekbones not caked in blood, it might have been the kind of smile that could light up a room. Shit. Looking at his toned arm muscles, she had to admit that – morbidly inappropriate though it most definitely was – he was disarmingly attractive.

Christ. Perving on the incapacitated; we're really descending to new lows, she thought as she let go of his hand and turned away to look for the ambulance again. As much as she tried to shake the thought from her mind, surely if she was finding so many other men attractive – dead or alive – was this not more proof that she was right to break up with Lawrence? Then she decided, thinking purely in medicinal terms of course, that it might be a comfort if she gently stroked the man's hair. So while Matron carried on wrapping the ridiculous Technicolor scarf around his leg, she kneeled down again, held his hand, and began to stroke his soft, brown hair in a completely non-sensual way.

'Thank you,' he said, his eyes half open, his expression ever more vacant, as though he was slowly slipping out of consciousness.

'Can you remember your name?' Matron asked.

'Aaron,' he said, then he stopped shaking and closed his eyes.

'Shit!' Holly said, still holding his hand. 'Where's he gone?'

'It's OK, he's just passed out,' Matron said as they heard an ambulance siren ascending in volume.

'Phew, that was fast!' Bella said.

The ambulance pulled up, and Holly slowly let go of his hand. 'You'll be OK,' she whispered to him as the paramedics got to work. The three women stood back as the professionals took over. After making some checks on him, they untangled him from his bike and hoisted him onto a stretcher. The girls watched, transfixed until the doors closed and the ambulance drove away.

Neither of them said a word as they walked back across the street to the bus stop, listening to the piercing siren fade away into the distance.

'Shit, that was horrible. I don't really feel like going swing dancing now, do you? It doesn't seem right. Not while that poor guy is in such a bad way.'

'No. Let's just go home instead, have a stiff drink,' Bella said, as the traffic gradually returned to normal.

They saw a bus headed for Tufnell Park and climbed aboard in silence. As they took a seat at the back, Holly contemplated the gravity of what they had just seen; of how the threat of mortality had stared them both in the face. Time to start valuing their life, stop moping around, start making the most of every minute…

'You're thinking it too, aren't you,' Bella said gravely.

'What?'

'Fit. As. Fuck.'

'Isabella Allen! You are an OUTRAGE.'

'He was BEAUTIFUL!'

'Stop it. You are beyond dark! You know there's a line – and you just went way beyond it!'

'No, you're right. Sorry. I'm being awful,' she said, shaking her head. 'It's just that he was just such a classic Hol-type. The curly hair, the stubble, well, from underneath all the blood, that is.'

'Not. Listening,' Holly said, putting her fingers in her ears.

'Hol, deny me to my face that he wasn't an absolute Adonis! And he seemed like such a nice guy, too! When you were holding his hand, he seemed so grateful and sweet!'

'There's a word for people like you. You're like – a borderline necrophiliac.'

'He's not dead!'

'Yet. You don't know the extent of his injuries. He may have internal bleeding.'

Bella fell silent.

'Well, that's put an end to my mission to take up cycling,' Holly said a few minutes later. 'No way am I riding in London after that.'

'Me neither. Think I'll put mine on eBay. Still, maybe there's a TV show in it for you, on the very real dangers of cycling in London?'

Holly stared out the window and closed her eyes, replaying in her mind the scene of the poor (stubbly) bleeding man lying in the road.

15. *Niche Quiche*

Olivia turned the oven dial to the Off setting, slipped some oven gloves on, and pulled out a large steaming tray. Then she proudly placed ten perfectly formed mini-quiches onto Holly and Bella's living room table.

'Shit Liv. These aren't half bad!' exclaimed Holly after taking a huge bite. 'Except I just burned the roof of my mouth. OW.'

'They're fucking delicious!' Bella squealed. 'Who knew our oven was even capable of producing something like this! Liv, you're the perfect woman!'

'Thanks,' Olivia said, beaming. 'I'm working on a special haloumi flavour for you, Holly. It's going to be called "You Had Me At Hellim".'

'That is literally the sweetest thing anyone's ever done for me,' Holly said as Bella guffawed.

'You're wasted in The Law,' Harry said. 'You should quit immediately. The culinary world needs you.'

'Oh, that's a tangible career plan. I can just imagine my parents now. "Dad, I'm going to BAKE my way out of the legal profession, after all those tuition fees you paid for. What do you think, Mum?" "Bye, bye now," they'll say, and I'll be ejected from The Mahoneys before you can say interfamilial divorce.'

No one had a counterargument for that one.

'So how's everyone else been getting on with their own creative exploits this last week? Are you all using the gift of time to its full potential?' she said, sounding oddly like a life coach from Malibu.

Everyone was silent.

'Holly, have you written your short yet?'

Holly shook her head. 'Still too soon for me, I think. Any day now though, I'm going to start.'

'We tried to do swing last week, but we ended up helping out at the scene of a bike crash,' Bella said.

'How awful,' Olivia said, 'was everyone OK?'

'Hopefully,' Bella said, looking pointedly at Holly. 'I still think we should ring round the local hospitals and check on poor Aaron.'

'Aaron? You talk about him like you know him!' Holly said. 'Come on, B. That is ILL behaviour. If I thought for one moment that your concern came from a Samaritan-like goodness, then I would let you.'

Bella smirked.

Sometimes, she was worryingly unaware of the fine line between fancying someone a lot and being a stark-raving stalker.

'Sorry. I just thought you guys looked good together. There seemed to be a real connection between you. In other circumstances…'

'Maybe you should track him down, Hol?' Harry said. 'Imagine if you ended up going out? Then it'd make another addition to your lovely documentary idea!'

'Oh, bless you for trying to help, but no, Jez blew that one out straight away. Anyway, shall we stop being morbid and move on?'

'No you're right,' Bella said. 'He's bound to have a girlfriend anyway. All the hot men in London in their late twenties do. Unconscious or not.'

'Well I hope he's OK,' Olivia said, before turning to face Harry.

'How about you? Have you done any work on your novel since we last talked about it?'

He shook his head. 'Still too raw.'

Olivia rolled her eyes. 'Tsh, you're all lazy twonks. Oh well. Who's in for seconds?' she said, having barely touched her own portion of quiche.

'IN!' Holly said, holding her plate out. 'So. I have a question: Is it just me, or are there loads of cosmic jokes going on at the moment?'

'What do you mean?' Harry said.

'Like, today, on my way to the meeting, I passed a new shop that'd just opened up. Do you know what it said on it huge letters?'

'What?'

'FOLLY,' she said, like it was the worst news on all planet Earth.

'So?' Bella asked.

'Well… you know… Lawrence used to call me Folly? It was his nickname for me when I was being a bit special.'

'OH! I've seen that shop!' Olivia said. 'Isn't it spelled F-o-l-l-i-e?'

'Possibly, yes… But still, the timing of it just opening up.'

'Strictly speaking it's two words, spelled F-o-l-l-i-F-o-l-l-i-e,' Olivia said, looking at Holly. 'I think it's time we had another talk about the rules.'

'Why?'

'Well, if you remember, some time ago, I drew up a provisional list of BUC rules for us all to abide by – mainly for our own protection, but I'm slightly worried that a) you're not all adhering to them and b) we maybe need to add a few more to the initial draft, to help us all keep our sanity a bit more in check.'

Holly stifled a yawn, and with it the urge to say 'someone's sanity definitely needs keeping in check.'

The others shifted about in their seats.

'Holly, I'm actually thinking of you in particular,' Olivia said sternly.

Holly sat up straight in her chair, suddenly aware she was slouching. 'Sorry, Miss.'

Olivia's eyes switched to 'evils' setting.

'Come on guys,' Bella said, 'I know all this seems a little officious forward-slash infantile, but I can't help thinking if I'd had some of these rules around when I was going through the worst of it with Sam, it might've helped?'

Olivia smiled at Bella like a teacher would to her pet. 'So,' she began, just as the doorbell rang.

'Who the shit's that?' Bella looked at Holly as if to say 'you go.'

'Maybe it's one of Daniel's girlfriends? I can't keep up with them all, he's like, Casanova MD at the moment,' Holly said, getting up and heading to the intercom. 'Hello?'

'Holly, its Jez.'

Her stomach lurched. She covered the mouthpiece and whispered to the others, 'Guys, it's my boss. What's he doing here? What have I cocked-up now?'

'Fucked if we know. Go and find out!' Harry said.

'Just a minute,' Holly said into the intercom, before heading down the stairs. She opened the door to a tear-stained Jeremy. He burst into fresh sobs as she took him in for an awkward hug.

'Jez, what is it, what's wrong?'

'My wife's left me.'

'Oh! Shit, I'm so sorry,' she said, relieved she wasn't in trouble again. She leant forward to give him another hug. 'Um, can I help? Is there any reason—'

'Well, it's Sunday night, so I thought...'

'You thought what?'

'I wasn't sure if you had a drop-in policy or not? You know, your Break-up Club?' he said as Holly's mouth dropped to the floor.

'It was presumptuous of me. I'm sorry, I'll go,' he backed away, his eyes watering again.

'No, no, don't be silly. Since you've come all this way...'

As they headed up the winding stairs, Holly wondered how she would explain to the others that they now had a fifty-year-old sociopath as their fifth member.

'Guys,' she said as she opened the door to the living room, 'this is Jeremy. He's suffered a recent heartbreak, so um, let's all show him the support he needs, shall we?'

Harry leapt out of his chair to shake his hand. 'Welcome, Jeremy!' he said as awkward claps spread round the room.

'Thanks mate.'

'How do you have your tea?' Harry said, putting the kettle on.

'Or perhaps something stronger?' Bella said, going over to the drinks cupboard.

'Whisky?'

'Sure. Double JD?' she said, pouring it out and taking it over to him.

Jeremy clasped the glass with both hands, then looked up to see who had handed it to him. He quickly became locked in a nano-trance at the sight of Bella in her blue polka-dot dress and its halter-necked cleavage, punctuated by her big brown eyes. 'Amazing, thank you. And you are?'

'Bella. And this here is Harry, and Olivia.'

'When you're ready, Jeremy, do you want to tell us what happened?' Olivia said.

He cleared his throat. 'Um, yes... Well, my name's Jeremy, and my wife has just left me after sixteen years of unhappy marriage,' he said, then downed the whisky in one go.

'Sorry,' Harry said, 'that must be tough.'

Then there was a long silence while everyone in the room struggled with what to say in the face of a grown-up drama of this magnitude. This was an actual marriage breakdown; not child's play. Suddenly they all felt woefully underqualified.

'But don't let me interrupt you. Please, just carry on as you were, pretend I'm not here!'

Holly looked at the others, her cheeks approaching fuchsia. 'OK Jez, if you're sure?'

Jeremy gave a firm nod.

'Okay, well, we were talking about the rules, weren't we Liv?'

'Yes, that's right. Jeremy – you can sit this one out since you've only just got here. But everyone else, I want each of you to think of one new BUC Ground Rule.'

They all looked down at their laps. 'Come on guys,' Olivia said. 'Try and think of them like The Commandments or something. You know, so that other people might benefit, in the future.'

Jeremy shot Holly a pointed stare.

'Come on guys, rules can be fun. Whether it's the 5-2 rule, or to never wear socks with sandals, these things just make the world a better, more controllable place. A little less catastrophe is good for everyone!'

Holly exchanged a look with Harry that said 'mad as a box of frogs'.

'I'm talking sense here,' Olivia went on. 'Just think, all the best civil societies were originally founded on strong codes. It's what separates us from savages. It's only through having a social contract of some sort that we can prevent chaos and preserve order. It's basic Rousseau. I think… but my degree was a long time ago now.'

'What the shit?' said Harry, while Jeremy pulled out a small notepad from his pocket.

'All right, I'll start,' Bella said eventually. '"Thou shalt not have a relapse with an ex only weeks after breaking up with them."'

'GOOD!' Olivia said, clapping. 'We'll call that Rule Number Twelve. Now, here are a few more I've already thought of. Like, the other day, when we were in that cafe in East London and the song came on and upset Holly. It made me think we need a rule like…' and she began to read from an A4 sheet, '"Limit your exposure to radio until your third trimester." Obviously you'll still need to go out in public sometimes, so it can't be helped in

203

those instances. But if you're just at home, it's worth bearing in mind.'

'OK so that's one covered,' Harry said, 'what else you got?'

'Actually, there's a lot more to it. If you'll allow me to elaborate, I'd like to talk to you about an expansion of Rule Number Ten. A little something I'm calling the "No-Go Zones".'

'Blimey, what are they?' Jeremy asked, scribbling notes onto his pad.

Olivia cleared her throat. 'We've touched on these before. But just to recap, No-Go Zones…' she resumed reading from her A4 sheet, 'fall loosely into three broad categories. One: the Locational Variant.'

Holly closed her eyes and began to seriously consider getting back together with Lawrence.

'By this we mean, be mindful of the geographical boundaries of your break-up. Avoid entering certain high-risk areas, for fear of memory bombs being detonated. For example – the bar where you first met your ex,' she paused for dramatic effect, 'or the street where your first kiss was stolen, or the borough where your ex currently resides, and so on. The reason for this is basic psycho-geography – the school of thought which states that traces of our memories can get left in places, as little fragments of your mind. That's why you can sometimes feel the energy when you go back to places of importance. Anyway, I digress.'

The others slowly nodded, and Olivia went on with her sermon.

'Next, the Musical Variant: It is often the case with break-ups that one's music collection takes a blow. Many songs inevitably fall prey to "our song" syndrome and must therefore be banished. In extreme cases, whole albums or back catalogues may face exile. Accidental exposure to certain songs – however fleeting – must be treated with absolute caution. And as I mentioned, for their own protection, members should refrain from radio exposure for at least one month.'

Olivia looked at Holly pertinently, while Harry gave her a reassuring pat on the back.

'I'm loving this,' Jeremy said, scribbling on his pad.

'Are you taking notes?' Holly said, noticing that Jeremy now appeared fractionally less wretched than when he'd first showed up.

'I am – this is all really good stuff!' he said, writing down the words Poss. on-screen chemistry between H & H – potential for breaking of rule no. 9? Beneath that was already written Bella – beautiful, vagabond kooky – show stealer. And Olivia – super-skinny, sexy in Made-In-Chelsea way, ball-busting legal eagle, control freak. Harry – the metrosexual, not-quite-gay best friend.

Olivia smiled at the newbie and went on. 'Moving onto the Gifting Variant: For a limited period, certain "sad" items of jewellery, accessories and clothing must face quarantine. The beautiful shoes or earrings your ex bought you must remain safely stowed at the bottom of the wardrobe. Or, better still, eBay. Even though they complement your favourite outfits perfectly, no good can come of you wearing these items while they are still "sad".'

'There's always Primani for interim replacements,' put in Bella, but Olivia's brow furrowed at the suggestion she would ever shop in such an establishment.

'Finally, a note about timings. All of this will go on for as long as necessary. Until one day, when you'll be able to assert the first major bastion of BUC law: that actually, The Ex is not legally entitled to custody of your music, TV shows or anything else. One day, when you're strong enough, you'll claim them all back.

You'll be there, shouting "This Is A Reclaim!" across a crowded dance floor, an incandescent smile on your face!' Olivia stepped down from her imaginary lectern, and took a deep breath and a long swig on her glass of wine.

Everyone remained mute for a good few minutes, drinking it all in.

'Wow,' Holly said. 'Reclaims. I like it.'

'Yes. You've really thought this through,' Harry said.

'Yah. I kind of want to give you a standing ovation. That was inspired,' Bella said.

'What she said,' Jeremy said, laughing. 'The public are gonna love you,' he added, before his face froze.

'Beg pardon?' Olivia said, shooting a look of alarm across the room at Holly, who was shaking her head at Jeremy in disgust.

Jeremy forced a smile as though this was all perfectly natural. 'Oh, did Holly not mention it? I was only saying to her the other day how all this will make a blinding reality show.'

As gasps filled the room, Holly said calmly, 'And that will be all from Jeremy this evening. I'll show you out.'

'Wait, I'd like to hear more about this,' Bella said, pouring him another Jack Daniels.

Jeremy sat forward in his chair. 'Well, we'd be aiming for a twice-weekly show on Sky to replace the *Prowl* slot.'

Bella's eyes dilated as though she'd just discovered the entire meaning of the universe. 'This is beyond exciting! Why didn't you tell us, Holly?' She scowled across at Holly. 'I'm a singer, but I suppose Holly mentioned that as a potential recurring storyline? My journey from the open-mic circuit, to being given a record deal as a result of being on the show and finally getting some exposure…'

'Um, no, Bella. Strangely enough that didn't come up.'

Olivia, Holly and Harry exchanged winces across the room, while Jeremy stared at Bella's chest.

'You do have a striking voice – and stage presence, I imagine.'

'Mostly jazz, blues, that kind of thing. Oh and some French pop. Gotta love a bit of Brigitte!' Reaching across the Jenga towers, Bella brought down a CD and handed it to him. 'Here's a copy of my EP I've just released,' she said, turning it over to point at the back cover. 'And you can find me on SoundCloud, here.'

'Erm, B, can we just stop you there?' Olivia said. 'I don't think you've noticed, but it's clear from the rest of the room that this

TV show idea is an absolutely diabolical one and won't be happening in a million years. I will testify to this in a court of law if need be.'

'In fairness,' Harry began, 'as a concept it's not so bad, if you made it into a comedy or drama you could keep the basic concept but fictionalise it all, keep everyone's integrity intact.' But no one could hear him through Bella's squeals of mounting desperation.

'Please, guys, this could fix my singing career! Give it the PR-injection it needs! Will none of you even consider it? For me?'

'Sorry B. It's not happening,' Holly said as a tantrum-ette began to percolate in the contours of Bella's face.

'Come on hon, you're not that desperate for fame. Have some dignity!' Olivia said.

'I thought we all signed that away when we joined the club?'

Jeremy downed his drink and stood up. 'OK, I can see I've outstayed my welcome. But if I could just leave you with this final thought…'

'Who is he, Jerry fucking Springer?' Olivia said, now red in the face.

'I do think you've hit upon something universal. Just think how many people there are out there that could really benefit from your club, and from all this wisdom you're codifying.'

Olivia looked at Holly as if to say, uh-oh, he's touched a nerve with me there.

'It reminds me of that moment in the film *Amelie*, when she asks "how many people in the world are having an orgasm right now?"' Jeremy's eyes widened. 'At this exact moment, any number of relationships and marriages are ending, all over the world. I put it to you – think of the thousands of people you could help with your little community!'

'He makes a good point there,' Olivia said, and Bella looked around at the others with her best puppy-dog eyes.

'Tie it all into a well-funded social media platform, and you've got yourself something massive,' Jeremy said.

'He's right! We could have a blog, and a message board. It would be nice to help others!' Bella said.

'Or, we could carry on quietly helping each other out in our own discreet little outfit,' Holly said, glaring at Jeremy.

'But think of all the people in Britain – the world – who aren't fortunate enough to have friends like you!' Jeremy said. 'Others who might be driven to do something more desperate without the support they need. And not to mention, there'd be a small financial remuneration to you all for taking part.'

'Our dysfunctional love lives are not for sale!' Olivia said at the same time as Bella asked, 'How much?!'

'OK, that's enough. At the risk of sounding inhospitable, Jez, Get tae fuck!' Harry said in full Scottish as he stood up. He wasn't quite tall enough to pull off intimidation, but it was better than nothing. 'Before you cause the Break-up Club itself to break up.'

'He's right, Jez. I'm afraid Break-up Club is now officially a private members' club,' Holly said. 'Say your goodbyes because I'm showing you the door.'

Just before she shut Jeremy out, she stopped. 'OK, hand it over.'

'What?'

'The hidden camera. I wouldn't put it past you.'

'Eh? What do you take me for!'

'If I'm honest, Jez, I really don't know what to take you for,' was what she wanted to say. 'On the one hand you're a manipulative psychopath and I'm terrified of you; on the other I feel desperately sorry for you.' But instead she said, 'No, of course. Sorry if I overreacted. See you at work.'

'Guys, I am so sorry about him!' Holly said, back in the room. 'The cheek! To try and make us feel sorry for him, and all along he's researching!'

'I do feel sorry for him. I think you were all far too hard on him. His wife's just left him!' Bella said.

'The man's a spineless manipulator,' Harry said.

'Obviously he's a bit creepy but I think he's got a good side, too.'

'He's brought his *alleged* divorce on himself though. I know for a fact he uses inter-marital dating sites,' Holly said.

'What, that's a thing now, really?' Harry said.

'Sadly, yes. Anyway, how about we all try and erase the last hour? Where were we before JezGate?' Holly said.

Harry stood up and poured new drinks for everyone.

'Well, now he's gone, we can ask you properly, Hol, how have you been doing?' Olivia said.

Holly sat down. 'Good days and bad days. I think it's just hitting me. I'm suddenly feeling scared I won't ever meet anyone, ever. Or worse, that actually, Lawrence was the one I was meant to be with for life, and make babies with?'

'Well, you know what they say – if you liked it, then you should've put an egg on it!' Bella said.

'For the love of shit, Hol, he wasn't anywhere near good enough for you,' Harry said, and Holly's mouth fell open.

'He's right, Hol. He was an absolute tool!' Bella said.

'And you choose to tell me now!?'

'We've all known for ages,' Olivia added.

'But we didn't like to say too much when you were together,' Bella said.

'Why?'

'You can't tell someone what to do about their relationship while they're in it. No one on the outside can ever really understand what goes on in the inner circle,' Harry said, a flicker of nostalgia in his eyes. 'But now you've seen it for yourself we can tell you.'

'What was wrong with him then?'

'Is there really any point going over this?' Olivia said.

'Yes! It will help me get over him. Seriously, anything bad you've ever wanted to say about him, let's have it. DO YOUR WORST!'

209

'All right then. You asked for it,' Harry said, looking delighted. 'Fig. 1. He was a financial fucktard.'

'Fig. 2, he was bad in bed,' Bella said.

Holly's mouth dropped open, as though she was shocked to hear that Bella had been trying him out.

'Don't look so surprised – you told us all about it! You used to say – and I quote – "He has the libido of a slug that has just OD-ed on Biryani."'

Holly couldn't help laughing. 'I don't remember saying that.'

'Oh Hol, you know we all liked him as a person. But he just sometimes didn't know when to stop,' Bella said.

'Er, pot, kettle?!' Holly said.

'I think the trouble with Lawrence was, he was a little too kooky,' Harry said sagely.

'Yes. With Lawrence, the fun would always end up overkooked,' Bella added, giggling.

'What, like that old saying? Too many kooks…' Harry said, and Holly mimed being sick.

'OK, enough now,' Olivia said, 'I think we get the point. Lawrence's kookiness was unmanageable.'

'Yes! He was an Unmanageable Kook!' said Bella, gasping as though they'd just landed upon the meaning of life, the universe and everything.

'I like it,' Harry said. 'So now all we need to look for is the opposite: a Manageable Kook.'

'Imagine finding someone who was that perfect balance of creative, yet practical,' Holly said, seeing an image of Luke flash up in her mind. 'Can such a person exist? Reliable without boring? Fun without exasperating?'

'There must be someone out there like that,' Bella added. 'What about, a producer on a film set? Or an architect?'

'That rare specimen of being. The Manageable Kook,' declared Holly, rather liking the way it sounded. 'Let us go in search of them!'

'Yeah right,' Olivia said. 'I'm sure you'll find one. Maybe in the local supermarket, RIGHT NEXT TO THE UNICORNS.'

'Haha. No, you're probably right, we're just dreaming. Can I change the subject please, to something much more pressing?' Holly asked.

'Of course,' Olivia said, who was getting used to her role as the lollipop lady of the conversation flow.

'This one's for Bella, really,' Holly said, 'Does the toothpaste thing really work? I might have to start doing it as my spots are now getting worse.'

'Not you as well? For Christ sake, we are too old for acne!' Bella said.

'It must be an offshoot of break-ups if you're all getting them,' Olivia said.

'But where are yours, Miss Pristine?' Bella stared up at Olivia's face, scanning her pores for any sign of imperfection, desperately seeking sebum.

'Nothing,' Bella said, frowning, 'she doesn't have ANY blemishes of any sort!'

'Well if the break-up spots haven't got her, the break-up diet certainly has – you look like you've lost a bit of weight,' Holly said. 'God, not that you ever needed to. There is no good way to say that sentence is there!'

Olivia smiled. 'Hardly. If anything I've put weight on! I can't get into any of my jeans anymore. And I might not have spots but I'm definitely starting to exhibit the signs of ageing.'

Bella's eyes brightened. 'Really? How so?'

Olivia pointed to her hair. 'I've been getting pop-up greys since finals. Been dyeing them for years!'

'She has a flaw! God bless us all,' shouted Bella, topping up everyone's drinks.

'That's not all though. I have to wax,' Olivia whispered, pointing to her upper lip. They all went quiet. 'Here. I have hair, here. Thick, dark little horrors. A big old tash, if you will.'

211

Gasps spread around the room like a bush fire in the Outback.

'And lately, I've been getting these weird soft, fine hairs on my face. So seriously, I'm thinking of growing them all out for next Movember. I bet THAT would raise some cash for charity.'

'It's fair to say we're not getting any prettier, are we?' joined in Bella. 'Every time I look into a mirror with good lighting these days, I see a new wrinkle.'

'Me too,' Olivia said. 'It reminds me of being in my new flat – I keep noticing cracks in the walls! My face is getting settlement cracks and going down in value.'

'Oh come on girls, you're all gorgeous, look at you,' attempted Harry. 'Can we talk about something else please? Or else I'm going to HAVE to ask that we advertise for another male member of the club. And I don't mean Jeremy.'

'Seriously, what if no one gets to see me in my prime?' Bella said, looking genuinely afraid. 'It's like Greg says, "Don't waste the pretty."'

They all turned to face Bella in slow motion.

'W. T. F.???' Olivia said, spelling it out like an actress in an American teen drama. 'Who the hell is Greg?'

'Greg Behrendt. He wrote an odious little book called *He's Just Not That Into You.*'

'Oh dear Lord,' scoffed Holly, 'I'd like to egg Greg, right in the face. That book is unadulterated baloney. It basically claims that if a guy isn't chasing you morning noon and night, then he's not interested. But the trouble is, it's culturally irrelevant to us, as it relies on men being the type who "step up" when they like a girl. And everyone knows only American men actually step up.'

'You're right! British men these days are so easily intimidated. I know so many guys who would rather wait for girls to make the first move,' Bella said.

'That book doesn't take into account the differences between confident, straight-talking Yanks, and the wussy, Hugh Granty spawns that us Brits have to put up with!'

'Ah, well now, there you might actually have a point,' Harry said. 'If I may, I'd like to apologise on behalf of my sex as a whole. It's true, we Brits are – barring a few exceptions – total weeds.'

'It's their loss,' Olivia said. 'I can't be arsed with guys who fanny about just wanting to be pen pals rather than actually meet up. In the dating apps I've been using, the guys just want to chit-chat! I'm offering full sex, and they're like "How was your week?" No. I have a simple rule that's served me well: Step up or step off.'

The others did a mixture of laughing and looking intrigued.

'Take Jonny, for instance. He may be the Archetypal Public School Boy but he's also a classic Stepper-Upper. He sees something he wants, and he goes for it. Hot. And yet we've got the perfect balance. I never stay over at his, and he never stays at mine. That way we avoid the problem of intimacy.'

'Wow. And they say romance is dead,' Holly said.

'It's just practical. We both have busy, demanding jobs. We both love sex. We just don't have time for being tired. So we don't do the cuddling bits in between. Let's face it, no one ever sleeps properly when they share a bed. We're just honest about it.'

The others looked unconvinced, and Olivia did a remarkable job of avoiding each one of their eyes. 'But enough about me, people…' she said as Daniel walked into the kitchen and headed to the fridge, where he stood slurping milk directly from the bottle. He then wiped his mouth with the back of his hand before returning the bottle to the fridge.

'You kids playing clubs again? Aww, so sweet. Have you got membership cards now and everything?'

'Ha ha,' Holly said as he headed back out the room, 'you're just jealous. If you have a break-up with any of your ladies, you know where we are!' she shouted after him as his laughter echoed up the stairs.

'Um, Holly, how are you doing that?' Bella was staring down at her phone. 'I just got an email from you.' She stared at Holly, who was neither using her phone nor anywhere near a computer.

'Maybe it's just a delayed one from the other day?'

Bella began reading. 'Wow. You really are officially the dullest person I know.'

'Don't be rude!' Holly said, leaning over her to read the message. 'Bella! Do you honestly think I would use the phrase "Very good price"?'

Harry joined them in studying the phone screen. 'Uh-oh. You've been hacked. Correction, you're being hacked right now!'

'Shit! My phone's too slow, does anyone have a laptop I can borrow?' Holly said, beginning to feel twitchy.

'Here. Use mine,' Olivia said, handing hers over.

'Oh my Christ,' Holly said, going through her sent items. 'I've sent emails to everyone in my address book about "very good price" laptops. Not only that, the first part of the email is phrased in a normal way. So some people will think it is actually me, having had some kind of breakdown!'

Holly sifted through the emails. 'Oh Christ no! Even the Head of Drama at Channel Four has got one! And OH GOOD LORD! Alain de Botton. I emailed him about one of his books, and my account automatically saved his address! Oh God.'

Harry let out a sinister laugh. 'HA! You have spammed Sir Alain of Botton!'

Holly looked like she was about to cry.

'You've spammed one of the eminent philosophers of our time!'

'All right, that's enough, Harry,' Olivia said.

'Sorry! I just like saying spam! SPAM!' Harry said, and everyone looked at him like he was deranged. 'WHAT? It's only a really famous *Monty Python* sketch! Plebs,' he said through laughter. 'Sorry Hol. But really, it's fine. It happens all the time, people know to ignore it now. You can email everyone to say sorry, or you can just leave it. Either way, don't worry about it.'

Holly clicked back to her inbox. Buried among the emails from friends and random people she'd not seen in ages kindly informing her that she may have been 'spammed', there was one very frightening message which made her heart leap into her throat.

'Hol, are you OK?' Harry asked. 'You've gone a little pale.'

She handed the laptop to him in silence. His eyes widened as he took in the email from TheRealLawryHill@gmail.com.

'Oh my shit. What's he doing emailing you? It's like he heard us slagging him off! Do you want me to open it?'

'No. Yes! No! I'll do it,' Holly said, practically hyperventilating as she clicked on the message, and waited approximately six years for it to open.

'"Dear Holly, Thanks for this. I didn't know you cared so much about my tech needs. Love, Lawry."'

'The fucker! He's just replying to the spam! Unless he's so thick he thinks it was me! Argggghhhh! I HATE SPAM MAIL! Oh. Oh no. He goes on to say, "P.S. You have been wandering through my thoughts recently. It would be lovely to catch up and talk about laptops among other things."'

'Oh fuck.' Holly clutched her stomach as though she had a sudden bout of food poisoning.

'The COCK!' Bella said.

'He's an opportunist, I'll give him that,' Olivia said.

'It's hard to know whether or not he's serious from that,' reasoned Harry.

'I think I'm going to be sick,' Holly stood up and started walking up and down the room. 'How dare he do this!? I've buried him. I've put him away in a little sealed box I can't ever go near. How dare he use this as an excuse to make contact, when he knows full well I'm not a laptop salesman!'

'He really is a proper scrote,' Harry said. 'This only serves to underline our earlier points a thousandfold. He's an absolute douche-merchant.'

'But maybe I should email him back?'

'NOOOOOOOOOO!' they said in unison, and Holly looked utterly dismantled.

16. *Like Buses*

Some days later, Holly was sat in her office attempting to salvage something from a hedonistic weekend's worth of *Prowl* footage. Meanwhile, in Camera Two of her mind, she was replaying in full the List of Lawrence's Faults the club had made her draw up at the last meeting. 'Anytime you're missing him or get tempted to engage with his spam,' they'd said, 'you just need to visualise the list and remind yourself what a numpty he was.' Just as she was mentally scrolling through the items, from 'unwashed hair' to 'financial fucktard,' there was a knock at the door.

'Hey,' Luke said as she opened the door. 'Sorry to disturb. Jeremy said that there was a scene I could take a look at. Apparently the Director's still not happy with that stupid flaring scene. So I was going to ask if I could just see where I was going wrong, if you've got time to play it back for me?' As he stretched into a yawn, she couldn't help spotting a flash of chiselled tummy and thinking, be still my loins.

'Of course. Let me just dig it out,' she said, gesturing to the chair next to her.

As she tapped away at various buttons and got the scene ready, she could feel his leg making contact with hers under the table.

'Here we go,' she said, pressing play and adjusting the speakers.

Just being in this small amount of contact was sending tiny shockwaves to all the skin around the neighbouring area. The rest of her body felt so mundane in comparison to that small highly charged area. Could he tell? Could he see the protons and neutrons bouncing about between them? What about moving a little closer, she wondered, so even more surface area could benefit? She stared at Luke's on-screen face, pretending that this was all in a work-related capacity. Then, she casually moved her chair a little closer to the desk. Bingo. Legs entirely in contact now, and a section of arm as well, to boot. Her heart beginning minor palpitations, she felt his leg flinch a little. She could sense his face turning to look at her, but she didn't dare move her eyes off the screen. Was he feeling it too? This was either the hottest thing that had happened to her in ages, or this whole infatuation was entirely in her head and she was carrying on like a cheap thrill-seeking perv. Both were entirely plausible at this point, this being the most bodily contact she'd had in about a century.

Maybe there'd be a clue in his expression? Fuck it, she thought, daring to turn her head and looking straight into his enormous blue eyes. Unless she was imagining it, she and Luke were inches away from unabashed dry-humping.

'All right, now I have to confess something, Holly,' he said, turning his face away.

'What?' she asked, barely able to breathe.

'What I did back there, that was me acting.'

'I'm sorry?'

He looked at his shoes. 'I don't really need to see the scene. It was just a ruse, so I could sit in a small dark room with you again.'

Holly grinned, hearing the crowd going wild and doing Mexican waves in her head. Quickly channelling her inner Olivia, she remembered the importance of not coming across too excited. 'Oh right,' she said, the very model of aloofness. 'But why would you waste my time like that?'

'Horribly cheeky of me, I know. It won't happen again. Maybe you'll let me apologise to you through the medium of a date this evening? If you're not otherwise engaged, there's a Linklater triple bill on at the BFI. *Before Sunrise* followed by the two sequels.'

'Yes, my friend told me about that! It's the rom-com about a girl and guy that just happen to meet on a train, isn't it?'

'It is not a rom-com! They are clever, arty films that just happen to be slightly romantic in sentiment. Although if you're going to be all cynical about it, I'm not sure you're the right person to see it with…'

'I'll try and be open-minded. I just don't really believe you could possibly meet the person you're going to grow old with on a train. Especially not on the Tube in London – they're about as romantic as rotting sardine cans!'

'I see your point, but that's all the more reason to come with me. I reckon I can convert you into a soppy romantic before the night is out.'

'Is that a threat?'

'It's a promise.'

'Well, I'll bet you one bottle of Pinot Grigio that you can't,' she said, smiling. 'Besides I'm still in post-break-up fragility – I don't think I can handle too much schmaltz. I might break out in a rash or something.'

'I'll go easy on you,' he said, and she almost swooned at the thought of any subtext.

Seven hours later, Holly's head was resting on Luke's shoulder as they lay back on a sofa at the bar in the British Film Institute, sharing a pint glass of chips.

'Did I imagine it or did I see you shed a little tear back there?' Luke said.

'All right, I have to admit it, the films were not entirely unmoving.'

'Really?'

'I bloody loved them!'

'Haha!'

'My favourite bit was when they're walking up those spiral staircases, you know, right at the end of the second one. The bit when she's holding the cat, when there's, like, ten years of sexual tension between them, and you genuinely don't know what will happen.'

'Nine years. But yeah, I know. It's all shot in real time, too. I did a film like that once. Bloody difficult it was, much more like stage acting than film.'

'That figures,' she said, then found herself telling Luke about her 'Mind the Gap' short film idea. To her amazement, he didn't just like the idea, but he suggested ways to improve it, such as telling the story in reverse.

'A narrative doesn't have to be linear. You can always muck about with chronology – whatever helps bring the story to life,' he mused, while she hung on his every word with wide-eyed wonder.

Shit, thought Holly as she listened to this very attractive man talk at length about self-shooting a film in his spare time which had cleaned up at last year's Sundance Festival. He stopped talking and lightly brushed her arm with his fingers. How amazing it was to be with a guy who was both talented and motivated. Someone who got off his arse and made stuff happen. Shit, she thought. This was all sounding a lot like Luke really might be that rare specimen – a Manageable Kook! She began to watch a trailer in her head for a feature film called 'Holly and Luke' about a Creative Power Couple who do creative projects together, go to red-carpet openings and live in a big house in Primrose Hill with nannies.

'Holly?'

'Yes?'

'I was just saying, have you heard any more about whether TotesAmaze have a replacement for *Prowl* yet? I'm only contracted for another two months of shooting, and I've got nothing else lined up yet. Jez said he might try and crowbar me into whatever they're working on next.'

'Oh, cool. No, I don't think the channel have bought anything yet. Hey, how about we have a shit-telly-brainstorm?'

'Yes! We both need a new job, let's write one into existence!'

So for the next five minutes, they both sat in silence, intermittently looking each other in the eyes and sipping their drinks until they were empty. Eventually, Luke spoke up.

'I've got one! So, I'm in a band in my spare time, and we're always joking about how it'd be fun to change things up a bit sometimes, bring in guest members to keep things fresh. Or to occasionally let our drummer play for a band of a totally different genre, for instance. See what difference it makes to our overall sound when he comes back.'

'Interesting! Or your singer could go from doing vocals in a jazz band to a metal one, and see how their style adapts?'

'Yeah! Could there be a show in that?'

'Sort of like musical swingers?'

'Kinky. Yeah – we play two very different bands against each other, then swap the singers or lead guitars.'

'We could call it Band Swap?'

'Nice! My housemate Bella could be in it! She's a singer!'

Holly wrote it down in her little book of ideas. 'Right, one more, then we've earned another drink!'

'Quite the taskmaster!' he teased, and Holly poked him in the six-pack. 'Let's see. Most popular telly starts with the word "Britain's" doesn't it?'

'Too true! That's our first word then.' She wrote it down underneath Band Swap. 'Oh, this might be something!' she said, remembering a recent Bella-ism. 'The other day, Bella was convinced she'd just heard the sound of her late tabby cat mewing.'

'Your point is?'

'Well. Bella's as mad as a sack of hyenas at the best of times, but at that moment she really did look like she'd seen a ghost. Of course it's all nonsense, but it does make me wonder if there are other instances where people think their late pets have come back to haunt them?'

Luke laughed. 'I mean it's obviously total dog-shit, but it could be worth passing to a researcher to see if there are any other alleged ghost pets across the country?'

'Britain's Ghost Pets! We're on fire! Do another one!'

'OK, I've got it. Staying with pets, how about, Through the Cat-flap? It's basically a furry friend equivalent of Through the Keyhole, where you have to guess the celebrity owner of the house, but the difference is...'

'That you can only see through the cat-flap! I love it! All you can see is a pet's eye view of what's going on in the flat. We'd pan over the hallway so the viewer can see the brand of shoes by the door; what kind of carpet they have; the type of catalogues that just landed through the letter box...'

'Exactly!' said Luke.

'That's our next drink in the bag, right there,' Holly said, just as the bell rang for last orders.

'Looks like I'll have to whisk you to Soho House instead. This victory cannot go uncelebrated.'

'It won't be full of pretentious arses?' Holly wanted to say but stopped herself just in time to realise that Luke was probably a paid-up member and might take offence. 'OK. Sure,' she said, remembering that, by contrast, the last bar Lawrence had whisked her to had been the local sports pub in Streatham.

Two hours later Holly was leaving Soho House, trying to remain calm despite the fact that they'd just been sat on a balcony within swooning distance of her childhood hero, Alex James from Blur. She was feeling proud for having contained her excitement enough to make it seem as though things like that happened to her every day.

'Shall we go for a walk? I'd love to carry on talking to you,

221

but everywhere is closing,' Luke said, his face so close to Holly's she could almost taste his Lynx.

And then they had the night. The night where you walk around a city for hours, talking inane rubbish and landing upon little details about each other, including the most important one of all – that your senses of humour are in perfect alignment.

Until hours later, when Luke broke the spell.

'Shit, it's 3 a.m., I should get home. I'm on screen tomorrow; if I don't get some sleep you're going to have one hell of a post-job to do on my dark circles.'

'Oh, you're so thoughtful,' Holly said, trying to hide her disappointment, and secretly wishing he hadn't been the first one to call it. 'How are you getting back? Where do you even live?' she asked, as though he had been magically wafted here from The Land of Perfect Men.

'Primrose Hill. I'll jump in a cab. You're Tufnell Park right? Here's a bus now!'

'So it is,' she said, wanting to sue TFL for delivering her a punctual 390 bus for the first time in her life.

'Well. I've had a lovely night, thanks Luke.'

'Thank you! Let's do this again soon.'

'Definitely,' she said.

She looked into his eyes. The bus had pulled up now. People were piling on. The doors were about to close.

'Well, see you at work,' she said, giving him a hug, edging her face near to his, an awkward performance which ended with her dispatching a limp kiss on the cheek. Forcing a smile, she climbed aboard and swiped her Oyster card. She took a seat on the top deck, looking down at him, a small piece of her dying inside as the bus pulled away, the sound of drunk kebab-swigging men adding to her torture as they headed north.

She got her phone out to compose a BUC bulletin. 'FUUUUUUCK! Most amazing night ever, but total and utter good-night-tumbleweed moment! I'm also shit at men!

Gaaaahhhh!' Just as she was scrolling down her address book to look for BUC members, she felt the phone buzz with a message. Who was texting her this late?

'Hey. Wanted to kiss you then, but didn't know if that'd be too much romance for you at the moment? If it isn't, get off next stop? PTB x'

Blimey, she thought, fumbling a reply. 'I think I can manage one kiss. Just. But where are you? I'll try and get off x'

'I'll walk up. How far you got? x'

'Not sure. Think I'm somewhere near the museum?'

'I've just gone past that 101 bar – the one that looks like a naff bar on a ferry. Walking along New Oxford St?'

'OK then. See you at Argos,' she wrote, pressing Send all too fast.

'Argos? REALLY?' she shouted out loud, staring down at her phone. Oh well. You can't always have a Tiffany's when you need one, she reasoned, gathering up her things and teetering down the steps, trying not to go pelting to the bottom deck as the bus jerked along.

Alighting at the next stop, she felt her feet picking up pace, as if they had a full tank of lust bubbles propelling her to her target. Where was Argos? Had it moved? It seemed implausibly far away now. She scanned the rows of stores up ahead – a generic stationery shop, an indiscriminate camera supplies shop, the British Museum, All Bar One and bingo... Argos. What was ordinarily a cathedral of pike now beamed before her like a beacon of erotica. Finally she was going to kiss the man she'd been flirting with for months! At last, the moment was going to happen! Right here, outside the nation's favourite budget home-furnishings store. And yet, how oddly clinical it was now that they'd both agreed, like a contract that, yes, they would kiss. She could see him up ahead. Kissing has been added to the agenda, she thought. It is written that we shall indeed kiss. She looked down to avoid seeing him too soon and combusting with anticipation. She began

223

watching the scene play out in her head before she reached him. Will we run into each other's arms for a full-on snog? she wondered. Will he sweep me up into a *Dirty Dancing*-style lift, followed by one of those Tango-esque Hollywood kisses where I do a massive back-bend, my hair sweeping the floor?

In fact what happened was they stood a metre apart and shifted their feet about.

'I'm sorry. I didn't know where your head was at. I should have just gone for it...'

'No, you're all right. It was sweet. Who's PTB by the way?'

'TV's Phil the Barman?'

'Oh of course!' she laughed, thinking, oh right, so we're just going to stand and chat then, after all that.

'Yeah, I thought it might've been too soon for you, it's not been long after you—'

'You know what I think? I think you should stop talking,' she said, interrupting him to pull his face towards her. Then they smooched by Argos for a full hour, barely stopping for air, their hands growing more intrepid with every kiss. Soon she wondered whether he was actually going to take her there and then, right in front of the window display for cut-price garden sheds and Dustbusters. But just before they got to that, he whispered, 'Did you want to come back?'

'I thought you'd never ask,' she said, leaning in to kiss him again.

17. *When the Night Meets the Morning Sun*

'What the blazes is wrong with you?' Bella asked as Holly hobbled along the street. Now that they were all single, they had made the executive decision to update their wardrobes and were about to commence a large shopping spree.

'Nothing.'

'Yes there is! You're walking like Pingu!' Olivia said.

'Piss off! I've got women's issues.'

A victorious smile broke out on Holly's face, and the girls turned to face her.

'Do we need to stop for coffee?' Bella said.

'I think so!'

They headed into the nearest cafe, ordered drinks and sat down. Holly began to fill them in on the night, right up until the receiving of the World's Most Romantic Text Message Ever™.

'So then we went back to his flat, which, I might add, was bloody amazing. Incredible king size bed, skylight and a lovely old gramophone, which we danced to!'

'I don't want to know about his flat or the dancing, what about the sex?' Bella said.

'Oh, it was just amazing – really heightened somehow, like sex in HD! But the best part is, I feel certain I did the right thing about Lawrence.'

'Oh that's great. I'm so happy for you,' Olivia said.

'Of course, the only snag is, I'm in a world of pain now! I think we might have overdone it somewhat,' she said, her face wilting in pain.

'So you went from crush to thrush in 24 hours?' Bella said, collapsing into snorts as the others shrieked with laughter.

'Something like that...' Holly said. 'Ow. It even hurts to laugh. You know, now I think about it, I don't think Lawrence and I were ever that connected during "business time". For one thing, he never wanted to look into my eyes.'

'Oh, you've got to have eye contact!' Bella said. 'First rule of Tantra!'

'Luke looked me right in the eye.' Holly continued as their coffees arrived. She took a sip and sighed. 'I feel in a bit of a state of shock, too. Almost like I've been unfaithful, after five years with the same person! Ah, here's the other one,' Holly said, seeing Harry walk in.

'Hello,' he said, pulling up a chair from a neighbouring table of yummy mummies. 'Christ, it's like Pram-ageddon in here,' he said a little too loudly.

'How was football?' Holly asked, kissing him on the cheek.

'Don't you how's football me! How did it go with Lukey?'

'Good,' she nodded, her eyes twinkling.

'Good? You're glowing.'

'There may have been some sexy-time.'

'Fast work, Braithwaite, well done!'

She glowed some more as she filled him in on the night's events, the highlight being their first kiss outside Argos.

'Wow, you got off the bus. Never get off the bus,' Harry said.

'What?' Holly asked.

'You see what he did there – he purposefully doesn't make a move on her at the designated goodnight-kiss-moment – no, he

226

waits until she thinks he's not that interested, then lets her make the move by getting off the bus. A clear signal that she wants it, that she's game.'

'Wow. For a bloke you are reading FAR too much into this!' Holly said.

'He's smooth! I like his style.'

'Style? There was no style! Are you saying this is a move guys pull? No – he didn't orchestrate it. It just happened. He was being sensitive, because he knows I'm not long out of things with Lawrence.'

'Or, that's what he wants you to think.'

'Shit off.'

'You slept with him didn't you? See, he made you trust him.'

'Bull. You're just jealous because I've had sex and you haven't.'

'Piffle,' Harry said, taking a massive bite of her cookie. And then he laughed; the kind of laugh he reserved for when he'd just thought of the most hilarious joke ever.

'You know what, he's ARGOS'ed you. Find it, get it, ARGOS it.'

Holly groaned. 'Not everything's a bloody advert Harry!'

'Yes it is. Same as how everything to you is a bloody TV show!'

'Touché.'

'By the way, didn't anyone ever tell you, never shit on your place of work?'

'I repeat: jealous.'

'No, in all seriousness. I think it's great you've had some fun and all. But it's a bit soon. Especially as you've kind of liked this guy for ages. I would just be a bit careful. I know how easily you fall for people.'

'Joy-killer! But yes, of course, I'll take it slowly. Anyway, we girls have some shopping to do... you coming?'

Harry shook his head. 'Mmm. Tempting. But I have a kettle that needs descaling, soooo...' he took the last bite of Holly's cookie and walked away.

'Ugh, I hate that boy sometimes.'

'He's just winding you up,' Bella said. 'That, and I reckon he's secretly a bit in love with you.'

'Don't be absurd. We're brother and sister.'

*

After an afternoon of shopping, having entirely restocked her wardrobe full of sexy, girl-about-town items of clothing for the summer, Holly was just about to climb into a bath filled with essential oils, soothing bubbles and excitement at all the possibilities that Life After Lawrence (avec LUKE) promised her, when her mobile beeped with a message.

'Hi Hol. Thanks for a great night ;) Been thinking – what with it being work and all, it's probably better if we just stay mates. You know what they say about not shitting on your workplace. Cool?'

18. *Back in the Foetal Position*

'I mean, what the actual fuck!?' she said to her laptop later that night, in between sobs, curled up in a ball on the edge of her bed. No one had been home, so she'd called an emergency Skype conference on her sellotaped-together laptop (luckily it still worked after being trampled on).

'Wow. I really did not see that coming,' Harry said on his mobile outside a crowded pub.

'Piss off Harry. I'm not actually sure I want you on this call?'

'Sorry. I was actually only teasing before. I didn't think he'd be this much of a prick.'

'Shit-sticks. He's that guy,' Bella said.

'What guy?'

'The Chase-a-girl-'til-she-breaks-up-with-her-boyfriend-then-lose-interest guy.'

'Oh. You think?' Holly said as sickness migrated through her stomach to her knees.

'Or… maybe he's just gone LukeWarm,' Harry said.

'Get thee to a punnery!' jibed Bella in disgust.

Holly glared at Harry's avatar and wished bad things on him.

'Sorry. Either way, he's an absolute C-word for doing this to you. Also, he's obviously a knob if he can't see what a catch he's just let go.'

But this just made Holly cry again. 'I'm so stupid. To think I was getting excited, then feeling guilty, all because I was moving on from Lawrence already. And now I miss Lawrence even more! For all his faults, he never once made me feel this shitty.'

'You know what this is?' Harry said, 'It's a fuckwit sandwich! You're the mangled bit of pastrami in between two fucktards.'

Holly laughed despite herself. 'You know what this all reminds me of? One of those hot towels you get given after an Indian. At first, he was this wonderful break-up comfort – cleansing and fresh like a new beginning where everything's going to be OK! But then straight away, just like the towel, he's gone cold, and I'm feeling even more wretched than before. Yeah. That's all Luke was to me. Just a sad, measly little hot towel.'

'I can't BEAR those creepy microwaved towels,' Olivia said.

'But we had tons in common! He grew up near me, we like the same Directors, the same bands—'

'Let me just stop you there. I was thinking about this the other day,' Harry said. 'The way most relationships begin with a long list of likes and dislikes, and then gradually you fill in all the gaps… a bit like a Panini sticker album, until one day, you've had all the same experiences, and like all the same things. It's as if we've got this underlying urge to create a carbon copy of ourselves in another human being.'

'So it's not so much dating as it is cloning,' Olivia said.

'Exactly. Same same, but different,' Harry said.

'Well,' Olivia began, 'I think in light of recent events that we need to add another BUC law.'

'Good idea,' Harry said.

'How's this for size,' Holly began. 'Rule Number Thirteen. Thou shalt not have rebound sex with an actor at work. However hot they are.'

'Perfect,' Harry said, 'and I'd like to also suggest a new motion, to do with having a Notice Period.'

Everyone laughed.

'I'm serious! It should be just like in a job. Depending on how long you've been involved with an ex, you need to serve your notice before you can start anything new. It's quite simple: no new dalliances before your time period has lapsed. Thus preventing the unfortunate "double-whammy effect", which poor Hol is having to endure now.'

'Too right. I feel like I've been WINDED or something. No one should have to go through this. You know, if just one person after me can be saved by this rule, at least it will mean my suffering has not been in vain.'

'OK. Agreed,' Bella said.

'How long should my notice period be?'

'Well, what was your length of service to Lawrence?'

'Five years,' Holly said with a gulp.

'I think about a month for each year you've served,' Olivia suggested, 'but maybe we can review your case and release you on good behaviour depending on how you're getting on. That's not to say you'll be over him at all after five months. But it gives you time to get him out of your system before muddying the waters again.'

'All right. But wait – this isn't exactly fair is it? Harry was with Rachel for years, and yet he's been online dating for a month now, sewing his wild oats around like some kind of exercise in sexual communism!'

'HA! He's like, Infidel Castro!' Bella shouted.

'Exactly!' Holly said. 'Plus Liv's been shagging Jonny. So tell me again, why is it that I have to go it alone?'

'The difference is simple,' stated Harry. 'Liv and I don't get emotionally involved with ours. And I don't see any of mine twice. The bigger issue, Holly, is that you seem to still be so emotionally hung up on Lawrence – and until you've had time to grieve for him properly, you should really wait to start anything else.'

'Fine. I'll start serving my notice. But for now, how do I stop feeling this bad?'

'You need to Break the Pain Chain,' Olivia said.

'Wean yourself off ALL men. Seriously, NO MORE WILLIES, not even casual,' Bella said. 'Go cold turkey.'

'Surely the phrase should be, go cold cock?' Olivia said.

'How will I do that, exactly?' Holly said.

'Get drunk. A lot,' Harry said.

'Go to art galleries and museums...' Bella said.

'I know what you need,' Olivia said, 'you need a pre-claim.'

'A what?'

'A pre-claim is like a reclaim. But rather than it being about you "taking back" a thing that's been tainted by a dead relationship, it's actually about claiming back an activity you used to do before they even came along; getting back a piece of you that went missing. You see, in bad relationships, you don't realise you're doing it, but you are letting little pieces of yourself go all the time. For example, before Ross I used to love cooking, but he always used to prefer ordering take-aways, so I stopped doing it so much while I was with him. Hey, that can be Rule Number Fourteen...' she said, dispatching a self-satisfied smile.

'Oh so that's what all your militant baking's been about then,' Harry said.

'Makes sense,' Holly said, 'except you're forgetting one vital detail. I don't do hobbies. I never have. My chief hobby of the last twenty-seven years has been, well, avoiding hobbies.'

'What about trying to write your short film?' Harry suggested.

'I haven't had time.'

'Bollocks, Braithwaite. You just don't believe you can do it. And I know you can! You were teacher's pet in A-Level English, remember? Have you even read that book I gave you yet?'

Holly bit her nail. 'Not yet, sorry.'

'She'll feel up to it soon; she's just a bit broken at the moment,' Bella said.

'I was depressed last week – now, with this dumping on top? This here is a one-way ticket to Beachy Head.'

'Holly, that is not funny,' Olivia said. 'Listen, at least you have a job right now. That's something. Especially when we're all about to endure some sort of "double-dip recession" thing.'

'She's right. They're predicting redundancies in the financial sectors,' Harry added, 'which will no doubt have a ripple effect on other industries.'

'Thanks, voices of doom,' Holly said. 'Next you'll be saying we're all being evicted, and our triptych of pain will be complete.'

'Hol. It's not that bad… yet,' Bella said.

'Sorry to cut you off, guys,' Olivia said, 'but I'm going to have to sign off now. I've got a not-date with Jonny to get ready for.'

'And me,' Harry said. 'But listen, Holly, remember what Louis Armstrong always says.'

'We have all the time in the world?'

'NOOOO! Don't worry, be happy.'

'I know what you need,' Olivia said. 'A haircut. Tomorrow after brunch. My treat.'

'That's so sweet of you! Actually, maybe it's time I did something drastic. I have had the same hair for fifty years.'

'Oooh, yes. Get bangs. They're very in right now,' Olivia said.

'I haven't had a fringe since I was seven. But why not, things can't get much worse can they?'

Everyone was silent.

'Fair. Well, guys, thanks again for being my lifeline.'

After they had all signed off, Holly shut her laptop and headed to the bathroom. She stared at herself in the mirror, and attempted to bend the front bits of her hair under, to simulate a fringe. It was hard to tell if this would be a good look or not.

She turned away from the mirror, noticing with sadness that the bathwater had long since gone cold. She stared at the floating tendrils of aromatic lavender as they bobbed about on the surface. She touched them with her finger and briefly debated getting in, so that at least they wouldn't go to waste, along with EVERYTHING ELSE EVER. Instead she pulled the plug. No need to wash anymore. For what? For whom? She went to sleep without doing her teeth, and wailed into her pillow – until she got a crying headache worse than that time when she was four and she'd dropped her mint-choc-chip ice cream in the sand.

*

Jeremy.Philpott@TotesamazeProductions.com to
Holly.Braithwaite@TotesamazeProductions.com
Subject: C5 Want in

Braithwaite,
Great news; just heard back from Channel 5. You and your mates are about to become reality TV stars! Got the impression you weren't all on board, but I'm sure we can make it worth all of your whiles. Except Olivia, but perhaps we can re-cast for someone that's a bit less of a rottweiler?

Let's chat.

Holly.Braithwaite@TotesamazeProductions.com to
Jeremy.Philpott@TotesamazeProductions.com
Subject: Re: C5 Want in

Jez,
My fuckwit friends and I are not for sale.

I don't really understand how it happened, but please can you UNDO whatever chat you've had with Channel 5 or anyone else?

As a humble alternative, here's an idea I think could be great. Please like it!

BRITAIN'S GHOST PETS – A documentary exploring all the haunted houses in Britain.

Not your normal ghosts though – the feline and canine ones! Think… Little Tammy comes back to visit the Joneses of Mildew Close. Young Boxer has some unfinished business in West Wycombe, and comes back to haunt the bloke wot ran him over on that country lane off the A40.

A quick dip into the research pool reveals that there are loads of true stories we could mine. Just think, even little ghost hamsters, or phantom bunny rabbits! It's cute meets scary.

I should add – I have it on good authority that our very own Phil The Barman is MEGA keen to be the presenter.

Holly.

Jeremy.Philpott@TotesamazeProductions.com to
Holly.Braithwaite@TotesamazeProductions.com

Did you not hear me, Braithwaite? This is TERRESTRIAL, BABY!

19. *Bang on Trend*

The next day Holly was up with the larks or, more specifically, the Camden Council Recycling truck. As she walked through the pristine glass doors five minutes ahead of the appointment time, she resisted the urge to publicly pat herself on the back for managing to not be late for an appointment for the first time in her short life.

Having taken her seat in front of the mirror, she was looking forward to ninety minutes of relaxation and pampering. As she began watching the cup and saucer of tea which Josie, her Welsh hairdresser, had put on the glass sill in front of her, she remembered that, actually, having your hair cut was anything but relaxing. For one thing, agreeing to drink a cup of coffee or tea was a decision fraught with ergonomic quandaries. Do I reach for the mug or not, she wondered as Josie savagely tugged a comb through her hair, clipping her ear each time in a way that made her want to cry out, but instead she smiled sweetly and answered questions about plans for Easter and the bank holidays. Then Josie started cutting Holly's hair, which involved her clamping Holly's head into a specific upright position. Holly went in for a sip of tea, but this meant moving her head fractionally, which resulted in a Josie emitting a discrete yet definite sigh, followed by Holly apologetically adjusting her head angle again. That one sip tasted so heavenly, but that would be the last, she realised as the lesson sunk in again: you're not meant to drink the tea they give you at the hairdresser – it's just for show.

After a while she turned to reading, and attempted to concentrate on her magazine. But she couldn't read it because Josie's scissors were now chopping away in her eyeline. Eventually, she decided to give up and close her eyes. Before long she drifted into a half-sleep, her mind serving up footage from the childhood archives, of a seven-year-old Holly with a fringe, on the playground with a young Harry who was trying to make her join his new club collecting Panini stickers, and she was telling him to bog off because clubs were silly.

'So? What do you reckon, my lovely?' said Josie, and Holly landed back in the present with a thud, to find a girl with 'bangs' staring back at her in the mirror. She looked every inch the same as the girl on the playground, with the ruler-straight fringe. The only differences now were the tell-tale bags under her eyes, a splattering of wrinkles, and a few extra pounds.

Holly thought for a moment, still lost in her daydream. 'I think, for the first time in my life, I actually feel like I belong to a club.'

Josie looked puzzled. Not the answer she'd been given to expect from new fringe clients. 'Of the fringe, my lovely?'

'Oh,' Holly said slowly, gradually realising an undeniable truth, that she didn't look like a sweet seven-year-old anymore. The fringe was an unmitigated catastrophe. 'It's great, thank you,' she said, preparing herself for a month of hibernation.

'It does wonders for you!' Josie said in that way hairdressers are so good at. 'Really lifts your face.'

Josie brushed off the last of the stray hairs before unfettering Holly from the shiny black straitjacket. The thing was, ever since the days of standing in a sports field at school in a minuscule netball skirt, thighs goose-pimply, nerves in shards as she became once again the last to be picked for the girls' hockey team, Holly had never managed to be the kind of person that – well – joined things. But now, twenty years on, she finally felt ready to be a fully paid-up member of a club. And that was rather a nice feeling, she was realising.

'Do you use any product on your hair?' asked Josie in that way that Holly had never understood. Surely it was a plural, wasn't it? Surely it's 'products', the octogenarian pedant within her wanted to shout.

'No I don't, actually. I'm all right thanks,' she said as Josie shovelled product onto Holly's head in spades.

'Oh, it's just lovely,' she said, smiling as Josie held up the small mirror behind, allowing her to see the back of the hair. The back was OK, but by Jehovah, the 'bangs', on the other hand, somehow conspired together to conjure up the vista of an emaciated heroin addict. Nope, there was nothing for it but to smile and nod, then get the hell home, dig out the Kirby grips and OD on St Johns' Wort.

Holly awoke four hours later with the afternoon sun blazing through the gap in her blind. She sat up and caught a glimpse of her fringe in the mirror on the other side of the room. She lay back down, closed her eyes and hoped that sleep would come soon and liberate her from the reality of her new appearance.

When she next opened her eyes and turned on Radio 6 Music, the Violent Femmes' 'Blister in the Sun' came on. One of her favourite songs in the genre of perky, quirky upliftingness, she took this as a cue from Broadcasting House to get her lazy ass out of bed and make something of her life. Yes. It was time to create.

With fresh resolve, she picked up the laptop that was still sellotaped together from the time she'd trodden on it. She turned it on – amazing, it still worked! As she waited for it to boot up, a new strategy popped into her head: she would simply avoid mirrors for a whole month. Genius! Other people might have to see her hideous fringe, but that didn't mean she had to. Also, there was one blessing: at least she wouldn't risk breaking her notice period again. No man would look at her now, let alone ask her to get off any buses.

Yes. The fringe represented a new start. New Holly was going to turn this shit around! There were only six weeks to go until *Prowl* came off the air, so she really should try and pluck one more idea out of the sky.

She opened up a Word document, and began typing up all the new telly ideas she'd had so far, ending with Band Swap, for which she wrote a quick blurb, ready to send to Jeremy. After trying to dream up some more telly ideas from scratch, she kept finding her mind drifting back to the short film idea. She opened up a new document and typed the words 'Mind the Gap'. Then she stared at the blank page some more.

What am I thinking, doing this in Times New Roman, she mused. She highlighted the text, right-aligned it. Then centre-aligned it and then changed it to Courier New, point size 12. There. Am now officially a scriptwriter, she thought, typing in her name underneath, hitting Return, and admiring her handiwork.

Although, strictly speaking, any scriptwriter worth their salt works in Final Draft, don't they, she thought, going online and downloading a free 30-day trial. Now what? Open New project. She retyped in her name and the title. Now we're cooking with gas, she thought as she began to type.

'Scene One. FADE IN…'

Fade in on what? Are we Interior or Exterior? What time of day is it? Are we starting on the Tube already, or are we starting with a flashback? Who is the main character, male or female? Who knew the answers? Why hadn't anyone told her this writing malarkey was full of so many arbitrary decisions?

She took out the notebook she'd started months ago and opened it to reveal some half-baked scrawls:

239

Short film idea – someone mourning their loved one who was once a TFL voice. Could be jobbing actor and this was one thing they did in between West End shows or Holby. Ended up weirdly immortalised by TFL. Show the widow on their journey of grief somehow.

How to magically transform these notes into an actual script, she wondered. She dug out the scribbles she'd made the other day about a woman named Clara Thomas, the voice of the Northern line. As it turned out, she sounded a lot more old-fashioned than she really was. In her thirties, she was a long way from leaving behind a widow. As it turned out, she wasn't trapped in a 1930s time-warp, but was just great at putting on old-fashioned voices. Which wasn't the most helpful of leads. No, the character in her film would be older. She'd have been recorded at least twenty years ago for the idea to have enough gravitas, she decided, scribbling down some more notes. But wait, maybe that was why Lawrence had said the idea was far-fetched and silly? Maybe the curly-haired one was right, she thought, grinding to a halt again.

She dwelled on this for a few minutes until she realised her gargantuan error. Of course, don't attempt anything without reading the Bible! She stood up and went over to her bookshelf to retrieve *Story*, the screenwriting tome that Harry had given to her. She opened it up, sat down on the floor and began to read. She wasn't two pages in when her eye drifted to the right, just enough to be struck by how messy the room was. The wardrobe – once reasonably tidy – now resembled the first floor of a Primark just before closing. Her underwear drawer was ajar, tights hanging half out, socks leaking out onto the floor. Her beanbag was piled high with discarded clothes and make-up. In short, it was not far off being a female replica of The Lawrence Pit.

Little wonder she couldn't write under these conditions! First things first then, a thorough spring clean – after which the script would write itself. She grabbed an empty carrier bag and began shovelling in old tissues and other break-up detritus.

Having hoovered the entire bedroom floor (with the nozzle attachment and everything), she moved to do behind the bed, which involved pulling it away from the wall. She wasn't prepared for what was down there. Buried deep among the dust balls and old coins was a time capsule of Lawrence. One of his old Sudoku books, a stray sock, and worst of all, his Che Guevara T-shirt, all crumpled up and smelling of Lawrenceness. She tried to imagine the last time she'd seen him wearing it – or worse, the last time she'd taken it off him. As she clutched it to her and inhaled its musty but manly scent, he was back in the room.

She sat in the middle of the floor, studying the plate of leftovers from her longest relationship. She opened the Sudoku book and looked at all the puzzles filled out in his spider-like scrawl. She turned to one that was half-finished. She grabbed the pen and attempted to complete it, before quickly remembering she was rubbish at them and Lawrence had always finished hers off. Just like he would have helped her write this script now. What was she thinking, trying to write a script without him?

Tears pressed at the edges of her eyes. No, don't fall off the wagon, she told herself. What do alcoholics do when they can feel themselves slipping?

Go to a meeting.

She grabbed the blue carrier bag, which already had some of his things in, and shoved it all inside, tying up the ends. Behold The Lawrence Sack, went the maudlin voice-over in her head. Five years of happy memories, bound in fraying polythene. She shoved it into the hall cupboard, next to Bella's More-reasons-to-break-up-with-Sam bag, which their house-mate Daniel had since dumped his ski-ing gear on top of. Poor Jezebel, the teddy bear that Sam had given Bella, was now buckling under the pressure, his beady, lopsided eyes peering out at her. Her heart ached for the poor teddy. Even he was feeling the blow, being caught in the crossfire of all the conscious un-couplings. C'est la vie, she thought, slamming the door and heading out, not before pinning back The Fringe with four hundred Kirby grips. Back in her bedroom, the blank page on the laptop got bored of waiting and turned itself to Sleep setting.

As she rode the escalator to the Northern Line, she resolved to try and think positive. Remember Rule Number Eleven: 'Eventually, you will be OK. You will recover.' She stepped onto the carriage and sat down, hearing Clara's familiar female voice announcing the stops, and finding it oddly comforting. She wondered whether hearing her voice again might magically stir something in the stagnant waters of her writer's block. She got her notebook out in readiness, her pen poised in the long wait for inspiration.

She looked across the carriage and her eyes landed on one of those lovely Poems on the Underground. She began to read, excited that she was about to have her creativity massaged into life by whichever uplifting verse just happened to be right in front of her on this particular tube train. And there it was, short, stark and staggering.

Separation

Your absence goes through me
Like thread through a needle.
Everything I do is stitched with its colours

W.S. Merwin 'Separation'

20. *When Harry Met Holly*

'For the love of shit! Even the Underground is out to get me now,'
Holly said as she, arrived at Olivia's newly decorated lounge and
helped herself to some baklava from the shiny new coffee table.
'Now even TFL is the enemy,' she said after telling them about
the psychic poetry incident.

'TFL is always the enemy,' Olivia said.

'It's like everything knows, isn't it.'

'No,' Olivia said, taking away the tray of baklava just as Holly
was going in for another. 'Oi missus. You'll ruin your appetite.'

'Sorry.' Her hands retreated.

'Just think about how ridiculous you sound,' reasoned Harry,
'Do you actually think that the universe as a whole, that's been
around for squillions of years, could possibly conspire to bother
you, little old you, with these things? It's almost a bit narcissistic
when you think about it.'

'Eff off Harry,' she said, although she'd never thought about
it quite like that.

'Maybe it's about being selective, Hol. You know, you have to
pick the coincidences to ignore, and the ones to take notice of?
The ones that are useful or actually life-affirming in some way,'
Bella said.

'As opposed to indulgent,' Harry added.

'OK, I'm going to try and be a lot more discerning from now on then,' Holly agreed.

'That would certainly be a start,' Olivia said, heading off to the kitchen and then re-emerging soon after. 'OK kids, it's Guac o'clock,' she declared, putting out a tray of fajitas and guacamole, which was then rapidly demolished.

'Yum, thanks Olivia!' Bella said as she took a huge mouthful and fajita juice dribbled all down her chin. 'Now, Holly. I've got an idea that might make you feel better. How about we ring round the hospitals, see if Aaron the bike boy is OK?'

'Bella, no!'

'Oh come on, I just think there was a real spark between you two – I know he was only semi-conscious, but guys, you should have seen them together, it was electric!'

'Bella – again, you're being inappropriate!'

'But he might take your mind off Luke? And Lawry? And—'

'END of conversation,' snapped Holly, 'you utter mentalist.'

Olivia looked at her phone and stood up. 'Sorry guys, but I've got to go and meet someone,' she said, looking uncharacteristi-cally sheepish, grabbing her handbag and stepping into her heels.

'But you've not eaten any of this delicious food you made us!' Holly said, pouring more tequila into people's glasses. She knew she should probably make them into actual cocktails but three margaritas in, she was way past being civilised enough for that.

'Oh, I scoffed a shit ton of it while I was cooking. What's that saying? A chef is never hungry…'

'Mmm. I wonder who Liv might be going to see at this hour,' Bella said, eyeing Olivia suspiciously. 'It wouldn't be a friend of our housemate's by any chance?'

'Maybe,' she said.

'Oh, I thought we were all crashing here tonight for some reason – I've even brought a boyfriend pack with me!' Holly said.

'Oh sorry. I'm a terrible host. Well you can all still stay. You can take the new sofa-bed. I'll get the spare bedding,' Olivia said, heading out to the hall cupboard, where she pulled out a duvet. Then she presented them all with matching guest towels, sheets and sets of slippers from posh European hotels that were still in their wrapping.

'Wow,' Holly said, 'I feel like we just took a wrong turn and ended up in the showroom at John Lewis!'

'I'll take that as a compliment. It does feel nice to finally have all my stuff out of storage! Seriously though, I'm sorry to desert you tonight. Help yourself to anything you need. Mi casa es su casa and all that!'

'Thanks Liv!' Holly said.

'Right, see you later then, fuck-ups,' Olivia said, dispatching multiple air kisses before slipping away.

And then there were three.

Bella sat herself down on the floor in front of Harry.

'Can one of you give me a back rub please? I've got all this tension in my neck – must be nerves for my audition tomorrow.'

'Oh I don't know,' Harry said. 'Massaging pretty ladies is such a chore. OK, but only if Holly does mine at the same time.'

'Oooh a massage chain, yay!' Holly said before doing the maths and realising that as Bella was right next to the table, she would be the one at the back who missed out. With a martyrish sigh she took a seat behind Harry and began kneading his shoulders like they were quiche dough.

'Tell me,' she said, her fingers beginning to dig into Harry's shoulders. 'Is it unacceptable that I keep finding James Blunt's "Goodbye My Lover" really comforting in my current state?'

'Yes.' Harry turned round to reprimand her to her face. 'Not only is it completely unacceptable, but it's entirely ancient! Either way, it will pass. All things must pass,' he said, staring into her eyes a little too intensely.

'I hear you. But there's this one line that kills me!' She stopped, feeling the floodgates open just behind her pupils.

'But,' Harry said, realising something, 'you know that Lawrence wasn't your "One", don't you?' he finished as though he was a lawyer backing his prosecution into a corner. 'You always said.'

Holly's eyes narrowed. 'So you know all the lyrics, hey? I thought you said you hated it?'

'I can't help it if our freakatron housemate Daniel keeps on tuning the kitchen radio to Heart FM, Radio Melancholy. That man has the strangest taste in music!'

'Fuck-sticks,' Bella said, 'is that the time? Sorry guys but I'm going to have to hit the hay – I don't want this massage to end but I need some sleep. I've not had paid singing work in months so I have to get this one!'

'Sure, why don't you crash in Liv's bed, you'll get better sleep in that one. We'll sort out down here.'

'Thanks guys.'

Harry stood up and pulled out the sofa-bed, while Holly unfolded the bedding and laid it out. Then they sat back down and resumed the massage chain, even if it was now only two people long. As Harry's hands took over from massaging duties, Holly wondered if there was a feeling in the world more blissfully smug than the moment you make the switch from the massager to the massaged, and all duties are over. She gave a happy sigh.

'Holface,' Harry began as Bella left the room and headed up the stairs, 'I know you don't want to hear it but I think the new do looks kind of hot,' he said, playfully pulling out some of her Kirby grips in order to set The Fringe free. It was a movement that felt out of the ordinary, and made her slightly uneasy. She shook out the last grip, so her hair fell in loose clumps around her eyes.

'Thanks.' She turned back around as his hands came back to her shoulders, pressing down on the concrete slab that was her thoracic region.

'It's very, um, hipster chic,' he said.

'Ha ha. Ugly chic, more like. Do you want a turn again?'

'Not yet. I'm enjoying giving you one.'

Holly felt something leap into her belly. Butterflies? Moths? Indigestion?

They could hear Bella's footsteps above. Then the running water of a tap, the bristling whirr of a tooth-brush, and finally the sound of a bedroom door closing.

'I wish you wouldn't be so hard on yourself, Holly. You don't know how lovely you are, do you? That's half the reason you're so lovely.'

Holly grimaced. 'Now you sound like that cheesy song! You're lovely too, you know that.'

'Thanks. Although, I'm really not dicking around. I do think you're gorgeous. You know I love you, don't you.'

'Of course. And I you,' she said, feeling nervous now.

Harry's hands were pressing harder, but she let them do their thing. Important to get out all the tension of the last few weeks, she decided. Yep, good for one's health.

'Oh, that feels fantastic,' she said loudly as if to assert just how entirely platonic this all was. But Lawrence never used to do that, she thought as another ripple of pleasure shot down her neck. Although, was someone softly kissing the back of your neck all part of the normal repertoire of medicinal massage? she wondered. Best to pretend you haven't noticed anything unusual, she decided.

But now she could feel his hands moving outside of what might be defined as the accepted territory of Western massage. As she gently cleared her throat, the hands moved from the small of her back to dangerously close to the edge of her right boob.

'Um, Harry…'

'Holly…'

'No, I don't mean, mmmm, I mean, um?' She turned to face him, gently coercing his hand away from Boobville and realising now why the Kirby grip incident had felt unusual. 'As in, um, is something happening?'

Part of her was now missing his hand and wanting it to go

back to where it had been. That whole area was tingly with withdrawal. Maybe it was actually OK to carry on enjoying the massage? Maybe, if they both just carried on pretending that this wasn't in any way sensual, that would be fine?

Harry leaned in, his face closer to hers now than it had ever been. She looked into his green eyes. What if this was actually her perfect rom-com hero, staring her in the face, and she was too stupid to notice this fact? Her eyes closed as his lips crash-landed on hers. His hand squeezed hers. Clunky, sweaty, a little clammy maybe, but sod it, she thought, switching into obedient romantic heroine mode and letting him wrap his other arm around her. As she tightened her arms around his broad shoulders, they kissed and it felt warm, safe and just nice, although obviously a little weird, but she wasn't going to think about that. For once she was going to live in the moment – do that whole 'Power of Now' bollocks. Stop worrying, start living. While she was getting busy living and running her hands through his hair, Harry's hands were going south. She stopped, pulled away again.

'Come on Hol. There's a recession on, you know.'

'What's that got to do with anything?'

He kissed her again, less like a friend this time. Then he pulled away, just as she could feel herself getting lost in the moment.

'Aye, remember what Keynes said. A country should shag its way out of a recession.'

'How very nationalistic of you,' she said, pulling away again, this time more defiantly. 'And I think the quote was "spend", Harry.'

'Och, semantics. Anyway, don't worry, this won't change anything.' And then he looked at her in a way she'd never seen before. Moments later, his jeans were in a pile at his feet. His hard-on was pressing against her leg through his navy blue boxers, and his hands were wandering towards her boobs, heading around the back to grapple with her bra fastening. It was happening – this weird thing that had once been so out of bounds and off

248

limits in her mind. She opened the door marked 'Don't Go In Here You Mentalist' and stepped, one foot at a time, into a parallel universe; into the aforementioned Circle of Sexual Disgust. Briefly, she let herself enjoy the moment, let herself be swept along by it. You never know, she thought – maybe there was something good in this – maybe this would take her mind off Luke, which would in turn take her mind off Lawrence, and in doing so remind her that she could do casual sexy-times and wasn't in some way remedial after all?

As they fell backwards onto the sofa, he leaned into her and began kissing her neck. She opened her eyes and had a proper look at him, viewing him for the first time as a sexual being. He was actually far more muscular and taut than she'd imagined. Ginger pubes (obv), but nice, strong, toned arms that made you feel safe when you were encased in them. And after everything they'd been through the last few months, it felt like coming home. Holly stroked his hair and began kissing his forehead, his cheeks, his closed eyelids, all the while thinking about how much she loved him as a friend. Of how precious their friendship was to her. Of how… Shit. Maybe crossing the line like this would turn out to be an epic fail? Holly opened one eye and watched Harry going through the motions of his Infidel Castro routine. Although the massage had got her going in some way, now she was starting to feel not so much sexy, but rather more like she was kissing her brother. And she didn't even have a brother.

But then, he was exceptionally cute, she noticed from deep within the circle. She kissed Harry back with gusto, sending her hands up into the unchartered territory under his ironic T-shirt that read, 'If you're interested in time travel, meet me last Thursday.' She pulled off the T-shirt and threw it to the floor. He pulled off her jeans and she did a grimace as she remembered what terrible knickers she had on.

'Sorry. It's laundry day… and I'm, er, a little behind with my waxing regime,' was the only elegant way she could think to phrase the fact her legs and lady-garden were presently more unkempt than the overgrown back yard of Harry's student digs in Oxford.

Harry smiled. His lips had moved down her neck towards her chest, and they were headed south. He took a pit stop in the boob area, and she had to admit it felt nice. Nice and a bit weird. She could feel his boxers pressing against her and she knew what was coming. It was probably too late to cancel now – that would surely just be rude at this stage, wouldn't it?

Holly took off her best friend's boxers. As she watched him fiddle with the little rubbery mood-killer, her head was spinning with tequila and confusion. She'd never dreamed of doing this even in her most Freudian of nightmares. Already this was feeling like Too Much Information and Not Sexy but Perfunctory. To be sure, this was definitely a mistake. Of this she was now abundantly certain. But surely you can't press Undo once you've passed this point? she wondered. 'OH – hang on, back up, back up, I've changed my mind SORRY!' she rehearsed in her head. What was the etiquette with this stuff? Perhaps, if she just kept on kissing him, did the deed, then all thoughts of 'This Is Wrong' and 'ICK!' would just go away? Diligently, as if to make a mark of defiance to that over-active party-pooping brain of hers, she took her right hand and placed it on Harry's Oh-my-days-really-rather-enormous-actually-cock and began to do what you were meant to do in this situation.

'Ow.'

'Sorry. You OK?'

'Yes. Just not so – um – tight.'

'Oh. Sorry. Actually, now you mention it, what you're doing could be a bit gentler.'

'Right,' Harry looked mildly affronted, as if to say, no one else has ever complained.

'Sorry Hol.'

Suddenly Holly let go and felt a smile appear from nowhere. She burst into rapturous giggles, just as Harry burst into uncontrollable laughter.

'What you thinking?' Harry said.

'What the fuck are we doing? You?'

'That this feels weird and we should probably stop, and, um, never drink tequila again?'

'Great. Now shut up and stop kissing me,' she said. Then she pulled on a T-shirt and pants, and threw Harry his boxer shorts. Once they were dressed, he leaned over and spooned her. Then he started laughing again, as though he'd just realised something ridiculous.

'What's so funny?'

'Oh, just that, these last few weeks, I've been harbouring a delusion that I was falling madly in love with you.'

'Are you shitting me? I'm so sorry, I had absolutely no idea!'

'Why else would I have been hanging around you and the club so much?'

'Oh. I thought you were into it…?'

'Christ no! Well, I thought it was ridiculous at first. But I had nowhere better to be, and it was a way for me to spend more time with you. Now of course I'm finding it genuinely useful. I'm not going anywhere.'

'Good.'

'Anyway. My point is, now I can see I was just really confused! It took getting our kit off and clambering around in the nude for me to realise I was entirely delusional. It was clearly just a strange transference episode, where my feelings for Rachel got discombobulated and projected back at you. No offence but being with you in that way just felt truly awkward and weird and wrong.'

Holly let out a gargantuan sigh of relief. 'Phew. Me too.'

Moments later, though, she began to feel panicky. Would they ever be the same again? This was one of her best friends! What if they'd ruined their friendship? She opened her mouth to speak the words, 'Christ Harry, we're going to go to Hell, we've broken Rule Number Nine!'

But the moment was killed by the sound of Darth Vader doing

his best heavy breathing. So Harry obviously wasn't losing any sleep over it. Maybe worrying could wait? She closed her eyes and attempted sleep. By 5 a.m. she was listening to a different breed of dawn chorus to the ones she was used to. Harry's arms were still enveloping her belly, and the warmth of his body was keeping her awake, but she didn't have the heart to unpeel them. At one point the Darth Vader noise stopped, and she felt his snoring turn into more regular, quiet breathing.

'Harry? You awake?'

'No.'

'Listen. I'm sorry if I misled you in any way.'

'Don't worry about it. You didn't. Sleepy Time.'

'I guess I was just missing bodily human contact... and affection from someone I can trust...'

'As opposed to Luke.'

'Yes. So, Harry. Um. I don't think we should tell the others.'

'Course not, we don't want them getting the wrong idea.'

'I'd hate for the dynamic to change.'

'Hey, it's no bother. Really, we're fine.'

And that was that. Harry had flicked this utter catastrophe away like a mildly irritating flea. Oh, to be a bloke.

'OK then,' Holly said quietly. 'Cool bananas it is.'

Harry tightened his arms around her and they continued spooning. She closed her eyes, her head spinning with regret. Maybe when the sun finally rose everything really would go back to normal. At dawn they would reinstate the original barrier of the Circle of Sexual Disgust. Like a railway crossing lever that had briefly come up, it would go back down again. Tomorrow, partially clothed cuddling would be weird. But today it was absolutely fine and normal, she decided, as she pulled the duvet over their heads and squeezed his hand into hers.

21. *She Who is Tired of London*

'You have to see this, Braithwaite!'

A week later, Jeremy burst into Holly's office, high on machine espresso, dark circles under his eyes. With a crazed expression, he leaned over her computer, logged into Vimeo and pressed play.

'It's a little sizzle I bashed together, just to get the commissioners even more excited.'

'A what now, for the who now?'

As Holly watched with eyes aghast, she heard The Beach Boys singing 'God only knows what I'd be without you', along with fast-cut clips of people having break-ups in various movies and TV shows. Then, some kinetic type came up on screen, along with some audible dialogue that was all very familiar. 'Thou shalt not have a relapse with an ex only weeks after breaking up with them,' went Olivia's voice, and 'One day, when you're strong enough, you'll claim them all back. You'll be there, shouting "This Is A Reclaim!" across a crowded dance floor; an incandescent smile on your face!' Then, the screen went black as some titles appeared. This went on for a few more seconds until Jez grabbed Holly's arm. 'Check out this last bit, Hol – it's a strapline Pascal thought up, based on an old AA advertising slogan.'

Holly's eyes widened as the words 'To our members, we're the first emergency service' flashed up, followed by the words 'Break-up Club, coming soon to Channel Five.'

'Well, shit the bed, Jeremy. You've really outdone yourself this time.'

'I knew you'd come around.'

'No. I meant, how the fuck have you got sound recordings of my friends? Could you BE any more morally emaciated?'

'You said nothing about not recording sound. Just picture!'

'Can you please take that down off the Internet. Now! And I WANT THOSE MP3s DELETED! Or I'll have Olivia file a lawsuit against you for life-theft!'

Jeremy sighed in a 'jeez some people are so precious' kind of way. 'They're on the server. I'll trash them right now.'

'And there's no way in hell you're taking this to Channel 5. Or anywhere else. Are we clear on that?'

'But IT'S TERRESTRIAL!'

'Jeremy. I don't know how else to say this but IT'S A NO FROM ME! And from the others! Well, except Bella, but we'd disown her…'

'OK, OK. I'll shelve it… For now. But neither Sky nor 5 were interested in any of the other ideas,' he said, pulling up a chair. 'So we're going to need to come up with something else, sharpish.'

'You didn't like Britain's Ghost Pets?'

'I've put it on the list. But it's quite a number to research.'

'Band Swap?'

Jeremy looked as blank as her GCSE maths paper.

'The one about musical swingers?'

'No. Look, there is this one half-thought that Pascal's had, but it's not really working just yet.'

'OK – let me at it! Let me help!'

'So, it's kind of *Embarrassing Bodies* meets *Big Brother*. A real-life challenge show, where people battle out their illnesses against one another. Only, they're all different types of – mental conditions.'

254

'Sometimes I really can't tell whether you're joking or not.'

'You know, insomnia versus OCD. And while all these people with "issues" try to form meaningful relationships with each other, the public gets to see which of these conditions is more bonkers than the other. Pascal's calling it Mentalist Top Trumps, he reckons it's got great merchandise potential.'

Holly shook her head in disbelief. 'Wow. Let me guess, instead of The Diary Room, contestants have one-to-one therapy sessions live on air that viewers can pry on? Then, as the weeks go on, the public vote off whom they think is least in need of clinical help? And the overall winner gets a year's stay at The Priory?'

'That's the stuff, Braithwaite!' he said, writing it down.

'Wait. You're being serious?'

'It's an absolute winner! But I don't think that title's working. Could you have a think, see if you can come up with a snappier name for it?'

'What like, The Funny Farm? Or, The Madhouse?' she said, joking. But he was already making a note of them.

'Oh yes! That second one's good. Plays off the Big Brother legacy nicely. And the strapline could be "You don't have to be bat-shit crazy to live here but it helps!"' He fell about his chair laughing.

'I was joking, Jez! You can't actually submit this? Surely you can see that it's monstrously insensitive and appalling?'

Jeremy rolled his eyes. 'You know what you can do if you don't like it, don't you?' he said, smirking as he looked at the BUC rules which Holly had since pinned back to the wall.

She sighed. How had it come to this? Lose any chance of working on a respectable show again, or lose my best friends in the world?

'OK. Madhouse it is. But don't say I didn't warn you.'

'How are the meetings by the way? Any inter-member liaisons yet?'

Holly felt her cheeks grow warm. 'No! Don't be revolting!'

'Is Bella still single?'

*

Some hours later, still in a mild state of shock at the boundless audacity of her boss, Holly headed to the bus stop outside work to meet the others for what Bella was dubbing 'Swing 'o'clock'. Today was the day that all four would attempt their first swing-dancing lesson, this time at a bar in Waterloo. Being south of her comfort zone, Holly had no idea how to get there. She hopped on a bus that looked vaguely relevant. She went up to the top deck and rested her head on the window, looking forward to seeing London by night, closing her eyes for just a moment.

But she never saw the view. When she opened them again, a large Hispanic man was sat next to her eating a kebab, and she appeared to be somewhere south of Brixton. She sat up with a jerk and blinked into consciousness. Looking out the window, she saw with alarm that the road signs all seemed to be pointing to Darkest Streatham. As was the bus, which was following in that direction. Uh-oh. Best get off before LawrenceVille, she thought, leaping up and descending the stairs as fast as was possible without falling arse over tit. She asked the driver if he could please stop at the next stop. He grunted back at her, something which sounded like, 'Can't, we're on diversion. The High Road's closed.'

Shit. 'Um, sorry, you don't understand. I need to get off this bus.'

The driver ignored her. The bus stopped at a red traffic light.

'Uh – I'm allergic to Streatham. It makes me – hypoglycaemic, I start to hyperventilate and stuff. It's really gross, sir. I'm sorry. Could you not just let me out at these lights, here?' she said just as an automated bus voice from up above said, 'The next bus stop is closed.' The driver looked at her, with a strange mix of smugness and pity.

The lights turned to green, and the bus pulled off again. Holly looked through the window. Here came all the famous landmarks, one by one, as they headed up Streatham Hill. The road signs pointing out the public toilet access in McDonalds and in Wimpy. Wimpy! The Beacon Bingo hall on Streatham Hill, followed by the Megabowl centre. Lawrence's idea of 'date night' had once involved a grand tour of both glorious places, she recalled, as the bus headed towards the turning for Telford Avenue.

As the bus drove towards what was essentially the Town Centre of LawrenceVille, Holly slumped down in the nearest available seat. She looked down at her hands as the familiar scenes began to play out on the screen of the bus windows.

She could only pray that Lawrence himself wouldn't be there, lurking around a corner. She sloped down lower in her chair just in case. As the moths flooded her belly, so too did all the memories. First came the exotic Indian spices, wafting through the window, from the curry house on the corner. Faster than a Tardis, the smell instantly took her back in time to Friday nights spent stuffing their faces on take-away and *Dr Who* triple bills. Then there was the multiple sclerosis charity shop next door, where they'd bought most of Lawrence's furniture. Looking into the shop now, she could see Lawrence and Holly in there, picking up that cranky old wicker chair between them and lugging it out together, giggling as it bashed against the walls. Then there was the Costcutter with the lovely Italian man that used to sell them marked-down bread before he was throwing it out. She could see him out the front, stocking up the tomato levels. She wanted to smile through the window at him and shout, 'So long, and thanks for all the focaccia,' but she couldn't because she had tears all down her face and she appeared to be coming undone again.

The pain went straight to her stomach, and the Boots honey mustard chicken sandwich she'd been nibbling at went straight into the bin. Everyone on the bus was no doubt staring at her as if to say, why are you in a state of mourning over Streatham? As the tears fell in droves, there then followed unbelievable, heart-melting kindness from a total stranger. While Holly sobbed like the self-indulgent numpty she was, a kind Afro-Caribbean lady next to her handed her a big wodge of tissues. As if that wasn't charity enough, she then took Holly's scraggy water bottle from her quivering fingers, filled it up with water from her own vessel and pronounced that, 'It will be OK,' like she knew it would. Holly burst into more tears before managing a snotty smile. 'Thank you so much. I'm so sorry to ruin your journey. I just wasn't meant to come this way,' she said while blowing her nose.

'Streatham's not that bad, darlin',' said the woman, and Holly collapsed with laughter.

'No you're right. It's lovely, really.'

And then there was little else to be done but to cry it all out, in loud unabashed tears. She'd unwittingly broken a fundamental rule. And as much as she couldn't bear the thought, she knew this would mean a setback of at least three weeks in recovery time. She climbed off the bus and into a cab, utterly exasperated with her sad pathetic self. Now I get Rule Number Ten, she thought. No entering zones of exes before the necessary time period has lapsed. Simple.

Twenty minutes later, as the cab pulled into The Cut in Waterloo and stopped outside a pub, her eyes were still puffy from crying. Her vision was so foggy that she didn't notice a man with wavy brown hair and a large scar across his cheek walking out of the double doors and heading to a bicycle on the other side of the street. Just as he bent down to unlock the bright orange chain, she stepped out of the cab, paid the driver, and walked into the pub. She joined Harry in a booth, where he was sat watching hipsters of all ages dancing around the room. The girls were sporting victory rolls and vintage dresses, while the men were rocking their braces and brogues.

'Hey, I'm sorry I'm so late. I just had a massive TFL fail.'

Harry shuffled closer to Holly and wrapped an arm around her. This being the first time they had come into such contact since The Incident, she immediately felt herself flinch and go red. 'Thanks,' she said, hoping no one would notice.

'You OK?' he mouthed, and she nodded quickly.

'So, we were just hearing from Bella that she went to see Sam again,' Harry said, shaking his head.

'What! Another relapse? After I've been so good at not replying to Lawrence's spam? Am I the only disciplined one around here?'

'Sure seems that way,' Bella said, 'but you don't need to tell me off. It's been a really positive experience!'

'How exactly?'

'Well, the good news is that Sam has well and truly gone off!' she announced, as though he was a piece of Camembert that'd been left out of the fridge too long. 'He's put on a lot of weight, and he's also just been made redundant, so he's living back home with his mum and dad in Broadstairs and has kind of let himself go a bit. I'm not being mean, but for someone that always called me Miss Piggy, he's looking distinctly pig-like himself!'

'Well maybe it's for the best that you saw him then,' Holly said.

'That's what I hoped you'd say. I think it was therapeutic. I can finally see that, all this time, I'd built him up to be this ideal man in my head – only now I can finally see, he really wasn't all that.'

Harry nodded. 'I did that with Rachel. I put her on a pedestal ever since I first met her in college. But now I can see she was actually entirely wrong for me.'

'You're doing a great job of taking your mind off her, aren't you,' Bella smiled.

'What do you mean?' Holly asked.

'Harry's been knobbing different girls every other night of the week, hasn't he? How many have you got on the go?'

'I would say there are about three I like at the moment,' he

259

said, avoiding Holly's eyes. 'But yeah, I've essentially had it with monotony.'

'You mean monogamy,' Olivia said.

'Yeah, like I said.'

'No, you said monotony,' Olivia said, exasperated. 'Holly, you're very quiet, are you OK?'

'Yes, sure, I just almost saw a ghost earlier. Had a bad episode, but I'm fine now,' she said, forcing a smile as Ella Fitzgerald began to blast out of the speakers.

'Oh, the next lesson's about to kick off. Here we go kids! Swing Swing Swing!' Bella yelled, tugging Holly's arm towards the dance floor. A pair of chirpy Australians named Scott and Ashley were wearing headsets and calling out for everyone to get into a circle.

'So it's triple step, triple step, rock step, with your feet, and then meanwhile you do this with your arms, OK?' Bella said, quickly filling the others in on the basics before they started. Holly looked blankly at Bella and attempted to do as she said. The others joined in next to her as they all tried to do the 'sugar-push' move.

'I'm just not getting it, am I?' Holly said, sighing and looking to her partner for help – a sweaty man with a name badge that read Nigel. Olivia and Harry mastered the 'throw out' move beautifully while she looked on in awe. Nausea started to take hold of her as Nigel swung her around in a circle and she almost fell over.

Triple step, triple step, rock step, she chanted along with everyone else, staring down at her two left feet as they struggled to keep up with Nigel's.

'OK, brilliant, guys!' yelled the tutor, Scott, from his microphone. 'Now, let's rotate partners again.'

Holly looked to her right to see who was next in the circle, and felt her cheeks flush to the colour of Bella's lips. This was the moment she'd been dreading. She knew everyone here would have to dance with everyone else at some point, but she'd hoped they might have somehow got away with it.

'Come on then Harry, show us how it's done,' she said with forced enthusiasm. Harry looked back, his eyes blinking nervousness.

As he took her in his arms, his hands a little clammy again, she instantly saw reruns in her mind of the other night. Of his moves, of his chiselled torso, and of his unfeasibly large willy. 'Triple step, triple step, rock step,' she repeated aloud like a mantra, trying to block out the weird incestuous-porn horror movie named When Harry met Holly that was playing in her mind. Try not to think about it, she told herself, attempting to focus on mastering the moves instead. Try not to drink tequila ever again, she also told herself. Again.

Harry grabbed her arm and spun her around.

'Woah, easy tiger!' she said, almost tripping up, but feeling a smile creep onto her face from nowhere.

'OK, I see what you're doing wrong,' he said. 'You need to keep your arms out here, at ninety degrees, and then fix them in that position. But mostly, you need much more tension in your wrists.' He grabbed her right arm and moved it into position. 'Here, see? Then it's about you just feeling for the tension in my arm – whether I'm pushing or pulling. Then you follow my lead and either do the footwork, or be spun around.' Holly nodded, tried again and somehow this time it was easier. Enjoyable, even.

'Yes! You're getting it!'

She got it again. 'Yay, this is fun!' she said, bouncing off Harry's arms, then unfolding out into a swing again. The more he flung her around, the lighter she felt.

As they tried a double turn, Harry shot her a smile that seemed to say everything was OK again, that the other night didn't matter anymore. Thank the Lord, she thought, smiling back.

'Hey, you've got it!' Bella said, who was watching them while rock-stepping like a pro with a new hipster friend she'd just made. 'Well done! Isn't this just the best natural antidepressant there is?!' she shrieked. 'I like it because you don't have to think – you just follow whatever the bloke is doing!'

261

'OK, that was awesome, guys!' said Scott as a Charleston track kicked in. 'You did great! But for now you can all just take a short break! The advanced class are just going to do a quick run-through of their routine for the Swing Ball!'

'Oh, I was just getting into it,' Holly said, as they all headed to the bar.

'We'll have to come again then, won't we!' Bella said.

'Mmm. Maybe,' Holly said, watching the advanced class, her mouth dropping to the floor. 'Although I can't imagine us ever being as good as that!'

'We can be if we put our minds to it! Anyway,' Bella said as they all sat down in a booth, 'Miss Olivia, how's it going with you and Jonny now?'

'Have you had "the conversation"?' Harry said, doing his Gay Best Friend act. 'Are you "exclusive" yet?'

'Christ no! I told you, we don't date. We just shag,' she said, repeating her mantra. But this time Holly detected a sense in which Olivia was trying to convince herself of this information more than them.

'Oh. Lovely,' Bella said.

'We have started to talk after sex though.'

'Has he stayed over yet?'

'No.'

'Have you stayed at his?'

'A couple of times. But only because I had meetings near his part of town so it made practical sense.'

'I shouldn't worry about it, Liv. If you're feeling something for him, that's OK. Just let it happen,' Harry said.

Olivia shook her head as though this was nonsense.

'Liv. Look us right in the eye and tell us you're not in love with Jonny The Archetypal Public School Boy,' Holly said.

'How can I look you all right in the eye?' Olivia said.

'Stop avoiding the question! Look at me then!' Holly said.

Slowly, Olivia turned to face Holly. There was a long pause.

'Go on then!' Bella said.

They all stared expectantly at her.

'I, Olivia Mahoney, do solemnly declare that… that… Shit. I can't do it. You're right. FUCK-STICKS. I've made a MASSIVE CLERICAL ERROR. I DO have feelings for him.'

'Hooray!' Bella squealed, and the others rolled their eyes.

'Rebound.com,' Holly said, shaking her head.

'I can see it all now. I must've never really loved Ross. I thought I did, but maybe I was just mistaking cosiness for love.'

'Oh that old chestnut. Easily done,' Holly said. 'Still, it's nice for you to know what actual love feels like. Congrats!' she said, and clinked glasses with a startled Olivia.

'No, not congrats! Can't you see, this is terrible news?! Jonny's nothing but a Cadbury's Flake – you've all said so. No, this bodes ill,' she said, downing Prosecco like medicine. 'Besides, it makes no sense! He was the one chasing me – I was never even that bothered.'

'Ah, you've had the FLIP,' Bella said.

'The what?' Olivia said.

'The Flip! Noun,' she continued, as though reading aloud from TheUrbanDictionary.com. 'The inevitable moment when, in a causal relationship with a man or woman, the one who really wasn't that bothered to begin with experiences an excruciating tip in power, and a swap of feelings from heady nonchalance to full-blown love and attachment. The other party simultaneously cools off at an inversely proportional rate.'

'Wow. Thanks for clearing that up,' Olivia snapped.

'It's just basic relationship maths.'

'Oh come on! You don't know that, guys! He might be just as into her as she is him!' Harry said.

'That would be nice, but this is Jonny we're talking about,' Holly said, 'The guy's a mandroid.'

'What is a mandroid?' Harry asked like he was from another country.

'The guy's emotionally bankrupt. Dan once said how Jonny's

263

ex-girlfriend broke his heart so badly that he physically swore himself off feelings for life.'

'But surely that was forever ago,' Harry began. 'Why don't you just tell him how you feel?'

Olivia stared at Harry as though he'd just solved a highly complicated simultaneous equation. 'You're right. I should try and tell him, shouldn't I? I don't care if I fuck it up, I'm going to HAVE A CONVERSATION WITH HIM!' She stood up and picked up her bag, looking quite the romantic heroine; gumption emanating from her every porcelain pore.

'WoooooHOOOO! Go Liv!' Bella said.

'Not now! I'm going to the bathroom. I'll definitely do it one day though. Soon,' she said as she walked away. The others exchanged looks.

'Car crash,' Harry said, when she was out of earshot.

'Tumbleweed,' Holly said. 'Liv, in love? I feel like something's been upset in the space-time continuum or something. Like, the whole natural order of things has been disturbed. If Liv's not a FemBot, then what else might be upside down in the world? Is the sky green suddenly?' She turned to look at Bella who was busy fiddling with a tube of glue, trying to fix the strap on her bag that had come loose. 'Er, B, you do realise that you are in fact super-gluing in public? You couldn't have waited to fix that at home?'

'God, anyone would think I was breastfeeding with my boobs fully out.'

Bella carried on gluing, a little bit of her tongue poking out of her mouth, in that way children did when they were concentrating hard on colouring in.

'This is Araldite, this one,' she said excitedly. 'It's meant to last longer. The trouble with superglue is, once you open it and close it again, it's pretty much dead. Such a waste of almost a whole tube.'

Holly nodded. As she watched Bella work, she wondered whether there was an Araldite in the world strong enough for what they all needed.

22. *Departures*

On this particular Sunday, in an alternative dimension, Holly and Lawrence were packing a suitcase. Alternate Lawrence was running around the house looking for his passport. Alternate Holly was decanting her shampoo and shower gel bottles into the miniature bottles from Bella's boyfriend pack. Lawrence was making playlists on Spotify, while sorting out his laundry, while watching Top Gear, while putting his PSP onto charge all at the same time, and asking everyone who'd listen where he'd left his foreign plug converter.

Then eventually an alternate taxi driver took them to Heathrow, where they rushed through check-in, cleared security, then made it to the gate just in time, after having spent too long in Boots and HMV and nearly lost each other. And then, in an alternate dimension, Lawrence held Holly's hand while their ears popped and they took off into the air.

Today was the day they would have been going to Cuba for the big trip. The one they'd been dreaming of for over five years, and been talking about since the night they met. Back in the regular dimension, Holly knew she shouldn't torment herself by screening footage like this in her mind, but it was just too tempting not to. She couldn't help but picture the 'other' them, had they not broken up… had she not made a different decision.

Closing her eyes, she could see them now, rising to thirty-five thousand feet while laughing at his lame jokes and tucking into trays of dubious food. And even though she knew she should turn off the Holly and Lawrence show, stop indulging in it and get on with her life in this dimension, she couldn't; it made such compulsive viewing. For the first time in her life, she had no editorial control over what her mind was broadcasting.

The patch of sand on the beach that would no longer be sat on. The waterfall that would not be snogged under, à la Tom Cruise and what's-her-name in *Cocktail*. The bedsprings that wouldn't receive a workout. The champagne cork that wouldn't go searing high over the rooftops. The mojitos that would remain undrunk. The floorboards that wouldn't witness their awkward attempts at salsa. The photographs that wouldn't collect up on her memory disc, some well composed, some with Lawrence's finger in the top right corner. One by one, she pictured all the scenes that would now never be.

Back in this dimension, she imagined the actual Boeing 747 bound for Havana at 1940 today, with its two empty seats and untouched dinners, and felt herself slip into another pity-party for one. As she was learning, when you're in the dungeons of despair, self-respect and willpower are not your friends. No – you won't see either of those little buggers jumping in to save you from doing things to make yourself feel worse. To that end, she picked up her laptop and fired up The Facebook for a nice quality session of Self-Harm.

'But you've done so well until now in not daring to look all these months!' sensible Holly told stupid Holly as she logged in. And yet still she went and did the one thing you must never do. She dared to check his Facebook picture, for any clues as to what he was doing with his life now. She tapped in his name, and there it was – camera one – Lawrence Edward Hill.

Even just seeing that he'd changed his Facebook profile picture

– it was like a weird unofficial window into his world. Within seconds, the questions began. Where is he? What are the other three walls? Whose bed is he on? Who is behind the camera and are they female? Who gets to look at his stubbly gorgeous face now? Why is he standing on his head? Why did he never do that with me? And most of all, does he not know that I can see this? Does he not remember I'm unhinged enough to stalk? Or is this his subconscious way of communicating with me? Of making sure I'll see he's just fine thank you very much, that he has moved on and he's living the life of the happy hedonist he always was? Or worse, he doesn't even think of that? He doesn't give two hoots? And a million other ludicrous thoughts of that ilk, many of which even a Harley Street psychiatrist would struggle to get to the bottom of.

I'll show him, she thought, opening up the folder on her desktop that said 'mixed photos from phone, must sort!' and beginning to hunt down that one definitive picture which would say, 'I AM PERFECTLY WELL AND HAPPY SINCE WE BROKE UP, I AM OFTEN OUT BURNING THE CANDLE AT BOTH ENDS AND GENERALLY SEIZING THE DAY AND HAVE MANY GORGEOUS MENFOLK ON MY TAIL EVERYWHERE I GO THANK YOU VERY MUCH.'

'Sweetie? What are you doing?' came Bella's voice.

'You're stalking yourself again?' Harry added.

Holly looked up to see that all of BUC had descended on her bedroom. At the exact same moment, she saw how insane she was being and slammed shut the computer.

'Nothing. I just accidentally slipped and looked at Lawrence's profile picture. And he looked good. Worse. He looked happy.'

'In the words of Damon Albarn,' Harry said, 'this is a low.'

'But it won't hurt you,' Bella added with a giggle.

'But why? How could you let this happen?' bleated Olivia like a disappointed teacher. 'You must always tell us before you feel tempted to self-harm again, OK?'

'I know, I know. THE RULES. But today was different. Today is the day Cuba was meant to be happening, so I can't stop thinking about him.'

'Have you cancelled it all?'

'No. The flights were non-refundable so I didn't bother. So I keep thinking about those two empty seats!'

'So why doesn't one of us come with you in his place? We'd have an amazing time!' Bella said, staring at her with puppy eyes.

Holly thought for a moment.

'It's a lovely idea. But – and I know this sounds tragic – I'd just be too sad, imagining us being there together instead. Plus, I don't have the spending money, as I'm so much in debt from the flights. And it's my last month at Prowl so I'm already bricking it about how I'll make rent next month. No – running away to Central America isn't going to solve anything,' she said as another tear of self-pity made a run for it.

'Oh darling,' Bella said, giving her a hug,

'And there are no other editing jobs out there?' Olivia asked.

'Not unless I want to go and live in Glasgow. And I think I'd unravel even more if I was that far away from my BUC.'

'Listen,' Bella said, stroking Holly's hair, 'I know today is a harder day than usual, but the past is behind you. You must try and leave it there. And as for what happens with your job – that's all in the future, you mustn't fret about it. You know they call it the present for a reason. It's the absolute best gift you can give yourself.'

Olivia stood behind Bella, miming projectile vomiting. Holly was inclined to join in. Surely a simple hug would have sufficed, she wanted to say, rather than a torrent of pop philosophy. 'Thanks sweetie, that's really helpful,' she said instead.

'Try and focus on what's happening now.' Bella began reaching into her bag.

'OK, Bella, I say this with utter love but what's happening NOW is that you're getting on my nerves. Please don't try and tell me to read *The Power of Now* again.'

Bella smiled and carried on looking in her bag.

'OR that *Excuse me, Your Life is Waiting.*'

Bella ceased rummaging in her bag and smiled resignedly. 'Suit yourself. Stay in your spiritual VACUUM.'

'I know what you need, Hol,' Harry said. 'What we all need. WHY DON'T WE ALL GO CAMPING!'

'Because camping in this country is hateful,' Olivia said.

'And we're all broke,' Bella added.

'Yeah, remember? I'm meant to be in Cuba? But I'm not, because my ex has EATEN MY MONEY and I'm unemployed in a few weeks' time!'

'OK, OK!' Harry said, ducking down to avoid imaginary bullets. 'All right, how about I look for something that's in everyone's price range, somewhere with a nice bit of nature to heal our broken souls. For next weekend. Leave it with me,' he said, placing the sellotaped laptop on his knees and Googling at hyper speed as though their lives depended on it.

23. *Bleak Camping*

'Really, Bella! We are ACTUALLY leaving the house now, right now!' Holly said, using up the last of the false deadlines.

'C'mon B, you big Faff Merchant!' Harry shouted up the stairs.

Harry and Holly were hoisting camping equipment and holdalls down to the bottom of the stairs, playing Harry's 'more than one journey is cheating' game by balancing as much as they could on their arms and hands. As Holly wedged the front door open with a camping gas stove, a catatonic Olivia arrived on the door-step.

'Liv?! I thought you hated camping!'

'I need the club, I need the club!' Olivia collapsed into tears on Holly and yelled into her hair, most of the sound being muffled by the curls: 'Take me away from this godforsaken town!'

'Oh dear. What happened?'

'That's the last time I tell ANYONE I've got feelings for them before they've told me!'

By now the whole crew of happy campers had assembled on the doorstep with their luggage.

'Whoops,' Bella said.

'Shit, sorry Liv,' Holly said, 'but at the risk of sounding rude, we have to go now or we'll miss our train. You can tell us all about it once we're on the bus.'

'Bus? No, I'll not be getting on any bus… not with all these…'
Her eyes darted towards her cavalcade of matching Louis Vuitton
shoulder bag and trolley, just next to the others' mismatched
rucksacks and supermarket carrier-bags.

'Oh not this again…' Bella began, 'Olivia. We don't earn a
hundred K a year like you. We are normal, humble bus-riding
folk.'

'Not today you're not!' she said. 'Today I am getting a taxi for
us. It's coming out of the Mandroid Foundation for the Broken-
Hearted,' she said as she stepped out into the street, scanning
Fortess Road for any amber oblongs of happiness.

'Hurrah!' Olivia yelled seconds later. 'Taxi, people, let's go!'

Holly's phone started to ring, saying 'Don't Answer' in the
robot voice.

'C'mon Hol we have to go,' Bella began.

'Shit, it's Lawrence! What do I do?'

'Don't answer. Just like the man says,' Bella said as they piled
into the back of the cab. Holly stared dumbly at the device until
Bella grabbed it and turned it off. 'There. Problem solved. Now
get in! We're going on holibobs!'

An hour or so later, they arrived at the 'campsite' in Waltham
Cross, which was essentially a car park that hadn't bothered to
be glorified. There were over fifty static caravans, all in awkwardly
close proximity. Enormous white satellite dishes balanced on top
of the caravans, like stars on unfortunate Christmas trees. Next
to them, a weather-worn lawn was dotted with rusty playground
swings and emaciated trees. Behind that, they could just make
out a bleak industrial park. Beyond that, the M11.

'You going to drink all that yourselves?' said the large, surly
campsite owner by way of a welcome as they wandered into the
site with their crates of beer. 'You'd better not make any trouble.'

The equally surly boxer dog next to him barked aggressively
as if to second that warning.

''S'not Glastonbury, you know,' the owner added, before

turning back to his mobile caravan to watch the match on Sky Sports. 'Pat!' he yelled. 'It's that lot from town.'

A moment later, a short, plump woman in a green velour tracksuit came out of the caravan with a rent book.

'Question,' Harry said afterwards as they trotted off towards their pitch. 'Why would you come all the way out here just to be in a box watching satellite television?'

'I have SO many more questions besides that,' Olivia said. 'Chief among them, why would you come here AT ALL?'

'He was right about one thing. Glastonbury this ain't,' Bella said.

'The only thing to do at this point is booze. Booze ourselves silly, in this poor man's Butlins,' Holly said, looking pointedly at Harry, along with everyone else.

'I don't know what to say,' he offered. 'Sorry guys.' He held out a can of Red Stripe to Holly by way of a peace offering.

'Thanks,' she said.

'You OK?'

She nodded. Somehow, the shock realisation that Harry had taken them for a holiday retreat at *The Only Way is Essex* meets *Scrapheap Challenge* had managed to diffuse any residual sexual tension between them.

'Oh, you're not serious. Is that all we've got to drink?' Olivia asked as they all started to unpack. 'Cheap multi-buy beer? No bubbles?'

The others exchanged eye rolls, while Harry popped open a can and slurped on it as it fizzed everywhere. 'You want bubbles?' he spat. 'Them's bubbles.'

'All right, all right!' she said, checking the alcohol content was high enough. 'Gimme beer,' she forced a stoic smile. 'Thank you.'

Four hours later, they had relocated to a scraggy patch of woodland just left of the car park, where they were dancing in the rain to a tinny stereo. They did a reclaim for Bob Dylan's 'Times They Are A Changing' for Bella. They bounced on a collapsed fence, which they had reimagined as a trampoline. They climbed really low trees. They held a weightlifting championship with an abandoned car chassis they'd found next to a burnt-out motor in the woods. They played the slowest ever game of Poohsticks, using bits of litter in the stagnant river. By eight o'clock, Holly was doing a booze run back to the tent for their final crate. When she returned, she stood back and watched the spectacle from afar. Olivia letting her hair down, pogoing to rock anthems and chain-smoking cigarettes. Harry sitting by the 'river' weaving a bracelet out of some long grass, while staring out at the motorway horizon as though it was the most sublime vista on Earth. And Bella dancing among them all, doing cartwheels and handstands.

Holly was about to jump on in there when an epiphany (and a bit of mud) stopped her in her tracks. I don't need a man to be happy, she suddenly realised. This is my family and I blinking well love them. Maybe this very moment, silly though it was, could be the high-water mark of their lives. For one brief moment, she saw how lucky she was. And how actually, one day, they might all be OK. One day, they might each find four completely deranged yet perfectly matched fuck-ups with which to settle down and spend their lives. And if they didn't, well then that was OK too. They'd have each other. And it would be one fun old people's home.

Just as she was enjoying the image of a wrinkly Harry and Bella dribbling into their slippers and Zimmer frames, she heard the opening beats to her and Lawrence's favourite Belle and Sebastian song, and burst into a run to join the others on the trampoline. As they bounced away and the song reached the chorus, she shouted 'RECLAIM!' at the top of her voice so that even the smallest animals in the woods could hear. All things considered, this night was a definite High Point (if not for the animals).

'You know what,' she said, feeling a pissed sermon brewing, 'Most people would have taken one look at this shit-hole and scarpered. But you guys – you saw it for what it could be – a gymnasium, a trampoline… Not everyone could do that. I've just realised, guys, I'm bloody well in love with you all!'

'Wooohooo!' Bella squealed, turning up the stereo, which was now blasting David Bowie. Holly bounced up and down as though her life depended on it, singing 'We can be heroes, just for one day,' as loud as her lung capacity would allow. Harry sang along with her, as he clambered onto the branches of a tree.

Later, when the heavens had opened beyond repair, they retired to the tent to enjoy a delivery from the Waltham Cross Tandoori House.

'So, Liv,' Holly began as they tucked into their tent feast, 'do you want to tell us what happened with Jonny?'

Olivia sighed. 'All right then,' she said, taking a long drag on a cigarette. 'We were at his house. We'd just had blinding sex. I was lying there watching him smoke. God, when Ross smoked I used to think how rank he smelled, but on Jonny it just looks hot. Anyway, so then I was like, "Jonny. Before I go, I was kind of hoping we could talk."'

The others nodded, listening intently.

'"Talk? What is talk?"' he goes, like he's a tourist trying on a new phrase. And I go, '"Talk. About this. Us."'

Olivia propped herself up on her elbow. 'And then I looked him right in the eye, in the naïve hope that I could somehow convey what I needed to say without words, and magically deliver it through eye contact alone. But no, nada. This man is DEAD BEHIND THE EYES!'

'Then what happened?' Holly asked.

'Then he's like, "What's with the deposition? I thought we were just going to carry on wordlessly fucking without any regard for the consequences?"'

'Bloody lawyers,' Harry said.

'I know, right? So then I said, "I thought that too." And then he went silent. And I was totally stumped. Me, the high-powered lawyer. Captain of the debating squad at Cheltenham Ladies College. Able to talk myself in, or out, of anything. Suddenly I need to defend myself against this shit-hot plaintiff, and I'm totes fucking flummoxed!'

'So?' Holly said. 'What defence did you come up with?'

'I went to pieces. I said, "Because I'm scared one of us could get hurt. And. I like you." And then he was like, "Oh, Liv. I like you too. But I'm really not in a relationship place…" And then, the more he explained why he was emotionally retarded, the more emotionally fucking needy I could feel myself becoming.'

'Wow. He's the ultimate mandroid,' Bella said.

'So it would seem,' Olivia said. 'He really is a proper Cadbury's Flake.'

Harry snorted. 'Wait. He's the crumbliest, flakiest boyfriend in the world!' and he carried on laughing to himself.

'So maybe in another dimension we might have had a future. But not in this one. He's like the Tin-bloody Man,' Olivia said, tears falling freely from her eyes.

'Oh, poor Liv,' Holly said, folding her into her arms.

'I just feel so naïve and stupid for ever thinking I could get away from this unscathed. Bella was right – when a woman has casual sex with a man, it's never as casual as they think.'

Bella was nodding sagely now. 'That crazy little thing called oxytocin.'

Holly looked blankly at Bella.

'Ultimately, women have different hormones to men. We get lumbered with the needy hormone after sex that they don't. That's all. We can try and have sex like a man but the hormones – the slippery little suckers – have other plans.'

'The science is stacked against us,' Olivia said, nodding.

Holly opened her eyes wide with interest. 'Okay. While we're doing psychobabble, I would like to posit a theory, if I may.'

'Can't we just do more tent-dancing?' Bella said.

'Stay with me, guys. I think it's a good 'un. I've been thinking about all our different break-ups, and I've decided there might be a mathematical formula.'

Olivia guffawed, while Bella shot her a 'give Hol a chance' look.

'My theory is this. Quite simply, if you are the inducer of the break-up, then sure, it may be easier at the moment of the break. But after that, when the grief sets in, then boy are you in trouble. That's when it gets harder, because you have yourself to blame for the pain, on top of the pain. Whereas, if you're the dumpee, then sure you've got it worse to begin with, because you probably didn't see it coming and they've gone and stuck a knife through your heart! But a few months in, it gets easier because at least you've got somewhere to direct your anger – you've got someone to blame other than yourself. I wish to God I could blame Lawrence for the way that I feel, but I can't because – I made this happen! I inflicted this pain on myself! I'm a dickhead!'

'But Hol, you're actually doing really well,' Harry said. 'Apart from the odd blip.'

Holly shot him an 'I think we both know that's not true' smile.

'It's a bit like a logic problem! Remember that, from our philosophy module? Let's see… if P is pain, and X is your ex, and D is the dumper, and L is how much you love the person, then the formula is P divided by L, multiplied by D, to the power of L. Whereas, if you're simply dumped the formula is much simpler. It's just P divided by L.'

Everyone stared at her, clearly awestruck by her brilliance. Or dumbfounded by how boring she was – one of the two.

'My. You're like the Carol Vorderman of break-ups,' Harry said finally.

'Oh my days. I've eaten so much, I'm in a korma coma,' Olivia said, putting down her bowl of curry and burping in a most un-Olivia-way.

Everyone looked at her in surprise.

'Pardon me. My stomach's really hurting, it doesn't know what I've just done to it.'

'While we're having epiphanies, I've got one,' Bella said, puncturing the silence. 'This trip has confirmed something for me.'

'What?' Holly asked.

'I'm BORED of my life. Just being away for this short time – even though we are in bleakest Essex – it's done me the world of good. And it's made me realise. I love you guys, but after all this crap with Sam, I need to get away. Properly.'

No one knew how to respond, so nobody did. Instead they carried on drinking, the hail pounding at the sides of their cheap Millets three-man tent.

The night passed in a heady medley of tent-dancing, tent-boozing, tent-poker, and finally, at Olivia's behest, tent-sleeping. It wasn't until they awoke early the next morning, feeling like four squished sausages in a too-hot toad-in-the-hole, that the wave finally broke.

'Eurgh,' Harry groaned. 'I can't breathe. What the EFF were we thinking – four men in a three-man? What time is it?'

'Sshhh, stop speaking. Too early,' Holly said, covering her head with her hoody.

'Too… hot…' Olivia moaned, having apparently stripped to her bra and pants in the middle of the night in an attempt to cool down.

'10 a.m. We can make it back in time for £2 breakfasts at the local greasy spoon if we leave now,' Bella said.

'I'll get the tent pegs out,' Harry announced, getting out of bed suddenly full of life and attempting to prise Holly apart from her sleeping bag.

'Oi!' she groaned.

Everyone else got up, while Holly remained welded to her sleeping bag. Eventually, they proceeded to take the tent down around her. Only when they started to roll up the groundsheet from under her did she finally give in and start to rub the sleep out of her eyes. 'OK! OK! Jesus!'

'Woooohooo. Let's get out of this wretched place,' Olivia said, helping peel a mortally hung-over Holly off the groundsheet.

Some thirty minutes later, Holly was staring out the train window at the Tottenham Hale sign, listening to the National Rail stops being called out and wondering if Clara had got herself another voice-over job, when something dawned on her.

'Wait. Guys. I've had a geographical epiphany. We could get off here and take the Tube. That would save us going all the way to Liverpool Street.'

'Oh yes. Where are we? Tottenham Hale?' Harry said. 'This is on the Vicky line isn't it. Good shout, let's do that.'

'Wow, Lawrence's train map-reading prowess has really left its mark on you, hasn't it?' Olivia said.

'Um, guys?' Bella said as they alighted all of three minutes later, at Finsbury Park. 'Speaking of maps… Are you thinking what I am?'

'That we could've actually just taken a cab the whole way?' Olivia said.

'That we've just gone on holiday THREE MILES AWAY FROM HOME!' Bella yelled as they headed towards a taxi rank.

'Ridiculous, Harry! Word of advice – never plan anything in your life ever again, OK?' Holly said, grabbing his head between her arms in a rugby tackle.

'Hey! That's not so easy, you know. I am an advertising planner – it's my job! Also, can I plead extenuating circumstances?' he said, directing it at the Lawyer.

'What do you mean?' Olivia asked.

'Look, we were all suffering from chronic heartache, we were in a hurry, and everyone kept saying they didn't want to spend much! So in my haste I picked one of the closest campsites in Google!'

Holly laughed. 'I didn't want to spend much, Harry, but that doesn't mean I'm about to go and erect a tent in the ticket hall of Holloway Road station, does it?!'

'IT DESCRIBED ITSELF AS A RURAL HAVEN!'

'Rural haven indeed,' Olivia said. 'We could sue for false advertising. Waltham Cross? Waltham bloody fuming more like.'

'You just took us camping in London!' Bella squealed. 'Hahahh!!!'

They fell about laughing.

'Had a bloody brilliant time though,' Holly said.

'Me too,' Olivia added.

'Same again next year then, yeah?' Bella said.

'What can I say?' Harry said. 'The inaugural Bleak Camping – it's the highlight of the British cultural calendar – second only to Ascot.'

'Love you guys,' Holly said, gathering them all into a big huddle just as a cab pulled up.

'You getting in or what,' grunted the cabbie.

'Bella,' Holly said as they squeezed into the back, 'can you remember your big speech last night? When you said you were bored of your life… what did you mean?'

Bella looked sheepish.

'Oh, she was kidding, weren't you B? She was six beers in!' Olivia said.

Bella shook her head.

'This going away thing – you're not serious?'

'I've never been so sure of anything. I need a break from the singing. Or the distinct bloody lack of singing! I was constantly in work last year. So I think while I'm in this quiet patch, and now I've finally finished the course at Guildhall, I should use the time to get away, rather than do any more gigs at the pub. If nothing else, I don't seem to have the willpower you guys do about not seeing the ex. Even though I know I said he's gone off, there's part of me that still loves him and still wants to keep seeing him. No, I need to face up to the fact that as long as I'm still living in the same TFL zone as him, I'm never going to get over him! So yeah… I'M OUT, guys,' she said in closing, like she'd just lost at a game of Twister.

The others were quiet while they took on board the notion of losing a core member. Holly felt like a piece of her arm was about to go missing. 'But you were only quoting Samuel Johnson DAYS ago!'

Bella looked puzzled.

'"He who is tired of London…" and all that?'

'Oh. I thought I came up with that?'

Holly tried another tack. 'But what will we do without you? You're like my lifeline!'

Bella looked down at the floor of the hackney carriage and studied the bits of dirt so no one would see her eyes welling. 'We're all each other's lifelines now. But I'll continue to be that from the other side of the world. The minute you have a crisis of any sort, or a 3 a.m. craving to talk, I'll jump on Skype! I'm sorry guys. It's not you. It's me – I don't like to stay in one place too long. I'm a Romany at heart and if I don't move every few years I start to feel like I'm gathering dust!'

'Oh, love you too!' Holly said.

'Oh, don't be like that.'

'No, it's a great idea,' Harry said, 'we're happy for you, aren't we?' He looked around the cab at their faces. The girls nodded, one by one.

'Ha. You're just happy because you've done the maths already and worked out who'll be taking my room!' Bella teased. 'Tssshhh! The bed's not even cold yet…'

Harry grinned as Holly realised the implications of this. There was every chance that their accidental foray into the Circle of Sexual Disgust was about to get an Nth degree more awkward, she thought, as her phone beeped with an email.

Jeremy.Philpott@TotesamazeProductions.com
Holly.Braithwaite@TotesamazeProductions.com; Pascal.
Brown@ TotesamazeProductions.com
Subject: The Madhouse

Team,
I bring triffic tidings. Channel 5 have BOUGHT The Madhouse. They've ordered a whole season, so it will be six months of solid cutting.

Because of the round-the-clock nature of the footage,

I'm going to need to keep you both on, for longer hours than on Prowl, too.

Good news is they want to move super-fast on this. We're straight into preproduction. Casting begins next week (we've got meetings at the Maudsley et. al.), and we're scouting locations already.

You're both pencilled to start w/c 13th July, so that gives you a couple of week's respite from when Prowl finishes.

All that's left to say is well done and thanks! Especially you Hol, I'd never have got that meeting with C5 without your Break-up Club as bait.

Jx

'Whoop!' shouted Holly. 'Not only has Jez said thank you for the first time ever, but I've also just got another six months' guaranteed work! Hurray!'

'That's great Hol!' Bella yelled, while Harry was frowning.

'Yay! Something's going right for once.'

'Are you sure you want to take it though?'

'It's security, Harry. In a time where I have absolutely none.'

'You don't think it's a tiny bit like building yourself a whole new prison, in which to serve a whole new sentence?'

'Or you could try to be happy for me. Hey, at least you won't have to keep helping me with my rent.'

'What's the new show about?' Bella asked.

'I'd rather not say. It's come from the land that taste forgot.'

Bella's eyebrows raised. 'You promise it's not Break-up Club?'

'NO! Look, maybe I'll let you see it when it airs, depending how bad it is.'

'Well, I think it's great news, Hol, well done!'

'Thanks, Bella,' Holly said as the truth finally hit her. She'd just agreed to spend another six months of her life alone in a broom cupboard, making morally destitute telly with a middle-aged sociopath for company.

24. *Leaving on a Jet Plane*

Holly was sat in the centre of the living room, surrounded by torn-up newspapers, brown tape and sheets of bubble wrap, which they were all trying their best not to jump up and down on. For the last few nights, they had gone to sleep with the sound of the brown tape dispenser reverberating in their ears.

'OK, that's the last one,' she said, wiping the dust from her face and leaving a trail of newspaper print all over her cheek.

'You're an absolute legend!' Bella said, throwing her arms around her.

'I can't believe you're going so soon. It's barely been a month since you first mentioned it.'

'Yeah, but I can't wait to go and get started on the work out in India.'

'You make it sound like you're going to work in an orphanage! Isn't it your mate's bar in Palolem?'

'Well, working in a bar is a step towards character growth for me!'

Harry popped his head round the corner.

'Hey, neighbour,' he said, smiling at Holly.

'How you finding your upgrade from the sofa?'

'Good thanks. Although there wasn't a mint chocolate on my

pillow? I rather hoped I'd get one for the inflated cost per night…'

'Oh hardy har,' she grinned. 'Bellarama, we need to get going if you're going to make your flight.'

'I'm just going for a swim but I'll meet you at the airport,' Harry said, who had recently signed up for a triathlon on a drunken whim with Olivia.

'OK, sporting mentalist!'

'Don't knock it, Holly. Sport has given me a PURPOSE these last few weeks. I think you'd benefit from it too,' he said, mid-lunge.

'GO Sport!'

'Piss off. I'll see you at T5.'

*

'God, airports are cathedrals of heartache, aren't they?' Holly said, looking around the crowded terminal. 'Checking in, checking out. Left luggage. Baggage reclaim… going in different directions… Christ, they're a metaphorical field day!'

'If you choose to see it that way,' Bella said, trying to remain upbeat despite Holly's exponential doom.

Staring at the revolving doors towards Departures, Holly couldn't help imagining she and Lawrence rushing through them, only just making the check-in deadline, racing to stock up on provisions from Boots and WH Smith – doing that 'divide and conquer' thing they always did when they were in shops and short of time.

'You're regressing again, aren't you? You're watching old movies of you and Lawrence?'

'You've got me. Sorry, it's just that being here is making me think about how me and Lawry were meant to be here together, going to Cuba…'

'Oh sweet Lord! Be kinder to yourself, Hol! You have to stop thinking like that; it's actually self-harm. Just do what you'd do at work. Delete the tape, or something. Wipe it clean!'

'You're right. And sorry, today is meant to be about you.'

'That's all right. But listen, you could quite easily have gone on another three years with Lawrence, larking about having fun, despite knowing that, deep down, you weren't right for each other long term. If you'd been to Cuba, all you'd have got would be three weeks of happy memories.'

'Which is bad, how exactly?'

'Hear me out! You see, happy memories have this bleak way of turning their back on you and making themselves into sad ones – they actually torment you! So by not going you've triumphed because you've got less in what I call the SadBank.'

'The SadBank?'

'Yeah, it's like a WankBank – you know, where blokes store pictures of their naked ex-girlfriends so they can check in any time they're having a play. The SadBank by contrast, is a receptacle of the happy times you spent together. So, when you're mourning someone, you indulge in memories of you together, which become sad by virtue of how you use them. So it's a relief you didn't go to Cuba, just to get three more weeks of happy memories. AND! Here comes the best part. You would have PAID two grand for the privilege! Seems like a steal now, doesn't it?'

Holly stared at Bella, feeling her eyes growing hot.

'Thanks, B. You know, in all this time, no one's been able to make me feel any better about my being essentially bankrupt. But now I can actually see some sort of bright side. Ball-bags, I'm going to miss you.'

Bella smiled and pinched Holly's cheek. 'And you, you massive wally. OH! Before I forget!' She delved into her bag and handed Holly a purple crepe paper oblong. 'Here. I got you something.'

'Oh, I didn't get you diddly squat!'

'It's nothing, really…'

Holly took the parcel and began tearing through the paper.

'I mean really. It's literally nothing,' Bella added.

Holly saw the words 'minty fresh' and her eyes welled up.

'It's a symbol of you making a new start.'

'I know what it is.'

'It's also the only tube of toothpaste I've ever bought for the house.' Bella smiled.

'There's that, too.'

'But hey, you always loved me for the emotional and humorous contributions I brought to the household, rather than my financial ones, didn't you?!'

'I'm almost certain poor Daniel saw it that way.'

'Oh! Plus you can use it on your spots!'

'That's so sweet. Thanks B.'

'Passengers on Flight BA305 to Mumbai please proceed to departures,' went the tannoy.

'Shit, that's me. Here I go then!' Bella said, suddenly looking like a lost child saying goodbye to her parents on her first day at school. Holly put her arm around her.

'Shit-sticks. What the FUCK am I doing?' she shouted into Holly's sleeve. 'I don't know the first thing about India, OR being an intrepid backpacker. This is madness, stop me!'

'Breathe,' came Olivia's bellowing voice. 'You're going to be brilliant!'

'Guys! You made it!' Bella smiled, her first-day-at-school nerves fluttering away.

'Sorry, we got stuck on the Tube! Signal failure,' Olivia said. 'I said we should have left earlier…'

'Oh, never mind, you're here now!'

'You'd better go if you're going to make it through security in time,' Harry said, looking at Bella's extensive luggage.

'Right. BYE KIDS!' she squealed, gathering her bags.

'BUC forever, yes?' Olivia said.

'What are we, eight?' Harry said.

'Oh there's no point trying to fight it anymore,' Olivia said. 'Shut up and huddle.'

'Shut up and cuddle!' Bella yelled. 'Love you guys.'

285

'OK. BUC forever,' Holly said, pronouncing forever more like 'whatever'.

'Remember,' Bella said from within the huddle, 'my little buccaneers, I may well be four thousand miles away but I shall be in each of your hearts the whole time.'

Holly mimed projectile vomiting. 'Just be safe, Belle. Try not to do anything stupid, please.'

'I won't. I'll be emailing or blogging as soon as I can get over my technophobia. Listen, all of you – be strong. We will all get through this godforsaken time, we will! See you on the other side...'

And with that she was gone. They all stared after her as she scurried towards security, fumbling with little plastic see-through bags while trying to down a two-litre bottle of water.

'And then there were three,' Olivia said.

25. *Somebody That I Used to Know*

A week later, Holly looked down at her brand spanking new tube of Bicarbonate of Soda Extra Whitening toothpaste, and had the world's first ever fluoride-based epiphany. She opened the tube and applied a hefty dollop of incandescent white sludge to her toothbrush.

It was time! Time to find a new man, she decided, brushing a bit too hard and getting a mild taste of blood.

Two minutes later, she knocked on Harry's door.

'OK then. It's time. I've more than served my notice now. Get me a date. Anyone will do, just get me back out there. I'm nearly 28! It's a numbers game now; let's get this party started!'

'Jesus, is it possible to come up on fluoride? I've not seen you this high since Glasto '08!'

'I'm just bored of being locked up,' she said, her face turning overcast like Swansea on a summer's day as she thought about her lacklustre love life. 'I've been celibate so long my hymen's almost certainly grown back. Let me at them! Militancy is all!'

'Not sure that's the way to a man's heart, Hol. Maybe you should redirect some of this wonderful energy at your new show?' he said, squeezing past her in the doorway. 'Anyway sorry, I'm late for work.'

'Ugh. Don't remind me. Rumour has it, today's episode features a woman with OCD cat-fighting a man who has ADD, over which of them has it worse off.'

'Brutal.'

'It's a career high, for sure…'

Later that night, at BUC, Holly tried again. 'Can't somebody gateway me? Anybody?' she cried out in their darkened booth at the Big Blue.

'What's a gateway when it's at home?' Olivia asked.

'Is it where we each bring a new friend to the club, someone's that recently become single?' Harry asked. 'If we're doing that now, I've got a mate at work that's just been dumped, and he's seriously keen on joining.'

'I'm not so sure. I think we've got enough on our plates at the moment,' Olivia said, doing her best not to look at Holly.

'That's charitable, Liv!' Holly said. 'Anyway, no that's not what gateway means. Gateway is something B. and I came up with, and means, Verb: to introduce a friend to an arena of new men, through someone you've met through work, your home life or any other means, with the express purpose of preventing them from having to enter the cesspit of online dating, or to have to confine themselves to a life spent swiping left with their finger.'

'Well that's a good enough cause if ever I heard one,' Harry said. 'I mean, online dating certainly isn't what I imagined ever telling my grandkids about.'

'But you may not have any grandkids if you don't,' Olivia said.

'And BOSH! Therein lies the paradox of modern mating,' Holly said.

And so began round one: the scanning of each other's Facebook friends. First up, they went through Harry's friend list, from which Holly selected a shortlist of singletons. The lucky ones were then messaged: 'Congratulations, you've been picked for a blind date with the lovely Holly Braithwaite!'

Minutes later, Archibald, the most creatively named of the

selection, messaged back to say, 'OK! But it's not blind is it, she's on your Facebook.' To which Harry replied, 'OK pedant, call it a "partially sighted" date then!' To which Archie replied, 'Sounds like a plan, what's her number?'

'EEK. Looks like The Hol's got herself a date,' Harry said, slamming shut his laptop.

'Hurrah. My first partially sighted date! Thanks Harry – I shall report back here in a week!'

'Is it me or, wasn't that basically like being on My Single Friend?' Olivia asked.

'Sshhh,' Harry said, in a 'don't let Holly hear you say that' kind of a way. 'It's nothing like it!' he added.

She was too excited to hear, anyway.

*

A week later in Stoke Newington, as the beginners swing class drew to a close, three sweaty musketeers sat down for a drink and a post-mortem of Holly's partially sighted date.

'So Holly – your first night back OUT there! How did it go?' Olivia asked.

'I know, right? A big day! But it was pretty much a disaster on every level. First of all, he showed up wearing these big framed glasses – and I was like, I didn't know you wore glasses? He never had them in any of his Facebook pictures? But then he was like, I got them in Top Man. So then I said, I didn't know they did eye tests now, and he said no, they're lens-free. I mean, are people doing that now? I thought it was just a Shoreditch myth?'

'No, no. It's all true,' Olivia said.

'Fake glasses indeed' Holly said. 'Honestly, it's like they're mocking the blind! What's next on the catwalks, EAR TRUMPETS?'

'WHEELCHAIRS?' Harry said.

'I do remember reading about a lovely line of neck braces at Stella McCartney's last show,' Olivia said.

'Really?' Holly asked.

'NOOOO!' they all yelled.

'Oh.' Holly sighed into her fruit beer.

'So anyway, what happened next with old Nathan Barley?' Harry asked.

'I went full nut-nut. I think to try and overcompensate for the fact I wasn't feeling it, I got a bit too chatty. He's in a similar field to me, as a TV producer – so we got talking about that. But then when he asked me what I did, I got confused and thought I was in a job interview. I forgot what you're meant to do on a date and turned into a talking CV! I guess because I'm worried what I'll do next if Madhouse bombs. But I couldn't stop myself. Kept telling him about all my previous jobs, where I wanted to be next; where I saw myself in five years' time. The poor guy just politely went along with it, and I could tell by then that he wasn't feeling it, at all!' Holly said, breaking into sobs of laughter and shame in equal parts. 'I mean, even though I knew I didn't fancy him, I still wanted him to like me! Is that fucked up?'

'A smidge,' Olivia said.

'It gets worse though. Then when I offered to buy him another drink, he said he wasn't feeling well and wanted to head home. I mean, am I that terrible company?'

She shoved a handful of mayo-laden chips into her mouth, one of them falling back out onto the table.

'No, Hol, you're scintillating, always,' Harry said.

'I can't even attract people I don't fancy. How am I ever going to nab one I like?'

'Maybe you need to try a little less hard. Maybe they can smell it on your pheromones?' Olivia said as a mobile phone rang out, making her jump.

'Fuck-sticks. It's Jonny.'

'Don't answer it,' Holly said. 'In fact. Go one better. Rule Number Six – re-save his name as "Don't Answer".'

Olivia smiled with approval and did as she was told. 'Done. Now, let's talk about something else.'

For one whole minute no one could think of anything to say. All they could see and hear was the buzzing and flashing of Olivia's phone on the table in front of them.

'Balls. Don't Answer has left me a message. Be rude not to listen,' she said, heading outside so she could hear over the Charleston music.

When she returned, her face had dropped.

'He's only gone and lost his job,' she said. 'He sounded dreadful. Like he's lost the will to live.'

'Not your problem,' Holly said. 'Don't engage.'

'He was all, "Can we meet up please? I'm lost without you." Poor thing. I really want to see him! Should I? CAN I?' She looked pleadingly at the others.

'No Liv. He doesn't get to see you now! He's not your responsibility,' Holly said.

'He's such a scrote. So typical of him to want you now he's down,' Harry said, shoving a drink into her hand while Holly physically restrained her from touching her phone by forcing her into a cuddle.

Once Olivia was suitably calm again, her phone stowed in her handbag, Holly turned to face the others. 'Guys, don't be upset, but I'm not sure I'm really feeling this swing-dancing malarkey. I might chip off. I mean, there's no one in the class that isn't gay or engaged.'

'I KNOW, RIGHT!' Olivia said in a tone that said, 'I think we should ask for our money back.'

'Woah! Back up, both of you!! You're getting it all wrong,' Harry said. 'We didn't take up swing dancing so we could fall in love. We took it up to enhance our lives, to find joy again, to make use of the gift of time, remember, Liv? It was your idea? And it was a good one, actually,' he said as the instructor started calling for people to come back into the class.

'You're right. Come on. Let's give it another go,' Olivia said, and they all slowly put their dancing shoes back on.

*

'Going, Going Goa', by @LadyGoa

Oh Hai!!!

    Sorry sorry sorry

    Sorry sorry sorry…

    Sorry sorry sorry…

    …that I've not written yet. But lots to tell!

    Actually, shit – this computer terminal that I'm on has a freaky countdown timer on it, so I'm gonna have to be real quick. More detail to follow in another email! But for now, a quick update:

    - I appear to have landed in some kind of theme park, populated only with people in Thai Fisherman's pants trying to 'find themselves'. So I don't need to tell you that the man thing isn't quite happening just yet. Nope. Bella Allen cannot get a wide-on from someone wearing pants so baggy they're adjustable according to how much curry-based gluttony goes on. Not sexy. As such, The Dry Patch continues unabated.

    - The curry's about as hot as Alan Titchmarsh's Y-fronts. But as someone who was always a bit of a lame korma gal, I'm quite OK with this.

    - I can't help feeling like a massive cliché for being in this part of India. It's about as intrepid as Center Parcs out here, so I needn't have worried about the lack of guide-book. Also, the Gap Yahs are everywhere (as predicted). They all have unlimited budgets and double-barrelled names (as predicted).*

    - I probably should go somewhere further afield. I could

try and go trekking in the Himalayas or go somewhere more remote, but to be honest even that's a cliché in some circles. So I'm just going to stay where the nice beaches are and eat curry and do yoga, meditate and most of all, get Sam out of my head.

(On this point – Sam, if you're reading this, sorry, but you're not supposed to be. That was the whole point of this exercise. You can live without me, but you love sex; and I can't live without you, plus have no shame, remember? So where does that leave us? Me: 4, 500 miles away and £749 poorer. And all because we lack the will-power not to see each other while we're in the same country. Dur! Now go on… off you pop.)

Ahhhh I just looked at the scary clock and I can prac-tically hear the *Countdown* theme music so I'd better sign off. Sorry this is a bit all over the place and has no real structure or purpose! In many ways, an accurate depiction of me in person then.

Bye for now. More soon, Namaste…. (yeah, insert all the other obvious hobo catchphrases.)

B xxxxxxxxx

P.S. Here's an idea – and possibly the only way you'll get through my travel posts without flatlining from boredom – shall we make a game called 'Travel Bore Bingo'? Then all my lovely devoted readers can cross them off as and when? First item on there – HENNA TATTOOS. Considering getting one? Or even a proper grown-up one, like one that I'll think means something deep in Mandarin but actually reads 'Chicken chow mein'? Talk me out of it?

P.P.S. How are my little buccaneeros doing? How are all the dates going? Are you still swinging? Miss your faces. Hope you're all looking out for one another and remem-bering THE RULES.

P.P.P.S. Hol – good luck in the new job, if you've started already I hope it's less direful than the last…

P.P.P.P.S. I've just realised that this ISN'T A LETTER. Sorry, I'm new to this blogging stuff.

BYE!

(2 comments)

Holly clicked to see who the comments were from. The first was from Olivia:

'Loving the blog, B. Am working on the designs for Travel Bore Bingo as we speak. Be safe and remember your malaria tablets, even when you're drunk please! xxx

The second was Sam:

'OK, OK, I'm just reading the first one then I'm out of here. Take care of you. Bon voyage ma cherie, Sammy xxx

26. Eating for Two

As anyone knows, a life in the shadow of a recent break-up is a life half-lived. Charismatically bankrupt, you're essentially the human equivalent of a dot dot dot… in a perpetual state of intermission, loading up on butterscotch ice cream while you wait for the curtains to open on the next act of your life. Of course, Holly's co-members had briefed her to expect a 'sad-gap' of some duration. But eight months? That was almost enough time to grow a small person in her belly! When all she felt was pregnant with regret.

Having made it through two whole seasons, Holly was now dragging her worn-down heels into autumn. This particular Thursday morning had begun like any other, with Holly waking up late, opening one eye to see The Alps spread out before her. The Alps being her very own mountain range of screwed-up balls of white tissues, whose only orienteers were little deposits of dried snot and tears. Were it not for them, she might have been able to forget that once again she'd wailed herself to sleep. But no, The Alps were her trusty reminder of a night spent wallowing in self-pity. The one thing casting some light over The Alps was a postcard tacked to the wall from Kerala, which said, 'STOP MOPING. Love you, bye, Bella x'

Five snoozes in, Holly peeled back the covers and slid out of bed to the floor. Slowly she raised herself up off the dusty carpet and walked over to the mirror. 'Mirror, mirror on the wall, who's the most remedial BUC member of them all?' she said aloud. She leaned into the glass and stared in at the cracked layers of make-up, each one shrouding the next; concealing layer upon layer of nights where she'd come in drunk, add to the base coat of make-up, then go straight out again for another spin on the dating merry-go-round. The more nights she went out, the more of a cosmetic Russian doll she became. Accordingly, the more she went out, the more her pimples had babies, and the more wrinkles shot up alongside them! How was it possible to have the youthfulness of acne, but also the lines of a wrinkly has-been? This was surely dermatological injustice of the highest degree, she lamented, staring at the mirror and sticking out her bottom lip.

Sometimes she toyed with the idea of completely removing herself from society for a year while the 'sad-gap' passed. She thought of a story her father had once told her, about when the composer Mendelssohn had just been dumped. Her dad's story had it that old Felix had headed for the Outer Hebrides to a place called Fingal's Cave, to hide himself from the world and have a proper good mope. When he emerged he wrote the 'Hebrides Overture', one of his most famous, beautiful pieces. So maybe she could do that – go back home to live with her parents in Sutton Coldfield, and re-emerge months later from the chrysalis like a creative butterfly, having finally come up with a feature film or TV drama that was going to change the world and liberate her from the world's most odious boss.

But then, as she pulled off her cocoon of leggings and tartan pyjamas and wrapped her threadbare towel around her shivering body, she realised that in her case all that would happen would be this: she would put on two stone from her parents' cooking, and re-emerge into the world, not a butterfly but a slug with a terminal addiction to *Jeremy Kyle* and *Loose Women*. No; far better to stay in London where there were distractions from her pain, and keep on trying to put one foot in front of the other. She'd just keep editing one dreadful episode of The Madhouse after another.

*

Holly turned the key in the lock, remembering to be quiet for Daniel and Harry, after another big fat NON of a night, unsealed with a kiss. Sealed instead with the vapid stench of broken dreams.

The thing was, a bad date was more than just a mediocre evening to go in the dusty photo albums at the back of your mind. It was actually a stinker of a setback, because it made you miss your ex more. No, a bad date could set you back weeks, she realised as she slumped onto the sofa and started flicking through TV channels.

Sure, they'd had their good points about them, the guys she'd dated. Some had been really cultured and well-travelled! And none of them had done that annoying clicky thing Lawrence used to do with his teeth when he ate too fast. Or – thank Christ – that jittery thing he did with his eyebrows. Or, come to think of it, tapping his feet under the table like a mad fidgeter even though there was no music playing.

But then, the flip side was that all the men she'd been dating would also have a whole bunch of stuff about them that was not Lawrence. Like, they'd order food without asking if she'd made up her mind. Or they'd make a loud remark about what a healthy appetite she had. Little things. Or, sometimes there just wouldn't be enough of a spark. Or worse, there wasn't enough nonsense chat, the kind that Harry had talked about. Sometimes the conversation was so wooden that Holly would get to the end of the evening thinking more than ever about the one person she was trying so hard to forget. About all the little things she used to

297

love about him, or still did. Suddenly she'd be forgiving him his every flaw, as though, if she could only have just one evening back with him, just to watch him tap his feet and do his eyebrow twitch thing, and his clicky thing with his teeth, she would jump at the chance. And by the time she was grovelling in her handbag for her keys at the end of the night, she'd be wishing to God she'd just stayed in and folded laundry while watching *Wife Swap USA* or some other mind-numbing rubbish. At least two dysfunctional, mismatched spouses from Minneapolis couldn't make you feel this low, Holly realised, heading to the fridge to spend some time with her NBF, the refrigerator.

Once she'd consumed some leftover meat pie, she opened up her laptop and turned it on. She spotted a document on her desktop called 'Mind The Gap' out the corner of her eye, and felt a twinge of guilt as she went straight onto Facebook to stare idly at her newsfeed – where she learned that her housemate in the room downstairs had 'just completed a five kilometre run with Olivia Mahoney'. She began to type in a comment, 'EFF OFF; I've just completed a really large pie,' before chickening out and deleting the post.

Sometimes, in the absence of any willpower, she toyed with the idea of asking Daniel if he'd mind them getting a lock on the kitchen door. Or even the fridge itself? It had become normal practice, this need to head straight to the kitchen as soon as she arrived home of an evening. Somehow it was OK when she and Bella used to raid the fridge together and sit up in the kitchen snacking after a night out. But now that she'd gone, the habit didn't seem fun anymore, just weirdly gluttonous; an act of staggering loneliness. Instead of coming home to feast on a big slice of a man, she would feast on a big slice of oven-roasted emptiness.

As she munched her way through the pie, she closed the fridge and leaned on it a while. A tear rolled down Holly's cheek. Bollocks, she missed Bella. The house was so horribly quiet without her. As she descended the stairs down to bed, she recalled all the things she thought she'd never miss. The sound of Bella's vocal warm-up exercises – 'AH AH EE EE OH OH' – over and over, louder and louder. The constant smell of popping corn in the morning. The toothpaste face-masks. She climbed into bed, and fell to sleep watching replayed footage of all the above.

The next morning, Holly awoke feeling with absolute certainty of two things: 1) this whole BUC business had been nothing but a curse, and 2) if she were to randomly see Lawrence in the street ever again, she would, without hesitation, run up to him, fling her arms around his legs, say sorry and beg him back. But why wait 'til then – surely now was as good a time as any? She looked at her clock to see it was 8.52 a.m. She picked up her mobile and began looking for his number in the 'L's. Then she remembered why she couldn't find it. He was still saved in the D's. Her finger hovered over 'Don't Answer', and touched it briefly. Calling… But then she cancelled it a second later. Maybe first she should kick things off with a breezy text about what do with the bag of Lawry leftovers?

Suddenly the phone began to play 'The Littlest Hobo', by way of a final snooze alarm, reminding her that she really needed to get up and go to work. She threw the phone onto the bed, resolving to call Lawrence later, when she'd had some caffeine to help her speak. She went to the bathroom. The door was locked, but there was a smell emerging from under it.

'Urggh, Harry! Are you smoking in the shower again? You rancid toad! To think, we took you in off the streets and this is our thanks…' Holly teased.

'Shit, sorry, I thought you'd gone to work!'

She heard the click of the lock, which in housemate code was the cue to open the door.

'No, I'm late again!' she said, opening the door to see Harry with a towel round his hips. 'Please don't look at my face. I'm subhuman.'

'Don't be stupid.'

'Anyway, that doesn't make it OK – if Dan knew, he'd throw you onto the street!'

'Sorry, I'm just a bit of an addict at the moment; I've ordered some patches. I'm going to quit any day now – I need to for the triathlon.'

Holly started brushing her teeth while he was towelling himself dry. She tried not to think about how close to his naked torso she was again.

'Well you've made me feel better about my increasing booze dependency at least,' she said, trying to avert her eyes from the way he was tying his towel around his perfectly contoured body, peppered with ginger hairs.

'Have you seen Bella's new blog post?' he said, oblivious to her gawping.

'Oh good, she's alive! It's been ages!'

'Such is Bella,' he said as he left the bathroom. 'I'm off in a sec, have a good day.'

Holly stepped into the shower, trying to be as quick as possible so she could get back to the computer to read Bella's blog; and trying not to think about her best friend's even-more-toned-than-before-tummy. Damn that triathlon. Damn it to high heaven.

'She's not dead!'(As Brent said to Gareth in *The Office*)
By @LadyGoa

Dearests,
It's with my tail between my legs that I address you now. I'm so sorry – I promised you a longer post ages ago. I've no excuse. I've just been in this massive whirlwind of amazingness. That, and I ran out of money well ahead of schedule, so I had to go to a more deserted resort. But it's not all bad – I got me a singing job in a bar with an old friend from drama school!

So anyway, the long version is in the post, as it were. I know I keep saying that, but my shift starts in fifteen minutes! So for now, I give you the news in brief:

* Did some travelling around. Saw some shit. Took lots of pictures. Lost camera and all the pictures on it. Made lots of friends. Took new pictures. Had new camera nicked. Gave up on photography; now committing things to own memory instead.

* Finished seeing shit, and am now two months into working at the bar which is owned by Keith from Wolverhampton and isn't as bleak as it sounds. I am lead waitress and lead vocals/ headline act! Have literally been singing for my supper the last few weeks! Awesomenal.

* Been eaten alive by mosquitoes – so far have acquired no less than 47 bites. On one forearm alone. See pic attached. Ridick! Deet does shit all, nor does that citrusy stuff. Oh well at least I've not got malaria… yet. And on the plus side I'm having some properly trippy dreams on the larium.

* Recently had to get the owner of beach hut camp here to hacksaw into my beach hut, as I'd left the key in my documents pouch in my hut for safe-keeping. Seriously, who'd be me? Still, owner was hot and let me buy him a drink to say thanks. (Note to BUC – hooray, am getting a tiny bit better!)

* Have found my favourite hammock – right down at the end of the beach, which is the perfect spot for star-gazing and composing. Here's an obligatory pic to make you all jealous while you're at work. SORRY. But it's not like I've not been working. The bar-shifts are loooong, and in my spare time I've written tonnes of new songs, many of which inspired by this special, magical place! Will upload them to my SoundCloud soon.

* One thing that's nice in all the bars and restaurants on the beach is that they have this rule that you can't enter unless you're barefooted. As a gesture of respect you all leave your flip-flops outside. My friend Hazel says it's like a modern-day Cinderella because you never know whose are whose flip-flops so you have to try and find the owners. Often, you end up having to steal through necessity when yours go missing – just so you've got something to walk home in. It's not so much that I've resorted to petty thievery – it's just that after a while it gets to the point where now no one's that possessive over them. A bit like biros or hair bobbles I guess… You just add your bit to the pool.

But I digress. You all have busy lives. You don't want to hear about flip-flops and larium. Also, this keyboard's sticking like a mo-fo and I can't find half the punctuation I need. LOVE YOU ALL. Oh and BUC – I hope you are looking out for each other and helping each other through the rancid turmoil that is life as a singleton in the big smoke. Lord knows I wish I had the BUC bosom with me right now. It's Sam's birthday and I'm missing him more than ever :((((

So much love and huggage for now, Bellington xXx

Holly experienced the usual pang of sadness coupled with guttural snorts that only a Bella blog could bring out in her. She briefly flirted with the idea of throwing in her job and flying out to join her, before remembering that Lawrence had cleaned out her bank account. As she clicked the Back button and returned to Facebook, her eyes landed on something on her newsfeed. Nestling in among the broadcasts of babies and engagements from people she hadn't seen since Double German, something caught her eye, and a new gaggle of moths arrived in the pit of her belly.

PART THREE

"Dance as though no one is watching you
Sing as though no one can hear you
Love as though you have never been hurt...'

Origin unknown

27. *Here's What You Could've Won*

Skype conversation between LadyGoa, DirtyHarry, and JustLiv.

JL: Guys, has anyone seen or heard from Holly?

DH: I don't think she's back from work yet.

JL: She was meant to meet me for a drink in town hours ago, but her phone's been off all afternoon and she's not answering texts.

LG: That's not like her! I hope she's OK! I've not heard from her in a while.

DH: I saw her this morning. She wasn't on the best form. Let me just go and see if her bag's still there. Back in a sec...

...Nope, the bag she always takes to work is still there.

JL: Maybe she just took a different bag to work? We're overreacting.

DH: I don't know. It's not like her to stand you up is it?

JL: Should we call her parents, see if they've seen her?

LG: I doubt she'd go to them. She said they've not been all that understanding over Lawrence... They keep telling her she did the wrong thing.

DH: Oh... actually. This is beyond ridiculous, but there is one place she could be...

*

Half an hour later, Harry and Olivia arrived at Hyde Park Corner station and began winding their way through the park towards the Serpentine pond. There, crouched under a tree with dripping-wet hair, was Holly. Her face was overcast and her eyes were as red as an old telephone box.

'There you are!' Olivia said.

'What are you doing here?' Holly said. Then, a beat later, 'Shit, Liv, I'm so sorry, I totally forgot about us meeting up!'

'God, don't worry about that,' Olivia said, 'what the hell's happened? Look at the state of you!'

Holly opened her mouth to speak, but a lump in her throat prevented her. Harry wrapped her up in his arms. 'How did you know I was here?' she managed through sobs.

'I had a hunch,' he said. 'Remember, you told me all about your dark secret once?'

Holly looked down at her shivering feet, embarrassed.

Harry turned to Olivia. 'Right before they went to sleep, they'd agree a place to meet up in their dreams. And the Serpentine was one of their many destinations.'

Holly nodded. 'It's all true. I would say, "See you in the Serpentine; don't forget your trunks…"'

'Blimey. That would be sweet if it wasn't so gay,' Olivia said while she mimed vomiting.

'Yeah. Well. It's not sweet anymore. I won't be saying it to him again. EVER.'

'What's happened?' Harry said.

Holly fell to her knees in a display of unabashed melodrama, the likes of which had only ever been displayed by Bella. Then, after a few minutes she realised she was twenty-seven years of age, wiped her eyes and apologised.

'Don't worry,' Olivia said. 'It's all part of the process.'

'Thanks guys. You're my lifeline, you are.'

'Can we just back up a bit?' Harry said. 'What exactly has happened?'

The three of them laid out their winter coats and huddled together under a tree, like a dysfunctional equivalent of school carpet story time.

'So,' Holly began, 'this morning I read Bella's blog. And then I accidentally went back onto EngagedBook, where she'd posted it. Then I started looking at my stupid newsfeed, and I saw something about how James, Lawrence's best mate, was "attending Lawrence and Anna's engagement drink". First of all I'm like, "who's Lawrence?" Because there's no way in the world those two words—"Lawrence" and "engaged"'belong in the same SENTENCE, RIGHT? But then I looked at the event. The PUBLIC EVENT, which any fucker can click on.'

'What the shit?' Harry said.

'You're having a laugh,' Olivia said.

'It was called Lawrence and Anna's Engagement Drink. Just "drink" mind, not "drinks", like they're trying to be all humble, with it… like it's just "a quiet little celebration, in a quiet little pub in Brixton".'

'Unbelievable,' Harry said.

'Who on earth is this Anna?'

'Fucked if I know.'

'What did you do? Did you call him an insensitive prick for not even trying to tell you first?' Olivia said.

'Well maybe he did try – in fairness, he did email, and tried to call the other day, but I wasn't allowed to answer!'

'Ooops, sorry Hol,' Olivia said. 'My bad.'

'So no, I didn't do anything. I went numb; I just sat there and kind of laughed. I mean, how is it that he's there already, and I actually haven't progressed at all?'

'If anything you've regressed,' Olivia said, prompting a prod from Harry.

'Fair,' Holly said.

'Did you go to work today?' Harry asked.

'I was about to, but when I saw the news I was actually almost sick and had to have a lie-down. Then I thought, hey, I've only had one sick day in two whole years, so I made the executive decision to press the Fuck-It Button. Rang in sick, came here with a bottle of wine, had a little splash about…' she trailed off, her eyes wistful, an unhinged smile dancing on her lips.

'Splash about? While under the influence of booze? You could have drowned, you numpty,' Olivia said, 'plus, it's Oct-Fucking-Tober!'

'Numpty Dumpty,' Harry said, taking his coat and draping it over Holly's shoulders.

'I know, I'm pathetic.' Holly wiped her eyes. 'It was just such a shock.'

'You had us worried. You went full 404.'

'WTF?' Holly said.

'It's Geek Speak for when someone goes missing. Sorry, another Ross-ism. It just slipped out.'

'Well, at least we're here now,' Harry said, 'so you're no longer a lonely tramp in a park. We're now a group of tramps in a park.'

'What's the collective noun for that, a group of tramps?' Olivia asked.

'Trumps?' Holly said. 'As in "old farts"?'

'Right,' Harry said officiously. 'I'm going to go and get us some ice creams, and the finest wine available to humanity. Back soon,' he said, heading off in search of the nearest off-licence.

'Poor Holly,' Olivia said, beginning to massage Holly's shoulders, which made her flinch for a moment, until she realised it wasn't Harry. 'Oh and there's more!' she said, remembering something. 'I heard the other day from his old flatmate that apparently Lawrence has really got his shit together. He's stopped drinking, joined a gym, AND has been taken on by a half-decent production company for commercials!'

'But he was a bum for the entire five years you knew him!' Holly nodded.

'This reminds me of something Jonny did that wound me up,' Olivia continued. 'When we finished the first time, he decided to tell me he'd bought us both boutique camping tickets to this amazing festival in the country. And then, instead of us going together, he went and put loads of pictures up on Facebook of him with this other bint that he took in my place.'

'No way!' Holly said. 'It's like that bit in game shows when they go, "Here's what you could've won!" before wheeling out the amazing prizes.'

'Exactly,' Olivia said. 'After all that good work we put in.'

'I KNOW! Tell me, why is it that we spend our lives educating guys, making them less emotionally bankrupt, sculpting them into functional adults, and then we never get to reap the fruits of our labour? Some other bitch is reaping them all around town. I know I sound like a bitter old cow and I should just be happy for him. But shoot me – I'm just not ready to do that yet. It's so frickin' unfair.'

'It's like when everyone's been trying to get a jar of marmalade open and then the lucky bugger that does it last opens it, just

309

like that, makes it look easy. When really we'd all loosened it up for them,' Olivia said.

'It's just like that!' Holly said.

'Or…' Harry said, reappearing with a box of wine and some Cornettos, 'this might sound radical, but maybe it's all just relationship politics – and maybe every one of them is shaping you up for the one you're meant to be with? Think of it as a training course – the only trouble is, you don't know how long it's for. Or when you'll eventually graduate.'

'Mmm, maybe,' Holly said, nodding slowly, biting into her ice cream. 'How much do I owe you for this?'

Harry shrugged it off. 'Think of it as my gift to the patient.'

'Thank you! Although I don't deserve it, after how I've behaved.'

'Pish,' Harry said by way of dismissal. 'Anyway, I've been thinking.' He began decanting Cabernet Sauvignon into plastic wine tumblers. 'I think this is a very positive thing indeed.'

'I wanted to get back together! This is positive how exactly?'

'The way I see it, it's like a rite of passage, this: finding out The Ex is engaged. Realising that yes, that's what they are now. AN EX. Not someone you were road-testing as an ex, but actually, they are now someone in your PAST. On with the future!' Harry said, raising his cup into a toast position, which the others clinked, by way of cheers.

'The future!' they shouted.

'I know you can't see this now, Hol, but it's truly the best thing that could have happened. I firmly believe it will be the catalyst to your recovery.'

'He's right,' Olivia said, holding onto her unwrapped Cornetto. 'Think about it. Deep down in the innermost chasms of your pain, there must be a hint of relief that now you can see you've done the right thing? Because if he could find happiness that quickly with someone else, then he clearly wasn't right for you. It goes to show you really didn't bring out the best in each other.

310

Whereas this Anna girl – maybe she just has the magic touch with him?'

'I have to admit, there is some degree of logic to what you're saying,' Holly said. 'It reminds me of that thing you said ages ago, that Lawrence and I weren't lifers. We weren't meant to push on to the next level; whereas him and this girl, they are.'

'Exactly,' Harry said. 'You'd lived out your sentence.'

Holly smiled wistfully. 'I've done my time! This means I'm now free from captivity! I'm free to roam!' she said, laughing and taking a massive swig of wine.

'Here's to that!' Olivia said, and they clinked cups again. 'And to Holly. Who went MIAFIH today,' Olivia said.

'What's that mean, Head of Pointless Acronyms?' Harry asked.

'Missing in Action, from Facebook-Induced Hysteria.'

'I went full nut-nut, is what I did.' Holly drank some more, then took out her mobile and scanned through the numbers. She found the entry 'Don't Answer' and edited it to say, 'What a Cock'. Not because it was grown-up or the right thing to do, but because it just made her feel better.

'I think we have another big learning from today's episode,' Harry said. 'I think we should all stop going on Facebook so much.'

'I never thought I'd say this, but I think he's on to something,' Olivia said. 'These days I can't go on there without people waving twelve-week scans in my face, or worse, full-grown pictures of their drooling little sprog-monsters.'

'I'd quite like a drooling little sprog-monster of my own one day…' Holly said. 'But OK, I'll try to cut down. Anyway, enough of The Holly Show. What's new with you guys?'

'Well, in between our triathlon training… I've been on SoulMates,' Olivia said, 'and Harry's been on Match.'

'We're both on Tinder too, obviously,' Harry added. 'We're testing them all out for you!'

311

'Thanks. Hey! Tell you what. If you meet someone nice, maybe you can just gateway me with one of their mates?'

'That's cheating, Hol!' Olivia said. 'You can't online-date by proxy! We're the ones putting in the hours!'

Holly stuck out her bottom lip in mock-sulk.

'In other news, I am going to see Jonny after this,' Olivia admitted quietly. 'He's still out of work, poor lamb.'

'Well, of course he wants to see you now. Men are transparent like that,' Holly said.

'You may be right, but he really needs a friend.'

'You do that… glutton for punishment,' Harry said.

'Are you sure this is a good idea, you going to see him, Liv?' Holly asked, her face puckering with concern.

'Red wine makes me randy, so…' Olivia smiled. 'Sorry. Look, in all seriousness. I know he'll dick me about again but I figure I'm allowed one relapse credit, aren't I?'

'Yes you are. Redeemable later this evening. Just the once, mind,' Holly said, grinning.

'Thank you, my trusty buccaneers,' Olivia said, refilling everyone's drinks. 'I'll have one more for the road, then.'

'Cheers,' Holly said, raising her glass and suddenly feeling like the luckiest girl in the world. 'Guys. I'm so sorry I took you for granted. I don't know where I'd be without you. Probably somewhere off Highgate Bridge by now.'

'That's not funny, Holly,' Olivia said.

'Sorry.'

'You know what I heard the other day? They've made the fence higher on that bridge now, so it's harder to commit suicide,' Harry said, deadpan.

'Thanks for the info, Harry,' Holly said. 'Good to know.'

'Anytime,' he said, swigging more wine and kissing her on the cheek. 'Come on. Let's go in.'

He began undoing his trousers, and Holly averted her eyes on reflex.

'IN? In where?' Olivia asked, her face creasing with worry.

'The water! Come on!' he said, taking off his sweater, goose pimples spreading over him like a rash while his knees began knocking.

'But it's almost winter, Harry. And there's no way I'm getting my kit off here!' Olivia said, tightening her coat around her.

'If she can do it, why can't we? Come on! We're all free from our sentences!'

'He's right!' Holly yelled, stripping off again down to her underwear. 'We are freer right now than we may ever be in our lives! Let's prove it! To ourselves, and to nature!' she said, jogging up and down on the spot, shivering.

'Oh, fuck it. All right then. I guess it's training, isn't it?' Olivia started pulling off her jumper dress, her lips turning blue.

'Wooooohoooooooo!' Holly squealed, tearing off her clothes and feeling the Siberian wind sting her bare skin again. As Olivia slowly peeled her leggings off, Holly couldn't help staring at her tiny shape. She tried to remember if Olivia had always been this skinny or whether it was all the training she and Harry had been doing.

'You are remembering to carb-load, aren't you—?' Holly began, but it was too late – Harry had grabbed them both by the hand and was dragging them, screaming and giggling, into the water. Then they frolicked, splashed about like hedonistic mermaids for as long as they could before being asked to leave by the park warden.

Later, at 2.08 a.m., Harry, Holly and Bella all received an identical text message:

'BUC Bulletin: I bring good tidings. We're giving it a go. Just had sensational make-up sex, after which, in our orgasmic haze, Jonny declared that he wanted us to TRY! Not for a baby. But for an Open Relationship. It was the sweetest five little words I think I've ever heard. I think the Tin Man has found his heart. Thanks for bearing with, Liv xxx'

Jeremy.Philpott@TotesamazeProductions.com
Holly.Braithwaite@TotesamazeProductions.com
Subject: What the bollocking hell?

Miss Braithwaite,
1. What happened today? Were you so ill you couldn't just come and sit in a dark room and press some buttons?

2. Yesterday's pictures came out all squashed. You must have exported it at the wrong aspect ratio. The episode where Terri and Tarquin were showing each other their slash scars, in their very own 'Bi-Polar-off' – pure telly gold – all ruined! Luckily I sorted it before it went to air. Just.

3. Be great if you could sort your shit out, Braithwaite. This is now an official written warning.

Happiness?

Jez.

28. *Mind the Gap*

'How can he be getting married before me?!!!!' she wailed at 3 a.m. that night, into her mobile phone. She was well aware of what a godawful bore she was being but was unable to do anything to circumvent it. 'It was my stupid idea to break up in the first place!'

'It's so obviously a rebound thing. Don't worry about it Hol...' whispered Olivia. Then, from two postcodes away, she proceeded to talk Holly down from the proverbial bridge.

After Holly had hung up forty-five minutes later, she heard a knock on her door.

'Jesus Hol, I could hear you crying! Why didn't you wake me up?!' Harry said, packing up a sobbing Holly into his arms. 'Come here,' he said as hot tears slid down her cheeks into his hair.

'I don't know. I guess part of me still feels pretty awkward – you know – after what happened. I thought you might think I was trying to come on to you,' she said, laughing.

'Hol! That's in the past. I'm over you! Seriously, you're one of my best friends. If you're upset, I want to know about it. Come on, let's have some tea.'

So at three in the morning, they sat on the balcony in their

315

pyjamas and slippers, sharing a pot of tea and smoking a spliff, setting the world to rights.

'I've met someone, actually,' Harry said suddenly, into the night sky.

'Really? Who? Someone online?!' Holly said, hoping her excitement was believable.

'No, analogue. It's this girl at work. Well, she doesn't actually work with me, but she's in one of the blocks in the agency opposite. It's crazy, our offices are basically level with each other, and I can see into her room clearly!'

'So wait… you've not so much met her as, you're stalking her like a Peeping Tom?'

'No. Well I'm convinced she's staring back at me, so that makes it OK doesn't it? I mean, I can even see what books she has on her shelves!'

'Have you ever actually spoken to her?'

'Not yet, no. But I'm pretty sure she's my dream woman. I mean, I think I can just about make out a hardback of *The Great Gatsby*.'

'Your favourite book; it must be love! So what's she like besides that?'

'Just breath-taking. She's this vision, with fiery red hair… She's basically like a smaller version of Christina Hendricks from *Mad Men*. That's why I've taken to calling her Christina. I don't actually know her name.'

'God, you're like Bella. Well. This all sounds promising,' Holly said, relieved to hear that it actually sounded tenuous and unpromising. 'So what do you intend to do about it?'

'I don't know. This week things progressed from me staring across at her, to her actually smiling back at me. I'm thinking the fact she didn't scowl at me for being a pervert is a good sign? Then, after a bit she kind of did this Pantene advert thing, where she took her hair out of its sleek high ponytail and let it bounce around her shoulders for a whole minute afterwards. I know she was half mucking about, but still, it was a sight to behold.'

Harry looked skyward and smiled. Holly couldn't tell if he was serious or stoned.

'She's clearly into you if she gave you the hair advert. I think you should put up a sign in your window saying "Pantene lady, fancy a pint?"'

'She might not be able to read it though – what about just a picture of a pint or a wine glass?'

'Yeah. It is an ad agency after all – you want to do something a bit smart, don't you?'

'I'll think about it, but knowing me, she'll actually have been flirting with the guy in the adjacent office.'

'That is a very real possibility.'

Gradually, their discussion regressed to sillier things, and they decided it was imperative that they retreat indoors to eat cookies and watch *The Magic Roundabout*. Soon it was inexplicably 5.13 a.m., and they were giggling outlandishly at Harry's Zebedee impression. Holly looked at Harry with utter love as he stuffed a cookie into her mouth. 'Can you never not be in my life please?'

As Harry opened his mouth to reply, Daniel stomped up the stairs, flung open the kitchen door and then slammed it shut behind him, hard. He then repeated the open and shut motion, over and over, getting louder and more forceful each time.

'Sorry Daniel,' Holly said slowly.

'Yeah man, we're sorry if we were being loud.'

'That's OK!' he spat. 'MAN, I'm only doing complicated surgical procedures tomorrow, which may or may not save lives. It doesn't matter if I get a good night's sleep or not. You two stay up all night and dissect your tedious break-ups!'

In the background, Dylan and Zebedee were prancing about. Holly had to try and look away, to prevent the laughter that was creeping through.

'Sorry Daniel,' she said, aware how obnoxious they were being but unable to stem the giggles. Damn that skunk. 'We'll go to bed now.'

They sloped off downstairs. 'Sorry Daniel. Really, we are,' Harry said as Daniel slammed his bedroom door shut behind him.

As they reached the junction between their two rooms, Holly went to hug Harry goodnight.

'You OK?' he said. 'Want me to sleep in your bed?'

'Do you mind?'

''Course not. Just try and keep your hands off me, is all. I'm practically spoken for now, remember.'

'Haha,' she said as they climbed into bed.

'It will happen for you Hol,' he said as they lay next to each other on the pillows. 'He is out there somewhere. But you need to work on you first. Maybe you need to stop moping, stop comfort eating, and look for another way to fill the hole.'

'I know,' she nodded, feeling embarrassed, and weirdly aware of her own – possibly much chunkier than before – body in front of him. She felt herself edge away and pull the covers up around her.

'I know what will sort you out!'

'What?' she said, opening her eyes and daring to point them right at Harry, lying face to face with him on the pillows.

'Natural endorphins.'

'Oh?' she said, butterflies stirring.

'Come for a run with me in the morning.'

Oh.

'Oh, no no no no no,' she said in the manner of the Churchill dog in those annoying insurance ads. 'The only running I do is for the bus.'

'Well that's all about to change. Seriously, training for this triathlon is helping me get over Rachel; I tell you, there's nothing like running away from your problems!' at which point he started giggling, clearly still stoned. 'I'm dragging you on a run if it kills me,' he said, poking her in the flabbiest folds of her belly. She quickly hoisted in her non-existent abdominal muscles.

'Um, how do I put this? Me and running: we just don't get on. If it's all the same to you, I'm booked in for a hangover tomorrow morning, and the only marathon I'll be good for is EastEnders.'

'OK. Don't say I didn't offer though. Night Hol. Sweet dreams,' he said, almost thinking of a place to tell her to meet, but stopping himself and turning away.

'Nighty night.'

And she lay there, staring at the strawberry-blonde hairs on his back, and worrying that maybe in some fucked up reverse-psychology way, she'd accidentally fallen in love with her best friend. Maybe it was just because he'd come to her rescue yet again, and she was growing more dependent on him. Or more likely, came another voice in her head, she wanted him because he'd just said he liked someone else. Textbook Holly. Same as wanting Lawrence back even though she'd sent him packing. Hi, have we met? The name's Holly Groucho Marx. She lay awake pondering over this, overthinking everything, vowing never to get stoned again, until the sweet sound of the reversing vehicle kicked in.

29. *Forrest Grump*

'Woah, there,' Harry said the next morning, coming into the kitchen. 'You all right, Grumplestiltskin?'

'Yeah, fine. I was just making coffee, doing the washing up.'

'Right; I could hear you banging cupboard doors all the way from downstairs!'

'Sorry, I didn't realise I was being noisy. But now you mention it, I am in a bad mood for some reason. I think I've entered a new phase all of a sudden. Anger!'

'Oh well, that'll make a nice change at least. Anyway I'm just off for a run. Sure you won't escort me? It might help you calm down.'

Holly opened a bottle of milk and tentatively lowered her nose to it. Yuck, definitely off. Which meant she'd have to leave the house anyway.

'OK, just a mini one. We can pick up some milk on the way back. Yeah, I'll come for…', and then, like she was trying on a foreign word, added, '…a… run.' She laughed. 'In the absence of a punchbag.' She chucked the milk into the bin and went downstairs to change.

'But listen,' she said as they were heading out the door, 'don't feel you have to wait for me. You know I'm the least fit person in the world.'

'Well let's just see, shall we?' he said as they set off towards the Heath.

After a whole minute of running down the steps in the flat, and then onto the crowded Fortess Road, Holly stopped.

'Harry. There's something wrong with my legs. It really ACHES to move them. Maybe I actually don't have any muscles. Just lead, instead??'

'You're just full of booze toxins. But they'll pass through in a bit and you'll loosen up.'

They started up again. As they reached the entrance to the Heath, the gradient got steeper, she could feel a stitch coming on, and her teeth were starting to go numb.

'Harry,' she said, panting and wheezing, 'now my teeth feel all weird. Is that normal?'

Harry grinned and started to speed up.

'You're enjoying this, aren't you? Shit. Why – don't – people – tell – you – it's – this – ex-haust-ing? Also, you didn't tell me there'd be a hilly bit! I need to work up to that! Can we stop? Here. Just by this fountain.' Holly drank from the water fountain as though she'd been trekking through Rajasthan for days. She splashed some water onto the back of her neck, and onto Harry, who was jogging up and down on the spot and doing star-jumps.

'Show-off.'

'Jabba the Hut,' Harry said, breaking into an uphill run. 'You really are immensely unfit, aren't you?'

'OI!… Wait! Not uphill!' she said as she ran after him. Although actually, it was a bit easier now. She was looser; he hadn't lied. She could even feel a small amount of – what was it they called it – stride?

Out of nowhere, an image of Lawrence with his stunning Facebook fiancée appeared in her mind. And then she felt someone pushing her. Maybe it was the ghost of Mrs Slydewell, her PE teacher from school, who used to run behind her in cross-country and force her to run by pressing on her back with both hands and brute force. Or maybe it was something else. But somehow, even after the agreed twenty minutes she had signed up for, Holly was still running. Mile after mile.

'Hey! Harry! I think I've been through the brick wall! The anger must be keeping me going!'

Harry turned to her and grinned. 'Haha! You're like, Forrest Grump!'

She started to laugh and couldn't stop. Then she realised it was exhausting to laugh and run at the same time, so quickly she visualised Jeremy and his audacious recording of their private BUC meeting, and there it was again – fuel through fury.

Flying down the main slope at the far side of the Heath, the wintry sun on her neck, she just could not stop. The anger was like guzzling six protein shakes. She felt an inner strength and a feeling that, just maybe, a small seed of defiance would one day bloom out of the wreckage, and with it the promise that one day she would love again. 'HOORAY!' she shouted as they reached the entrance gate and began a gentle hobble home.

When they reached the flat, Harry couldn't help laughing. 'Hol, your face is redder than a genetically modified strawberry!'

They headed straight for the kitchen, where Harry began preparing a huge feast with which to reward himself. 'Want some?'

'No thanks. My insides are still in shock. In fact I'm starting to feel quite nauseous.'

'You should make sure you stretch out.'

'Oh I intend to.'

She showered and headed into her room, to lie down for a long time.

As she pulled back the covers, her phone rang, and the auto-mated robot voice began calling out, 'What a cock. What a cock. What a cock.' She laughed out loud, before turning her phone off and closing her eyes.

Later, she hobbled into the living room where Olivia and Harry were drinking tea before the week's meeting. Despite half their members being either geographically or mentally absent, Olivia had insisted on continuing with a skeleton BUC service.

'Wow! This running lark's something else. I feel like a born-again Christian; I just want to praise everyone and everything!'

Holly smiled and kissed each of them hello on the cheeks. In return, they looked at her as if to say, what have you done with Holly?

'Seriously. I feel all happy and floaty!'

'Jeez, calm down. Next you'll be running a marathon!' Harry said.

Holly raised her eyebrows. 'It's all right this, though isn't it? It's like a natural high that you don't need anyone else for. Mmm, maybe I'll get one of those Nike Fuel bands. You know, to help me train.'

The others looked at Holly like she'd just spoken Swahili.

'You've changed,' Olivia said in mock disillusionment. 'Seriously, you look dead skinny, so it must be working!'

'As if, Liv! I think you've got reverse-body-dysmorphia-by-proxy!'

At this point Holly noticed that Olivia was also glowing.

'Have you been working out too?' Holly asked in mock-Californian.

'If you call break-up sex exercise, then yes,' she sighed. 'It's all off with Jonny again,' she announced, pinching a cola bottle sweet from the bowl in the centre of the table.

'Oh no,' Holly said, giving her a hug. 'I'm sorry.'

'What's happened now?' Harry asked, handing out wine glasses. Olivia shot him a look as if to say, 'Oh I'm sorry, am I boring you?'

He filled her glass first by way of apology.

'Oh, it's fairly predictable stuff,' she said, taking a sip. 'He's got a job again, and all of a sudden he's stopped being all needy. Turns out he just wanted mothering for a bit while his ego recovered from the shame of being made redundant.'

'No. What a knob!' Holly said, doing a good job of surprise.

'That's it now. I was totally kidding myself. I really thought we could do the whole open relationship thing.'

'I don't understand the point in them. Surely they just mean you don't love each other enough?' Holly said.

Olivia shook her head. 'I used to be all about the open relationship before Ross. But now I've stopped even looking at other men. And the thought of Jonny with anyone else makes me feel physically sick. How did this happen?'

'Well, if you want my two-pennies' worth again,' Holly said, 'you're just a knob that's never properly been in love 'til now.'

'Had to pick a mandroid for my first time, didn't I?' she sighed and took a large sip of wine. 'And yet when we're together, it feels so connected! You know, when he's looking in my eyes I think he really does feel it too. It's like I almost come close to this secret part of him. But after it's over, that bit of him shuts down, the mandroid armour seals back up and he's gone. Then he's doubly cold afterwards, I barely get a kiss on the mouth then if I'm lucky.'

'Wow. He's like, Vivian in *Pretty Woman*.'

The girls turned to Harry.

'I had two sisters, OK?'

'Anyway, back to me please.'

'Sorry Liv,' Harry said. 'But hey, maybe it's for the best. You know, quit before you fall any deeper?'

Olivia looked at Harry and nodded, her face gaunt and sad.

'Now you sound like Will Young!' Holly said.

'Are we sure he's not gay? Harry, that is,' Olivia said to Holly.

Holly shook her head. 'Oh no, he's not gay all right,' she said, giggling, before feeling her cheeks go red. WHOOPS.

'What makes you so sure?' Olivia said, looking suspiciously from Holly to Harry. Holly's heart began thumping and she prayed that a) the others couldn't hear this and b) Olivia wasn't about to uncover The Dreadful Secret.

'Oh, let's just say the walls are thin,' she said.

Harry shot her a look that said 'good save' and her heart rate began to return to normal.

'Hey, isn't it your first episode tonight, Hol?' Harry said, heading over to turn on the television.

'Yep it is, but I'd rather you didn't watch it.'

'Have you actually made a secret camera show about us anyway?' Olivia asked.

'No I swear! It's just so abominable, I don't want anyone to see it. I've been thinking about asking if I can be called Olly Braithwaite on the credits, it's so awful.'

'OK. Nuff said,' Olivia said. 'So how is crazy Jez these days?'

'Oh I'm fairly sure he wants my head on a stick. Partly my fault, but partly that he's more mentally unstable than any of the contestants. Did I tell you he secretly recorded the sound from that BUC meeting he dropped in on? Then made a trailer out of it all, to send to Channel 5. I can tell you this now that Bella's gone!'

'Holy fuck. That's illegal!' Olivia said.

'How are you still working for him?' Harry said.

'I have no choice. Lawry cleaned me out. I'd need to get myself out of the red before I could even contemplate leaving. No, I need to stick it out 'til the end I think.'

'Fucking phone,' Olivia said out of nowhere. She stared down at it willing it to beep in some way.

'You know, it's not the phone's fault you're upset,' Harry said, 'That's just you, projecting onto the phone. You're choosing to filter your experience of the phone in that way.'

'Qué?' Olivia said, in the manner of Manuel of *Fawlty Towers*.

'Seriously, if we can all learn to control how our thoughts influence what we see, we might be able to control our break-up woes,' Harry said. 'We just need to reset our filters.'

'Where's this all this coming from?' Holly asked, shaking her head in wonder.

'It's basic NLP.'

They all looked confused.

'Neuro-linguistic Programming. I did a minor module in it at uni.'

Olivia turned to him. 'Oh Harry, can't you, won't you, gateway me, please? You must have some single mates?'

'Oh Christ. Now you as well?! Look I'm sorry, my friends are all either engaged, married or boring, I'm afraid. Why else do you think I'd be hanging out with you losers so much?'

No one batted an eyelid.

'Fair,' Olivia said.

'Are none of your married lot divorced yet, though?' Holly asked, half joking.

'OK enough about boys,' Harry declared.

'You're right, Harry. We'll stop now. Let me cook something for everyone – Liv, when did you last eat? You look positively skeletal.'

Olivia blushed, but nobody noticed because a shadow the size of Ben Nevis had just passed across Harry's face.

'Um, Holly,' Harry said, 'do you happen to follow Stephen Fry?'

'What do you mean?'

'On Twitter. He's just, um, tweeted about your show.'

'Oh really?!' Holly's heart stopped; first in a good way, then bad. 'Oh, fuck. He's a poster boy for mental health awareness, isn't he. This is bad, isn't it?'

'Um, it's not one hundred percent complimentary,' Harry said, beginning to read aloud from his phone. '"#TheMadHouse is the most morally reprehensible tripe I've ever encountered. Genuinely thought was watching ep. from @Aiannucci's Time Trumpet."'

'Oh dear,' Holly said, 'I totally saw this coming.'

'It's been retweeted 1,437 times. So far.'

'I'll never work again. Argh, I have had it with shit, brain-dead telly!'

'So do something about it,' Harry said. 'Write your way out of it.'

'I would! But I need Lawrence to help me.'

'Can I just stop you there?' Harry interrupted.

The girls went quiet. Holly watched him expectantly. He picked up his drink.

Moments later, Holly nodded. 'You're right. How long before I stop saying shit like that? What a waste of life this is.'

'I'LL SAY,' Olivia said, her eyes catatonic with boredom.

'How long does it take to get over someone? How do you even know when you're over them?'

'You just know,' Harry said. 'The other day, I had this annoying wodge of Sellotape stuck to my shoe. It'd been there so long, dangling along, not enough to trip me up, but just enough to make me aware of its presence and piss me off by making me slightly off balance. Then, after walking around all day, I noticed it wasn't there anymore. I hadn't noticed it go. It's a bit like that, I guess.'

'That's beautiful,' Holly said.

'Beautiful in a "sponsored by Ryman's" kind of way,' Olivia said.

'Don't be mean,' Holly said.

'I'm just saying. It's about as profound as Tippex.'

'You have no soul!' Harry said. 'FACT.'

'Oh don't do that. Lawrence used to say "FACT" all the time.'

They all glared at Holly. 'Oops. I'm SO sorry.'

'You know, Holly it's ironic,' Harry began, 'considering you're an editor for a living, you're pretty sloppy at editing your own thoughts.'

Holly stared at Harry as though he'd just seen right through to her soul.

'He's right,' Olivia added. 'You need to look at all your memories of Lawrence and instead of replaying them and torturing yourself, kick the fuckers to the cutting-room floor. Leave them there, like the deleted scenes they deserve to be.'

'That's your problem, Hol; you're an emotional hoarder,' Harry said.

Holly looked down at her feet. 'Blimey. Nail. Head. It's like I need to just clear the hard-drive of memories in my head! So what are we going to do about it? Does anyone have one of those machines they have in *Eternal Sunshine of the Spotless Mind*? That would be the answer.'

They all fell silent. After a while, a glint appeared in Harry's eyes.

'I've got it. The next best thing!' he said, rubbing his hands together. 'I've got the perfect wee plan for how we can all move on quicker.'

'OH GOOD!' Holly said, her eyes lindy-hopping with excitement. 'Anything you can do to help me pull myself out of my arse. What is it?'

'Mmmm. You've got exactly the same "cunning plan face" on that you had with Bleak Camping,' Olivia said.

'Is this going to be as well-thought-out as that?' Holly asked, her eyes narrowing.

30. *The Ex-orcist*

'Holly!' Harry yelled after work a few days later. 'Roll up, roll up, it's the fifth of November! Know what that means?'

Holly placed her bag on the hallway floor and scrunched her nose at Harry. 'Fireworks?'

'Liv's here, I've got a box of wine, a cheap grill, and we're officially declaring an ex-orcism!' he said, throwing his head back and doing a 'Muwhaahaahahah!' evil laugh like they do in bad horror films.

'Ooooh. Actually, that does sound like my kind of Bonfire night.'

'None of this, "remember, remember the fifth of November." This bonfire night is all about forgetting.'

'I'll drink to that!' Holly said, her eyes widening. Harry passed her a glass of red wine. 'Oh, actually, not for me thanks.'

'I'm sorry. Have we met?'

'Seriously. I've been thinking I need to cut down a bit.'

'Don't be ridiculous.'

'Yes, you're right. I'll start cutting down after tonight.'

'That's the spirit,' he said as they clinked glasses. 'I'm actually quite excited about all this, in a sick way. I feel totally ready to burn Rachel's things. It's perfect timing too, as things have slowly been progressing with Window Girl.'

'Oh?'

'Yep. She was in the same lift as me at the station the other day. There were too many bloody people in the way so I couldn't say hi though. But something's on the cards, I can feel it. Anyway, on to the matter at hand. Pyromania!'

'OK. I'll just go and get the break-up bags,' Holly said, heading to the cupboard of broken dreams.

When she came back up the stairs, the smoke was already filling the living room, and with it a trail of laughter. She followed the sound to the roof terrace. In one hand was her break-up bag, which she hadn't dared open since its first collation. In the other was the lighter, no less festering one of Bella's. She could already sense the familiar stench of the singular mouldy Adidas from within the flimsy Morrison's bag.

Arriving at the scene of the fire, she placed both bags down on the ground, and took a swig of JD from the bottle Harry was holding up at her.

'I'm the fire-starter. Twisted fire-starter,' he sang, a maniacal expression in his eyes. Huge orange flames were billowing everywhere, clouds of black smoke trailing off into N19.

'Now, as we know,' Olivia began as if she was centre stage at an awards ceremony, 'our dear Bella couldn't be here tonight, but I know she would if she could. And as I don't have any Ross paraphernalia, I shall be burning Sam's things on her behalf.'

'In an important practical demonstration of our absolute allegiance to Rule Number Ten,' Holly added.

'Yeah. What she said,' Olivia said, smiling in approval.

As the others applauded, Holly opened the bag and began to place the little pieces of Sam onto the fire. The birthday, Christmas and Valentine's cards were the first to go. Then the pack of Embassy cigarettes, which they divvied up and lit on the flames. Then poor Jezebel. 'Aw, Jez!' cried Holly, covering her eyes. There was a small, mean part of her wishing that it was evil Jez there instead. Then all three of them watched the remaining Sam debris snap, crackle and pop, while they smoked their cigarettes and

Harry held up his camera phone to capture it all for Bella.

Harry took a large glug from his beer. 'Burn baby burn!' he sang out as the others cheered and Holly took over from filming. She looked through the lens at her friend's most heartfelt memories as they turned to embers. She zoomed in on poor Jezebel, who was slowly morphing into a teddy-shaped pile of ash. 'There he blows! Bye bye Sam!' and so on, they sang out.

As the flames died down a little, she reached for the bag-au-Lawrence, with a heavy heart.

'Wait,' Harry said. As though he was manning a barbeque, he grabbed a tray and began to fan the flames. He took a utensil and pushed the smouldering matter around to make space.

Holly slowly reached into the bag. First, she pulled out five years' worth of sweet, adoring cards written from him to her, and a wodge of 'I love you' notes that he'd left under her pillow over the years (one of them written on a sheet of toilet roll).

'Look at this one here,' she said, holding up a birthday card. 'There's even a little smudge on the writing from where it made my eyes water.'

'Awwww.' Everyone took a moment to feel sorry for the card that was about to be incinerated.

'BURN!' Olivia shouted, making Holly jump.

'Right! Yes, let's burn the lot!' One by one she tossed the artefacts into the flames.

Then she added the rest of the miscellaneous Lawrence items, and watched through wet eyes as Che Guevara's iconic face crackled and peeled, along with the little book of Japanese puzzles that would now never be solved. Her face grew hot from the fire. While the others cheered on, a tear slipped down her cheek. But this time it was a tear of letting go. Not of regret but of acceptance. Somehow, seeing each item being physically destroyed before her eyes, the memory was scorched out of existence, removed from her brain, no longer capable of administering torment. For one brief moment, she felt a little like Jim Carrey's character after his turn on the Eternal Sunshine machine.

Then when she looked up at her friends dancing among the flames, seeing all those memories of Lawrence go up in smoke, she felt a sense of peace, that finally she was free from the agonising possibility of them ever getting back together. Harry had been right – that was the most liberating feeling of all.

'Wooohoooo!' she called out as they jumped up and down in the air.

Amid the cacophony of cheers and screams of manic enjoyment came the distant sound of sirens. Seconds later, in among the red and orange glow, there came a blue and red flashing light.

*

BellaAllen247@hotmail.co.uk
HollyBraithwaite25@gmail.com

Dearest Bellarama,
I'm writing this email from my cell in Holloway Prison.

Well, I nearly was.

Two weeks ago, we had a small bonfire. Just a cosy event for the three of us, you know, to finally get rid of our break-up bags. (We did le sac de Sam as promised – btw did you still want me to get an urn for Jez's ash? Let me know. It's in a Tupperware for now).

Anyway, it was surprisingly therapeutic! I felt cleansed somehow, and lighter, like I'd shed a load of weight! Only, then it got a teeny bit out of hand… when the fire was at its biggest, suddenly, not one, not two, but THREE fire engines pulled up and drove past the flat, slowing down, the firemen gawking out the windows. Then they drove past and we all said to each other, ah it's fine, they must be here for a real fire somewhere – until the POLICE VAN rocked up. Then an ambulance! Naturally, like the responsible citizens that we are, we all ducked down. Then we heard a policeman yell out that they'd heard reports of a fire on one of these balconies. Luckily, our fire was just at the tiny embers stage by then. But someone had to answer – so I heard myself say, 'We were just toasting marshmallows I assure you officer!' Then I probably pushed my luck by offering them some.

Later, in the police interview room, I told the nice policeman all about what had happened with Lawrence. How he owes me a grand, and how he'd just carelessly announced his engagement to the world on Facebook! I told him all about BUC, and what a headcase I've been lately, and how this bonfire was basically just an absolutely essential procedure to give us all our sanity back.

And do you know what he did? He said, 'Christ on a bike, in that case, off you go. Clear off and find yourself a nice boyfriend that deserves someone as pretty as you.'

Then, after that we all ran down the street screaming and laughing, our arms linked. Do you remember that moment at the end of *Stand By Me*, when the narrator says, 'I never had as good a group of friends as I did when I was twelve… does anyone?' It was just like that! Only we're not twelve, we're coming up to bloody well twenty-eight, and I feel even less sure of myself as I did when I was an awkward little runt scared of my own shadow! But hey, we're all in it together, and I'm starting to feel a little less wretched. Which is nice!

Truly though, Belle, it was special and I wish you'd been there. It made me realise, I really do think I've never had as great a group of friends as we do right now – I know that we'll never forget each other, even years from now when we've squeezed out some puppies and are living in our dream homes by the sea.

You know, there might be new people joining BUC one day; there might be old veterans passing through. But deep down, I don't think any of us will really leave. Not even you, even though you're a few thousand miles away!

In other news… just this week, our Harry seems to have got himself a girlfriend. I'll let him tell you about how he got a date with her – it was dead romantic! It's got quite serious with them, quite quickly. The least serious part being her name. It's Harrie – I shit you not – short for Harriet. It must be so odd when they call each other's names out in bed. If they do – ew, I don't want to think about it!

Me, I've given up militant dating and replaced it with READING. Remember Harry bought me that book that's longer than the Bible? Well I've finally started it. It's all about how to structure a story for screenwriting, and now that I've finally got into it, it's amazing. Still not sure how to apply it to actually writing the short, but I'm hopeful the magic will happen somehow. I've GOT to get away from my job and evil Jez one way or another. The show is diabolical; like, beyond offensive. But it's not just that. I just keep fucking things up. I'm either exporting things wrongly, cocking up the sound levels, or worse, not putting the cut together as punchy as he wants. Starting to really wonder if a job is this hard, maybe it's not right? Shouldn't the thing you do day in day out come naturally to some extent? I mean, with you, you just open your mouth and sing – the most natural thing in the world!

All this time I've been blaming it on Jez for being a grade A C-word, but maybe it is me being in the wrong job? Have I been busting a gut to save a career that actually isn't what I'm meant to be doing? Is it just because I did all those unpaid internships that I'm forcing myself to stick with it – out of kindness to my younger self?

Sorry. That's enough now – I've rambled on. We're really missing you, B. Hope to god you're safe. OH AND HAPPY EFFING ALMOST CHRISTMAS (trying my best to ignore it this year!)

Xxx Hol xxx

31. *Ctrl Alt Del Ldn*

It's a quirk of the British winter that, every year, when the curtain has finally been drawn on it, people remark to one another, 'Brrr, that was a tough one, wasn't it?' But on this Sunday night, as Holly threw yet another inside-out umbrella into the bin by her flat, she felt confident that this particular winter – with its infernal cold, its epidemics of unemployment and swine flu – was definitely worse than any other. It was like winter, squared, with knobs on. The schools were closed. No one could get to work. Theatre shows that had been rehearsing for weeks were cancelled, never to have another outing. By mid-December, the coat of gloom had worn everyone down; you could see it in their faces. Still, mustn't grumble. Drink less and whinge less: those were her twin goals this week, she reminded herself as she opened the front door.

'Christ! Enough with the white stuff!' Olivia said to Holly as she walked in.

'I know! I'm so bored of everyone saying how snowy it is! Get over it!' Holly let slip as she took a seat in the cosy lounge, which – Harry having had his wicked way with it – now looked like Christmas on heat, with paper chains, a fully decorated Christmas tree, and silver tinsel hanging from all the walls.

'And all that's on the news now is SNOW. Narrated by Jon Snow!' Harry said, emerging from the kitchen.

'OK. Successful dates, anyone?' Olivia began.

'Nada,' Holly said, taking her second piece of quiche and hoping no one was counting. 'Currently going through the most epically long dry patch.'

'Waiting for a wet patch, then?' Olivia asked.

'Ugh, Liv. Nice to know you're filling the lewd gap now Bella's away.'

Olivia did a mock bow. 'I like to do my bit. So, I have a suggestion. Why don't we all go out dancing on New Year's Eve?'

'That's a good idea,' Harry said, 'maybe not actual hectic clubbing. Or swing dancing. But just some low-key pub-dancing, forward slash, going to various house parties?'

'All right,' Holly said. 'It could be a nice thing to do to together after our enforced separation.'

'Are you not looking forward to Christmas? I am!' Harry said.

'That's because your family is The Waltons,' Holly said, looking at him as though he was from another planet.

'For the last time, it is not my fault that I came from a two-parent family!'

'Sorry. It's just… Christmas is to those with dysfunctional families what Valentine's Day is to singletons.'

'BAH HUMBUG!' Harry said.

'I'm with Hol on this one. My parents are spending Christmas in Aruba! So I'll just be at my aunt's house in Gerrards Cross, with my twin cousins who are incapable of conversing about anything other than reality TV. So I suspect we'll be mostly stuffing our faces and watching shit telly all day.'

'I'll probably do a double-decker,' Holly said. 'Christmas Day with my mum and stepdad, then Pretend Christmas with my dad on Boxing Day.'

'Double the fun!' Harry said.

'No. Double the pain.'

'OK, in that case we'll have to have a big one, to celebrate the family getting back together. As in, our Chosen Family,' Olivia said.

'Deal,' Holly said, nodding in approval.

'Big enough for Class-A's big?' Harry said, taking out his mobile phone and scrolling through his address book.

'Now you're cooking with gas,' Olivia said.

'Mmm… a little MDMA might help see us through to the other side. But I don't know – I'll only do some if Liv signs off on it,' Holly said, turning to Olivia to see if she was also up for turning their depravity up a notch.

Olivia shifted about in her seat for a moment. 'Oh go on then, you've twisted my arm,' Olivia said with a naughty glint in her eye. 'I'll try some, just this once.'

Later, once the last drop of mulled wine had been sunk, and the last mince pie scoffed, the three of them resigned themselves to the reality that, until they were all a little happier, the only festive spirit they were capable of conjuring up was probably eggnog, and that this Christmas just wasn't going to be one to remember. So they began their goodbyes, and agreed that Break-up Club would have a brief recess for the holiday period.

Harry stood up. 'Gather ye round.'

'Let's huddle,' Holly said, opening her arms out.

'Merry Cocking Jesus'-Birthday,' Olivia said as they hugged.

'See you in a week, my babies,' Harry said. 'Good luck with your fuckwit families, one and all. Be sure to bring back some good stories. And maybe we'll give a prize to whoever wins "family most likely to go on *Jeremy Kyle*".'

*

BellaAllen247@hotmail.co.uk
HollyBraithwaite25@gmail.com
Subject: Bombay Mix-up

Dearest Hol,

Hello? Is that the international BUC helpline?

Am really struggling at the mo. Really missing the boy; keep Face-stalking him, instead of focusing on this amazing place that I'm in. Please can you tell me I've done the right thing again? Or send me one of those 'More reasons to break up with Sam' lists that we wrote? He has stopped all contact with me now, which I know I wanted, but still it hurts, bad! Think I'm only now seeing the wisdom of Rule Number Six – otherwise, it just comes back to bite you later, and you have to do delayed grieving, which is where I'm at now – on my tod! NOT FUN.

Anyway, thank you for your gorgeously long email. Try not to overthink it on the job stuff, and just see what happens. What will be will be. Who has been evicted from The Madhouse though? Is Borderline P.D. still winning?

It sounds like things are getting a bit intense with the old BUC… Bonfires? Burning rituals?? Really? Are we turning into some kind of cult? Only kidding. We all know it's been a cult from day one – it's just a question of where and when the mass suicide will take place… :)

By the way, do you know who popped into my head the other day? That bloke, Aaron, from the bike accident. I had this horrible larium dream – a really vivid flashback of him lying there in the street. Made me wonder if he was OK or not. I still think we should've gone to try and find him in a local hospital. You never know – you might have nursed him back to health and fallen in love in the process?! It's just so hard to meet men in London, I wonder if you missed an opportunity there? Perhaps you could still find him? If you work out where the nearest hospital would have been, they might give you info if you say you helped at the scene of the accident? Or is this one of those times when you're going to try and talk to me about boundaries again?

To be honest, Hol, I'm really missing your bones. I wish I was back home sometimes, and I've never EVER felt homesick before!

Although, there might be another reason I wish I was home: I've recently committed a Bella Allen Fail of epic proportions. I'm road-testing my description of it with you now, as I'm scared it's just TOO AWFUL AND NO ONE WILL EVER WANT TO BE FRIENDS WITH ME AGAIN.

So, here goes… let me know what you think, and whether I should tweak before posting??? Love you, bye,

me xxxxx

Bombay Mix-Up, by @LadyGoa

Namaste,*

Hope you're well. So I'm still having an amazing time and have seen a lot. Recently went down to Lakshadweep, an island off the coast of Kerala, to do some scuba diving. I swam with Butterflyfish! They swim in pairs, and they say here that if you see one on its own then it's broken-hearted! I hope butterfly fish have a BUC of their own!

FRIENDS AND FAMILY DISCLAIMER:

So, I don't come off well in this next part – AT ALL. In fact you'll probably disown me. But I'm going to tell it anyway, in the hope it'll be cathartic? Anyone lily-livered is advised to look away NOW.

It all began the day before yesterday, when there was a massive festival on the beach. It was awesome. Fireworks, barbeque, everyone dancing in the water. Even the locals were there paddling in their suits and saris, while we smutty westerners waded around in our hot pants and bikinis.

Anyway, my friend Hazel and I were dancing in the shallows (trying to not notice the guys weeing in it like it was one big urinal) when I spotted this Adonis of a man in the water, in a black trilby hat. Easily one of the most beautiful men I've ever seen. I managed to talk Hazel and the others into us doing a subtle relocation so we were dancing nearer him. I was swimming in my hot pants (complete with dorky money-belt that my lovely sister Daisy made me take to ensure I don't get my money nicked). I ended up chatting to Mr Trilby and discovered that he was from Amsterdam, he was a photographer, and his name was Yann (name changed for humiliation-prevention purposes). We hit it off, and one of the last things I remember is us kissing for hours under the stars, in the seawater, that I remember even now, felt silky and warm like a bath.

But friends, that's where the Romance genre ends, and the PSYCHOPATHIC THRILLER kicks in. After heading back to my hut for more 'kissing' we then fell asleep. We woke up the next day, still in each other's arms (I NEVER do that, I'm a need-my-space sleeper), and I remember him saying he was just going to his hut and then he'd come back in a bit for breakfast.

I slowly peeled myself out of the sweaty mozzie net chamber and began to try, with the worst hangover I'd had in some time, to piece my world back together. As you know, I can't see shit without my glasses or contacts, and I had no idea where either of them were. So you can imagine the kind of slow-motion hangover fog we're talking about here. No bother, I thought, I'll be able to find them after a nice cold shower. Then I'll be able to find my – come to think of it, my thing that I've not seen in ages - my money belt. It then hit me that I had absolutely no memory of taking it off, or when and where that could possibly have occurred. Surely it should be screwed up in a wet heap on the floor along with my shorts and everything else? But it wasn't. I began to feel panicky and a little bit sick as I realised it was nowhere to be seen. Trying to keep calm and do lots of that deep Ujjayi breathing business, I began ransacking the room. No money belt, but I did find my glasses – hurrah! With renewed vision, I then noticed the time. It was a whole hour since he'd left, saying he would 'pop back to his hut'.

When I came out of the shower and he'd still not returned I began to panic and the truth hit me: of course this ridiculously good-looking Yann hadn't been interested in me. Me, Bella Allen, certifiably crap at men! No! I'd robbed him by punching so monstrously above my weight, and he robbed me right back, of nearly all my money and my cards! With the remaining 200 rupees I had stashed in my rucksack, I headed out to the internet cafe.

As I was logging into my bank on a terminal, I caught something out the corner of my eye. Someone much like the man who had laid next to me all night long was sat right there, on the computer next to me. He was like, 'Oh Hai! I was just coming to get you. I just had to check my bank; I'm waiting for some money to transfer.'

I bet you are, I remember thinking.

Then he asked me what was wrong, and I had to basically fess up that I'd lost all my money and then, in the nicest way possible, accuse him of taking it.

What happened next was most unexpected. First, he swore blind to me that he would never do such a thing. Then, after helping me search my hut, he insisted on going back to his own hut that he was sharing with a friend.

And then he made me stand and watch while he emptied every zip, pouch and vacuum-packed bag in his rucksack, all the while his charming and embarrassed friend is looking on in amusement, no doubt wondering who this silly British slapper was. Then, he pulled out all of his possessions – photos of his family, rolled-up pictures he'd bought on his travels, diaries – which he flicked through to demonstrate that no money was hidden in the pages of them – and a copy of Martin Amis' *The Rachel Papers* (he has good taste!), a bootleg CD of Floyd's *Dark Side of the Moon* (again with the good taste!), an elephant statue for his mum (and by now the heartstrings were being tugged as I was thinking, Fuck-sticks! Here was a genuinely nice boy!). After half an hour of me getting to know him better via the medium of unpacking, it became candidly clear that he hadn't robbed me, and that I needed to get my proverbial coat.

So I apologised profusely and said I'd go and have a lie-down.

He told me not to worry, and said he'd come by my hut again later to help me look. Bless him. He kept saying, 'I really want you to find it! I don't want you to think I'm some thief, or have my ass thrown in jail!'

I'm so confused now. I don't want to think he did it but I'm about to go and cancel my cards anyway. What do you think? Did he do it? Use the voting buttons to the right of the blog! Also, you can watch the song I wrote about the whole sorry ordeal here.

Happy Chrimbo from your idiot slapper friend,

B xxx

* Yep… Travel bore bingo-tastic.

Holly.Braithwaite@TotesamazeProductions.com to
Jeremy.Philpott@TotesamazeProductions.com
Subject: Same Same

Hey Jeremy,
Not sure if you've seen the news about Stephen Fry? Has the show responded officially yet?

Either way I've just had an idea for another show. What about a reality thing about backpacking? There's not been one of them, has there? Lots of funny stuff happens out on the road. Gap Yahs, Trustafarians, piss-heads 'finding themselves…' all that jazz… It could be set in Goa, or even Thailand. It could be about how travel's never quite as different as you think it's going to be and playing with Alain de Botton's premise that travel is always better in your head. What do you think? Oh, and I'm calling it 'Same Same' (as in, But Different).

One vital piece of information – it could be starring your favourite person – Bella Allen. She's living out in Goa at the moment, working as a singer and barmaid. Have a look at her @LadyGoa blog here, her pics and a bunch of her songs she's been writing out there. If any of that appeals I could put you in touch – I think we both know she'd jump at the chance!

Holly

Jeremy.Philpott@TotesamazeProductions.com to
Holly.Braithwaite@TotesamazeProductions.com
Subject: Re: Same Same

Think it might be too much of a tall order production-wise. Not without Channel 4 or Sky Atlantic's budgets.

But if we can strip it right back, keep it a small Reality unit then we might be on to something.

Lose the de Botton stuff. Still too cerebral.

I do like it though. I'll drop Bella a line. Could work nicely as the next project after Madhouse. On that – don't worry about Mr Fry. No idea who that Armando character is that he keeps banging on about! Either way it matters not – our ratings are sky-high now – he did us a favour!

Happiness?

J.

32. *Out With the Old*

By the time Christmas rolled around, the snow had covered London in a thick blanket of at least fifteen togs. To those outside the duvet, the general consensus was that 'London was closed due to adverse weather conditions.' Holly had pretty much given up trying to get anywhere, and had taken to hibernating at her parent's house in the Midlands. The amount of layering up required, coupled with the extra travel time, had turned even the most outgoing of them into hermits. But eventually, from the three corners of Britain – Scotland, Sutton Coldfield and Gerrards Cross – BUC was reunited again. Come New Year's Eve, Holly was welcoming the others back into the flat with open arms and mulled wine. Along with Bella, who was sat on the coffee table in Harry's laptop, appearing live via Skype. She was on her fifth Tiger beer, it having already turned midnight where she was. But as soon as they had all taken up their respective seats in the lounge and lined up their alcoholic offerings on the table, Olivia began to complain of being feverish. 'Sorry people. I'm only going to come out for one. I've got the vilest of colds at the moment.'

'Oh that's a shame. It's NEW YEAR'S EVE!' Harry said, as though it was the millennium and Elvis himself was going to be in attendance.

'Yeah, come on Liv, don't be lame!' Bella added from Goa.

'Sorry. But I can't help it if I feel rough,' she said, heading to the bathroom again.

'What's up with her?' Bella asked, while Harry poured out some tequila.

'She's got some kind of a cold,' Holly said. 'Says she's suffering with "exhaustion". You know, like the slebs do.'

'And she tells Bella off for being a drama queen!' Harry said.

'Oi! I am here you know!' Bella said.

'Ha! We're only kidding, B. But yes, we should give Liv a bit of a break,' Holly said, 'she's probably still getting Jonny out of her system. Again.'

'Oh, the old Break-up Flu,' Harry said.

'She's due a bout of that,' Holly agreed.

Olivia re-emerged from the toilet, looking more alive, owing to a smattering of bronzer on her cheeks. 'Well, that was NOT regular.'

'Poor you. Do you think you can manage to stay out for more than one?' Holly asked.

'I'll try and manage 'til midnight, if only to see the back of this godforsaken year.'

'I'll drink to that!' Holly said. 'Adios, Year of Cack!'

'And Hello, Year of Cock!' Olivia added, a glint in her eye.

After applying the necessary six layers, they kissed Bella goodbye and headed out. Everyone seemed to know a friend's house party to add to the mix, and they did their best to drop in on all of them. The final stop was 'Feeling Gloomy', a pub night in Kentish Town that Harry's workmates had suggested. It prided itself on playing music that was both cheerfully upbeat and yet melancholic in sentiment, which seemed to match their mood perfectly as they danced away; sometimes on tables, sometimes on the crowded and sticky dance floor.

At ten o'clock, just as she was coming up, Holly heard the familiar bittersweet tones of The Cure's 'In Between Days' kick in, and felt an undeniable urge to do one of two things. One, curl up into a foetal ball on the floor, begin rocking and sobbing for all that was lost. Or two, jump down from the table and onto the dance floor, dragging her friends in tow. Once out there, release the song from quarantine – the song she and Lawrence had their first kiss to – and dance like no one was watching her.

She plumped for the second, and it became her new favourite memory. As she bounced up and down alongside two of her best friends and they hollered, 'This is a Reclaim' in unison across the dance floor, she forgot all about it being New Year's Eve. Never mind 'Auld Lang Syne'; to her this Reclaim was better than any new beginning. Shimmying in time with the chorus and screaming, 'Without, without, without YOU!' she locked arms with Harry and felt more and more like she was flying. Hooray, everything was going to be alright! Robert Smith was hers again and she was finally, finally moving on.

'It's all going to be OK, man!' she screamed in Harry's ear, picking up speed with every word. 'There's so much exciting stuff going on and I feel driven, like really driven you know, to make the most of these last two years of my twenties! Bring on next year! I'm gonna finally try and get myself a better quality show to work on, somehow!' She stopped for a much-needed breath, and to take a sip from her bottle of water.

'Yeah! That's the stuff! Get in!' cried Harry, his jaw moving from side to side, tiny warts of sweat forming on his forehead.

Olivia smiled and nodded as though she totally agreed, but that she wasn't on quite as many Class-A's as them. She smiled and took a long glug on her bottle of water.

'YEAH! The Break-up Club! I am in love!' Holly squealed, high as a Red Arrow doing a loop-de-loop.

'With us!' Harry yelled, completing her sentence for her while she grinned inanely.

'Yes! AND now that we're almost in a new year, I can say that

347

Lawrence belonged to another year. He lives there now, IN THE PAST! Wooohooo!' Holly looked up and saw Olivia coming over, also drenched in sweat from dancing.

'Yay, I'm so glad you stayed out Liv!' she said, engulfing her in hugs before shouting 'I love you!' over the music.

'Yeah!' she said, then adding, 'It's really hot in here, isn't it?'

'Um, not so much – do you want to go and get some air? I'll come with you?'

'Yeah, let's go for a fag.'

'You okay?' Holly said, giving her a hug as they walked out to the balcony. 'Here, you're shaking. Have my coat.'

'Thanks,' Olivia said, tightening it around her and lighting their cigarettes.

'Maybe drink some more water?' Holly hoped her face was managing to exhibit concern despite having recently relinquished all control of her facial muscles in favour of gurning for Britain. 'Are you having a bad reaction?'

'Maybe. I've only done a couple of bombs, I guess my body's not used to it,' Olivia said, taking a seat on a nearby chair, still shivering. She emptied the rest of her bottle of water into her mouth. Then she inhaled deeply on her cigarette as though that might warm her up. Instead, it set her off into a gargantuan coughing fit.

'Jeez, maybe lay off those? You sound like an old man!' Holly said as Harry came out to join them. He grabbed the cigarette and took a sneaky drag on it.

Olivia finally stopped hacking and frowned. 'Yeah. I'm going to take up vaping soon, that's probably a much healthier idea.'

'Me too,' Harry said, giving Olivia the rest of his water bottle, and starting to rub the back of her neck in an attempt at a relaxing massage. He stopped after a few seconds and looked at Holly, his eyes widening. 'Liv, you're shaking quite a lot now. Have my coat,' he said, wrapping a third coat around her so she now resembled the Michelin Man on an Arctic expedition.

'Actually, I'm still really cold. I might go back inside,' she said, beginning to sound breathless.

She stood up, but then sat back down again. 'Why is the world spinning so much? Can you make it stop spinning please?' She broke into another coughing fit. 'I wish to god I'd not taken any now. This is really not fun Harry.'

'Shit, Liv. I think we should take you home,' Harry said.

Holly felt a sudden surge of paranoia. What if Liv was having a terrible reaction to the MDMA? What if they were all duff ones? Were they all going to collapse in a minute? Was this a mass cull of the broken-hearted, she wondered, before mentally berating herself for being so self-absorbed. 'Yes. Come on, let's take you home.'

They headed through the club and out to the street, Olivia leaning on Harry's arm for support.

'Shit. There are no shitting cabs,' Holly said what felt like an hour later.

'Of course there're no shitting cabs,' snapped Harry. 'It's New Year's Fucking Eve.'

'You guys stay out, enjoy your night,' burped Olivia. 'Especially you Holly, I've not seen you on this good form in ages; don't let me stop you please.'

'No, we're coming home with you, don't be ridiculous.'

'Yeah,' Harry said, 'you're dripping with sweat, and it's zero degrees. No way we're letting you go home on your own.'

Olivia smiled at them as her eyes closed and she slid towards the ground. They caught her just in time, and leaned her on each of their shoulders like a stoned rag doll.

'OK, this is silly, we have to do something,' Holly said, taking out her phone.

'Call a cab, good idea,' Harry said.

'No, fuck that, there won't be any. I'm ringing NHS Direct.' Then she whispered to Harry, 'Do we ply her with water? Or will that make it worse? Remember Leah Betts from the nineties? She died from drinking too much water after a pill. We're walking a fucking tightrope at this point.'

'No, she's been dancing loads. It's important she drinks enough. Let's give her the rest of your bottle, too.'

They gave Olivia a sip more water, and a little more colour returned to her cheeks.

As a cab with its light on came around the corner, Harry jumped up and waved his arms about until it pulled up. He opened the door, and helped Olivia into the back seat.

'Thanks guys. Happy New Year!' she said, 'I feel a bit better now. You two stay out, enjoy the rest of the night. I've got this, really! As they say in the American sitcoms…' she said, breaking into laughter, then another shivering fit. 'Have a great night,' she said, her voice getting hoarser.

'You in or out?' said the cabbie, looking at the others as he revved the engine.

'They're out,' Olivia said. 'Can I go to London Fields, please.'

'Not on your tod you can't,' grunted the cabbie. 'I'm not having her chucking up all over my seats. At least one of you has to look after her.'

'That settles it,' Harry said, climbing in. He sat next to Olivia, squeezing her hand, while Holly sat facing them.

As the taxi headed up Kentish Town Road, the countdowns were beginning all around them. 'Ten, nine, eight.' As they sat in traffic in the slush-lined streets, the bursts of cheers and Auld-Lang-Syn-ing escalated while Olivia's condition deteriorated.

'Hello, yes. Thank you for answering!' Holly said into her phone 'I'm calling about one of my friends… She's taken a few bombs of MDMA… about two hours ago… but she's shaking and her temperature is really, really high. We might be overreacting but,' she said, turning round, 'she's shaking uncontrollably now, and she had a small cough earlier that's turned into a crazy coughing fit.'

Harry put his hand on Olivia's forehead. 'Tell them her temperature is off the charts. I don't have a thermometer but I'd say she's pushing forty here. My hand is soaking wet. That's bad, isn't it? Ask them what we should do?'

'Shh! Hang on! I can't hear what they're saying.'

'Fuck this, I think we should go to hospital.'

Holly got off the phone and turned to the driver. 'OK, they just said to go straight to A & E. Can you take us to the nearest hospital?'

He turned the car around with a screech and headed back towards Euston. As they drove on, Holly's pulse began to race at a rate faster than when she was a speed-freak in her mid-teens. Eventually the green-tinted windows of the University College Hospital tower loomed ahead of them. The cab pulled up and she jumped out, leaving Harry with an unconscious Olivia as she raced through the revolving doors.

'Our friend's outside in a cab, she's in a really bad way,' she said to the triage nurse standing in front of reception, 'full disclosure: she's had a third of a gram of MDMA...I'm sorry.' Then she watched as two paramedics pushed a wheelchair out to the taxi.

'What time did she take it?' the nurse asked.

Holly answered to the best of her ability. Meanwhile in her head she was walking an emotional tightrope between guilt for having less right to be there than everyone else, and fear that they'd be arrested for possession any minute.

'Have a seat, someone will be with you when they can,' said the nurse as Olivia was wheeled inside, but all Holly heard was, 'you and your friends are an abscess on the economy, recklessly draining the resources that are paid for by the hard-working taxpayer.'

'Thanks,' she said as they sat down in a noisy waiting room filled with a heady cocktail of shame, graphic-looking injuries, and magazines from 1998.

351

Sometime later she and Harry were still slumped in a dark corner, drinking bad machine coffee and Googling 'symptoms of adverse reactions to MDMA', on their phones because they didn't know what else to do. The minutes went by like hours, but none brought news.

Just as Holly was attempting to make herself care about an article on celebrity cellulite in a trashy magazine, a sombre-faced female doctor came up to them and asked them to step to one side.

'Is our friend OK?' Holly said. 'Do you know what's wrong with her?'

'I'm afraid we don't know yet. She has a very high temperature and she's having trouble breathing, which we're trying to control with CPAP.'

'C-what?' Harry said.

'CPAP. It's a respiratory mask which forces air into the system It's not the most pleasant thing in the world.'

'Is this all because of what she's taken?' Harry asked. 'I feel terrible…she would never have taken any drugs if it wasn't for me.'

'We never normally take the stuff. It was just a one-off!' said Holly, as though that could possibly make any difference now.

The doctor shook her head dismissively. 'The effects of that should have worn off long ago.' Harry allowed himself a brief exhale.

'Has she got swelling of the brain from drinking too much water?' Holly said, her eyes stinging with tears. 'Is this all our fault for giving her too many bottles of water?'

'Holly, stop it,' Harry said. 'I think you've got early-onset paranoia.'

'It is too early to say what's exactly wrong with her at this time,' said the doctor.

'Can we see her yet?' said Holly.

The doctor shook her head. 'She's been taken into quarantine for now. The infectious diseases doctor is coming to see her next. We can't rule anything out at the moment. You're better off coming back tomorrow morning, when we'll have moved her to ICU. We'll know more then.'

'Quarantine? Infectious diseases?' Holly said, but the doctor was gone.

*

'Send for the men in white coats,' by @LadyGoa

OK, I literally don't know how to say this. I've found my ARSING money belt. It was hanging next to the loo all along, draped over some pipes, its sickly grey colour having camouflaged itself in the sickly grey pipes. I can only assume I must have taken it off when I first went to the loo after the party, but I was so twatted I didn't remember.

And yet, by some bizarre twist of fate, The remarkable Yann has forgiven me AND allowed me to buy him lunch by way of apology. He keeps saying that he'd have done the same if it was him. And that more than anything, he's just totally relieved I'm not going to turn him in to the Goan police.

To conclude, as if there was ever any doubt, I am a mentalist of the highest order. Clearly the only remaining option is now to replace all alcohol and drugs with transcendental meditation and yoga, as a matter of urgency.

P.S. Breaking News - I might be about to be the star of a pilot for a brand-new reality show about backpacking! A cool TV exec called Jeremy (thanks Holly!) wants me to shoot an audition tape in a matter of days. So am madly rehearsing – this is finally a chance to get my music out there! Halle-fucking-lujah!

33. *Resolutions*

The next day, instead of joining the rest of Britain in a synchronised New Year's Day fry-up followed by an afternoon chasing the hair of dog while surgically attached to the sofa, the remaining two musketeers headed straight back to the hospital.

'Don't be the one that spreads it,' they were told at every turn as they passed posters warning of MRSA, en route to the Intensive Care Unit. As they reached the waiting room, they took it in turns to get a squirt of disinfecting fluid from the dispenser on the wall.

'Hey,' Harry said as he rubbed the fluid into his hands, 'this is like the stuff you get in Portaloos, isn't it? It's like being at a festival.'

Holly turned to him in slow motion. 'Yeah Harry. It's JUST LIKE being at a festival.'

'Shhh,' he said as they entered the waiting room. Inside, a middle-aged lady was mopping her eyes with a screwed-up tissue that wasn't fit for purpose, and next to her, a young girl was choosing a new ringtone on her mobile phone. Just as Holly was debating asking her to put it on silent, a short, rotund nurse with a name-badge that read 'Shauna' popped her head into the room. 'Is anyone here the family of Miss Mahoney?'

'We're basically family,' Holly said, standing up. 'How is she?' she said as Shauna ushered them outside.

'I'm afraid we are not at liberty to divulge confidential information to those who are not next of kin. Are you her next of kin?'

'Well not exactly,' Holly said, looking defeated.

'Her only official family members are in Aruba at the moment,' Harry said.

'May I ask what is your relationship to Miss Mahoney?' Shauna said, a little too snootily for Holly's liking.

'We're very close friends. As I said, we're basically her only family.'

Harry raised a cautionary hand, lest Holly launch into any more detail about the nurturing bosom of the BUC.

'Well. In that case…' Shauna said, beginning to thaw a little around the edges.

'Can I ask what do the doctors think it might be?' Harry asked. 'Was it a reaction to the drugs?'

'At this stage, everything is pointing towards swine flu.'

'What?' Harry said.

'Influenza A H1N1. Pig flu,' Shauna said. 'The Flu of the Swine,' her Caribbean accent inflating with every syllable.

'Right, thanks. I think we've got it now,' Harry said.

'Let's hope you haven't.'

'Um, don't take this the wrong way, but… isn't swine flu a bit, um… five years ago?' Holly asked.

'Yeah – I thought that whole thing had cleared up by now,' Harry said, as though if it had been Bird Flu that might have been more on trend, and therefore more Olivia's style. Holly suppressed an inappropriate giggle at the thought of Olivia having an out of date illness, and how that wouldn't do at all. Then she felt a wave of guilt for doing so, followed by a sudden burst of motion-sickness.

Shauna looked to the ceiling. 'You'd be surprised. The strain returns every winter in small doses. All the more reason for looking after yourself – eating well and keeping warm so you don't get run-down. Now, do any of you live or work in close proximity to her? As a precaution we will need to give you a dose of Tamiflu.'

'Um, just so we know, how worried should we be?' Holly asked. 'On a scale of one to ten?'

'It's too soon to know,' Shauna said. 'In the meantime if you just wait here.' And then she was gone.

'Shit,' Holly said quietly as they returned to the waiting room. 'Swine flu, really? People can die of that. Do you remember when it was all over the bloody papers?'

'Liv's not going to die, don't be ridiculous,' Harry said. 'Anyway, how did she even get it? She hardly ever takes public transport? This is beyond ironic.'

'It's not a joke, Harry.'

'I know. It's dreadful, that's what this is.'

Holly's throat began to feel dry. 'I can't breathe,' she said, winding her curls around her fingers at hyper speed. 'Oh god. Do you think I can't breathe because I'm worried, or because I've contracted swine flu?' She stood up. 'I'm going to go and get dosed up now, just in case,' she said, running off towards reception.

As she and Harry sat in silence some two hours later, she couldn't help noticing the small round stains on the wall above some of the seats. The more time she had to stare at them, the more she wondered how they had got there. Another hour passed while they sat and waited. Her eyes kept landing back on the marks on the wall. Eventually, she figured it out. The marks were there to signify the sheer length of time people had to sit in one spot, their head slumped against the wall with worry. A greasy reminder of the prolonged, agonising wait for news. Just as she realised this, Shauna reappeared.

'OK, I have some news for you, if you'd just like to step outside again.'

They left the room, and the nurse began to speak softly. 'Miss Mahoney's condition has deteriorated I'm afraid. The oxygen level in her blood isn't what it should be, so a respiratory doctor is coming to see her. Then after that you may be able to see her.'

'Respiratory doct—?' Holly said, her hand moving to her chest as she tried to concentrate on her own breathing.

'Do they know if it's swine flu yet?' Harry asked, his face creasing with concern.

'We won't know for certain for another twenty-four hours,' Shauna said, looking at her watch before striding away again, leaving them alone.

'I can't believe we've been here for over three hours and still haven't seen her,' Holly said, feeling the room spin and sitting back down. She grabbed hold of the underside of the brown plastic chair to anchor herself.

Harry sat down and squeezed her hand tightly. 'Should we try and get in touch with Bella? You know. In case of…'

'Yes. I think we should,' Holly said, getting her phone out and starting a Skype message. 'What about Jonny?'

Neither of them knew what to say to that, so the question was left to hang in the silence. They heard some footsteps approaching, and Holly stood up to see if anyone was coming for them. Nope. Nothing. After a while, she became obsessed with the Footsteps Game – the crescendo of hope as footsteps came near the waiting room, and then the disappointing diminuendo as they got further away and as you realised there were no news-bearing humans attached to them. Although the truth was, she was dreading actually hearing any kind of news. In here, tucked up in the waiting room of ignorance, she was shielded from the worst thing ever. Part of her wanted to stretch out the bubble of not-knowing a little longer, so she could carry on living in a world where everything was still OK. A world where one of her best friends wasn't stood at the border control of Death, deciding whether to go in or not.

Just as she was beginning to think the unthinkable, the footsteps began to get louder and clumpier. Shauna peered around the door.

'You can go in now.'

They stood up and walked towards the door marked ICU.

'Uh-uh! You'll need these,' Shauna said, pointing to the dispenser of attractive blue robes, and handing them both a face mask. Holly pulled on the 'robe', which looked more like a festival poncho made out of up-cycled blue corner-shop plastic bags.

Harry smiled at the sight of Holly in hers, and opened his mouth to speak.

'Don't you dare liken this to a festival again,' Holly said, and Harry closed his mouth.

'Follow me,' Shauna said, and they walked into the intensive care unit.

So as not to have to see all the bodies lined up in all the beds, Holly stared directly at the neat bun at the back of Shauna's head in front of her, focusing only on her thick brown hair while they walked, until eventually they reached the furthest bed in the room. Even then she didn't dare look at the patient in the bed. Instead she studied Harry's face first, for any reflection of how bad it was. A shadow crossed over his face, and slowly, she turned to face Olivia. Her eyes like coal, she was pale and gaunt; the illness having robbed her complexion of its former radiance. Tubes ran from her arm to a drip, and an oxygen mask was clamped to her face. Beside the bed, a veritable cockpit of controls beeped away, monitoring her vital statistics. Briefly,

Olivia's eyes opened, and she managed a slow smile of recognition, before they closed back up again.

BellaAllen@LadyGoa:
Fuck. Bad news from home. Bad.

The next evening, they were back at Olivia's bedside again. The doctors had confirmed it was swine flu, and Olivia had acquired a new neighbour in the next bed along. On the other side of a lemon yellow curtain, an elderly lady was attached to various machines. At regular intervals, she emitted an unfortunate loud wailing noise while convulsing in her sleep. Holly and Harry looked at each other.

'She doesn't know she's doing it,' Shauna explained, while checking various dials on Olivia's monitors. 'She is very uncomfortable. She has the same thing as your friend, but the doctors don't think she has very long,' Shauna added, writing notes onto a clipboard. Then she looked at her wristwatch. 'Miss Mahoney needs to go for some more tests now, if you want to come back in an hour?'

Holly stood stunned, unable to speak. Eventually Harry took her hand and led her back to the waiting room. They returned to their old seats, and Holly lay her head on Harry's shoulder.

'Why are they doing more tests? If they know it's swine flu, what else are they looking for? Why won't they tell us more?' Holly lifted her head up and turned to face Harry. 'Is she going to end up like her neighbour?'

He shook his head unconvincingly. 'I don't know if I should say this, but I overheard the doctors talking about her breathing problems. They said if they get much worse then there's a risk of it becoming pneumonia.'

Holly's eyes welled up.

'Hey, hey…' he said, putting his arm around her, 'I'm sure it's one of those things that sounds worse than it is. You know, pneumonia was a killer in Dickensian times, but these days, people get over it, provided they're strong.'

'Liv's not that strong though, is she? You heard; the registrar took one look at her and said she was underweight, and that could be why she was more susceptible.'

'That makes sense,' Harry said.

'God, I thought it was all the triathlon training – but looking back, it's so obvious now – she just wasn't eating. Why didn't we all just try harder to force-feed her?'

'I don't think that's quite how anorexia works,' Harry whispered, and they fell silent.

'We've fucked up, royally, haven't we?' Holly said. 'Why didn't we notice?

'She just always seemed so on top of everything. But looking back, I don't think she ever really processed the break-up with Ross. All she did was bury it and jump straight into things with Jonny.'

'And she did a very good job of seeming OK, of keeping up the veneer.'

'If anything, it's my fault for encouraging her to train with me! I should have been more strict about the carb-loading.'

Just then, Holly's footstep receptors – by now finely tuned from what felt like weeks of waiting for news – picked up on some distant feet in the hall. But there was something different about these ones. They were more like the pitter-patter of tiny flip-flops.

She peered her head out of the waiting room. Down the hall, in the distance, was a sight to behold. A lady with jet-black dreadlocks, a deep tan and love-beads was hobbling up the corridor. She was weighed down by an enormous rucksack, an ethnic-patterned red guitar case, and various hessian holdalls hanging from her arms.

'Oh. My. Shit! BELLA!' Holly yelled, before remembering she was in a hospital and apologising profusely to everyone around her. Then she ran down the corridor, trying to suppress the urge to scream.

'HOLLY!' Bella shouted, running into her arms.

'Sshhhhh! Ick, you smell of Camel!' Holly said a beat later.

'Thanks, nice to see you too!' she whispered.

'Here, let me help you with these,' Holly said, and Bella offloaded her entire rucksack onto Holly's shoulders.

'Ow. Christ, what have you got in here? An actual camel?'

'Almost. Sorry.'

'Here, we're just in this room,' Holly said, leading Bella back up the hall to the waiting room. Bella peered her tanned face around the door.

'What the—?!' Harry whispered, standing up and rushing over to Bella.

'Say nothing about my dark circles, I came straight from Heathrow and haven't slept in two days.'

Holly and Harry threw their arms around her.

'I cannot believe you came back!' Harry said from within the huddle.

'Liv's family; of course I had to come back! As soon as I heard how serious it was, I got on the first flight I could. BUC forever, remember?'

Holly squeezed her tight and started sobbing.

'OK, I have an idea,' Harry said eventually, 'don't laugh, but it's Sunday... what say we... have a meeting?'

Holly rolled her eyes. 'Really? But Liv's lying there!'

'All the more reason to pull together. She wouldn't have us miss a meeting, would she?'

Holly looked him in the eye to see that he was actually being serious. Then, slowly, she began to talk. 'All right then, if you insist... But let's keep our voices way down. So, OK kids... welcome to BUC. Could I begin this week's meeting by saying that I take it ALL back. Whatever it was I said earlier about break-ups being worse than, well, you know... it seems so trite now. Ridiculous, even. Sitting here in this dingy room, faced with the prospect of losing one of our best friends in the world, I can suddenly see what a bunch of self-indulgent arses we are! We've had our head up our bums for way too bloody long now.'

'I hear you,' Harry said, giving her a hug. 'Maybe it did all get a bit out of hand.'

Holly gave him an awkward laugh, and felt the need to change the subject. 'So how was India, B? Until all this happened, I mean...'

'Amazing, thanks! Yeah, until the roof fell in, I was actually doing pretty well. I was basking in the glow of my backpacking epiphany. In fact, I've decided I'm going to do something drastic.'

Holly and Harry looked at her as if to say, 'Oh?'

She cleared her throat. 'At the risk of going a bit Clichés-R-Us: Liv being in here like this, it's made me realise that life's too short. I'm going to quit pub singing. There's something much more worthwhile that I can do with my life. The answer's been staring me in the face.'

'Good on you, Bella!' Holly said, slapping her on the back.

'Yeah, that's a brave decision, well done,' Harry said. 'So what are you going to do?'

'Get down the job centre for starters! I'm sick of being piss-poor. No, I'll take you through the master plan later. It feels wrong discussing the ins and outs of my career while Liv's lying there...'

Harry raised his white plastic cup of water. 'Fair. Well here's to getting off our arses, and to not being such a bunch of fuck-ups. We owe it to Liv.'

'To Liv,' they said. Then as they all 'clinked' their white plastic cups of water, Holly's phone buzzed with an email. She clicked onto her inbox.

'Shitting fuck,' she whispered moments later.

'What?' Harry said.

'I've just been dumped. It seems that OfCom – the TV complaints board – have received over 21,000 letters after the whole Stephen Fry thing... and as a result they've had to take The Madhouse off the air. So Jez says he's now only able to keep Pascal on. After all the effort I made to save his manipulative little arse, I've got one month left!'

'So you've essentially just been fired by Stephen Fry,' Harry said, helpfully.

'It's a claim to fame if nothing else. Get this though. There's a postscript: if I'm willing to let him use BUC, he'll keep me on. At almost twice my salary! I hate that arse-faced weasel!'

'Have you told him Liv's in hospital?'

'I suspect that's what made him up his offer, the sick fuck.'

'Hol, I know you can't see this now, but it really is a blessing in disguise,' Harry said.

'Yeah. You can take some time out, work out what it is you want to really do,' Bella said. 'Or just come to the job centre with me! Broke-up Club, anyone?' she said, a massive grin spreading across her face as a doctor walked up to them with the opposite expression.

'Excuse me. Do any of you have the contact details for Miss Mahoney's next of kin?

'I do,' Holly said, opening her handbag. 'Why, has something happened?'

'There has been a change in Miss Mahoney's condition I'm afraid,' said the doctor very quietly. 'Please try not to be alarmed,' she said, in such a way that the only possible outcome could be gargantuan Belisha beacons of alarm. 'Miss Mah—'

'You can say Olivia. That's her name,' Harry said. They all looked at him in surprise, and Holly 'shushed' him with her eyes.

'Your friend is very poorly, I'm afraid. She's been getting tired from breathing so fast for so long. So in order for us to help her, the doctors have had to insert some breathing apparatus into her throat to make her lungs oxygenate her blood better. In other words, a life-support machine.'

Bella looked at the others as if to say, what the fuck have I missed?

They all looked at the doctor in silence, as she went on. 'In order for this machine to help your friend with her breathing, we have had to temporarily paralyse her muscles. As a result –

this may come as a shock – Ms Mah— your friend is now in a coma.'

'BUT SHE NEVER EVEN TAKES THE TUBE!' Holly shouted. Then, more quietly, 'How can this be happening?!'

Bella burst into tears, Holly turned the colour of a Milky Bar and Harry took both of them into his arms.

He looked up at the doctor. 'Um, can I just ask – I thought that swine flu only affected really old or really young people?'

'Yes, that's certainly been the case with previous outbreaks. Usually, if you're young, fit and healthy you should be able to fight it. But Olivia was, sorry, is quite underweight. There is also another reason why her symptoms could have been exacerbated.'

'What's that?' Holly asked.

'Well. Is there any chance that Miss Mahoney might be pregnant?'

34. *Broke-up Club*

When Bella and Holly arrived, the queue to take a ticket was already way out the door. Bella attempted to keep on walking, past the concrete cathedral of gloom, but Holly grabbed her arm.

'No you don't, Allen. We can do this. I'm right behind you, every step of the way. We're the Broke-up Club, remember? We're unstoppable.'

Bella smiled and gave Holly a squeeze. She took a deep breath and entered the stuffy waiting room that was filled with people of all ages, each bored and depressed in equal measure. They each took a ticket and sat down.

Holly gave the jobs wall a tentative scan – from nightclub toilet cleaners to bus drivers to call-centre workers – before making the decision to sit down instead. She opened up Story and picked up where she'd left off weeks ago. She didn't get further than five words in before she noticed Bella's eyes filling with tears. She followed her gaze to see a newspaper headline on the table in front of them: 'FIVE MORE LOST TO SWINE FLU AS LATEST EPIDEMIC GRIPS YOUNGER GENERATION'.

'Don't, B. Don't look at it.' Holly swiftly turned the page as if this would make it all go away.

'It's been two months, Hol. Two months she's been in a coma

now! Two months we've been going out of our minds with panic! What if she never wakes up? How long do they leave it before deciding – you know?'

'I know, B, I know. I mean, I don't know any of the answers,' she said, giving Bella a reassuring cuddle, 'but I know what you're feeling because I'm thinking all the same thoughts too.' She stopped, having run out of useful things to say or do, and sank back into her chair as a new, equally shocking headline beamed out at them. 'WIDOW "MINDS THE GAP".'

'What. The. Shit?' She grabbed the page with both hands, her pulse quickening. 'Oh my god, this is just like my film idea. How weird!' She began to read. 'It's exactly my story! Only it's the other way round. Here, listen to this… "Margaret McCollum, who used to plan the route of her Tube journeys so she could hear her late husband's voice, was devastated when she found out his recording was no longer being used. She wrote to TFL for a copy of the iconic recording so she could keep the memory herself. But they only went one better than that and actually reinstated it at Embankment tube station."' Holly read on, her heart pounding as she took in all of the facts.

'His name was Lawrence! Well, all right, Oswald Laurence. He was an actor, and was the life and soul to all who knew him. He died fifteen years ago.'

'I bet none of his films ever reached such a wide audience as those three little words,' Bella said, leaning over Holly's shoulder to see the article. "To know I was going home and could just go to that station and hear his voice was really very special,"' continued Bella, reading aloud. 'How beautiful is that?'

Holly nodded, a lump forming in her throat.

'SEE? Your film – it is a good idea. And it is plausible. Lawrence – your Lawrence, was wrong all along.'

'Yes – this does make it feel more like a story that needs telling now.'

'Too right. It's a sign! Fate himself has decreed that you must make this film. It is written!'

'I wish it was bloody written already.'

'Plus the fact someone else might read this and think of the film idea now – you'd better hurry up and write it first.'

'Shit, you think so?'

'Yeah, probably. Oh, that's my number!' Bella stood up. 'Right then, positive mental attitude here I go!' She made the long walk of shame to the allocated desk, where 'Hello, my name is Bernice' raised an eyebrow by way of a welcome.

'HELLO!' Bella said to Bernice, who had sallow skin, a beard of croissant flakes and the kind of vapid eyes that said she'd worked at Harringay Job Centre her whole adult life.

'What do you do, Miss Isabelle?'

'Whatever I like,' Bella said, giggling.

Bernice did not look up, and did not smile.

'Sorry. I've just always wanted to say that. And you walked right into it…'

'Are you actively seeking gainful employment?' said Bernice while tapping away and avoiding any danger of eye contact.

'Yes.'

'Do you have any distinguishing skill-sets?'

'I've worked as a pub singer for the last six years. And I graduated with a degree in Music.'

'So you're looking for work in the Entertainment sector?'

'Actually I'm after a new departure.' Bella cleared her throat and smiled. 'I've just been out in India… where I had a bit of an awakening.'

Bernice's eyes glazed over.

'I've realised that I want to help people for a living. After spending the last year consoling my friends through some pretty dark times, I've come to realise that I'm actually quite good at helping people. It's also the one thing that seems to stop me being such a self-obsessed nincompoop. Putting this together with the fact that I have an incredible singing voice, it suddenly came to me – I should be a music therapist! To heal those less fortunate than I, through the wonders of the noblest of art form!'

'OK. So let me see if I've got this. You're going to enrol in a Music Therapy course?'

'Yes. But they don't start 'til September, so I need to find something in the interim.'

'Right…' said Bernice, tapping the keyboard with purpose. 'OK then. I might have something for you that could be a nice stepping stone in the meantime.'

'Really? Great!'

'Telesales Marketer for a pharmaceuticals firm. Lots of benefits if you meet your targets. Temp to perm, starting AY-SAP.'

Bella forced a smile. 'While that sounds absolutely brilliant, Bernice, I'll have to be honest and say it's not quite what I had in mind.'

'Things are very quiet at the moment.'

'OK. I guess it wouldn't hurt to give it a whirl…' Bella said, feeling her soul wilt a little.

'There is one thing. It's in Friern Barnet.'

'Right. Is that in London?'

'You can get the number 43 all the way there from Holloway Prison.'

Bella nodded, feeling her soul keel over.

'That's if you get it, mind. There are one or two candidates down for interview. In the meantime, if you'd like to fill out one of these for me, and we'll see if you can't qualify for Jobseeker's Allowance.' Bernice held out a clipboard with a form and Biro attached. Bella took the form and went to sit back down next to Holly.

'I appear to have picked the absolute worst time ever to try and change my career,' she mumbled.

'You're doing the right thing,' Holly said still eyeing the article, 'you're doing the right thing. Say it with me now.'

'Right. I'm doing the right thing. Thanks Hol.'

As Bella began to fill in form JSA1, she realised her Biro was one of those special ones that only worked if you intermittently dabbed at it with spittle to stop it from drying out.

'Hol, I don't suppose you have a functioning pen, do you?'

Holly scrambled in her bag, then shook her head. Bella sighed. She was just getting into a nice rhythm of filling in a box, scribbling on the back of an envelope, licking the pen nib again, filling in a box while suppressing a huff, and so on, when she found herself staring across a crowded job centre at a beautiful blonde man who looked like he'd stepped straight off a surfboard, having ridden a wave all the way here from Newquay. She thought about risking a smile, then felt the urge to check there wasn't actually a Babylonian goddess more befitting of his calibre sat right behind her. She turned around. All she could see were more depressed unemployed people with clipboards. She turned back round and delivered a broad smile, showing off a full, gleaming set of teeth. Having had her adult braces removed only a year ago, this was still a novelty.

'Hey, did you want to use mine?' Surfer Dude asked from across the way in a thick Australian accent. 'I think there's a little more life in it yet.' He stood up and traversed the brown synthetic carpet in order to take up the orange plastic seat next to her. Which was possibly the single most romantic thing that had ever happened to her.

'Thanks,' she said, taking his chipped Biro and trying it out. As she went to look back down at her form, she caught a wink from Holly.

A few moments later Holly's number was called. Looking from side to side, she smuggled the newspaper into her bag. 'Woohoo, that's me!' she said, but Bella didn't hear her; she was too busy marvelling at the bone structure of Surfer Dude.

'What are you even doing here?' Bella blurted. When he looked startled she added, 'I mean, what brings you here?'

'Well, since you ask, I'm a stand-up comedian. Except, most of the time I'm sitting down, doing crap temp jobs. It's turned out to be a lot harder to get good gigs out here than it was in Melbourne.'

'Well, there's a cracking telesales job in Friern Barnet that's all yours. I can't face the interview. Being here's made me realise, I was perfectly happy in my old job as a penniless pub singer. I'm calling my boss tomorrow; see if he'll have me back.'

'Strewth. But you must have thrown in the towel for a reason, surely?'

'Well, yes. I've decided I want to retrain, to be a Music Therapist... But now I've realised that I'm twenty-seven years old and this is the plan of a crazed lunatic!'

'Hey! No idea is crazy. In fact, they say it's the crazy ones who change things don't they?'

Bella smiled at him, noticing that he had one green eye and one brown.

'Surely the real madness would be for you to not give it a try?'

'You really think so?' she said.

'I know so. I was a management consultant back in Oz for five years on a ridiculous salary, until I realised it wasn't making me happy. So I quit to do comedy.'

'And now look at you...' she teased.

He smiled, sending a swarm of butterflies to her stomach.

Were they having a moment? Bella smiled back at him and prayed she wouldn't mess things up this time. Then, pretending just for a second that she was Olivia-on-form, Bella tried something she'd not done in years.

'Um. Don't feel obliged to say yes, but... once you've filled in your JSA1, would you like to go and get a coffee? Or what is it you call them, flat whites?'

'I don't have anywhere else to be. I am an unemployed bum, after all.'

Hurrah! Finally she had achieved a certifiable, ask-a-man-out-without mistaking-him-as-a-criminal moment! Liv would be so proud, Bella thought, filling out the rest of her form as fast as her fingers would let her.

35. *Traffic Wardens*

'I can't believe her parents haven't come back from Aruba for this,' Bella said. It was a week later, and the three remaining muskahounds were sat on the bus, on their way back from the hospital, sharing a bottle of wine.

'I know! Poor, poor Liv,' Holly said. 'She officially wins the Jerry Springer trophy for having the worst parents out of all of us.'

'What are we meant to do? All this waiting is killing me.'

Holly shot Bella a glare.

'Sorry,' she said sheepishly.

'We should just keep having meetings, think positive and keep busy,' Harry said.

'He's right. How are you getting on with penning your amazing short film, Hol?'

'Not so well actually,' Holly said, feeling a small gaggle of moths return to her belly.

'What? I thought that freaky news story would be the making of you. The key to unlocking your creativity!' she said, her eyes lighting up.

'At ease, B. Nope. Turns out it's still too blooming hard to turn into a script. Lawrence was right. He always said how executing

371

an idea was so much harder than having one. Anyway, none of that matters now because I've got an INTERVIEW later! For a call-centre job. Jesus, it sounds even worse saying it out loud. Does anyone have any happy news?'

'I do!' Bella was now grinning like a Cheshire cat that had found a large tub of double cream on special offer in Aldi. 'I smiled at a traffic warden today.'

'What?' Holly said.

'You know, after I left Joel's house, I just felt so at peace, and so happy for the first time in ages, that I just found myself saying, "Hi, how are you? Have a great day," TO A TRAFFIC WARDEN as I passed him in the street!'

They all looked at her in confusion.

'I know it sounds bonkers. But the world IS just better now.'

'Sorry…' Harry began. 'Can someone fill me in please? Who the EFF is Joel?'

'Joel is a very lovely man that I've been seeing.'

Harry listened in shock as Bella filled him in on her P45 romance. 'Wow, so romance really does happen where you least expect it!'

'Indeed! But listen. If anyone should ever ask how we met, remember it was in the street OUTSIDE the job centre in Harringay. Not actually INSIDE. OK?'

They all nodded.

'Have you done it yet?'

'Oh how I've missed you, Dirty Harry! Actually, since you ask, we want to wait. It's going to be so special, we don't want to rush it. He's been so sweet and caring about Liv, too. He's basically perfect.'

Holly grimaced. 'I feel queasy. I'm either contracting swine flu. Or you're just being über-nauseating.'

'Joy-killer!' she yelled, 'You'll feel like this one day, I promise. You'll feel a rush of the good butterflies again. And when you do, you won't look back.'

Holly gave Bella a 'you've changed' look, as she went on.

'I'm telling you. I know it's not been long, but I've never felt like this. It's changed my whole state of mind. And all because I decided to change my career!'

'All right, can I just stop you there?' Harry said, and Holly winked at him with relief.

'We're going to have to ask you to leave the club,' Holly said, 'I'm sorry. We just can't be around you when you're so happy. It's giving off completely the wrong vibe.'

'Oh shush guys, that's mean. I actually think it's healthy for you to be around something slightly more uplifting than usual.'

'You may have a point,' Harry said. 'But Bella, with respect, you haven't known this guy long, so just be careful. Especially since you'll have all sorts of visa problems if it does get serious. Not to be the Voice of Doom or anything… just don't be thinking to yourself Joel is "the one". Not yet, anyway.

'No?' Bella said, her eyes belying that it was probably too late for that. 'Harry's right. He doesn't have to be THE ONE. He's just THE ONE AFTER SAM.'

'The one after Sam,' Bella repeated, liking how it sounded.

'Exactly. Take the pressure off!' Harry said.

'OK. Please can I just say one more revolting thing before we move on? I had a bit of a realisation, right. I never truly understood why people get married. Now I get it! It's not just because you've decided they'd be a nice match for you. Spending your life with someone – it's actually just about wanting to spend more time with them. And instead of days, weeks, years it's, well, a lifetime. It's just a way of saying you really, really like spending time together. Do you know what I mean? It's your way of declaring that forever has really got started.'

'OH! I want my forever to start!' wailed Holly, overcome with the cheesiness, and taking another huge swig of red wine to wash it down with.

'We can't rush these things, people. Remember what the great

Diana Ross once said…' Harry mused sagely as they stepped down from the bus.

'Every time you touch me, I become a hero??' Holly said, blankly.

'No, you numpty. That Motown classic, "You Can't Hurry Love"!'

Everyone was silent and contemplative for a few minutes.

'Wasn't that Phil Collins?' Bella said, who was promptly hit on the head by Harry.

'Guys. Can we make a pact?' Holly said as they began walking up the road towards Boozenest. 'And I'm directing this to Olivia too, even though she can't hear us… But, if by the time we're of proper settling age, we still haven't met anyone we'd like to do the whole forever thing with, we'll just all live together in a massive pile-on? Can we all go and live in a commune in the country somewhere, with sheep and chickens and LAND? And then, after that, shall we all try and make sure we get a place in the SAME OLD PEOPLE'S HOME and everything? I don't ever want to be without you guys.'

Having initially expected a cacophony of enthusiasm, she instead became aware of two things. One, that possibly she was alone in this dream. And two, that Harry looked distinctly uncomfortable.

'What's up?' she said as she turned the key in the lock.

'Actually, Hol,' he said as they all began walking up the stairs, 'I was having a chat with Harrie the other day, and we said we – um, might move in together at some point.'

Holly's face fell. 'The Harrie you've known for a matter of weeks?' she wanted to say. 'After what you just said to Bella?' Instead, she said 'Wow, that's great.'

'Yeah. Her housemate is moving out in a few months, so there'll be a spare room, so it makes sense. Gather ye rosebuds and all that! Plus it also means Bella can have her old room back - and you won't have to put up with me smoking in the shower anymore!'

374

'Oh, you're right, it's win-win,' she said, hoping it sounded convincing.

*

Later, the feeling she was failing in class again was keeping her awake. By five in the morning, Holly gave up on the dream of sleep, and went to the kitchen for a drink. Her long-suffering housemate, Daniel, was sat in the lounge, watching late-night poker.

'Why are you up?' she asked.

'I've just been on lates all week, so I'm too wired to sleep. There's some chamomile tea if you want some.'

'Rock'n'roll, Daniel.'

'Piss off, it helps me sleep.'

'Well in that case, I might get involved! Thanks.'

'You OK?' he said as she perched next to him.

'Well let's see. Liv's been on a life-support machine for almost three months now. Why am I telling you, you work in the same sodding building! Anyway, as you know, she's showing no sign of improvement... which is pretty much the worst thing that's ever happened. And aside from that – there's no way to say this without sounding entirely pathetic – but everyone I've ever met seems to be settling down. So I'm on track for being a sad old spatchelor 'til the end of my days, scraping at the date-tritus at the bottom of the barrel. And that there is my lot in life.'

Daniel laughed and poured out some tea for Holly.

'I'm glad my life is providing you with entertainment.'

'Sorry. I didn't mean to laugh. And hey, I can't promise to be an expert on swine flu – it's not my area. But I do know that Liv's young enough to fight this thing. I'm sure she'll pull through.'

'Thank you. That helps to hear.'

'As for you and your Break-up Crew...'

'Club.'

'Sorry, Club. I know I've always taken the piss out of it, but in all seriousness, I think you need to try and move on now. Not just from Lawrence, but from "the BUC" itself,' he said, acting out speech marks with his fingers.

Out of nowhere, a re-run started playing in her mind, of that first day on the Heath, all four of them lying back in the long grass, drinking and making daisy chains. Strangely, what was originally such a sad day, replete with grief and emotion, now seemed so carefree and happy. It was just like Bella had said – a happy memory seen through a prism can so easily become a sad one; and vice versa.

'I see your point. I have come to depend on it a worrying amount, whereas I can feel the others starting to need it a lot less. It's like they've all taken off their stabilisers and are merrily riding around on their bikes, while I'm still clinging on to mine for dear life, afraid of falling off,' she said, laughing. 'How is it possible I could miss being in a club that you need to be a massive loser to even be part of?'

'Blimey. Your Groucho Marx complex just went into overdrive!' Daniel looked pensive for a moment. 'You know, in my ward, we deal with a lot of crack and heroin addicts. They come in from the streets mostly, looking half-dead. We give them a bed and a course of methadone. At first it's brilliant, it gets them off the heroin. But then some have an even harder time coming off the methadone.'

'That must be rough,' she said, not quite getting the relevance.

'I feel like, to some extent, that's where you are. I think it's time to wean yourself off the methadone. It's time you broke up with the Break-up Club. They can still be your mates, but just try and tone down your dependence on them. Learn to stand on your own two feet a bit.'

'Holy shit, Doctor Daniel. I've never looked at it that way but yes. I am in fact a massive addict. I'm no better than Lawrence was at drinking!'

'Not to mention, you're putting away a lot yourself these days.'

'I didn't know you cared! So OK, you've got me. How the hell do I wean myself off it then?'

'I don't know. What do we tell our patients? Start taking walks in the park, drinking in fresh air, smelling the flowers. Go and stand in the rain, listen to music – sad and happy music. But most of all, you need to find a way to be happy within yourself! Maybe that's by doing something creative. I don't know, is there a way that you can use everything you've been going through lately as material for something; channel it somehow?'

'Mmmm. These are all good suggestions. Right. I shall start trying to wean myself off tomorrow. Thank you.'

He smiled. 'You're welcome,' he said, before drinking the last of his tea and leaving the mug in the sink.

'I might just have one last glass of red wine first though. Help me sleep.'

Later that night, as Holly sat up on the balcony, eating a whole bag of microwave popcorn and watching the pink and orange hues of the sun rising over the rooftops, she hoped this was finally a new dawn over more than just N19.

Back in bed, the red wine was failing to combat her insomnia. Whenever she closed her eyes she saw Olivia in her regulation blue and yellow gown, all those tubes strapped to her face. Then she'd open her eyes again for a minute, before closing them and finding a different piece of footage playing out: this time a funeral, with the three of them sat together in the second row. She imagined what music would be playing, what eulogies would be read. There were Olivia's sun-tanned parents in the front row, and there was Bella, clearly finding it the hardest to keep it together out of all them, slowly breaking into the worst tantrum-ette any of them had ever witnessed, about the injustice of it all.

As she lay there staring at the cracked ceiling, she tried not to think about what they'd all do if Liv didn't wake up. Never mind how it would affect the Club, how would they all cope without one of their best friends? She sat up in bed, and began to think about earlier that week, when she'd been sat by Olivia's bed. She'd been chattering away to her, rambling on about the week's news, no idea whether she could be heard or not. But she'd liked to think that in some small way her voice had provided comfort. Which reminded her of something.

She grovelled around for the newspaper article from the job centre. She re-read the story of Oswald Laurence, and thought about his widow being comforted by his audible leftovers. She opened up Bakerloo Bob's forum, pressed play on some of the YouTube recordings, and made some notes. Then she read about all the different voices of the Underground and National Rail. She tried to imagine them all as real people, each of them with lives, hopes and families who loved them, who couldn't live without them.

She picked up her laptop from the floor, turned it on and opened up the document named 'Mind the Gap'. Rubbing her eyes, she began to type.

Five hours later, she woke to find Harry holding out a cup of tea for her, while the laptop lay snoozing next to her on the pillow.

'Well hello there!' she said, pretending to be a perky morning person.

'You look like shit. Are you still not sleeping?'

'Yes. But it's OK. I've been up writing!'

'How did that happen? Writing what?'

'Well, I couldn't sleep, and I kept on thinking about Liv, and what if she never wakes up, and how ironic that was – I can't get to sleep, and she can't bloody well wake up! And then I got to remembering being in the hospital, trying to talk to her, and not knowing whether she could hear me or not. I started thinking about the importance of voice, and of being heard... And then it was like it unlocked something, somewhere. For the first time ever, I finally found a way to script that idea I had forever ago. Then I just started writing a whole torrent of rubbish, kind of a stream of consciousness at first, and then it twisted and turned its way into what might actually be a script.'

'Well fucking done!' Harry smiled and sat on the floor next to the bed. 'What did I tell you? So what's the synopsis?'

'OK. It's probably total horseshit, but it's about this guy who just rides the Tube all day long, listening to the TFL voice calling out the stops. Slowly we see his appearance deteriorate. He begins to look less and less well presented, then after a while his stubble goes full-beard. Only, it's all done in reverse, so that at the film's beginning he just looks like one of those unhappy tramps you see on the Tube. The more we see him deteriorate, we gradually see that he's not a tramp at all – he's just addicted to aimlessly riding the Northern line all day for some reason, and he's really let himself go. Eventually we see him wearing a suit, looking really attractive and like he has his shit together. Then later, we might see him step off the train and change to a different line; the Victoria line. A sign that he's finally starting to be able to move on with his life, and to put the past behind him. Then we see a flashback to him and his wife together, of a scene where they were at their happiest. And you hear her saying sweet nothings to him. The first and only line of actual spoken dialogue, which is when the audience will hear her speak, and realise it's the same as the Tube voice that was calling out the stops. Ultimately, it's about the depths you sink to in grief, and the importance of voice as a comfort.'

Harry nodded. 'Wow, you've really moved it on. I love the idea that these people who did seemingly meaningless voice-over jobs are now actually immortalised in some way by Transport for London.'

'Exactly! I'm wondering about that "reveal" scene taking place on the Heath, on one of those real halcyon summer days where they're just lying back in the long grass...'

'Like we all did a year ago?'

Holly nodded, her eyes brightening. 'And then, if it's not too cheesy, maybe some titles appear over the top… "Though nothing can bring back the hour of splendour in the grass, we will grieve not, rather find strength in what remains behind…" '

'Well, as I always say – there's nothing in life that can't be improved by with a bit of Wordsworth,' Harry said. 'Anyway, I like it. Can I read the script?'

'I would love you to.'

Harry took the laptop and rested it on his knees. 'Mind the Gap, by Holly Braithwaite. Oooh, hark at thou, screenwriter!'

'Piss off. Like I said, I'm confident it's mostly cack. But you're welcome to have a read while I'm in the shower,' Holly said, jumping out of bed.

When she came back from the bathroom, Harry was staring at the screen, his eyes lost in thought.

'Well? Say something.'

'Yeah. The idea's good.'

'Really?'

He nodded. 'Yeah. It's strong.'

'But?'

'But the execution isn't quite there yet.'

'See! I told you, it's a pile of turd!'

'Stop it! It's a solid first draft. And you definitely did not need Lawrence! I love the scene where he eats his dinner off a plate, on the actual Tube, just because he's used to them eating all their dinners together every night, for forty years. That actually made me cry. Yeah, I just think it could be helped by adding in a few things here and there, like, I think you need to see him doing more in between the journeys. Maybe we see him shedding stuff, clearing out her clothes into bin bags, slowly editing her out of his life, smelling her bottle of shampoo one last time before he throws it away – minding the gap, if you will. Then you're laying clues that he's lost someone and he's not just lost. And then you could even misdirect the audience a bit, to make them wonder at first, has she left him?'

'Until we see the lilies and sympathy cards and they work it out.'

'Exactly. And maybe we can also see him burning some of her things.'

'If he can manage to do so without the fire brigade coming.'

'Then, maybe we should try and make this.'

'Make it?'

'YES! That was the idea, wasn't it? When's the next Future Shorts competition?'

'I love you Harry, but, dream the fuck on! We'd be doing this on a shoestring. Worse than that – the little bit of plastic at the end of the shoestring!'

'Oi, less of the pessimism! Sometimes low budgets can actually push creativity! Remember the Pythons. Those coconuts in *The Holy Grail* only came about because they couldn't afford to have actual horses on set. FACT.'

'Really?'

'Besides which, if we do it soon, you can borrow all the camera kit from work, can't you?'

'Guess I might as well screw them for all I can before I go.'

'Great! And I might be able to rope in one of the TV Producers from work to help. One comment – and this is a purely logistical thing. I know from whenever my agency has shot ads on the Underground that it's expensive, forward-slash, impossible to film there. I think we'd be better off rewriting it to be set on a London bus. The idea still holds.'

Holly nodded slowly. 'So then we just need a director. Shame I don't know any of them anymore!' she said bitterly.

'Or, you could direct it. You know what you want, don't you? Why not give it a go?'

'I'm an editor, Harry, not a director!'

'Labels, schmabels. OK, forget who does what. Between us we'll do the role of a first assistant director and director. We'll just be a team and we'll pull it off somehow. Think how amazing you'll feel – and you never know where it might lead!'

'Shit, the deadline's next week! There's no time,' she said, quickly Googling the competition website.

'Ah, but you've got to have a deadline, otherwise you won't do it. If you don't have a deadline, how you gonna make your dream come true?' he sang. And in spite of the fact this reminded her of Lawrence, Holly broke into laughter.

'OK, you've got me. Let me see – I can probably borrow a boom and camera kit from work. Then I just need an actor. Someone dark, tall, in their late twenties, with a sexy smattering of stubble…'

'Mmm. Who do we know that would fit a casting brief like that?'

'Ha! And who just so happens to owe me a favour!' Holly said, picking up her phone and dialling.

The next few days unfolded in the manner of an episode of the classic eighties show *Challenge Anneka*. Bella had placed an ad at Guildhall School for some extras. Somehow, a friend of a friend knew someone who had access to a double-decker bus that they could film in. And Bella herself was to play the part of 'the Voice', which they would record using the sound booth at work. Before long, it was shoot day and Holly was smuggling camera kit out of the studio and onto the back of a van, praying Jeremy wouldn't see her. Next thing, they were filming, guerrilla style, on London's South Bank.

'Fuck-sticks. We don't have a dolly,' Holly said an hour before they were due to start shooting. 'I knew there was something! This isn't going to work; it'll look far too jumpy and amateur!'

Harry looked up from his call-sheet. 'Don't worry, we'll find a way to improvise. How about, Holly, you can just hold the camera guy tightly, to try and stabilise him while he walks, and then we'll pull him along slowly. That way the camera will be a bit smoother. Not perfect, but better than nothing!'

Holly nodded slowly. 'It's worth a try I suppose. Thank you, Harry. Again.'

'See, improvisation!' he said, chuckling in advance of his own terrible pun. 'We don't need a dolly. We've got a Holly!'

Holly allowed a laugh to seep through her shell of pre-shoot nerves, and glanced up to see Luke arrive, looking extra stubbly and a stone thinner.

'Hello!' he said, giving her an awkward hug with his now bony frame.

'Hi! Hey, you've gone full beard! I like it!' she said, relieved there hadn't been an influx of butterflies upon his arrival. 'And you're gaunt!'

'I've been on a strict diet for the part. I figured my character wouldn't have been eating much.'

'You're a true pro, thank you! Did you bring your razor for the clean-shaven scenes later?'

He nodded.

'Ace! We're just about ready to start turning over. Thank you so much for doing this, Luke.'

'Hey, it's the least I could do,' he said, somehow not needing to explain why. 'And I always said it was a nice idea. So which way's my trailer then?' he joked.

'Actually, we're all using that Starbucks over there as our dressing room and unit base. Hope that's to the talent's liking?!'

'Perfect,' he said, heading off to get changed.

When he came back, Holly took a deep breath and took up her position behind the cameraman and the director of photography, both of whom were friends she'd drafted in from *Prowl*. Once they were all fed, watered and in first positions, she began.

'Everyone! So HI! Thank you all so much for giving up your time for this. The first thing to say is, please bear with Harry and I, as this is actually our first time playing at being "Director and First AD". I won't lie, there's going to be a fair amount of making things up as we go along. So if I say something you don't understand then please don't be afraid to pick me up on it!'

'OK, let's go for a take. Sound speed… turning… mark it…'

Harry opened and closed the clapperboard with a loud clunk. 'Camera set.'

'And, action,' she said, feeling like a total fraud but somehow managing to convey a semblance of confidence.

After a few hours of filming, they stopped for a food break.

Holly bit into a sandwich while looking over the shot list, trying to figure out how they were going to get it all done in time.

'More food, Hol?' Harry said, offering her a huge tray of delicious-looking bagels and sandwiches.

'No thanks,' she said, looking at her watch. 'I'm stuffed, and we're losing light, and we've still got to get to the other side of London for the scene on the Heath! No, eating can wait.'

Harry stared at her with his eyes wide open.

*

By late afternoon, they were all out on the Heath, racing to get through the last scene before sundown.

'OK, let's just do this last take, and then we'll call it a day,' Holly said. 'Any longer and we'll have a hell of a time adjusting the sky in post!'

Later, after she had yelled, 'OK everybody that's a wrap', and felt like a cross between a pretentious twat and a movie sensation, they had an impromptu wrap party picnic. They chose a spot overlooking the ponds, not far from where four broken-hearted friends had gathered one Sunday, over a year ago.

'Hey, massive well done today, Holly,' said Luke, handing out glasses of Prosecco to everyone. 'You'd never have known it was your first time. Well, except maybe when you gave me that note to "Keep it light-hearted, but with gravitas!"'

'Yes, sorry, I'm the queen of conflicting feedback, aren't I? I just hope we've got the film we want out of it, and that it's something for both our reels.'

'Sure we have. This job will shine in the edit, that's what they say, isn't it?' Luke smiled, opening another bottle of Prosecco, sending the cork flying over the Heath, narrowly missing a passing Labrador.

'Hopefully, yes.' She smiled, taking a cup and clinking it with his.

*

For the next week, Holly didn't see daylight. Every spare minute at work was devoted to the edit in the broom cupboard, switching between The Madhouse and Mind The Gap at every opportunity. When she came up for air again, she had one painstakingly edited film on her computer.

'What do you think?' she said to Harry, who had just watched the full thirteen minutes.

'Yeah. It's beautifully shot. Good choice on the music. Love a bit of Eno. You've done a great job.'

'But?' Holly said, her stomach tightening.

'But it feels too woolly. I think it'll have far more punch if you cut it back a bit. At the moment it feels indulgent and you start to lose sympathy for him.'

'Right.'

'So. I think there are quite a few scenes you could let go of, and the overall impact will be much more memorable. For example, towards the end, maybe it's enough that you see him take the wedding dress out of the box – you don't need to see her in the photo frame wearing the dress. That way, when you see him taking it to charity, you've only hinted at the significance of it. You imagine her filling it, which is more poignant than if you'd spelled it out.'

Holly scrolled back through the timeline and nodded. 'You're so right. I was really labouring it wasn't I!'

'Sometimes what you don't say is even more powerful. Brevity is the soul of wit, and all that! As true as life as it is in art,' and Harry looked at her in that way where he saw right into her soul again.

'Right. Bugger off then while I give it another go.'

'Don't be disheartened though. It always takes longer to make something shorter. Remember what Pascale said: "I would've written you a shorter letter, but I didn't have the time".'

'What? Pascal? When did you meet him?'

'No! Blaise Pascale! The seventeenth-century philosopher?'

'Oh! Right. Love you, you big pontificating idiot.'

'Love you too,' he said, giving her a hug before leaving her alone.

Holly disappeared back into her editing bubble for another few hours. This time when she came up for air she had a much punchier seven-minute version. Then, after ironing out the usual issues to do with aspect ratios, and export formats without getting into a flap, she uploaded it to the film competition website just in time for the deadline. She closed her eyes, rested her head on her ergonomic wrist cushion and felt her phone beep.

'Amazing news! Liv is awake. Harry x'

36. *Alight Here*

Bella and Holly walked into the ICU ward as they had done every day for the last month, walking past the lemon yellow curtain, past the bed where Olivia's noisy neighbour normally lay. But today the yellow curtain was drawn wide open, and the bed was empty. She tried hard not to think about why this might be, as she walked on towards the next bed along.

Olivia was sitting up, the cannula tubes winding from her nose to her ears, and a small dressing over her throat, just below her Adam's apple. She turned towards them and managed a smile.

'Liv!' Holly said as she reached her. Cautiously she planted a kiss on her cheek.

'Happy New Year,' Olivia said, her voice so hoarse it was essentially a whisper. The others stared at her, not sure what to do next.

'Yes. Happy New Year indeed!' said Holly.

'It's safe to hug me. I won't break.'

'Sorry.' As Holly hugged Olivia tentatively she felt caught between the desire to smother her with affection and kisses, but also to shout about how incredibly thin and frail she was. She plumped for neither.

'What's this for?' Holly dared to ask, pointing at the dressing on her throat.

Olivia shrugged. 'Oh, it's nothing,' she said, looking at the nurse.

'It's where we had to go in for her tracheotomy,' said Shauna.

Holly's eyes widened.

'It's just a small breathing tube,' said Shauna. 'Don't worry. It's not painful. You might hear the wind whistling through it, but not for long. No smoking for you, Madam!'

Olivia managed a meek smile.

'Well this really is the least glamorous-sounding disease, isn't it,' Olivia said after a long silence. 'I mean, can there be anything more gross than Influenza of the Pig?!'

They laughed uncomfortably.

'It's actually kind of funny, isn't it – you'd have thought Miss Piggy would wind up in here, not Liv.'

'Humour now, Bella, really?' Holly said.

Olivia broke into an enormous smile. And, like it was the first time in months, she began to laugh hysterically, before stopping and looking exhausted.

'Hey, love, don't overdo it, please!' Holly said, stroking her forehead. 'Still, they do say laughter is the best medicine so maybe I'll let you off that one.'

'I still can't believe you left your trip for me,' Liv whispered to Bella.

'Er, you did almost pop your Jimmy Choo clogs, Liv.'

Olivia shrugged this off as a trifling detail. 'Well it's very kind of you. Not sure I'd have left a tropical beach… even my own mum and dad couldn't do that,' she said, her smile not quite reaching her eyes.

'I'm so sorry. We did try calling them, but we could only get hold of your housekeeper,' Holly said. 'She said she'd tell them to come and see you when they're back next week.'

Olivia forced a smile. 'Oh, that's good of them.'

'But it's like we kept telling the nurses. We're your family now,' Holly said.

'How are you feeling though? Don't speak too much if it's tiring – you should rest your voice,' Bella said.

'They're saying I'm out of the danger zone,' she croaked. 'I just need to really rest for a few weeks. And put some weight on.'

'That sounds like a good idea,' Holly said. 'Oh, Liv. You gave us such a scare. I'm so sorry if we weren't paying you enough attention. Things got a bit carried away with the Club…'

'Yeah but whose fault was that? I turned into a complete control freak.'

'Hey,' Bella said, 'I think we all went a little crazy in our own ways.'

'The irony is, I've really got my appetite back now, despite all this hospital food,' Olivia said. 'Do you know, they serve curry every night as the main option for the evening meal? Really spicy curry, even though half the people in here have heart conditions?!'

'At least you're eating, that's the main thing,' Holly said.

Olivia nodded slowly. 'They keep trying to give me all these funny little pamphlets. And they want me to see some sort of counsellor. Which I think is a bit excessive. Not sure how I'll find the time once I'm back at work. But we'll see.'

'Sounds like it would be worth making time for,' Holly said.

'I guess I can use the sessions to work through some of my deep-rooted parent shit. Either that, or I just officially divorce the fuckers and be done with it.'

'That's an option! You can represent yourself, too,' Holly said while fluffing Olivia's pillows. Then, while Bella gently tipped Olivia forward, Holly made a big performance out of repositioning all the cushions. She took the first pillow and changed it so it was vertical, then moved the one on top to be horizontal. Somehow it worked, and Olivia smiled.

'Oh that's so much better, thank you,' she said, motioning towards the cup of plastic water on her bed tray. Holly picked it up and held it to Olivia's mouth.

'So what have I missed so far in this brand new year then?'

As they filled Olivia in on everything she'd slept through, the cannula kept on falling out of her right nostril. Holly soon became master of putting the small tube back in and fiddling with the cord around the back of her head to adjust it.

'Oh, girls, I was having the weirdest visions though…' Olivia said. 'While I was unconscious, I dreamed that Jonny was sitting by my bed. Telling me that he wished he'd not dicked around all that time! And that he wished it wasn't so late – and that if I woke up he'd be a better man. Or something like that. I mean – as if.'

'Sshhhh, Liv, breathe,' Holly said, stroking her hair. 'Take it easy, lady; you've been through a lot. You're bound to have had some weird visions. You're going to be OK though.'

'Where's Harry?'

'He's coming later. You're only allowed two visitors at a time, so we've staggered it. But hopefully when Sandra's back on duty she'll let Harry in at the same time as us. It is a bit quieter in here today.'

'Yes, Sandra's the more laid-back nurse,' Bella said, 'we love her. She used to let us hold Club meetings round your bed!'

'You're not serious. You made all the other patients listen to you dribbling on about your tedious break-ups?!'

''Fraid so. We kept it up in your honour! We kept our voices really low though…' Holly said.

'We thought it might help bring you back!' Bella added. 'And maybe it did,' she whispered.

At that moment the nurse came over. 'Ladies, you're going to need to resume the lonely hearts' club another time for me. There's a gentleman here to visit Olivia. Only two at a time, remember.'

'Oh,' Holly said. 'I told Harry to come at seven. Boo. Oh, well, bye Liv. We'll come and see you tomorrow, same time-ish.' She leaned in to kiss Olivia goodbye, and gave her another cup of water. 'Drink lots of this, remember. And stuff your face like there's no tomorrow.'

Olivia rolled her eyes.

'Yes. The quicker you do, the sooner we get you back!' Bella said.

As they headed out the ICU ward, disposing of the plastic gowns and masks in the special bins on the left-hand side of the door, they saw a familiar face sat on a plastic chair in the hallway. He was holding a huge bouquet of flowers and a grave expression. He was unshaven, his shirt was crumpled and his eyes had huge dark bags under them. At first Holly thought it was the main character in her film, but then she realised.

'Jonny!?'

'Hey girls,' he said as he stood up, and Holly gave him a hug.

'Shit, I'm so sorry, we were going to try and get hold of you, but what with one thing or another we hadn't got round to it.'

'Don't worry, Dan called me. He said he'd seen how sick she was, and that it was against his moral code not to tell me!'

'Oh, good, I'm glad. So you've been in already?' Bella said.

'Yeah, I came in yesterday briefly. I'm so glad she's woken up.'

Bella was looking at Jonny oddly, as if calculating something.

'What?' he said.

'Nothing.'

'So how is she today?' he asked.

'She's a lot brighter,' Holly said. 'The oxygen level in her blood is still pretty low, so they're monitoring her and giving her regular nebulisers.'

'To keep her airways moist, or something like that,' Bella added. 'It's not nice, but at least they've stopped giving her those CPAP mask things – she said it was like sticking your head out of a car in the fast lane on a motorway. Horrible!'

Jonny went a shade paler. 'Shit, poor Liv. It sounds so awful.'

'But she's getting there, Jonny,' Holly said, resting a hand on his shoulder. 'I think she's finally over the worst of it, luckily.'

*

391

'Well Liv, this place is much more you, isn't it,' Bella remarked, sitting next to Olivia's bed and feeding her triangles of daintily cut smoked salmon sandwiches.

A week later, Olivia had been discharged from ICU and relocated to a clinic on Harley Street, for a period of convalescence. In a true testament to friendship, Holly had spent the afternoon helping a much healthier-looking Olivia to wax her secret upper lip hair, while they waited for the full BUC complement to arrive for the Sunday night meeting. Well, if they were still calling it that. Holly was trying to reframe it in her mind as simply a warm gathering of friends.

'Well, I figured I've been paying extortionate healthcare insurance for so long that I may as well be more comfortable!' Olivia said, her voice now much less hoarse.

'Exactly,' Holly said.

'Um, if it's not too inappropriate to do so, I'd like to share some news,' Bella said. 'Jeremy has just said he wants to fly me out to Ko Pha Ngan for a month! To star in the pilot for his reality show about backpacking!'

'What, as in Jeremy, the reason there is evil in the world?' Holly said.

'He's not that bad!'

'No, he really is. To start with, that was my idea, and he's not even told me he's still progressing with it, despite having fired me.'

'I'll have a word with him, Hol, make sure you get to be the editor on it. Don't worry!'

Holly pretended to mop her forehead with relief. 'Phew, thanks B.'

'Bella, you'll let me read your contract before you get on any planes,' Olivia said. 'I don't trust that letch as far as I could throw him.'

'Here, have some more sandwich,' Bella said to Olivia, who looked apprehensive but took one anyway.

'What about your new career? And what about Joel?' Holly said.

'The music therapy course doesn't start 'til September. And don't worry – Joel is coming with me! We're going to nip to Australia once filming's wrapped, and go and meet his folks!'

'Well, while we're doing announcements. I also have some news for you. Bear with.' Olivia looked even more nervous. 'You might want to sit down, actually.'

There were only two visitor's chairs in the room, so Holly sat on Bella's lap.

'OW! OK. What is it?' Bella said. 'Whatever it is we won't love you any less.'

'Yeah. I just waxed your lip hair, for the love of God. Nothing can be worse than that,' Holly said.

'Jonny and I are together. I mean, properly this time.'

Nobody spoke.

'WOW. That was biblical!' Harry said, emerging from the en suite bathroom with a white fluffy towel around him and a grin on his face. 'I just had a shower SITTING DOWN on a chair!' Having run all the way to the hospital and arrived dripping in sweat, Harry had decided to take full advantage of the benefits of private medicine. 'What's happened?' he said, seeing everyone's shocked faces. 'Liv? Are you OK?'

'I think our Liv's got something to tell you, Harry,' Bella said.

'What? Don't tell me you're pregnant. The nurse said that might be what caused you to get so sick, but we didn't like to pry until we knew if you were going to make it…'

'Christ no! That was just speculation! Thank the Lord,' she said, as a chorus of 'phews' ran around the room. 'No, I would like to formally announce that Olivia Mahoney is now in a relationship. And it's not even complicated.'

'No fucking way,' Harry said.

'Yes. Me and the mandroid are actually going to give it a proper go. Crazy, huh.'

'I think I love you a little less,' Harry said, shaking his head, while Holly laughed.

'Oh come on, people. He said he loved me!'

Bella cooed, while the others said nothing.

'Yeah, I know, he's been a massive twat. But you can't help who you love. So I have to give it a go.'

'So it took the flu of the swine to unlock the tin man armour!?' Bella said, marvelling at the true romance of it all. 'I know I never approved and it broke all the rules, but I suppose some were meant to be weren't they?'

Holly and Harry looked at each other, eyes smiling.

'Well this is all very Jane Austen, isn't it? People becoming ill and well again, all in accordance with the slings and arrows of Cupid?' Harry said.

Olivia grinned. 'He says he's going to take us to Tuscany, just as soon as I'm feeling up to it. To fully recuperate.'

'Recuperate, eh?' Harry said.

'Yeah. Well. You know what they say about flu,' Bella said, winking. 'Lots of bed rest.'

EPILOGUE

(three months later)

'The camel became lighter and lighter as it walked through time,
it kept shaking memories and photos off its back, scattering them
over the desert floor and letting the wind bury them in the
sand... and gradually the camel became so light that it could trot
and even gallop in its own curious way – until one day, in a
small oasis that called itself the present, the exhausted creature
finally caught up with the rest of me.'

Alain de Botton, *Essays in Love*

Reader, I Left Him

Holly was sat in the centre of the room, surrounded by brown tape and boxes. But this time it was her old friend the broom cupboard she was packing up and this time, for a good reason. She was so excited she couldn't stop herself from re-reading the email for the fourteenth time that minute.

Hi Holly,

Congrats on the festival win. I was proud as punch when I saw your name on the credits. Almost jumped out my seat.

I can come out and admit this now: I always hoped you'd write something of your own one day. Had a hunch your strength was more in idea generation than in cutting.

Tell me to mind my own if you like. But in my experience, all the best editors have a quality about them of, how do I put this – ruthlessness, quick decision-making. Knowing instinctively what to keep and what to cut. Not dwelling on things too long – that's what separates the mediocre editors from the Walter Murches. If I'm being brutal, I'm not sure these are qualities you have in spades. I think your (considerable) strengths lie elsewhere.

My point is, I'm setting up a new, smaller production company. We're specialising in pitching new Comedy/Drama ideas to places like the Beeb and C4. We've an opening for a writer/developer (paying more than your junior editor role, too!). In particular, we're focusing on ideas about groups of friends in their late twenties – something to try and fill the British Girls gap, which every man and his dog is scrapping for. If anything springs to mind?

Anyway, if any of this makes any kind of sense to you, I'd love you to come on board. That's if I can drag you away from Reality…?

Look forward to hearing what you think.

Mark.

Even now, three weeks later, this was still giving her the good kind of butterflies as she put down her mobile phone and caught sight of The Rules that were still tacked to the wall. She smiled, took the piece of paper down and put it into her bag. Then she felt a craving for one last shopping spree in Room G.E.13. Nothing too crazy, mind – just one or two trinkets to kit herself out with for the future. Soon she was face to face with the hallowed stationery cupboard.

Moments later, she was rifling through supplies. This time she took only what she needed. Just a couple of envelopes, batteries and some pens. Oh and five of those A4 ideas pads. On the walk back to her office, she noticed a Diesel-clad figure skulking by her door.

'Been to the sales?' asked Luke, smiling his Hollywood smile.

'Hello again! Actually, I'm stocking up. Where I'm going they don't have a huge superstore like here.'

'Where are you off to?'

'I'm going back to Drama. In development this time, though! If this year's taught me anything it's that I'm an appalling editor.'

'Well, I don't know about that. But congratulations on the move!'

Holly blushed. 'What about you? How are things?'

'I've just been in for a meeting about this backpacking reality show. It's only at pilot stage but Jez wants me for the presenter, if it gets picked up.'

'Great!'

'No, brutal, but actors can't be choosers can they! It's not that I'm averse to fucking off to a Thai island for a bit, but it's still not why I trained at drama school, is it! Though, it's not all bad. I managed to bag a new agent after Mind The Gap cleaned up at the festivals. For which I only have you to thank.'

'Not at all. It's all down to your amazing acting.'

Luke gave a nervous smile. Then he made to leave, but something pulled him back. 'Can I just also say that I'm sorry about what happened with us? It was textbook knobhead behaviour. The pathetic truth is, I lose interest in girls after I sleep with them. It's a condition.'

'You're all right. I think I took it badly as I wasn't in a very good place. Luckily I'm just about back from there now.'

They gave each other the slightly awkward hug, as was customary in these situations.

'Keep in touch, yeah?' he said into her shoulder blade.

'Of course,' she lied, as was also customary in these situations.

'Well. Good seeing you...' he said, looking at her in that brooding, come-to-bed way again.

Oh no. Don't let's start this up again, she thought, her eyes darting to the ground.

'Yeah. You too,' she said as she shoved the last layout pad into a cardboard box.

The door closed behind him, and she went over to her computer. She saved the latest version of where she'd got to with a project called 'Prowl13marchFinalVersion', then closed down her machine while doing inner star jumps. Then she looked around the room, shoving the last lot of things into her bag. Only one item remained on the desk: the tiny womble that Lawrence had bought her. It seemed to be looking up at her, its eyes pleading with her not to leave him. She picked it up. He was covered in dust, and one of his eyes was hanging half out. There was a small space in her bag just the right size for it.

Half an hour later, Holly returned her newspaper to the paisley-upholstered train seat and looked out the window. The sun was peeping out from behind a solitary gap in a sky of continuous cloud, for the first time that year. It was still freezing, but she couldn't help feeling like it was the universe's way of confirming it was soon time to move to another season – the season of finally, finally being over the curly-haired-one.

And now she was totally ready, she realised with a smile, just as a man climbed onto the train and bustled through some people to find a seat.

'Is anyone sat here?' she heard him say.

Without looking up, she shook her head and moved her bag from the seat to make room. Moments later, her eyes drifted to her side, settling for a while on a woollen catastrophe of colours – yellow, pink, russet, gold, amber, purple and then a lurid green, all thrown together in thick stripes – creating the overall effect of a bad replica of a *Dr Who* scarf that travelled all the way down to the floor. Not unlike a scarf she'd once owned.

Wait. That was the scarf she'd once owned – the same one she'd given to a semi-conscious man named Aaron over a year ago.

She let her eyes drift upwards from the neck the scarf was swaddling. Yep. That was the man who'd fallen off his bike. Wavy brown hair, stubble and a tiny scar just below his right cheekbone. That's some powerful washing powder, she thought, looking back at the scarf, then into his eyes – at which point she noticed he was staring right back at her.

Holly looked away and pretended to organise her bags and

boxes into more of a coherent pile. Were they having a moment, she wondered, trying to repress the miniature die-hard romantic that was providing the Special Features-style Director's commentary in her head. She looked back across the carriage at the gorgeous man staring at her. As their eyes locked, Holly smiled, daring to hold his gaze. He smiled back, and she felt something flood her belly – not moths, but their friendlier, prettier counterparts.

The train was approaching the next station already. Aaron grabbed the sheets of paper he'd been reading, which were covered with what looked like architect drawings, and zipped them up into a portfolio. Then he did up his coat and tightened his scarf around his neck. As he stood up to leave, she opened her mouth to speak.

Meanwhile, back in the broom cupboard, the womble stared up out of the bin, thinking, it's dark in here.

ACKNOWLEDGEMENTS

This book would not have happened were it not for three life-defining break-ups, and two life-defining friends - Mark Hermida and Curly Katie Sheasby. The kindest, funniest two people I've ever met, who taught me that a break-up shared is a break-up halved. You guys make the worst of times into the best of times, and I'll love you 'til death do us part'. Mark, you're the top (pig) dog. Katie - I owe you a dog.

Soppy thanks are due to so many other people for their help along the way – to name a few: Nathalie Turton, Ben Westaway, Lauren Taylor, Emma McMorrow, Jose Gomez, Mark Lunney, Hannah Marshall, Vicky Grut, Miriam Berry, Lucy Beevor, Donna Amey, Vicki Lines, Sarah Morris, Tom Hyde, Christopher Keatinge, Charlotte Eaton, Rick Johnson, Beattie McGuinness Bungay, Laura Lockington, Phillipa Ashley, Broo Doherty, Sarah Collett, Natasha Harding, Eli Dryden and everyone else at Maze and HarperCollins.

Thanks to Charlie of Pure Evil, for granting permission to quote his kick-ass street art. And to Alain de Botton, for the kind permission to quote him. Incidentally, his book *Essays in Love* is essential, beautiful reading that I would prescribe to anyone with a broken heart.

And thank you to all The Mathias Clan. The ones in this world – Mum, Camilla, Emil, Danny, Sarah. And the ones in the next - my daddy, who half-way through this book, suffered a much worse kind of heart-ache than any silly break-up could bring. But

I know he'd have been smiling to see this now. As would my dear step-mother Evie, who so recently joined him. Sincere thanks to you both for your never-ending belief and encouragement. I just hope there's a kindle up there with a big enough font for you both.

'Out-Breaks' – Scenes from the cutting-room floor

Deleted Scene 1:
"Mont Blanc, and Other Low Points"

Eventually, Holly arrived at work with only minor bruising. The rest of the morning was spent in and out of the toilet, in thrall to the ebb and flow of her nausea. In between that, she mostly watched Youtube links from friends, finding them all far funnier than they were. But by mid-afternoon the hangover had changed gear and an unrelenting doom took hold.

This was the trouble with Happy, she was slowly realising. Happy was all well and good, to a point; but you never knew when its sell by date was. The trouble with feeling happy when you were heartbroken was that, at some point you'd remember you were heartbroken again. So any elation was like a rising balloon that you desperately wanted to hold on to; but the higher you got, the steeper the drop would be. You could enjoy the temporary feeling of lightness – but eventually you'd remember again, you'd lose your grip of the balloon, and back down you'd fall.

Maybe, just maybe, alcohol wasn't actually her friend, she

wondered as she tried to distract herself by checking her emails. But all she had was a message from 'Laterooms.com,' telling her that there was a brilliant offer on this weekend at The White Room Hotel, St.Ives. As ever, the Internet seemed hell-bent on delving into the vault of romantic e-commerce and spitting out reminders at random – of every mini-break, present and thoughtful little thing she'd ever done for Lawrence in their five year tenure. She quickly deleted the email in the hope that it would stop any happy memories from being stirred. But she was too slow; she'd already been accosted by the thought of an evening they'd spent in one of their favourite restaurants in St Ives. Despite herself, she pressed Play on the memory, sat back and watched.

Holly had arrived late to meet Lawrence, and was stood in the doorway of the restaurant, faffing about with her bags – trying to find her mobile, losing a war against gravity with the many layers she was juggling in her arms. Looking around for Lawrence but unable to see him, she had then begun that funny pantomime-esque dance; the one where you're walking round the restaurant, knowing full-well that the person you're looking for can see you and is probably waving at you like mad. Meanwhile the whole restaurant is laughing their head off at how silly you look, because *you just can't see them anywhere*. So when Holly had finally reached Lawrence after about three hours of flapping, he was grinning at her, a look of adoration in his blue eyes, and just out of nowhere he'd said,

'I love you.'

Like he'd just thought of it, that second. She'd been floored at the time. It was just so wonderfully *not* the way you'd normally say something like that for the first time. Its spontaneity was what she'd loved most about it. What she'd loved most about him.

'Thank you!' she'd said, 'Love you too,' and she'd kissed him on the lips, leaning across the table, her long hair only just avoiding a dalliance with the cheesy garlic bread.

As the balloon went rising into the air, Holly decided it was time to take herself to the toilet, to be alone with her pointless reminiscing. You and Lawrence have done your time. Your sentence is over, she kept telling herself. But the finality of it, and the knowledge he was with someone else already; it was too much.

She headed down the corridor, not before clocking Luke ahead of her in the hallway. Which was brilliant timing, considering she had pretty much never looked worse. She thought about saying hello, but she couldn't find her voice box, so instead opted for the much more mature approach: lowering the eyes, and marching on prudently. Excellent, good save.

Moments later she was sat in the warm bosom of the women's toilet. She had a nice long, cathartic cry. She opened her mobile phone and began to flick through to see which BUC member to call. If only Bella was around to speak to. She tried logging into Skype to see if she was randomly online, but her new-fangled smart phone kept on asking her to log in again and asking her to type in security words that really weren't words, which was all too complicated in her present state of mind. So she gave up on Skype and put her phone into her pocket, realising her nose was in urgent need of blowing.

As she dispatched another batch of snotty tissues into the toilet, she looked down. Oops. She'd blown her nose so many times, and mopped her tears up with such a mountain of toilet roll that it now seemed as if Mont Blanc had sprouted up then and there in the toilet. Uh oh, time to go, she decided, leaping up and flushing the chain, twice.

But it wasn't having any of it. She flushed it again. Nothing. In fact, if anything, Mont Blanc was now even sturdier. She began to prod at the mountain with the toilet brush. Nothing. Worse, even. Soggy little bits of loo roll were now caught up in the tendrils of the brush.

Could this get any worse, she wondered, bending down to get a better purchase on the u-bend. As she leaned in, naturally, her new smart phone fell into the toilet, landing at the summit of

Mont Blanc. She fished the watery phone out and dumped it in her bag, too exhausted to react. She returned to the blockage.

After ten minutes of pretending to be a plumber, she gave up and returned the sopping wet toilet brush to its mother ship. And ran.

Two hours later, she saw through the gap in her doorway that there appeared to be water seeping down the corridor, from under an adjacent doorway. Oops. Maybe the time has come to stop drinking so much, she decided, as she heard a beep and saw a new email come in.

Through the fog of her hangover she could just about make out the words.

'(High Importance): ALL STAFF: the ladies toilets are currently out of service while we tend to a major blockage/flooding incident. In the meantime we are allowed to use the conveniences in Princely Productions next door. Thanking you, Anthea Jessops, Head of Facilities.'

Holly pressed delete and buried her head in her arms.

* * *

Deleted Scene 2.
"Nutrition Advice"

'I'm serious. No food has passed my lips in days. Unless you count my own mucous, from crying so much,' Bella said. 'Does nasal mucous have any nutritional value I wonder? It must do. That's all that's in me, and I'm still going, aren't I?'

'Well, it's either nutritious or you're living off fat reserves,' said Olivia.

'It's quite an efficient system,' said Bella. 'First, I cry my eyes out for hours. Then the tears begin the mucous production, and that's enough to give me enough energy to keep crying the whole day. Kind of like a deranged version of The Water Cycle, like you did in school.'

'Shall I make a diagram?' asked Bella, reaching into her bag for her notebook.

* * *

Deleted Scene 3.
"The Name Game"

'Jenny Microwave.'

Holly exploded with laughter. 'Alright. That's a good one.'

'Yeah Hi! I'm Jenny Microwave!' he said through laughter. 'Now you.'

'Oh, I can't think of any more just now. I'm not really in the zone. How about, Peter… no. Francesca… Francesca Upholstery.'

Lawrence guffawed. 'Jimmy Cutlery,' he retorted, barely missing a beat. 'Hey, I think Jimmy and Jenny would make a nice couple, don't you? And if Jimbob ever made an honest woman of Jenny, she'd become Jenny Cutlery! Awesome. Your turn.'

Holly thought for a moment, then gave in. 'I'm sorry, I can't think of any more. Maybe we can leave it there for today?!' She gave her boyfriend a nudge.

It was infantile at best, but when no one else was around, Holly and Lawrence would play a few rounds of The Name Game. It was their dark secret, but the rules were simple. You just had to say the most stupid fictional name that came into your head. Usually, the optimum humour could be derived by juxtaposing a regular forename with a surname comprising a domestic appliance of some sort. No one else knew about this game, which had passed the time for them over many a journey on the London Underground.

'Oh, OK. We need to get off in a few minutes anyway,' said Lawrence.

Holly was puzzled. 'No, we don't. We're nowhere near Tufnell Park!'

Deleted Scene 4.
Free-Wheeling"

'Yeah! I so know what you mean!' said Holly. 'Like, the other day, I was on my way to work when I saw this girl riding past on her bike, pulling a wheelie bag along with it on the ground, while she was riding. It looked so awkward and cumbersome, but she was smiling away, so somehow, she pulled it off! And I just thought, that's awesome! And I laughed out loud with her, she caught my eye and smiled as if to say yeah, why not… and I got my phone out to ring Lawry and tell him, and then I remembered.'

* * *

Deleted Scene 5.
"Eff-Off"

'Well at least you're not being E-persecuted,' said Bella as she poured out some Margaritas to accompany the Mexican themed dinner which Olivia had been preparing. 'Even Amazon is out to get me these days. Through the medium of 'past-buyer mailings', it sends me 'thoughtful' suggestions related to every gift I've ever bought Sam on there. Which is a lot of things.'

'I mean, really,' said Holly. 'What really gets me is when Facebook sends me 'friend suggestions' – you know this person and this person – 'why not add Lawrence Edward Hill as a friend'?

'You're kidding? I wish FB would F OFF, sometimes!' yelled Bella, drinking her Margarita like water.

* * *

Deleted Scene 6.
"Admin Error"

'OK…well, you're going to think I'm pathetic beyond belief, but… I haven't been able to stop thinking about Mr Film Buff… So I did a very sad thing. I searched through the 'groups' on Facebook around the Hackney and Dalston area, and it turns out there is actually a group for the 'The Film Shop' on Broadway Market.'

'Oh B, you're actually ill,' said Holly.

'And guess who the Admin of the group is? ADAM! His name is Adam! And it's him! How mad is that! So I've added him as a friend.'

'You really must stop spoiling the surprise about all your prospects!' reprimanded Harry. 'Stop stalking them – I bet you know all about his life now don't you? Also, is he not going to wonder how on earth you found him?'

Bella looked a little worried, as though she'd not quite thought of that. 'It's fine. He'll probably just ignore my friend request anyway.'

'You can find ANYONE these days,' said Olivia. 'Even if they don't want to be found.'

* * *

Deleted Scene 7.
"Sweet Dreams are Made of Cheese"

An hour later, Harry came into the kitchen to see her lying on the sofa, an empty packet of Cheddars at her feet. She opened her eyes to see distinct disappointment on his face.

'Holly, beautiful girl. I don't think you're getting on that well without BUC, are you? This compulsive dating certainly isn't helping. And neither is all this late-night bingeing.'

'Yes,' she said as he sat down next to her.

'Cheese isn't going to fill the hole, Hol. Temporarily, yes. But not long-term,' he said slowly, as though it was an ancient Sanskrit proverb. 'Neither are cheese-ball men, come to think of it.'

'You're right,' she said, mulling over each word, marvelling at his profound wisdom.

She hugged Harry as they both looked out the window over Fortess Road. 'Jesus Harry, is this a break up, or a quarter-life-sodding-crisis?'

Harry laughed and squeezed her hand. 'Come here,' he said, folding her into his arms, as her hot tears slipped down her cheeks and into his hair.